EVACUATION PLAN . . .

Ehren and Laine looked over the crest of the hill, and assessed the situation. The woman guarding Shette was rummaging in a stack of goods. Ehren caught Laine's eye and nodded. Laine began stealthily making his way to the other side of the outlaw's camp.

Waiting while someone else took action had never been Ehren's strong point. He eased his sword from its scabbard and followed Laine's progress.

Her eyes darting desperately from one end of the camp to the other, Shette saw Laine. She stiffened, and her mouth dropped open. For a moment Ehren thought she would give her brother away, for she half-rose.

"Sit yerself back down again," the outlaw woman guarding her said gruffly.

Instead, Shette stood all the way up, walking to draw the woman's gaze away from Laine—and heading straight to where Ehren waited. He froze.

"You just went. Sit down."

"I can't help it. I'm scared. I have to go!" Apparently not trusting herself to keep her face schooled, she turned her back on the woman and her brother, right in front of Ehren.

And she gasped when she saw him.

The outlaw's head rose sharply; Ehren didn't wait for her to spot him. He surged up from the trees, and shoved Shette back the way he'd come. "*Run!*" he told her, moving to block the outlaw woman. "Just let her go," he warned the woman, standing ready but with his sword to the side, point down. *I'm willing to do this without a fight if you are.*

"King's Guard," she sneered, clearing her own sword of the scabbard.

Baen Books by Doranna Durgin

Dun Lady's Jess
Touched By Magic
Changespell
Barrenlands
Wolf Justice (forthcoming)

DORANNA DURGIN
BARRENLANDS

BAEN

BARRENLANDS

A Baen Books Original

Baen Publishing Enterprises
P.O. Box 1403
Riverdale, NY 10471

ISBN: 0-671-87872-7

Cover art by Darrell K. Sweet

First printing, April 1998

Distributed by Simon & Schuster
1230 Avenue of the Americas
New York, NY 10020

Printed in the United States of America

This book is dedicated to the people who held me up when
my own legs wouldn't do the job,
especially my family—Mona, Chuck & Nancy—
and Pat, Jennifer, Judy, Beth & Di.

LORAKA

Eredon
Delta

Eredon
River

Lake
Everdawn

Kurtane

SOLVANY

Lanes
Route

Trade
Road

hidden
pass

Valleydwell

Clan
Arial

Clan
Grannor

THERAND

Tieranguard

Clan
Portan

Clan Shahinian

Torra
Cove

Clan
Midde

Clan
Blake

N

Prologue

Answers at last. And maybe . . . maybe, a chance to eliminate the Barrenlands.

Benlan tried to turn that hope into something more reasonable. An experienced king ought to know better, at least until he learned just what this clandestine meeting would yield. He walked the muddy path from the lodge stables to the hunting lodge itself, not so keyed on the meeting that he neglected to enjoy a spring day when the sun was out and coming strongly through the still-barren branches of the trees.

Behind him, the silence of the King's Guard shifted to quiet conversation. "Where's Ehren, anyway?" Gretna said in a low voice, probably not meant for Benlan's ears. "He's the only one of us not here."

"Some foolish errand for the Upper Levels." Herib sounded grumpy. Well he might, as a master of guards who'd had no say in the matter. "Special request."

"Odd," Gretna said, while others murmured agreement around her. Benlan strode through the mud as if he wasn't hearing a thing. "Just like this trip."

"He don't think this is the regular spring lodge inspection, either," a third voice added, one Benlan didn't immediately recognize. "The queen always comes along for that one."

"That's why Ehren should be here," Herib said sharply. "There are a lot of things that make this—"

"Odd," Greta said again.

Benlan smiled, knowing they couldn't see it. His Guard was nothing if not devoted; they knew when something was up no matter how many other people he had fooled. And they were right, too. After months of subtle clues and warnings and an underlying uneasiness in court, he was finally taking the first aggressive steps to deal with it. True, the information he would get here was old, generations old, but if Benlan had learned one thing in his reign as king, it was that unresolved conspiracies at court tended to have their own lives, passing down from one set of ministers to another. He might learn nothing of importance . . . and he might learn everything.

Benlan stopped outside the lodge, sweating slightly despite the chill spring air, and breathing deeply just for the enjoyment of it—and because it fit his hope. *Peace . . . and a chance to break the silence with Therand.* The notion was as invigorating as the air. The Guards stopped a fair distance back from him, at his request; Benlan had the feeling his informant wouldn't show if he felt crowded.

What—? Something stirred the air, no normal breeze. Benlan stood straighter. Magic? Varien, ever-competent First Level wizard, had assured him the area would be shielded. It was a strong shield indeed, if Benlan could sense it.

Ehren should be here. Ehren, who offered not only the best protection any other man could give, but friendship and unquestionable personal loyalty as well. When acting in the King's best interests conflicted with the politics of a situation, he did what had to be done, without hesitation. The others were more intimidated by the Upper Levels, and Benlan supposed that was just as well. It wouldn't do to have a whole Guard full of Ehrens causing trouble.

But it was very nice indeed to have the one.

One of the Guards harrumphed, as if to remind the king he was still standing before the lodge, doing nothing. Benlan gave him a distracted nod.

"Odd," Gretna mumbled, apparently her refrain for the day.

If only Benlan's informant was right, that the material he offered meant an opportunity to work together with Therand's leader. *Sherran*. Benlan had heard she was strong and protective of her country, but reasonable as well, and neither of them had done anything to challenge the other since she'd taken the role of T'ierand years earlier.

It was hard to challenge their neighboring country with the Barrenlands dividing them, of course. The Barrenlands were an abomination, an ugly, dead region where nothing grew and no living creature stayed for long. No man could tread that ground, save for the ruling line in either country and those they gave limited dispensation—and it wasn't easy at that.

But it could be done. Benlan's brother, Dannel, had done it, had run away with his unacceptable Therand love. Benlan lost his brother; the Barrenlands had done that. Their age-old feud with Therand had done that. It was time for things to change.

Magic surged around him, making the Guards stir uneasily. Benlan frowned. The man he was meeting didn't have magic. He wasn't learned enough in his writing, and Varien had declared his numerous notes free from magical influence of any sort.

When the first shout hit his ears, Benlan drew his sword without hesitation—and barely unsheathed it before the alarm turned to an unmistakable death cry. It came from the stable area, and his Guards, torn between helping their own or protecting their king, turned to Benlan with faces grim and anguished—and then shocked. Soldiers in unfamiliar uniform were gliding out of the woods, solidifying into flesh from air, rippling into shape already on the run, swords already raised. *Magic*.

Benlan's Guards didn't have a chance. Neither did he. *Ehren!* Benlan blocked a death blow and missed the second attack, the one that sunk deeply into his arm. He was alone, the Guards outnumbered by two and three to one. Their cries of anger and agony filled the air. *Ehren, I need you!* His sword sunk deeply into the back of the man who would have hamstrung him, notching bone to stick there; Benlan wrenched it loose and staggered around just in time to look into the fiercely grinning eyes of the woman who sunk her blade into his belly.

The strength drained from Benlan's legs and pooled onto the ground with his blood; he fell to his knees. Beside him, a Guard thumped face down to the ground, dead before the liquid mud oozed into her mouth.

Someone behind him jammed a knee between his shoulders and wrenched his head back, exposing his throat to the tickling warmth of spring sunshine. Warmer yet, then, as blood coursed down his skin, sprayed up against his jaw, pulsing from a cut so clean he'd barely felt the blade slide across his throat.

The bracing leg disappeared from his back; the hand on his head shoved him down so he flopped against his own heels, feeling the sharp pop in his knees as they tore.

As if it mattered now.

Peace . . . the Barrenlands . . . lost.

Benlan lay in the mud while his blood drained away, and as his body turned into a remote, lifeless thing, he was suddenly aware of more magic, someone watching him. Of the cold satisfaction in those eyes, the cruel dispassion for the slaughtered Guard.

The eyes of someone he knew.

Chapter 1

Spring in Kurtane was as it had always been. The courtyards and gardens were awash in green, the white flagstone pathways sluiced clean by rain. This day was pleasantly cool, with just the faintest of breezes, barely enough to stir the fronds of the vine-draped arches shaping the traffic-ways of the palace yards. The odor of the stables was barely noticeable beneath the sweet scents of carefully tended flower beds. The kind of day to be savored.

Ehren sat on a comfortable wooden bench in the midst of it all and wondered when it had ceased to feel like home.

Not that it had ever been his *home*, as much time as he had spent here. But there had been a time when he *fit*. Now, the flirting young nobles strolling these famous walkways gave him glances of polite disregard instead of respect. His dark grey gaze was hard in return, and they invariably contrived to forget they'd been looking at him at all.

He knew what they saw. One of King Benlan's men, out of place in what was now his successor's court. A dark blue shirt of fine material that nonetheless showed wear, the shirt of a working man, and not a mere court accessory. Tall boots that were about ready to be resoled again, with worn straps hanging loose at the calf and ankle where metal greaves were often buckled on. Ehren's black hair, tied back for the moment, hung well past his shoulders; braided into it was his honor feather. These days the members of the King's Own Guard tied their feathers to wool beret caps, since not one of them had enough hair to do the job.

But his worst offense, Ehren knew, was something he could do nothing about.

King Rodar's court was a young court; his Guard consisted of young men and women. Most of Benlan's sworn had been killed in the fight that took the king himself, a fight Ehren had missed. Now the faint lines beside his grey eyes, the hardened quality of his face, the number and age of the scars he carried—all spoke of a maturity that most of Rodar's sycophants lacked.

Their problem. His was to figure out why Varien had summoned him. Had summoned him an hour ago, in fact. Most of that time Ehren had spent on this bench, his arms spread along the delicate curving back of the seat, his leg crossed ankle over knee, his broad shoulders relaxed against the wood. Watching Rodar's court, marking the new faces as he had not had a chance to do while scouring the coastal villages for remnants of the faction that had caused Benlan's death. Wondering why the court wizard had need of him, when their paths had scarcely crossed before.

Well, that was perhaps not strictly true. They had seen enough of each other. They had simply never had any use for one another.

Speculation got him nowhere. He'd waited long enough. Ehren uncrossed his leg and let the foot fall to the ground with a thump, rising to stretch as though there weren't three sets of eyes on him—at least two of which most certainly thought they were unobserved. He settled his sword belt a little lower as it slanted across his hips, and moved with unconcerned strides into the first of the open archways that preceded the palace proper. There were seven of them, placed closer and closer together until they merged into the building. At the last two were guards; in Rodar's new court they were more decorative, matched in feature and beauty, than functional. Ehren nodded at them and walked on.

He could hear them behind him, the hesitant step of boot on stone, as they struggled with the decision—call him back or let him go? By custom, he should have stopped and stated his business.

But these men were from the Kurtane Ready Troops— the Reds—and Ehren was ranking King's Guard. No voices were raised. Ehren smiled a tight, private smile, and turned down the airy hall that led to Varien's suites. He passed no less than three work crews that were, as far as he could tell, gilding perfectly good stained wooden crown work.

Changes. *Inevitable.* He shook his head; he couldn't help it. It seemed to him that his steps echoed too loudly as he came to the open door of Varien's anteroom. He stood in it and waited.

Varien's apprentice measured a small quantity of dried leaves on a tiny scale, engrossed. When she noticed Ehren, she fumbled her weights. The scale platform jerked; the dried matter spilled over her blotter-covered desk. She bit her lip, glancing over her shoulder to the closed door behind which her master waited. "We were expecting you earlier," she said, her voice low.

"What made you do that?" He leaned against the door frame and rested one relaxed wrist over the stirrup hilt of his sword. She was in mid-adolescence, blonde and light-boned, and looked small among the plain but heavy furnishings of the room.

"Why . . ." she bit her lip again and tucked a strand of hair behind her ear. "He sent for you over an hour ago."

"Yes," he agreed. "And I'm here. But I've never jumped at his bidding."

She stared at him, aghast.

"You're new, aren't you?" Ehren asked. New, young, and completely intimidated. "He does go through apprentices quickly. Don't worry about it—you just do what you have to when the time comes."

She dropped her gaze to the spilled plant matter. "I'm

here to learn from a master," she said resolutely. "This is the opportunity of a lifetime. You do Master Varien a great disservice to suggest otherwise."

He smiled. "Do you want to tell him I'm here, or shall I just walk in?"

"I'm sure he already knows you've arrived." But she went to the door and knocked quietly anyway.

The response was muffled; Ehren couldn't make out the words. She winced at it, then smoothed her features and pushed open the door, stepping back and giving a slight curtsy as Ehren passed. He paused in the doorway, very close to her. "Don't take it all so seriously," he told the top of her bowed head. When she lifted her eyes, surprised, he gave her his best rakish smile, the one that so angered the First Level ministers when it was his only response to one of their demands. Her surprise turned to a sudden shy smile of response, and he left her standing there, looking after him.

He'd never known a wizard as neat and organized as this one. Of course, the actual workroom was something he'd never seen, but this office was meticulously appointed, from the thick carpeting to the matching seat cushion on the desk chair to the distinct walnut grain of each piece of furniture. It was a place he'd been but half a dozen times, and one he meant to avoid in the future.

Varien stood by one of the heavily curtained windows, his hands clasped behind his back. His knuckles, Ehren noticed, were white. Like everyone else in Rodar's court, his hair was nearly shorn—a new style for the wizard, but one that went far toward hiding the grey in his dark blond hair. It was often difficult to remember that the wizard was in his ninth decade, when he looked only ten years older than Ehren's thirty-three years. Ehren stopped before the dark wood of the substantial table that stood between them, and said congenially, "What can I do for you?"

Varien turned abruptly. "You can start by not ignoring my summons," he said, biting the words off as precisely as he'd decorated the room.

There were many things to say to that. *I'm not yours to command* was the most polite of the replies that sprung to mind. So Ehren said nothing. After a moment he raised an eyebrow, and put the conversation back in Varien's hands.

The wizard turned back to the window. He was a small man, but not one Ehren took lightly, despite the understated subtleties of his magics. When he looked at Ehren again, his expression indicated that their first exchange had been dismissed. "Benlan has been dead a year now."

"Nearly."

"And you have been given the freedom, since his death, to track down those responsible for it. I am given to understand you've had no success."

"That depends on your definition of success," Ehren said. A clear lead to a dozen conspirators, scattered throughout the coastal cities, questioned and formally executed. And the trail? The trail was so dead that he knew he'd looked in the wrong direction from the start, been *led* in the wrong direction. His return was not an admission of failure. After a year, someone here was bound to figure they were safe, let down their guard . . . and here he was, to pick up the trail anew.

"My definition of success is the same as anybody else's," Varien said with a smile, but did not elaborate. "The point is, your current chances of discovering who had Benlan killed are remote. And there are other things that need to be done, things more crucial to the security of Rodar's rule."

Ehren pulled out a chair, invited himself to sit, and rested his forearms on the table. "As you said, I've been away. So you'll excuse me if I'm more blunt than you're used to." He paused, leaned forward, and said, "Why am I *here*? This conversation is not yours to hold."

Varien's laugh was short. "Whose, then?"

"The Guard answers to the king himself, as well you know."

"Rodar is seventeen years old." Varien seated himself opposite Ehren, placing a small silver ring between them. It had been Benlan's, a token from Queen Wilna. She hadn't wanted it back. She hadn't wanted anything to do with

Ehren, or the court. She was gone, and only rumors told
where.

Varien said nothing of the ring, but regarded Ehren with
his head tilted to one side, considering. "You know as well
as I that our young king is slow to maturity. He yet plays
with his powers, delighting in his effect on the most shallow
aspects of this court. That Solvany remains stable is a
testament to Benlan's ministers. If it seems to you I have
stepped out of place, well . . . perhaps it is so. But often
these days, it is how things are accomplished in Kurtane."

Ehren remained silent at first, measuring the expression
on Varien's face and discovering its sincerity somehow
grating. That a wizard should have even the faintest hint
of decision-making power settled ill with him. As far as he
was concerned, Varien's only official duty requiring initiative
and independence was the handling of Solvany's share of
maintenance spells on the Barrenlands. The other First
Levels—the Minister of Diplomacy, the High Secretary,
and the Military Commander—had plenty of influence over
any monarch's rule; when banded together, few were the
kings and queens who would—or could—go against them.
But the wizards had always been held apart. Most reckoned
a wizard of the Upper Levels had enough power already.
Ehren was among them.

He picked up the ring Varien had placed between them,
a smallish ring set with a beveled emerald and a band of
intertwining ivy. A woman's ring. It had always looked like
it belonged with Benlan, anyway, right along with Wilna's
love. And now, it somehow connected to whatever Varien
had to say. Ehren placed it back on the table. "So," he said.
"There are other things more crucial to Solvany than
punishing the conspirators who killed her king. Enlighten
me."

"I'm surprised to find it necessary. You, after all, are the
one who has been traveling through the land. Surely you
have observed the unrest, the dissatisfaction with Rodar's
rule—such as it is. Surely you have heard Dannel's name
come up, again and again."

Unrest, indeed—Ehren had fended off three attempts to kill him on the way home. He snorted. "There are always dissatisfied voices when something changes. It happens every time one of the First Level ministers is replaced. It happened when you replaced Coirra, if you remember."

"I do," Varien said. "But I'm surprised that *you* do. You can't even have been born."

"I wasn't." Ehren let the words sit there a moment, making their point. Then he said, "Dannel is gone. Benlan talked of his older brother often enough; the man wasn't suited to rule, even before he fell in love with a T'ieran daughter and ran off to who-knows-where. He won't be coming back to snatch the throne away from Rodar."

"And his children?"

Ehren snorted again, showing a little more derision this time. "That's what this is all about? You're worried Dannel's children might make some sort of play for the throne?"

Varien's eyes narrowed. "There will be no better opportunity."

"Granted. A good reason for all Rodar's ministers to be prepared with their best rhetoric. Supposing these hypothetical children should appear."

"We have no intention of waiting for them to *appear*," Varien snapped.

Finally, then, here was some of the temperament Ehren knew to be Varien's. He gave the wizard an even smile. "Most of the Guard is unblooded. Half of them haven't spent three nights in a row under the stars. If you want to waste time and Guards looking for Dannel, you might as well get some training done while you're at it. Which brings me back to my original question—why am *I* here?"

Varien didn't answer right away; he seemed to be tucking his temper away. Ehren found his eyes narrowing at the satisfaction that found its way to the wizard's soft features. Varien said, "You will be doing the searching, Ehren."

While Benlan's killers still live? While the conspirators who had seen to the death of half his fellow Guards, his friends, *still gloated over that victory?* His jaw set hard;

he deliberately had to relax, to force a calmness—of sorts—into his voice. "If you're concerned about the king's safety, this is where I need to be. If those First Level fools hadn't sent me off on a trivial errand last spring, Benlan might yet be alive." Ehren's bitter voice held accusation. "Do you want to make the same mistake again?"

"I've heard you say this before," Varien said coolly. "Do you really think your presence would have made the difference, simply because Benlan considered you *friend*? And do you really think the ministers care to deal with you, ever reminding them of the possible truth behind your words? Do you think the new Guard is eager to have you here, breathing over their shoulders and reminding them they have no experience?"

"To the lowest Hell with what they want," Ehren said. "The important thing is the safety of the king."

"It will be hard to keep the king safe if his ranks are in disruption," Varien said. "Your very appearance reminds everyone who sees you that you were Benlan's man. And there are plenty who will remember how difficult you were, even then. Who *do* remember, and don't want you here."

Difficult? Perhaps. He did what was necessary to keep Benlan safe. Ehren sat back in the stout chair, holding Varien's gaze. "Difficult will be as nothing, if you continue talking about sending me on another fool's mission while Benlan's killers run loose and Rodar turns this throne into an adolescent fantasy."

"It's been a year, Ehren!" Varien stood and leaned over the table. "What do you suppose that looks like? A year, and you're still searching? You're already *on* a fool's mission!" He took a deep breath and straightened, resting his hands lightly on the back of a chair. "Frankly, you don't have much choice. There are plenty of First and Second Level people who see you as a threat right now—a disruption that Rodar's rule is not capable of handling. Don't underestimate the lethal dangers in those scheming Levels—forced resignation is the least of what you're facing. I hope I make myself clear."

So that's how it was. Take this assignment, and lose his chance to track down the conspiracy—or refuse it, and lose everything. Ehren stayed where he was, leaning back in the big chair, eyeing Varien, barely aware that his jaw was set. "Are these *your* words?"

"They're my words, yes. But they come from the mouths of others as well. In fact, it was my idea to give you this last chore. You'll be gone some while, and perhaps by the time you return, things will have settled. Consider this before you refuse us."

He'd consider it, all right. He'd consider the fact that he'd never judged Varien a man to do something that benefited only one person, unless Varien was that person. If searching for Dannel was Varien's idea, there was more to it than one last face-saving assignment for Benlan's favorite Guard.

Which, perhaps, was reason enough to do it. How else to discover what the wizard was up to? Besides, once he was through, he could return here and pick up where he left off. Someone here in Kurtane was frightened enough of him to drive him out, and that was the best lead he'd had in months.

Ehren leaned forward, picked up the ring, and studied its flawless emerald. "Tell me about the ring," he said.

<hr />

"Lain-ieee!"

"Not now, Shette." Laine frowned at the slight shimmer of the ground in front of him, barely discernible in the morning light. It wasn't Shette's fault she couldn't see it, but her timing was characteristically awful.

The caravan stretched out behind Laine, several dozen uninspiring but sturdy wagons carrying Therand goods bound for Solvany, via the bordering mountains of Loraka. They waited with an impatience that was almost palpable. It was his job to guide them through the magic of this tricky, hard-country route, and their hurry was of little concern to Laine when he felt something amiss before them.

The spells were several hundred years old, things that

had been loosed during the same war that had wrought
the lifeless, magic-made Barrenlands between Therand and
Solvany. The Barrenlands made travel between the countries
impossible; the spells made travel through the mountains
perilous. But there would always be a market for fine
Therand cloth goods and precision trade work in Solvany,
just as Therand took in a steady supply of hardy northern
breeding stock and quality wines from Solvany. Commerce
always found a way.

Until recently, that way had been a triangular route along
the Lorakan Trade Road—a slow and costly journey capped
with tariffs. And then Ansgare had stumbled on to Laine,
and his quick merchant's mind had divined a way to take
advantage of the younger man's Sight.

When Laine's Sight happened upon a lurking spell—
something that tripled a traveler's weight, or turned his
boot soles to ice-slick uselessness—it was like an itch that
couldn't be scratched, or spotting something out of the
corner of his eye at night, and then watching it disappear
when he tried to focus on it. Seeing through a spell took a
careful balance of not looking too hard at any one thing
while concentrating on all of it. Laine went about it patiently,
and never took himself or the job too seriously.

"Lain-*ieeee.*" Shette's voice, drawing out the last syllable
of his name again in the way she knew he hated. This was
her first trip further than the village closest to their family's
mountainous pasture land, and patience was something she
had yet to acquire when it came to waiting out his Sight.
Or anything, for that matter.

"Not *now*, Shette," Laine said with a touch of irritation,
eyeing the rutted road ahead and heeding the silent,
disquieting voice that warned him there was magic tangling
their way. The ground shimmered faintly, subtly. The route
was only in its third year of use, and though Laine had
come to recognize the flavor of the old Border War spells
drifting through this region, this one—if it indeed was a
spell—was new to him. Harder edged, it made some spot
behind his eyes twitch, and gave him a cold, hard knot in

his stomach. With his younger sister at the wagon behind him, he wasn't about to get careless. Slowly, he closed his left eye, the blue one, and after a moment switched and closed the right. The old habit seldom worked, but he couldn't help from giving it a try. A little concentration and he'd see the right of it—

Behind him, a mule grumbled, punctuating displeasure with an explosive snort. Shette gave an equally explosive sound of dismay. "He did that on purpose! You *know* he deliberately snorts all over me! Laine, why do I have to—"

"Shut up?" he finished, rounding on her where she stood by Spike, the near-side mule, in front of his small four-wheeled wagon. She was the picture of irritated sibling—irritated teenaged sibling at that. Shette's loose trousers were rolled up to the knee, her sandy hair tied off at the base of her neck. Her expression was graphic revulsion as she vigorously rubbed her shoulder off against the mule's lower neck. For its part, the mule did indeed wear a half-lidded expression of satisfaction. It had probably been as tired of Shette's whining as Laine. "If you're not quiet, we'll be here for the rest of the day. Do you want to be the one to explain that to Ansgare?"

Sometimes the five years between them seemed like a century.

Shette made a face, and pushed the mule's head away from her. Whenever Laine was out of the wagon, Shette stood with Spike, who often took advantage of her hesitant authority. His partner, Clang, was happy to follow Spike's lead.

Even now Spike flopped his jagged namesake of a mane back and forth to rid himself of a fly, and gained a sneaky foot in the doing of it. "Shette," Laine said, and his teeth ground together a little as he strode forward, caught the mule's lines under the animal's chin, and backed him the exact step he'd stolen, "you've *got* to watch him. If I can't trust you to keep him back, I'll swap you with Dajania—she doesn't let him pull anything. You can ride with Sevita."

"Laine, I don't want to ride in a whore wagon!" Shette said, truly horrified.

Her reaction was so satisfying Laine regained his normal good humor at once, and merely smiled down at her despite the threat of the spell tickling at his back.

"It's all your fault, anyway," she grumbled, seeming to remember that the women in question had actually been quite kind to her on this trip, and embarrassed by her condemnation. "There's nothing up there, and Spike knows it."

"Laine." A new voice, startling him from behind the wagon. Ansgare. Of course. Riding his big cat-footed pony, the merchant-turned-caravan owner never failed to take Laine by surprise once Shette got him distracted. "Seems we've been here quite a while."

Laine gave Shette a quick warning look and moved back behind the wagon with Ansgare; there was no room for Ansgare's little horse to make its way alongside the wagon to join them. On one side was a jut of granite that rose far above their heads, and the other was such a jumble of fallen rocks and tall grasses that riding it was the same as begging for a broken leg. It hadn't been easy, finding a decent route through the Loraka mountain chain.

Laine put his back to the rear panel of the wagon and gave Ansgare a shrug, rolling his long sleeves up around his biceps, where they were just a little too tight but much cooler. Even at twenty, Laine's was a casual approach to life, reflected by the frequent humor in his eyes. "Whole trip is going slow this time, Ansgare. Someone's been playing with these mountains. Loraka's turning all the apprentices loose to practice, I'll bet."

"It doesn't take this long to unscramble apprentice spells," Ansgare grumbled, rubbing a hand over his short, grey-shot beard. He glanced back over his shoulder. The view was blocked by Kalf's squat, solid wagon of fine Therand mercantiles, but Laine knew Ansgare was mentally placing the caravan's strongarms—Machara and her two men, Dimas and Kaeral. Likely they were spread evenly among the wagons, as was their pattern. When he turned back, it was with a shrug, as though, defenses set, he could afford to take Laine a little less seriously. "Loraka's never minded us here before. Take a drink, close your eyes a few minutes. See if it's still there."

"Have I ever been wrong?" Laine asked, more amused than offended.

"No, son, but Guides grant us, things change. It never was natural, you being able to See things with no training, and no call to magic."

"Natural, maybe not. But it's shown no signs of deserting me. Patience, Ansgare." Laine grinned at the man, knowing the merchant's thoughts well after two years together. "You're not carrying goods that spoil. You're just restless from winter."

"That's a certain fact. And so's this—your old Spike mule decided to move ahead without you."

"What?" Laine spun around to see the wagon creeping away from him. "Damn," he said, slapping a hand to his short sword. "Shette . . ."

Her rising voice grew clearly audible. "Spike, whoa, you stupid mule!" A loud grunt of effort, no doubt from a correction Spike didn't even notice. "Spike, would you—"

Laine scrambled alongside the wagon, stumbling on the stones there, as Shette's words stopped in a gasp, then escalated. "Spike, get back, get *back*, *get*—" Spike's alarmed snort overrode her, and Laine was just close enough to glimpse his sister over Clang's back when she screamed.

The quaver of resolving magic in front of her was all too clear. The path suddenly tracked left, through what *had* looked like solid stone, and the ruts Spike had been following phased to sparsely grass-edged rocks. Clang's foolishly floppy ears went back and he reared, nearly concealing the coalescing boil of darkness that appeared only a few feet away from Shette.

Laine slapped the beast's rump on his way by, with little hope of having any effect. "Stand, Clang! Stand, Spike!" He pulled out his sword, an unblooded thing with a sweeping basket hilt, and when he threw himself between Shette and the smoldering darkness, it seemed an insignificant weapon, indeed.

"Laine," Shette gasped, staring at the unknown that towered over them and tugging at his arm. "Laine, come *on*."

He shook her off. From behind, he heard Ansgare's bellow. "We're coming, Laine! Hold on!"

Machara, he hoped, and hoped fervently, as the darkness solidified in front of them, choosing form and texture. A dark beast, bristle-hided with ichor dripping from its short-muzzled mouth and reddish piggy eyes that seemed quite happy to see them. Shette snatched Laine's arm again, dragging him back; he didn't hesitate, but shoved her, as hard as he could, toward Spike, never taking his eyes off the oddly assembled beast before him.

Its batlike face bobbed up and down on a short neck; Laine took the gesture for uncertainty, as Ansgare and the three fighters clattered over the rocks behind him. But its lips drew back, an absurd parody of a grin, and—

"*Duck*, Laine!" Ansgare roared, so close to him that Laine flinched away, and so was caught only by the edges of the spittle aimed at his face.

"Sacred shit!" he yelped, swatting at the fierce burn along his upper arm and nearly dropping his sword.

Shette's scream of "Laine!" overlapped someone's "Watch it!" and Machara's light, commanding alto, shouting "Spread out!" The strongarms were a flurry of uncoordinated movement facing off a hunch-shouldered beast that appeared more amused than threatened by them. Laine ended up on the far left, his venom burns forgotten, on the balls of his feet and waiting for opportunity while the others baited the creature—but something was *wrong* with it all. Machara feinted at the thing when it had clearly been sizing up Dimas, and Ansgare was completely unaware when it turned on him, its face drawn up in the grimace of its spitting attack.

No time for words; Laine shoved his boss aside, bringing his sword across in a quick backhand sweep that cut deeply into the thing's neck. At that one instant, everyone focused on the creature where it was, and then just as quickly they were feinting at phantoms again.

They don't see it! Startled, Laine closed an eye, leaving himself open to attack—and there it was. While the bulk of the thing's body was the same to both Sight and sight, the head whipped around in two different patterns—the truth, and what his companions saw instead. Only Laine saw the reality within the illusion.

But Shette's rock pinged solidly enough off its hide, bouncing on the bony point of its crouching hip, an area protected from sword that it did not bother to defend with illusion.

"Be careful!" Laine shouted at her as she flung another rock, totally unaware when it lurched heavy shoulders around to face her; as far as she could see, it was still angling to reach Machara. Laine's first instinct was to go after it—but if he let it think it was unobserved, let it commit itself to attacking his little sister. . . . He swallowed hard, pulled himself up short, and joined the others, battering the empty air while he watched the true beast out of the corner of his eye. Certain it was unobserved, the beast gathered venom with each bob of its head, drew back its lips—

Laine whirled and brought all the momentum of the movement down through his arm as his sword connected with bone just behind the creature's skull. Shette jumped back, clearly surprised by the sudden flash of Laine's sword at nothing, at . . .

*Some*thing.

A handful of startled exclamations joined Shette's as the creature collapsed on itself. Its heavy skull thunked off the ground, nearly separated from its body, with Laine's sword imbedded in its neck and wrenched from his grasp.

Machara stared at the empty space she'd been so successfully engaging and said, "Well, I'll be damned."

For the moment, that seemed to be the general consensus. Shette ran to Laine and made fussing noises over his arm, which then, of course, started to hurt. Spike postured behind them, little half-rears of threat accompanied by the sharp tattoo of his front hooves against the ground.

"Never seen anything like that," Kaeral pronounced finally,

still breathing heavily. He and Dimas had worked under Machara, guarding caravans, for many years longer than Laine had been guiding for Ansgare. Laine glared at the creature, hands on hips, panting. Something Kaeral had never seen. Wonderful.

"The thing had us completely bamboozled," Dimas said, shaking his head in disbelief.

"No," Ansgare said, crossing in front of Laine to jerk the short sword out of the thing's neck. He handed it to Laine, moving up close to look directly in his eyes. Looking, Laine knew, into eyes of two different colors. A black eye and a blue so dark you had to be this close to see the difference. "No," Ansgare repeated. "Not all of us."

He moved through the caverns from a viewpoint that seemed a little taller than normal, and he was happy and excited—and scared. He'd taken Jenorah from a life of ease and comfort, and together they were entering more than a cavern that led from one country to another. It led them into another life, a voluntary exile. He held the lantern up a little higher, and felt the soft touch of Jenorah's hand on his arm.

"Together," she said.

Dannel stopped, then, and put the lantern on the ground, turning to face her. She was a sturdy young woman, the best of Clan Grannor. Her long black hair was tied back, and her equally black eyes glinted in the wavering light of the lantern, looking at him with such love he felt himself nearly overcome. He put his hands alongside her face and smoothed her hair back, all the impossible wisps that had come loose during their wild ride to this place, through both borders and into the Barrenlands. She tilted her head back and looked into his eyes, and wry amusement gathered in her gaze, until it overflowed her eyes and came out in a laugh—and not one of those fake little court laughs, either. An infectious laugh that caught him up in its wake and played with them until they were breathless and clinging to one another.

"We did it," Jenorah said through a contented sigh. "For all of their stupidity, we managed this. And if we can do this, what is there that we cannot do?"

He drew her close and rested his cheek on the top of her head. "Nothing," he whispered. "Nothing at all."

"Nothing," someone repeated, only with someone else's voice altogether. He was looking not at Jenorah, but at a man. Tall, dark-haired, intensely angry, and armed with plenty of blade. "Nothing should keep me from your side, and running errands for the Upper Levels least of all."

"Relax," he said, not feeling all that relaxed himself. He'd been about to discuss the day's plans with this man—this friend—but that would only make things worse, now. "Someone's playing games, pulling strings to prove they can. If we cut them off, we won't have a chance to follow the strings, will we, Ehren? Ehren?"

"Ehren!" He cried the warning out of habit when the attack came, aching for the solid feel of his friend against his back, fierce and capable. The world filled with the sounds of fighting men—blades and shouts and death cries, the worst of those coming from his own throat as his body took cut after cut. Someone jerked his head back, put a blade against his throat—

Pain. He was choked with it, his body stiffened and jerking with someone else's death. It burned in his belly, his arm, his throat. Death, reaching for him—

"Laine!" Shette's annoyed voice, the not-so-gentle prod of her finger. "Wake up, Laine, you're doing it again!"

"Huh?" He jerked upright, nearly smacking his head on the bottom of the wagon, and let himself flop back to the ground again, dazed. Laine unclenched his fist, flattened it on top of his stomach and the phantom pain there. No blood. No.

A mule snorted on the other side of the wagon, a wet

and unhappy sound. For a moment Laine stared at the darkness of the wagon slats overhead, his hand resting on his dry, whole torso, listening to the uneven patterns of gusty rain overhead.

Shette, her voice tinged with sisterly disgust, said, "You and your dreams. Between that and the rain, I don't know how we're supposed to get any sleep."

Laine's thoughts were far away, picking at the details of the death scene he'd just witnessed—Hell, been a part of. Out loud, he merely said a mild, "At least we trenched uphill." If they'd skipped it as Shette had wanted to, they'd be on wet ground right now.

When she spoke again, her voice had changed, grown tentative. "What do you see, Laine, in those dreams of yours? Mum and Da thought you'd outgrown them."

"And you're to tell them no differently," he said, abruptly rolling over to face her in the darkness.

"But what do you *see*?"

He hesitated. "I see *them*, sometimes. I see them when they ran away together, and how frightening it must have been—and exciting, and happy. Sometimes I see them building our home, or the first time Papa found the way to the village." He wasn't sure what he'd seen this time. When Shette poked him awake like that, sometimes he lost it all.

"Dreams," she said, sleepy again.

No. Not like a dream at all. *True* Dreams, they were. "Yes," he said. "Dreams." He shifted to his back again, looking for a comfortable arrangement of his body on the subtle dips and hollows of the ground.

"They don't sound all that bad to me," she said, pulling her blanket in close. "Not worth so much fuss and bother."

"Sometimes they change into nightmares," Laine said shortly. "Now go to sleep. It's not me that's keeping us awake now."

Shette murmured, "Bossy older brother," and was apparently content to leave it at that. Her breathing lapsed into light snoring, a gentle sound that he could barely hear above the rain as he stared into darkness and tried to remember just when the Dreams had changed. He wondered whose death he was feeling, night after night. Whose eyes was he trapped behind—and would he ever get the chance to turn and face their betrayal?

Chapter 2

Parry in fourth position, rotate wrist—riposte. Parry in first, riposte to flank; a little awkward, that move always was, so do it twice for every one of the others. Parry three, riposte, and there goes your head, sir. Quickly, easily, never the same sequence in a row, Ehren ran through the standard parry positions and their direct ripostes. With his arm relaxed, his mind relaxed, his moves fast and controlled—the practice dummy was doomed.

His saber was a heavier weapon than the ones the new Guards were making popular; theirs were basket-hilted creations with complex quillons and numerous counter-guards, and fine blades with barely enough width for a good fuller. Their movements, in practice, were just as fine; they pit themselves against one another in bouts that were punctuated by triumphant yells and dramatic shouts of attack.

Herib, the Guards' master, had died with the others. Most of those who hadn't died had left the service in the year Ehren had been gone. And the remainder were like him, serving the king in new ways, ways that took them from the suddenly too-familiar grounds of the palace, and the ghosts that walked them. The current master was imported from Loraka, and had brought his own styles, his own type of weapons. These young men and women . . . they were pretty enough, they moved well—although Ehren would set them to a month's practice on distance drills. And they were brash and proud, and probably as loyal as any king could ask for. But . . .

Ehren remembered fights when the ground beneath his feet was uneven and slippery, sometimes with his own blood. He remembered grunts of pain, the quick panting of fear, and solid blades taking life from endless practice drills, moving quicker than thought, sliding along each other to break through guard and into flesh. Maybe he was old, and old-fashioned to boot, but he preferred to have a solid piece of metal in his hand, and not some stick. And among those fighting at his back, a certain number of scars was not a bad thing.

He realized he'd stopped killing the dummy in front of him. His sword was lowered, its tip hovering just above the floor. Time for a good bout with a whetstone instead. He looked over at the huddle of men and women who had stopped their sparring and were joking around, a shove here, a nudge there. It occurred to him that Varien, whatever his scheming—and Ehren was certain there was more to it than Varien claimed—was right in one thing: Ehren didn't seem to belong here any more.

He closed his hand over the ring, the emerald set in vines, that barely fit over the small finger on his left hand. For reasons of his own, Varien seemed certain Dannel and his family lived over the border, in the steep ridges of the Lorakan mountains that hugged both Solvany and Therand. A long journey from Kurtane, and a place filled with old magics.

Not anywhere Ehren wanted to be. But as his visit to Rodar earlier in the day had proven, he didn't have much choice in the matter—not if he wanted a chance to come back and continue the search for Benlan's killer that was, as far as he was concerned, still priority.

Rodar had been in his semi-formal receiving room, making a seamstress' life Hell by gesturing freely while she tried to fit the sleeves of the colorful shirt he wore. The person on the receiving end of the gestures was a First Level minister, and not one that held Ehren in any favor. Halden was First Level Minister of Diplomacy, and Ehren had disrupted more than one of his functions, implacably unmoved by Halden's protests when Ehren spotted something—or someone—that he felt might create a problem for King Benlan.

Halden had glanced away from Rodar just long enough to give Ehren a cold look and a nod of greeting. Rodar, when he saw Ehren standing in the doorway, greeted him cheerfully enough. "Ehren! It's about time you paid a visit to your king, instead of skulking up and down the coast."

Ehren held his tongue on the reminder of the *reason* he'd been skulking along the coast; Rodar was sincere enough in his grief for his father, but had been very good at pushing it to the back of his mind. Instead he said, "It'll be the last visit for some time, unless your majesty does something about it."

Rodar frowned. His face was long and narrow, and the fuzz-short hairstyle he'd adopted did nothing for his features. He flapped an arm in protest—narrowly avoiding the stick of the needle, to judge by the seamstress' alarm. "What do you mean? I was counting on you to stand with me for the fete next week. Halden's managed to gather all the First and Second Level families together—no simple task, ey, Halden?"

Halden turned a poisonous gaze on Ehren. "Indeed, quite a difficult one, your majesty. Pinning down your First Level secretary and the Second Level commanders took considerable persistence. But the effort is well worth it, to celebrate the start of your second year of rule."

"Exactly. It's an important occasion, and I want Ehren there." Rodar's jaw set, but it only served to make him look slightly petulant instead of determined. For once his arms were still, his fists resting at his waist, but the seamstress had paused in her efforts to look at Ehren with an expression that wavered between intimidation and curiosity.

"Varien has other plans for me," Ehren said. He'd come

straight from his discussion with the wizard, fully aware that he was carrying weapons only the King's Guards were allowed to bear in the king's presence. He rested his palm over the cold, smooth curve of his sword hilt; a subtle reminder of his status that Rodar missed completely but Halden did not. The smaller man's nostrils flared slightly, and he looked away. Ehren said, "Yours is the final say in this matter, Rodar. The Guard is yours."

Halden shot him a quick look of anger, and suggested, "I'm sure Varien has good reason to request Ehren's services, your majesty."

"What could be more important than having him at my side?" Rodar asked, in complete sincerity. "He's ranking Guard, and he was my father's most trusted protector."

Halden contrived to look reluctant; Ehren suppressed a flash of irritation as Rodar picked up on it. "What's wrong?" the king asked. "Is there something I should know?"

Halden said carefully, "There has been some discussion of this, your majesty. While it's true Ehren was an important part of your father's court, some of the First Level have been concerned about the appearances of maintaining his presence."

"What do you mean?" Rodar demanded. "How is it *supposed* to look? All of Solvany's monarchs have had their Guards beside them."

"Exactly." Halden nodded with satisfaction, as if the conversation had taken just the spin he'd been aiming for.

Ehren gave him a cold look, entertaining a brief fantasy of breaking the man's nose. *That* would have shut him up quick enough. . . . The seamstress, a mature woman who knew well enough when to disappear, quietly moved back from Rodar's side to discreetly fiddle with some bright corded trim in her basket.

Halden seemed oblivious to Ehren's inner seething. "Ehren is your father's Guard, sire, not yours. It might not be the wisest thing to retain him. And celebrating the onset of your second year of rule by reminding the Levels—and all their family—that you have come upon your rule young, and through the tragedy of your father's death, cannot be a good thing in any case."

"My age has nothing to do with it!" Rodar said, but his voice squeaked a little in the saying of it. He gave Ehren a worried glance. "Do you really think . . . ?"

"I think," Ehren said without hesitation, "that a king should weigh the advice he's given against his own judgment. And I think your father would prefer to see you as well-protected as possible, given what *did* happen to him."

Halden ignored Ehren. "It's time to establish your own court, sire, and your own Guard. All the rest of the palace shows the force of your personality; no one would mistake it for your father's." He left the conclusion dangling.

Rodar glanced at Ehren and then quickly away, perhaps knowing the decision was already in his eyes. "I'll have to think about this, Ehren."

And Ehren knew when there was no point in pushing a young monarch's patience. He might need it for another time. "Thank you, your majesty," he said. Halden, he gave a hard look, and no acknowledgment.

A few hours later Rodar sent Ehren a sincere but firm note validating Varien's assignment. And Ehren, exasperated and angry, went straight to the Guard practice room. If nothing else, it was time for him to check in with the new Guard master, a position that had not been filled between the slaughter of Guards and king, and the time Ehren had left Kurtane, hot on the heels of fleeing conspirators.

Now, his frustration appeased through physical effort, Ehren shoved the dummy back against the wall. When he turned around, the little group of Guards was moving his way. He recognized a few faces then—at least two of them had started training before Benlan was killed. Jada and Algere were their names, and it was Jada who stopped in front of him, her broad, pleasant face troubled beneath its freckles. As he recalled, she was normally cheerful, more than a little flirtatious, and unquestioningly dedicated.

"Ehren," she said. "You've only been back a few days, and we've heard . . . already you're off again?"

"We wanted to see you," Algere said. "We've honed our swords down to nothing, waiting for you to get back with some word of Benlan's killers."

"Is that what happened to those weapons?" Ehren said, deadpan. "I wondered."

It took them a minute; it was one of the young women in the back who giggled. Then Algere snorted, and nodded back at the other end of the paneled wood floor, where the Guard master was checking the practice equipment. "Varien seems to have connections in Loraka. He's been encouraging Rodar to make more open trade agreements. You should stick around, and get an idea of just how many things have changed around here."

Ehren gave a short shake of his head. "Politics," he said. "I'm off over the border myself. Have a couple of things to check out."

"Benlan?" Jada asked, coming alert. "Or the border gang we've been hearing about?"

Border gang? "Neither that I know of. But I get the feeling . . ." Varien wanted him out of the way, all right, and Ehren was beginning to understand why. There was too much happening here, too much that needed careful watching. He didn't complete the thought out loud, but instead said, "If any of you need to get in touch with me, you can have a message sent to the border crossing. I'll get it."

Jada and Algere exchanged a puzzled look; the younger Guards behind them didn't pretend to understand.

"Listen," Ehren said. "Rodar is a young king. No younger, perhaps, than his father when he took the throne, but sometimes age isn't all in your years, if you take my meaning. There are plenty of people who'll see this as an opportunity. Preventing such opportunities is what the Guard is all about."

"Ehren, if you know something, maybe you should tell us," Jada protested.

Ehren shrugged. "If I knew something, I would."

"Then," she said calmly, her hand on the hilt of her sword,

"we'll be forced to beat it out of you." Behind her, the other young Guards stared at her in alarm, and then at Ehren, to see how he would take it.

"Will you, now," he said, a slow smile finding its way to his face. He didn't feel like playing, not now. But this was an opening—an invitation back into the world that should have been his—and he wasn't about to ignore it. He took a deliberately menacing step forward, raising his sword into second guard. The group scattered as Jada abruptly realized she'd neglected to free her weapon before she'd started this game, and she back-pedaled furiously, trying to unsheathe it before he was on her. It was a quick-paced contest; they kept an open distance in unspoken regard for the fact that while Jada had on a leather practice brigandine, Ehren did not. Her moves were cat-swift and light, and he kept his the same, using wrist and fingers instead of brute strength—though she kept him on his toes with her frequent use of the sword point.

Around them, the others shouted encouragement, and Ehren laughed when she managed an especially quick disengagement and slipped through his guard; his parry was a close thing. She was laughing, too, but her eyes widened in surprise when his riposte tagged her side. She gave a theatrical death groan, but Algere was ready to take her place, and the battle raged up and down the practice room until Ehren ended it by dramatically disarming his fifth—sixth?—opponent and saluting them all.

"Now," he grumbled loudly, "I'll have to rest for an extra day before I leave."

Jada was on the floor, giggling. Unrepentant. Ehren grinned down at her. But her expression suddenly faded and Ehren followed her gaze to find the Guard master coming up beside him—he didn't even know the man's name, for glory's sake—holding out one of the extra practice brigandines.

"I would be honored," the man said, his Lorakan accent strong. "Someone should have seen to our introduction when you first returned. My name is Gerhard."

Ehren looked at him a moment, seeing in the man's almost expressionless face a resolute duty. Of course Gerhard would feel obliged to offer himself for a bout, after this. And in the man's expression, as well, was a glimmer of resignation, which could only mean one thing. Ehren gave Gerhard a sudden grin, and shook his head, blowing the drop of sweat off his upper lip. "If you'd managed to save me from *them*, perhaps," he said. "There's not much left of me, now."

Gerhard lowered the brigandine; if there was relief on his face, it was well hidden behind his amiability. "Another time, perhaps."

"Another time," Ehren agreed. He looked at the Guards before him, and nudged Jada with his toe, catching her eye with a look that stopped her amusement cold. "You remember what I said," he told her. He stepped over her, raised his sword in a brief salute to them all, and left the practice room. There were still some places in this palace where he belonged, after all.

The bright chestnut gelding gave the mildest of impatient snorts and tried to rub his nose on the inside of his foreleg. Ehren let the reins slip through his fingers to accommodate the horse, a sensible but often hot-blooded creature named Shaffron. Today, however, Shaffron was tired. It was the end of a long day, and Ehren was stretching it out even longer to get to the station at the border crossing. Seventeen days of travel, taking back roads across the breadth of Solvany from coastal Kurtane to the eastern border crossing into Loraka, and he was too close to the border station to stop for the night in the middle of nowhere.

Shaffron, satisfied his nose was properly tended, commenced to shake, rattling Ehren's teeth with the unexpectedness of it. Ehren swore mildly at the horse; Shaffron lowered his head, jingled the loose shanks of the bit, and waited for Ehren to decide what would happen next. Thrushes rustled in the underbrush around them, offering occasional liquid notes of evening song.

"You should have been born a mule," Ehren told his

mount. "Ricasso never does things like that." Ricasso was a stouter, taller gelding who had never decided if he wanted to be brown or black and thus was a muddle of the two; he waited at the end of his lead with palpable patience. Today he carried supplies instead of carrying Ehren; yesterday he had taken the front. The two horses had served him like this, sharing pack and saddle duties, for the year Ehren had moved along the coast. They were a team, now, well-trained and in superb condition. He conversed with them without reservation and on occasion would have sworn they spoke in return.

But when he nudged Shaffron forward, Ricasso followed grudgingly, and his first step made a clinking noise. *Damn*. Loose shoe. Ehren had a moment's wistful thought—he might make it to the border station just fine, since they were on the main road now, smooth and well-tended— but it wasn't worth the chance the shoe might tear off, taking with it crucial chunks of Ricasso's hoof. "All right, boys," he said out loud. "That's it for the day."

He found a place in the scrubby woods to lead the horses away from the road. No water, but they'd watered thoroughly within the hour and done nothing but walk in the cool of the evening since. He'd eaten well at noon, too, paying king's coin to a couple making a go of it on this hard soil, in the shadow of the mountains. Those jutting Lorakan ridges rose suddenly at the border, as though some force had wrinkled the earth like a piece of cloth, and Solvany west of the mountains was an arid place, little populated.

Amidst the ever-bolder thrushes and a quietly calling cuckoo, Ehren built a small fire for some tea and went about unsaddling the horses. As the daylight faded, he applied a brush to the sweat marks on Shaffron's back; Ricasso was browsing, trailing his lead rope and never straying far from his partner. It was Ehren's thoughts that kept straying, back to the young couple that had fed him. They'd been so nervous at his approach, even though he'd been wearing ailettes—painted leather squares tied off the point of his shoulder—with the Guard crest on them. *Just imagine if you'd been wearing your mail or brigandine*, he told himself, working at the crusty hair across Shaffron's loins while the horse stretched his lips in silly foal faces of enjoyment.

But a moment later the animal's head went up in the air, his diminutive ears pricked tightly up and forward. Ten yards away, Ricasso mirrored the movement.

"Company, then, boys?" Ehren murmured. In a moment he heard it, too; conversation, a little loud, and only two of them unless the third simply never got a word in edgewise. There was barely enough daylight for him to pick out their shapes as they approached, on foot, and then stopped, looking at his fire. Shaffron snorted; Ricasso echoed it.

"That decides it," one of the men said. "Care for some company?" he called to Ehren.

"As you please," Ehren told him, not particularly pleased himself.

They blundered through the brush toward him, and Ehren sighed, resigning himself. "What's on the fire?" the second man said, a solidly padded outline with a voice that sounded head-cold hoarse; an assortment of snuffling sounds reinforced the impression.

"Not much," Ehren said. "Tea, if you'd care to share it."

"Oh, good, he's a generous sort," the first man said. They arrived in the firelight; the first man was scruffy and sported an ill-tended beard, while his well-padded partner was vigorously wiping his nose on his sleeve. Charming. They wore rough brigandines with ailettes Ehren couldn't read in the darkness; he tried to remember if the border was patrolled this far out.

"Border patrol?" he asked, setting aside the horse brushes to pour himself some tea. "You'll have to provide your own cup, unless you care to wait for this one."

"Yeah, a patrol of sorts," the allergic one agreed. "Never mind the tea. We've got our own drink." And so they had, a leather bota with something stronger than tea, no doubt. With any luck they'd fall asleep early and not snore too loudly.

Ricasso gave a mutter of a snort, letting the world know he wasn't sure of these newcomers.

"He's got two," the bearded man said. He looked at his companion and without a word they jerked their long narrow swords free of their scabbards. Ehren froze.

"No harm to you, fellow, unless you give us trouble," the stout man said. "All we want's your horses. Seems fair, don't it, the two of us with no horses and you with two all to yourself?"

"Fair depends on your point of view, I expect," Ehren said, holding his arms out to the side, one hand still gripping his cup. He could *probably* clear his sword before either of these two could reach him, but—not just yet.

"You just move aside," the bearded man said, edging toward Shaffron, waving his sword to herd Ehren to the other side of the fire. Step by step, careful not to offend, Ehren moved, gaining a little more distance between them.

Covered by his partner, the sniffling stout man did a quick search of the ground around the fire. "Got saddles?" he demanded.

"Two," Ehren said. *But you've got to get the horses first.* "And don't mix them, or the boys will get saddle sores."

"The boys," the bearded man repeated mockingly. "Isn't that sweet." His eyes still on Ehren, he groped for the saddle on the ground by the horse, fighting the tangle of girth and stirrup leathers. As the man tugged the saddle blanket free and tossed it at Shaffron's back, the horse snorted. Jerking against the insubstantial tree that held him, he neatly stepped sideways. The blanket slid to the ground.

Ehren smiled. The stout man scowled at him and muttered at his partner, "Hurry up, will you?"

But when the bearded man reached for Shaffron's lead rope to steady him, the horse grunted and struck at him with a front hoof; the man leapt back with a curse. Ehren dipped his tea at the stout robber in toast and took a sip.

"Ninth Level, just get the beast!" the stout man snapped, and wiped his nose again, shifting his gaze between his partner and Ehren, between impatience and growing uncertainty. What to do with a man who drank his tea as he was robbed? "Try the other one first."

With a glance at Ehren, and another at the snorting, walleyed prancing of Shaffron, the bearded man sheathed his sword, an angry motion that jammed the weapon home. He grabbed up both saddle and blanket, heading out for the rustle in the scrub that was Ricasso.

"Wrong saddle," Ehren said.

The stout man snarled, "Shut up!"

They could see nothing of horse nor man, despite the clear light of the brightening stars, but the course of events was obvious without such cues. Ricasso's snort, the man's harsh command to *stand*, the slap of the saddle against the horse's back. A peculiar, solid thud, the snapping twigs of a body falling through brush. Agitated hoofbeats and a fading sigh of a moan that was not repeated.

Ehren looked the stout man in his piggish little eyes and said, his smile suddenly gone dangerous, "I told him it was the wrong saddle."

The stout man hesitated; his sword wavered. "Endall," he called uncertainly, and turned his head ever so slightly, as if he might see through the dark brush to his partner. Ricasso snorted.

Ehren had the distance that made it safe to unsheathe his weapon; he threw the tea on the ground, reached for his sword hilt—and the stout thief broke. Dropping his guard, he turned and fled.

Ehren's sword rang free of the scabbard; he leapt over the little fire and ran for Ricasso, unwilling to expose his back to the bearded man however unlikely the threat. He tripped over the saddle, a dark bundle on the ground, but saw the man clearly enough—a bigger dark bundle of flaccid muscles that did not respond to the nudge of his toe. Maybe dead, maybe not; certainly hurt. Ehren jerked the man's Lorakan-style sword free of its scabbard and threw it into the scrub. When Ricasso jigged up to him, rolling high snorts of excitement, Ehren grabbed the lead rope and swung up onto the animal.

The sturdy, big-boned horse crashed through the brush as though it wasn't even there, the wide warmth of his body solid between Ehren's thighs, his movements full of power. His heavy hoof-falls steadied as they gained the road, and though he snorted eagerly, his canter remained even as they reached and passed their quarry.

The stout man had taken a quarter mile at full run and his stride was turning to a stagger. When a shift of Ehren's weight brought Ricasso broadside in his path, the man stumbled to a stop, almost losing his balance.

Even so, it was only an instant before he managed to reverse track and head for the brush—though suddenly Ricasso was in his way there, too. It took three such tries, with Ricasso cutting him off more quickly each time as he understood the game. Finally the thief stood still, panting. Without much hope, his eyes half closed and his head tilted back with his exhaustion, he said, "Please . . . don't kill me."

"If I killed you, I'd have to carry you," Ehren said. He rode up close and nudged the man with his booted toe, nodding back the way they'd come. With resignation and no few furtive glances at the brush, the man obliged.

They'd only gone a few steps when Ehren realized Ricasso's gait was subtly uneven. Grabbing the horse's mane, he leaned over the sturdy line of Ricasso's shoulder and looked at his foot as it stepped in and out of view. In the darkness it took several paces, but by then he was sure. "Damn," he muttered, and at that moment, he saw a dark flash of movement on the other side of the horse.

Ricasso sprang forward instantly, and Ehren reached down to haul the thief back by his greasy shirt collar. "Don't tempt me," he growled, giving the man a little shake. "Now that Ricasso's lost that shoe, I'm *really* mad."

※　～～✦～～　✕

Morning confirmed Ehren's hope that Ricasso's hoof had taken only minor damage. He pulled the shoe off the other front hoof to balance the horse out and resigned himself to walking until he reached the border station. Shaffron bore the pack and Ricasso carried his own saddle; the thief's bound hands were tied to one stirrup, and after his surreptitious attempts to loosen the rope annoyed the horse into snapping at him, he was docile enough.

The second robber was dead and still lay where he'd fallen, his chest crushed and bearing the clear imprint of two hooves. In the daylight, Ehren discovered their ailettes were nothing more than a meaningless combination of crests— Border Patrol, King's Guard, Local Guard—enough symbols of authority to catch the eye and make any law-abiding man at least hesitate.

It made him think of the young couple and their trepidation at his approach. And that made him wonder what was going on in the borderlands, and what news he had missed as he'd scoured the coastal areas of Solvany. But gentle prodding got him no answers from his prisoner, and he left it at that. For now, it was the Border Patrol's problem.

Ehren crossed the Eredon River bridge and reached the border station at midday, his feet more sore than he liked to admit. He turned the thief over to the youth and middle-aged veteran there, told them of the body alongside the road, and wondered out loud at the paucity of traffic that morning. He got plenty of cooperation with handling the thief, but only shrugs in response to his deliberately idle questions, so he took Ricasso into the crossroads beyond the border station. It was actually a small collection of amenities—an inn, a modest number of merchants under one roof, and what Ehren was looking for: a series of corralled shelters with a grain shed and a farrier's anvil and forge in the midst of them. Behind it all was a barn for the higher paying customers.

He hitched Shaffron outside one of the corrals and had to stop the farrier's hand as it reached for Ricasso's lead. "She's safe," he told the horse distinctly, not once but three times, waiting for the animal's ears to swivel forward again, and then pressed the rope into the burly woman's hand within the horse's field of view. "Just don't let anyone else try to handle him," he told the woman dryly as she eyed the horse askance.

Ricasso calmly eyed her back. At sixteen hands and with

a trace of draft blood in his veins, his superbly conditioned bulk was more than intimidating. But in the end the woman sighed and bent to examine the horse's hoof, having apparently decided to trust Ehren's confidence in the matter.

She grunted over the chunks of missing hoof—Ricasso's hoof walls had ever been liable to crumble—and said, "I'll have to make him a pair. Don't have anything this big on hand right now."

"He toes in a little on the left side," Ehren said. "He'll do better if you leave a little length to the shoe on the outside."

She grunted again, a noise he took to be assent, and led Ricasso to the hitching rail by her anvil.

Ehren stripped Shaffron of his packs, gave the horse a quick curry, and saddled him up again. Then he hesitated, looking at the ring on his little finger.

Just as Varien had told him, it pulsed against his skin. No longer just a ring, it now had many roles. Somehow Varien had used the ring, and the blood tie from Benlan to his brother Dannel, to create the vaguest of guides. Ehren didn't understand how it worked; nor did he understand why it was then necessary to trigger one last spell to confirm the bloodline when he was with the royal family in their self-imposed exile: Dannel and his T'ierand-blood wife, with whatever children they might have had. Varien wanted them confirmed, and would know when the spell was triggered.

And then, he told Ehren, Ehren was to make sure there would be no interference from them, no threat to Rodar. In whatever way was necessary. He made it just as plain that failure in this matter would be considered the same as treason; at the very least, Ehren would be cast from the Guard.

"I'm no hired killer," Ehren had told him, as bluntly as was his wont. And Varien had just smiled. For the Guard . . . the Guard had been his life. Benlan's trust in him had fueled bone-deep loyalty at an early age, loyalty to the royal blood— even if the current king was in fact a royal pain in the ass.

Ehren frowned now, at the memory, and swung into the saddle. The ring nagged at him, and although he expected it would lead him in the obvious direction—through the trade route pass to Lake Everdawn, and down through the gentler hills beyond into Loraka proper—he intended to ride the area around the border station, and see if the feeling waxed and waned. It had certainly done nothing but intensify as he approached the border, so Varien had, indeed, aimed him in the right direction.

Shaffron bobbed his head impatiently, his fine neck arched and as noble as he could get it. With his copious copper-flaxen mane and tail and the fine T'ieran-bred features that hid the true wealth of sturdiness beneath, he was a lady pleaser, the horse that drew the attention—though Ricasso was the real pet, the one who wanted scratches and murmured words.

Ehren gave Shaffron the slight shift of leg which meant *go*, and Shaffron, pleased to be free of the pack and ever the glorious show-off, jigged a fancy sideways prance down the Trade Road.

Ehren let him play. He was more interested in the ring against his finger, and the careful inspection he received from the few travelers he passed. Suspicion seemed to be the one thing that united them; he noticed not one of them was traveling alone, but always in pairs—or more. He didn't spend much time in this part of the country, but even so their sullenness, the quick glances of distrust they gave him, struck him as odd.

But what was even odder was the road branch he ran into a quarter mile out, off to the south and into territory that had been largely impassable since the Border War several hundred years earlier. There were too many stray magics floating around, fading ambushes and spells of confusion, ready to snare the unwary traveler. Someone, it appeared, was overcoming the dangers.

He kept Shaffron to a cautious walk, and investigated half a mile of the new road, finding that it turned rough fast, with barely an impression of wagon wheels as a guide.

The established Trade Road to Lake Everdawn, worn to stone and dust and wheel ruts, ran along the pass made by the Eredon River. East of the lake, the hills turned mild enough that passage into Loraka had been forged by man, and not water. But *this* road . . . well, calling it a road was generous by any standards. Once it crossed the river—via a crude, man-built ford that wouldn't last long against the rush of the water—the north-south line of ridges rose again, enfolding the twisting road and any unwary travelers upon it. Complete with wild, leftover magics.

And there was no doubt the ring was happy about Ehren's course. It practically purred upon his finger. The moment he turned Shaffron north to return to the station, it quit. Sulking, he would have called it, if he was wont to make light of Varien's magic. Shaffron settled into a steady, rolling canter with his characteristically high leg action, leaving Ehren plenty of opportunity to digest what he'd learned.

There was a new road. It led south into the Lorakan mountains, a rough territory of unfriendly magics; its end point was unknown. And it was where he had to go.

<hr>

"No, sir, you can't mean to do it." The young Border Guard gave an emphatic shake of his head and spat around the corner of the guardhouse, into the weedy growth that held its ground despite heavy traffic.

Ehren raised an eyebrow, amused. "Why, I guess I do, at that." He waited for the man to check a small wagon for signs of contraband—mostly, materials too similar to those Solvany produced on its own—and said, "Tell me about that road. Until this afternoon, I didn't even know it existed."

"Ain't but two years old," the man said. He was young, without much more than a scraggly assortment of hairs on his upper lip, but he talked as though he'd been in the Border Patrol guard forever. Ehren kept his amusement to himself. "Some Therand merchant—guy named Ansgare—found himself a fellow who can See the magics and avoid them, even with the way they wander around."

"Any half-trained apprentice can do that." Ehren felt horse lips nibbling surreptitiously at his shoulder and twitched his shoulder up to bump Shaffron away.

"Not this, they can't. This fellow—he's young, too, maybe a couple years older'n me—just Sees them naturally. He don't know a thing about casting spells, or setting charm warnings. He just *sees* the wrong places, when everyone else'd walk right into 'em. So he guides Ansgare's merchants straight from the Therand pass, along the mountains to us. Cuts off a lot of time, and they aren't paying any of the Lorakan road tariffs."

No small matter, and no small advantage. Since the Border Wars, the man-made, magic-kept Barrenlands had separated Solvany and Therand. Trade between the two countries had been forced to circumvent the barrier by swinging east through Loraka. Loraka had kept well to itself during the Solvany-Therand conflict, and was further isolated by the abrupt and rugged series of ridges between its inner lands and its western border against both Solvany and Therand.

The mountains restricted travel to only one route—from the Therand pass northeast to Lake Everdawn, and then along the Eredon River to the Solvany pass. It was a long trip, over a month, and though the road was kept warded and safe by a bevy of Lorakan wizards, there was a high price for using it.

But the very difficulty of obtaining Therand products created a demand for them—horses of Shaffron's breeding, or fine, soft woolen cloth—while the Therand-born developed a taste for the salted, north coastal fish of Solvany's fishing fleet. Running goods from one country to the other had become a major source of income for the entrepreneurs of both countries.

Ansgare's route cut his travel time in half, Ehren guessed. An advantage worth the risk of following some youngster's unusual Sight. Ehren fingered the ring on his little finger and thought of Varien's veiled threats, layered on top of one another, the hints that many of the First Level no longer trusted Ehren—the most visible of the King's Guards, and

the one who hadn't been there when Benlan died. That
they were looking for a reason to cast him out of the Guard,
and maybe into a dungeon.

The road forward was uncertain. The road back . . . was
rutted and filled with dangers he had not untangled yet,
any more than he could untangle the magics ahead.

He gave the Border Guard a wry crook of his mouth.
"It can't be any worse than what waits for me back in
Kurtane."

"Yessir," the guard agreed, patently not understanding
in the least. "Can I offer you any provisions to get you
started?"

"That would be welcome," Ehren said, pushing Shaffron's
questing lips off his shoulder again. *Do better to lay in a
supply of luck.*

Chapter 3

Laine looked at Shette and blinked. For a moment, she'd been someone else, a young girl with vacant eyes and the look of old Solvany about her clothes and hairstyle, things he recognized from the few precious books his parents had collected. Her expression was dull; in her hand she held some kind of toy—a wand with brightly colored tassels, meant for a child half her age or less—and she'd been hitting her leg with it in monotonous rhythm.

And now he saw Shette again. Sandy-haired, light brown eyes, and built like their mother. Not very tall. Definitely not the lithe look she pined for, but instead sturdy, and just a little bit broad despite the lack of excess flesh on her frame. And, at this moment, definitely annoyed.

"What're you staring at?" she demanded, squatting by the fire to reposition the heavy iron fry pan over the hottest coals. Despite the fact that she was the daughter of a beef cattle farmer from westmost Loraka, she had a ribbon woven into the complicated plaits that were all the rage among the Solvany upper class.

"Not your hair," he told her, knowing that was her suspicion, and then winced inwardly—that'd teach him to get caught off guard.

She gave him a mighty scowl. "You mean you think it's so awful you can't even bear to *look* at it?"

43

"It's *not* awful," he said lamely, because, in truth, it was too delicate and fanciful to compliment her strong features, and Sevita, one of the whores who'd been coaxing Shette into friendship, should have known better. "It's—" and the other girl was back, sitting by a window, looking out without seeing as she slowly, deliberately, brought her head into contact with the brightly painted stone wall of a child's nursery. Again. And again. A smirch of blood stained the paint; behind her, there was some sort of crest, something he didn't recognize.

"*What?*" Shette said.

He shook his head and stood, although the fried ham was almost cooked, and the sliced potatoes he'd been watching on his side of the fire would surely burn without attention. He felt, suddenly, the need to get away from her, lest she turn into that other girl yet again.

"You're really getting strange," Shette muttered as he walked away from their fire and down along the string of wagons and fires on the road. They'd stopped early tonight for Bessney's loose wagon wheel, and there was plenty of light left to walk ahead on the road—but not until he told Ansgare he was going out. Ansgare usually ate with Machara and her sword company of two, whose small wagon brought up the rear of the caravan.

Halfway there he paused at Sevita and Dajania's colorful, enclosed wagon. They weren't immediately to be seen. Entertaining, probably, although they supplemented that profession by treating the minor ailments among the merchants. Well, maybe it was none of his business if they encouraged Shette to try out fancy styles her life would never have a need for. He was turning away when Dajania popped around the end of the wagon and said, "Laine!" in a delighted voice. He was not surprised to see her hair done up like Shette's. Sevita's work, all right.

"You two don't do her any favors, you know," he said.

Her mouth pursed in an exaggerated pout. Unlike Sevita, who was light on the powders and face paint, Dajania was bold in her appearance. Plump in all the right places,

cheerfully inoffensive but not taking any slight without
an instant response, Dajania co-owned the wagon she and
Sevita worked out of—although Sevita's quiet voice always
seemed to have the last say. Dajania trailed her hand along
the edge of the wagon and sauntered out to him, hips
a-sway.

"She's a girl, Laine," Dajania said. She stopped directly
in front of him and draped her arms over his shoulders
without invitation. "Girl's got to play with her hair and face.
And she's a lot more grown up than you think she is."

Dajania was *not* the person he wanted to hear *that* from.

She grinned slyly, reading it on his ever-revealing face.
"Poor dearie," she said. "Do we make you worry? And here
we, of all people, should be giving you *other* things to think
about." She pulled his head down and kissed him.

And kissed him.

"Dajania," he said, against her lips, holding his arms out
to the side in supplication of sorts. "Mmph. Dajania—"
Oh, what the Hells. He let his hands fall on her soft, ample
hips and kissed her back. After a moment she came down
off her tiptoes and pulled back from him.

"See?" she said. "You see what you're missing? And that
was *free.* It gets better when you pay for it, dear."

Laine found himself unable to think clearly right at that
moment. "Umm," he said. "Right. Ummm . . . have you
seen Ansgare?"

She was laughing, quiet but taking no pains to hide it.
" 'Course, dear. He's right where he always is, with Machara
and her two. But he'll be round later this evening . . . why
don't you stay and wait a while? I'll make sure you don't
get bored."

Laine wiped the back of his hand across his mouth. "Not
tonight, Dajania," he said as he stepped back from her,
stumbling a little.

Another pout, but there was still amusement in her amber
eyes. "I'll get you in that wagon yet, Laine-dear. And I'll
enjoy the look on that handsome face when I do."

Not while Shette is in this caravan, Laine told himself

quite fiercely. The first year or so with the caravan, Laine had been faithful to his sweetheart at home. She'd gotten tired of his traveling ways and married someone else this spring—but by then the game between Laine and the whores was set, and he figured he enjoyed it as much as he would any single hour in their bed. But sometimes . . . well, sometimes they came very close to winning.

Fortunately, his brain was back in place by the time he made it down to Ansgare, along the second half of the caravan, another eleven wagons. Biggest train yet. As far as Laine was concerned, it was as big as it would get, no matter how the profits beckoned Ansgare. The travel was rugged but not impossible, but the magics were unpredictable. And as recent experience had shown, they were becoming more . . . *focused*. He wouldn't want to guarantee the safety of anyone as far away from him as the back of a lengthy caravan, not anymore.

It made him wonder if their very presence here wasn't stirring something up.

"Sit and have something to eat," Machara told him, when he'd arrived and said nothing after several minutes. Too lost in thought, even if it was no longer of Dajania's obvious skills.

He shook his head. "Shette's got something going up front," he said, and let Ansgare know he'd be walking ahead a way, scouting for spells in tomorrow's path. "Not that it'll mean we're safe in the morning," he added. "Not the way things have been going. But I'll sleep better all the same."

"Go ahead, son," Ansgare grunted around a mouthful of tough meat—fresh, at that, a mountain hare the tin merchant's young son had brought down with sling and stone, and presented to the caravan leader. "Just don't go so far a good yell won't bring someone running."

"No fear of that." He wasn't even wearing his sword. "I leave the fighting to those who do it best."

"Oh, you did well enough," Machara drawled. Short-cropped red hair, pale blue eyes, and generously freckled skin went far to hide the steel and professional skill that was Machara. Ansgare, a wiry man whose fencing skill lay in words and bargains, was smitten with her, for all that she was a decade his younger. If Machara had thoughts on the matter, she kept them to herself. "That was quite a pretty kill you made, that monster-that-wasn't-where-he-was."

He sketched her a noble bow. "Kind Machara. Just don't stop listening for that yell."

She raised her meat-tipped knife in acknowledgment, and he grinned back. But he thought, as he walked back along the line of wagons, that he would pick up his sword before he left Shette again.

He stopped long enough for some of the ham and potatoes—Shette had managed to keep them from burning despite his precipitous exit—but not any longer. "I'm going to walk on a ways," he told Shette, sticking his dish in a bucket of water to soak a while. Strapping his sword belt on, an act that was finally beginning to feel natural, he was walking away from their wagon when Shette's voice followed him.

"I want to come, too."

Spike snorted loudly, as though in emphatic agreement.

"Shette—" he started, and fortunately stopped before saying, *It's you I'm trying to get away from tonight,* because no matter what he really meant, he'd never explain his way out of that one. But over his quick meal, that vacant-eyed girl had returned yet again, this time allowing her limp limbs to be dressed by hands whose owners he couldn't see.

This sort of thing had never happened to him before. It had to be the area they were in, the vestiges of some strange spell, maybe one that had faded and eroded into something other than its original form. In any case, it wasn't something he wanted to deal with. It was distracting, and . . . disturbing.

"Shette," he said again, and firmly this time, "it's your turn to do the dishes." That, at least, was true. And by the angry mumbling behind him, she knew it as well.

Laine stepped out onto the path ahead. It was clearer here, for it wandered through a thick grove of sumac. The first year of the caravan, Laine and Ansgare had spent no small amount of time and effort cutting through it, and every time they came this way, they had to take hand axes to the stubborn, quick-growing saplings that had sprouted anew. There was a quarter mile of the stuff, set on the slight slope sumac always favored. They gave way to grassy, scrubby rock soon enough, and not long after that, the path intersected the main Trade Road and led to Solvany.

He was nearly to the end of the sumac grove when his eyes got that strange, hard-to-focus feeling that meant there was magic around. He stopped short. No matter what was going on around him, when the magic tickled his eyes, he always stopped and added the extra bend of will that let him see what waited.

This time, he hesitated first. There was a sharp feeling to this spot, similar to what had surrounded the area where the acid-spitting creature had nearly gotten Shette. Laine rubbed his arm appreciatively; it was healed, but the skin was still pinkly shiny where the thing's spittle had landed. There was a certain subtle clarity to the feel of magic there— and here—that he'd not encountered in the previous two years of travel.

Feeling just a little silly, he drew his sword, and looked through the trees before him. Ordinary sumacs, the tallest of which was perhaps twice his height, dripping elongated spears of leaves and a few dried, leftover berry bunches from the previous fall's seedfest. And then . . . not. Suddenly, darkly reaching branches writhed before him, just out of reach—and by the Hells, they *did* try to get him, stiff wood turned to flexible tentacles and oozing . . . something.

Laine took a step back, his face scrunched in revulsion. An odor drifted out to him, a thick, gagging smell; he brought the back of his hand up to cover his nose and mouth. Not that it did any good. Something flittered across his vision, darting among the trees, and he didn't think it was a bird.

Ugh, he'd had enough. He stumbled back a few steps,

and then a few more, before he dared to turn around and trot away with his back to the spelled area.

Once out of the sumacs, he moved up the hill a few feet and sat, only then discovering his sword was still in his hand. Carefully, he laid it on the hill, rescued it when it started to slide, and found a bit of grass hummock against which to rest the forte of the blade. *Think, Laine*, he told himself. *Tomorrow we've got to get a caravan through here.*

They could always accept a day or so of delay and cut a new trail—after all, there were more hands here than when Ansgare and Laine had first cut their way through. Laine grimaced at the thought nonetheless, and then realized that wasn't really what bothered him the most.

It was the feel and nature of the magic.

Until this point, the spells had been limited to one or two per trip, and always felt worn from years and miles of wandering the currents of the mountains. And they weren't site specific; they might trigger monsters from another plane of existence, or they might bring down blindness upon all within the influence of the spell, or they might make everyone too heavy to move. They rarely had a direct effect on the environment.

Rarely isn't the same as never. But *never*, he had to admit, had the spells felt so . . . anchored.

In the distance, a loud snort. Spike, Laine thought, distracted. But then the noise repeated, and it held the edge of alarm. Scrambling to his feet, Laine realized that the mountains had twisted the sound on him, and that it had come from the sumacs. Someone else on their road, coming from the other side? Who would dare it, without a guide?

The shout of alarm he heard was human, and he didn't hesitate any longer. He scooped up his sword and ran for the sumacs. And this time, when he reached the spell, he didn't have to make any effort to See it. It was triggered, all right, and there were figures within the odiferous, magicked sumac, thrashing against the twining limbs that reached for them, ducking the swirl and loop of a darting, airborne horde of . . . Laine squinted. Of . . . something really ugly with teeth and claws.

He set his jaw and ran into the dripping trees, heading for the man and his two horses. His sword ran interference for him, and he ducked and slashed, creating enough noise so the man heard him coming and froze an instant, focused sharply on Laine. Then the heavy-boned horse beside him screamed a challenge—a branch had draped over his poll and oozed down his neck, spiraling a tendril around the rein that rested there—and the man was in motion again, leaving Laine with the impression of economical deadliness.

"Let me help!" Laine yelled over the huff-huff-grunt of the lighter horse; it reared, kicking its hind legs out behind before its front legs touched back to the ground. Something grabbed his ankle—Hells, were the roots doing it too?—and Laine hesitated just long enough to slash it away; when he straightened he had to duck a flurry of leathery wings and grasping talons. But he was still moving, and as he reached the besieged trio, the man said, "Take him!" and nearly flung the big horse's rein at Laine, pausing at the last minute to shout, "It's safe!"

Laine was about to shout, "No it's *not*," as if that hadn't been obvious, harried as they were by tree and creature, when the big dark horse snaked his neck forward and snapped at him. Laine back-pedaled furiously, smacking into a tree and then reflexively leaping forward out of its unnatural grasp.

"He's *safe*, dammit!" the man said, and smacked the horse's butt as it passed him, still on its way to Laine. The horse pinned his ears, shaking his head in threat—but when he snapped, it was at the creature flapping above him.

Laine had no intention of trying to figure it all out. He reclaimed the rein he'd dropped and turned for the edge of the sumac, hauling the horse for only the first few steps. As soon as the beast realized he was heading for safety, he spurted into a powerful pounding trot, dragging Laine the last thirty feet. The sumac clung to Laine, ripping his shirt, a noise which only spurred the horse on. Once on a clear path, the horse snorted loudly half a dozen times, and when Laine would have turned to check on the animal's companions, he discovered the horse had other ideas. He scrambled to stay on his feet as the rein jerked him onward, and was unable to stop the horse until "Ricasso, whoa!" rang through the air from behind him.

It seemed, then, that they'd all made it out. But Laine suddenly felt like he was getting *into* something just as dangerous.

The big dark horse jigged beside him, and Laine kept an ever-wary eye on it as they finally approached the wagons he and the oddly familiar man from the sumacs. His wagon seemed innocuously out of place compared to the horror they had just run through. It sat at the head of the caravan, square and solid, a sturdy four-wheeled box with a springed seat up front. The edges of the wagon body were lined with deep compartments that held provisions and equipment, and still left room for passengers or hay in the center. All very homey looking, and far too calm to be perched a quarter of a mile away from the hellish sumacs.

This particular camping spot was unusually generous with its space, a nice wide spot in the narrow valley they followed northward. There was even room to picket Spike and Clang between the wagon and the mountain that rose abruptly to the west of the trail. The couple dozen merchants and wagons strung out in a line behind his own wagon were barely visible; it was the everyday supper time noise and clatter that gave them away.

Shette was nowhere to be seen. At the back of the wagon, no doubt, cleaning up after supper, or using the dishwater, if it was clean enough, to do some laundry. She'd been bored lately. Well, he was bringing her something to make the day more interesting.

Spike's head jerked up from the hay Laine'd spread out for him, his ears perked at full forward. He gave a challenging snort loud enough to pop Laine's ears; there was a clatter from behind the wagon—Shette, no doubt, startled by the noise. *That'd* put her in fine fettle.

In a moment she came out from behind the wagon, the laundry bag still in her hands—but her purposeful strides immediately faltered. Laine didn't think he'd ever seen that stunned look on her face before.

He rather enjoyed it.

It was easy to put himself in her place, to see himself leading the big, handsome horse. Behind him was the stranger, leading a spirited, high-crested chestnut with a flaxen mane and tail. He was taller than Laine, and despite the bulk of the leather, metal-studded brigandine he wore, it was clear he was broad-shouldered, lean-hipped, and long-legged. His boots were faced with metal greaves, and his strides long and self-assured. *Surprise, Shette.*

Shette took a few steps closer to them, her mouth hanging open, and Laine smothered a grin. Then the big horse behind him stepped on his heel, and he had to take a few quick steps to keep his feet; when he looked up again, Shette had recovered her wits. She'd dropped the bag of laundry and was waiting with arms crossed.

Laine stopped at the wagon tongue, offering no explanation of it all but a tired and wry grin—not that Shette gave him a chance. Her eyes widened, and she blurted, "You *stink*!"

Laine's sharp reply, half-framed, was drowned out by Spike's abrupt braying, a greeting to the two horses who were wet with nervous sweat and not particularly interested in introductions. Behind Laine, the man snapped his horse's lead rope and said firmly, "Settle down." Shette's eyes went to him, and her face had a strange expression—almost disbelief.

"Are you all right?" Laine asked her, amused—and then amused again at the incongruity of the question. *He* was the one with smelly sumac ooze on his shoulders and muck on his boots, his black hair ruffled and messed, sweat dripping off his nose . . . he thought Shette did well when she stifled her sudden laugh.

"Am *I* all right?" she repeated. "I should be asking *you*! What's going on, Laine?" She gave the man and horse behind Laine another look, one that grew bolder when no one challenged it. "Who's this?"

"Ehren," the man said. "Your brother helped me out of a bad spot. I'd heard there was magic wandering around, but I never expected such an . . . intense spell."

"Neither did I," Laine grumbled. Or such an intense *smell*, for that matter. "We need to talk to the caravan master, Ehren, and let him know you've joined us. Not to mention that we've got to find another way through to the trade road."

"I'm not at all sure I've *joined* you," Ehren said. "But we'll talk to the master. After I've checked my horses."

"I can go get him," Shette said. "And I'm sure I can find someone with supper still on—I'll bet you haven't eaten."

Laine raised an eyebrow at her, suspicious of such cooperation, but said nothing except a mild, "Let's take care of the horses first, and give Ehren a few minutes before he has to face Ansgare." Ansgare was likely to react strongly to the notion of a blocked road and a stranger on it, no doubt about that. She made a face at him, but it was a quick one, and then her eyes were on Ehren again.

"Just pull that saddle off," Ehren said to Laine. He was already working at the ties on the chestnut's pack—though the animal didn't strike Laine as a pack horse at all. "We'll hobble Ricasso; Shaffron won't stray from him."

The horses were still nervous enough that Laine never would have chosen to leave one of them untied, but he didn't say so. Instead he flipped the stirrup over the saddle and tugged at the girth. When he glanced up, he discovered Shette had moved closer, and was extending a hand to pet the big black horse, murmuring some soothing nonsense.

"No, Shette!" he cried, lunging for the reins underneath the horse's chin just as the animal laid its ears back, flinging its head up and baring its big yellow teeth. Shette stumbled back in astonishment as Laine was swept off his feet and tossed to the ground, but Ehren was swift on those long legs, and left the chestnut to snatch the cheekpiece of the black's bridle. He snapped something quick and hard and gave the bridle a meaningful shake.

The horse subsided; it lowered its head and flapped its thick mane against its neck as though nothing had happened. Shette stared at the creature, appalled—an expression she couldn't manage to tuck away before Ehren glanced at her.

"I'm sorry," he said. "It's best if you don't try to touch them. I should have said something right away."

"That's all right," Shette said, her voice uncertain; she glanced down at Laine as though looking for guidance. "I . . . imagine you had other things on your mind."

From the ground, Laine grunted, recovering from his awkward sprawl. "This horse has given me more bruises in one evening than Spike's managed in the last month," he said wearily. "And that's saying something."

Ehren's mouth quirked—humor, and apology as well. He leaned down to take Laine's arm and help haul him up.

At Ehren's touch, Laine stiffened, every muscle jerking to attention. *The clash of steel and eyes watching him and blood and cries of pain and fire across his throat*—his legs gave way, his arm slipped out of Ehren's grasp, and he landed in a heap, on the ground again. Ehren hovered over him, surrounded by an aura of dark and ominous colors. Dangerous.

"Laine?" Shette's concerned voice sounded so very far away.

Laine took a big gasp, and blinked, and then frowned to find the earth so near again. "What the Hells?" he muttered.

"Battle shock," Ehren said, his voice sounding deliberately even, and extended a hand again. This time Laine made it to his feet without incident, though the world around him seemed further away than the images and sensations in his mind. He shook his head, a dog shaking off water, and reached for the saddle again, forcing his body to behave.

"Just what did you run into up the trail?" Shette asked suspiciously, holding out her arms for the saddle Laine pushed at her. Ehren continued to watch him, obviously not sure it was safe to leave Laine to his own devices just yet.

"Nothing you want to get close to," Laine assured her, finding that intense and recent experience to be something he could focus on. "Some kind of spell on the sumac grove. The trees were . . ."

"Alive," Ehren supplied, finally turning back to the chestnut, whose fidgeting had not taken him all that far from his equine buddy, after all. "Slimy and alive."

"Blackened, slimy and alive," Laine decided, seizing the chance to act like a big brother instead of a vacant-minded clod. "Their branches were like cold, oozing fingers. Just imagine, Shette—going through that grove at night, with sumac fingers reaching for your neck . . . in the darkness . . . silently. . . ."

"Stop it," Shette snapped.

"And what were those bat things?" Laine said, a genuine question this time, and aimed at Ehren. "Have you ever seen anything like that before?"

Ehren flipped the pack tarp neatly off the chestnut's load; it settled to the ground behind him. His face looked strained, Laine thought, finally noticing the details of this world again. "Not before, and never again, if I have a choice. They were quick. I'm lucky they only got me once."

"You were bitten?" Shette asked, and hastily set the saddle on end just beneath the wagon. "Are you all right?"

"Bitten or clawed, it's hard to tell," Ehren said, glancing down at his wrist as he finished unloading the horse. The pack frame fit around the animal's very normal saddle, and Ehren lifted it off. "It's not deep. But I suspect it's some kind of poison."

"Why didn't you say something?" Laine asked. He'd been about to lead the big horse to the side of the wagon where Spike wasn't, but he stopped short.

"Either it'll kill me or it won't," Ehren said, pulling the saddle from the chestnut's back and handing it to Shette, who hadn't managed to move after the revelation that Ehren had been injured. Laine saw the wound then; it didn't look deep, but the parallel marks were vivid, raised and puffy— and the whole wrist was swollen in an alarming—no, wait a minute. That was just the thick, strong wrist of a swordsman. Still, the poisoned scratches needed tending.

Shette exchanged a look with Laine, and he suddenly knew what she was thinking. Dajania was as close as they got to a physician on this caravan, and he bet she didn't want to let Dajania anywhere near this man.

Ehren smiled, a wry expression. "If it was going to kill me, I imagine we'd know it by now."

"You don't look very good," Shette said doubtfully, and he didn't, Laine realized. All that sweat wasn't from their exertion, and that sudden flush of color wasn't, either.

"I don't feel all that good," Ehren said. "But I've lived through worse."

"Oh, I don't know," Laine said brightly. "You haven't met Ansgare yet."

Ansgare turned out to be a spare man, bearded and probably older than he looked. Ehren respected him immediately; his expression was a keen one, and he didn't waste much time bemoaning the turn of events, despite Laine's warning. Ansgare wasn't happy at Ehren's appearance, but as he pointed out, the road belonged to no one, and any fool was welcome to bumble along without so much as a cottage witchy to help him. His real concern was getting around the sumacs, and to that end, he left Laine's wagon to gather up the caravan members and total up their hand axes.

Ehren did not give any explanation for his presence—he wore his King's Guard ailette, and that was enough. No one pushed him, although Shette's curiosity was almost palpable. She was a sheltered young woman, one who seemed to know the practicalities of life but had obviously never suffered greatly because of them. She and Laine were manifestly of the same blood, and Shette was a feminine version of Laine's sturdy muscled form, of medium height and with the same general cast of feature.

It had grown dark while Shette scavenged some semblance of a meal for their guest. By the time she presented it to him, Ehren was no longer in the mood for eating. His wrist throbbed with pain and his blood pounded in his ears, but when Shette fretted about it, he shook his head. "If it was going to get worse than this, I expect it would have done it by now," he told her, once again. He was even pretty sure he was right.

He was sure about something else, too. This road was the quickest way to Dannel, and therefore the quickest way to get this over with, and back into Solvany doing what *needed* to be done. But every throb of his wrist reminded him it wasn't a road he could take alone. As cavalier as he'd been about the wound, it had been a much closer call than either Laine or Shette knew—the beast who had done this had barely touched him, just a whisper of claw against skin that hadn't even left a mark. At least, not at first.

No, this wasn't a road he could take alone. But it was a road he had to take. And that meant staying with the person who could See the dangers of the road and avoid them. It would slow him down—but in the end it was still faster than taking the Trade Road.

Shette had said something; Ehren missed it. He shifted his weight, resting his wrist across his knee, and gave her a quick smile. Not encouragement, exactly; reassurance, perhaps, for the worried expression that had appeared on her face. They sat together on the other side of the wagon from the mountain, where the boys were hobbled for the night—away from the mules. The night was warm enough and bright enough that neither had suggested stirring up the dying dinner fire, but other cookfires were still blazing away. Dots of light traced the slightly curving line of the caravan behind Laine's wagon, and someone near the middle was playing a cheerful air on a stringed instrument, occasionally accompanied by a chorus of untuned but enthusiastic voices.

They were alone; Laine had recently taken his blankets and said his good nights. Shette seemed apologetic about it, when in fact Ehren was wishing he could do the same without slighting the girl. But Shette was wound up and talking on without the benefit of encouragement.

"He hasn't been sleeping well," she told Ehren. "It's been such an odd trip—not that I'd know, it's my first time out. But all the magic we've been running into has been hard on him, I think. He dreams . . ." she trailed off, creating a sudden silence that even the faraway singing didn't puncture. One of the tiny scrub owls finally filled her silence with its call.

But she'd given Ehren something to think about—her brother. He had plenty of questions about Laine, and wasn't quite ready to ask them straight out. Sideways, for now. "He mentioned the monstrosity you ran into earlier," Ehren said; it'd been a brief exchange of words outside the sumac grove. He looked over at her, caught her staring at him in the darkness, and let her go when he could see from her expression that she was probably blushing. "I gather he has some sort of Sight."

"He's the reason Ansgare can run this caravan," Shette said, with a touch of pride Ehren doubted she would show in front of her brother. "He's always been able to See things. That's what makes it so strange . . . he doesn't have a drop of wizard potential in him—at least, that's what the old village witchy said when he was my age."

Ehren shifted on his borrowed blankets. Touchy moment here, when asking more could clam her up, just on general principles. Not everyone who was brushed by magic wanted to talk about it. Off to the side, both his horses heard some sinister noise, and snorted suspiciously. "All right, boys," he murmured to them, and added casually to Shette, "It took that long to get him to a wizard?"

Shette's mouth opened, but closed again, and she looked away. Sudden discretion, then. "We only went into the village once a month or so," she said finally, her voice low. "We live in the foothills of these mountains, just this side of the Therand border. There aren't a lot of people there, and the village isn't close."

Ehren knew of the area. To some extent, it explained

Shette's unworldly ways. Not many folk chose to live in the hard border mountains when lusher Therand land was so close—only those of scrappily independent bent who were not inclined to pay the clan tithes, nor want the clan protections.

She dared to glance his way again, and seemed reassured by the bland interest on his face. "It didn't come out strong in him till then," she added, though it sounded lame to his ears. It must have to hers, too, for she suddenly stood, and said, "Ansgare's going to get us up early, I bet. Best go to sleep. I'm going to."

She left Ehren to his aching wrist and thumping head, and the quiet conclusion that Laine, at least, had more of a story to tell—and it was a story Ehren knew he had to hear.

It was Shette's curse to be a light sleeper, and to be lying out under the stars with her brother. When her eyes flew open, she knew she'd heard something; it was only when Laine, lying ten feet away on the other side of the mostly dead fire, grunted again, that she realized what it had been. Dreams again.

With a sigh, Shette sat up, letting her blanket fall to her waist. It was a dead calm night, with no breeze against her face to stir the warm humidity, nothing to cover Laine's noisy dreams.

Or not-dreams. Dreams were what she called them to annoy him, to be little-sister smart. They both knew that whatever he saw in the night, it was more than simple wanderings of his mind, no matter what that old village witchy had said. Their parents had realized it early on, when Laine casually referred to things in their own past that he'd had no way of knowing. And since they'd seemed upset, Laine had become careful not to let that dream knowledge slip any more. But they all knew it was there—just as Shette knew, without being told, that those moments from the past were not for the ears of others.

He seemed to have quieted now. Good. It was a shame

they'd started to come back, these visions of his. As he'd grown, they more or less faded, but starting with the previous spring, two years after he'd left home to guide the caravan through the magical hazards with his unmatching eyes, they'd been back in force. Wintering at home had made their reemergence obvious to a light sleeper like Shette, if not to their parents.

Such knowledge had made good ammunition when she was pestering him to take her on the route this year.

She flipped a hand at the bug whining near her ear and considered her brother. As brothers went, she supposed he wasn't so bad, but their isolated childhood left her little to compare him with. He was handsome enough, in a brawny sort of way; at fifteen years, Shette was discovering she preferred to eye a man built long and lean—Ehren flashed unbidden through her mind's eye—so it had taken the earthy teasing of the caravan whores to make her see anything in her brother. They liked his eyes, which were nearly always filled with guileless humor, and which had slightly down-turned corners that at the same time made him look puppy dog sad. And they especially liked the way a body had to get close to tell the difference between the black eye and the blue one.

Laine made another little noise, as if someone had stepped on his stomach. Shette sighed, a dramatic sound. Despite the irritated way she occasionally poked him awake, she'd learned long ago that it was best—and safest—*not* to disturb him in the middle of these spells. Once he'd blacked her eye; once he'd been dazed for hours. It never lasted long, anyway—in a few minutes she could go back to sleep.

Another grumble of sound from Laine, another sigh from Shette, as only a wronged fifteen-year-old can sigh. She hadn't taken the stupid dreams into account when she'd begged to see a little of the world with her brother. Of course, she hadn't taken magical monsters or handling Spike into account, either.

Laine jerked; the faint starlight dimly picked out the features of his face, the tightened muscles of his neck. The noise he made was harsh, torn from deep inside. Shette didn't like it.

"Laine?" she said. "Laine, wake up."

His body arched and jerked, and suddenly she didn't like it *at all*. "Laine!" she said sharply, getting on her hands and knees and leaving the blanket behind. She heard the dull thud of his head hitting the ground as he spasmed again, saw his fingers splayed out stiff, then suddenly clutching at nothing. "Dammit, Laine!" she cried, forgetting she wasn't supposed to use such language. She grabbed his arm, finding the muscles clenched so tightly she might as well have been holding oak. *Thud* went his head on the ground, as he arched back so hard she swore she heard him creak.

"Laine, stop, *stop!*" In desperation, she threw herself over his broad chest and held him tightly, riding him as she would a pony. "*Laine!*"

He gave a great gasp and fell limp, drawing in air as though he'd been drowning, his chest heaving up and down beneath Shette. She held him tight, feeling very much five years the younger, and at the same time somehow older, protective. "Laine?"

"Shette. What . . . ?"

"Dreams is what," she said, anger stirring in the wake of her fear. "I hope it was worth all this trouble, whatever it was."

"Not a dream," he whispered, still breathing heavily, bringing one arm up to rest over the back of her shoulders. He patted her once or twice in an absent and consoling way. "Definitely not a dream."

She knew. And she sure didn't like it.

Chapter 4

Laine spent the morning dazed, Shette talked too much, and Ehren, though patently miserable, spent more time watching Laine, his expression unreadable, than he did getting the rest he ought.

Laine knew he should make something of that. He should have been amused, too, at the outrage on Shette's face when both Dajania and Sevita showed up in the early morning to inspect Ehren's wrist and concur he would, indeed, live. They left a pack of herbs to soak compresses in and promised to return in the evening, although Laine frankly thought the women would have their hands full with merchants whose aching muscles needed massaging. As rough as this travel was, none of the men and women were used to the particular labor of clearing wide trail.

But the fact was, Laine couldn't concentrate hard enough to work up to amusement. He'd tried Ansgare's temper sorely first thing after breakfast, when the two men went ahead to scout out the exact path of the new road. The impression of the spell lingered strongly in the area where he'd found Ehren, and Laine simply couldn't discern whether it was a long-lived spell, or the aftereffects of the day before. Neither man cared to chance triggering it again for their answer.

That meant scouting a new route. They couldn't stray

too far from the old; the terrain wouldn't permit it. They moved as far down the slight slope as they could, before the ground grew too rocky for the wagons to handle. Progressing step by step, they blazed the trees while Laine tried to focus on the here and now, scanning for the edge of the old spell, or the advent of a new one.

For once, it was damnably hard work. There was something pulling at him, teasing at the edges of his mind, and it had nothing to do with malicious spells. It was flashes of memories that weren't his, and faces he didn't know, all wandering through his thoughts. It was the odd, sharp pains that assailed him, flitting away as suddenly as they came—in his arm, or throat, or belly. Ansgare's prodding and eventual temper didn't have a chance of keeping his attention, and finally the smaller man flung his hands up and chased Laine away. There was enough distance marked to keep the group busy for a while, and when they broke for lunch, why maybe, just maybe, Laine would be able to keep his thoughts together long enough to check out the rest of the route.

Maybe not, Laine thought, sitting against the tongue of the wagon and scrubbing his hands through his hair. But they didn't have the fodder to linger here more than a day or two, and they all knew it. At least they didn't have to feed Ehren's beasts; the two were at liberty, picking their way through the tough grasses in the rocks above and below them.

He tried to remember just when this feeling started, this out-of-control waywardness of his thoughts. The twisted sumacs, he decided. He hadn't really felt right since he'd come out of the spelled area Ehren had triggered. He felt his eyes glaze over again, beyond his control, as a man's face appeared to his inner eye, a quick impression with eyes that lingered. Reflected in those eyes, somehow, were a handful of gory bodies, sprawled around a central figure who'd fallen back from his knees in an impossible death pose, his rich clothing soaked with blood and his throat a gaping wound.

"Laine?"

Not Shette's voice, but still filled with concern; Laine blinked, and felt Ehren's hand on his shoulder, saw the injured hand resting over Ehren's thigh where the man stooped slightly to reach Laine's level. The emerald glittered greenly before his eyes; Laine winced. "Wilna's ring," he murmured without thinking, barely realizing the name meant nothing to him.

"What?" Ehren's voice was suddenly sharp; it made Laine blink out of the halfway world he was in and focus on Ehren's dark eyes, a gaze as sharp as his voice.

"I'm not sure," Laine said, looking up at Ehren to close one eye in doubt. Just looking at Ehren made him uneasy, and he wasn't sure why. "I suppose the shock of fighting with trees has gone to my head."

Ehren just looked at him, then finally stepped back a pace. He shook his head. "Something's gone to your head," he said. "But I'm not sure that's it." And he left, before Laine could question the statement.

Just as well. There were too many questions already bouncing around in his head.

───～◆～───

The next morning, Ehren took off the ring—Wilna's ring. Its constant nagging had grown irritating; it seemed happy he was with the caravan, but still wanted him to move south, instead of back to the Trade Road. Besides, Laine's problems had started not after the encounter in the woods, but after Ehren had tried to help him to his feet, using the hand that bore the ring. There was no reason to subject the young man to further befuddlement; clearly, his Sight made him sensitive to the thing.

He thought again of the night before last, when Shette's alarmed cries had woken him even through the haze of the venom in his system. Laine's thrashing had been almost as loud—Ehren was on his way to help when the murmur of the younger man's voice let him know it was over. Whatever *it* was. A fit, perhaps. But Ehren didn't think so.

Ask him about it, his inner voice suggested. *You've no reason to hide anything from them.*

But Shette obviously felt they had something to hide from *him*, even if he did drive her to distraction—an embarrassingly obvious situation. No, a little watch-and-wait would help to puzzle things out. Besides, Ehren's prime objective was to get to Dannel, and Ansgare's wagon route was the best way to do it. He'd pay his way with work and coin, and follow the wagons back to Therand when the merchants finished trading in Solvany.

With the ring on a loop of tough, braided grass around his neck, his gear tossed into Laine's wagon and Ricasso trotting along unburdened behind Shaffron, Ehren slid into place behind Shette and Laine. The new route had been finished the evening before, accompanied by blisters and blistering oaths alike, and the day of rest had reduced his wrist wound to something merely stiff and annoying. By the end of the day, they'd be back at the border station, and the merchants would split up. Laine and Shette preferred not to travel into Solvany—or Laine did, and none of Shette's pestering could make him change his mind—and the two prostitute healers, as well, would stay by the border station. Some of the merchants preferred to camp out there as well, the ones who had no regular buyers and who had come along on speculation—it was worth a lower price to find buyers here, than risk a fruitless journey into Solvany, paying Solvan tariffs on goods that didn't sell.

The wait was fine with Ehren. It would give him a chance to look into the suspicion that there was some sort of organized banditry occurring along the border. And it would give him time to watch Laine.

Shette sat on the tailgate of the wagon, her legs dangling over the edge. She studied her ankles. They weren't thick, but they weren't thin and dainty, that was for sure. She would never be like the high-blooded Solvan nobles Sevita talked about, the willowy young women in their lacy,

beribboned dresses—styles that were not suited to her own
sturdier frame. She was like her mother, Shette was—of
moderate height, and perhaps not quite through growing
yet. Like her brother, too—her frame layered with muscle
that was more substantial than lean. All well and good for
Laine—plenty of women liked the feel of muscle beneath
their hands. But men wanted softness, and soft, Shette was
not.

She glared at her sensible footwear—low, laced shoes
with hard leather soles that had once been black, but now
had much of the dye worn off. Maybe that's what was on
her ankle, smudged up the side of her calf and disappearing
into the loose trousers she had rolled up to just below her
knees. Not exactly proper, but in the midday heat, Shette
didn't much care. The shirt she had on was Laine's; he'd
worn through the elbows, and she'd claimed it. Cutting
off the arms at his elbow wear still left her with a respectable
amount of material, and she'd used the leftover material
to fashion cuffs of a sort.

She'd also stitched a series of flowers across the shoulders
and winding around the collar. At Sevita's wistful admiration,
Shette had stitched her some, too. Her fingers weren't
slender, but they were long and sturdy, and nimble enough
to handle any needle.

The offering had started the awkward friendship between
herself and the prostitutes, one they were still defining.
Shette had always been told that women such as Dajania
and Sevita were loose and wicked, and spread disease. They
in turn were well accustomed to rudeness from those who
considered themselves respectable. But Shette had also
been taught not to judge people without understanding
them, and when it came right down to it, she hadn't had
enough friends in her short life to be turning down the
opportunity Dajania and Sevita represented. It just took a
little practice—and she still sometimes caught herself
fighting old prejudices.

Not that she couldn't do with a little company right now.
Laine was at the blacksmith's, getting Spike shod. That was

always a big production, he'd told her, and one Shette preferred not to experience. She could hear Spike's protests from here. No, thank you.

She pushed off the end of the wagon and made her way past the building that housed the merchants—some of them looked a little rough, and she didn't want to go in there without Laine. But she was tired of watching the travelers go by, few as they were today, and the caravan merchants who had stayed to trade were in the inn, eating a noon meal. Nothing interesting would happen until they came back out. So she wandered down the hard, spell-preserved road to the border station, to watch the Border Guards inspect the travelers for contraband.

The border station was a small, white-washed building with a second building tacked onto the back for guard quarters. She'd met both the guards working out of it— one of them was hardly any older than she was, and the other was a grizzled veteran of a woman who brooked no nonsense, and whose stout form held more than enough muscle to back up her attitude. Both were Solvans; the Loraka station was set at Lake Everdawn, and the territory between, if technically Lorakan, was effectively neutral.

"Look at this, Shette." It was the young border guard; he seemed glad to have her for company. He met her at the side of the building, leaving his older partner going through travel cases she'd spread on the ground. It was a much more thorough inspection than normal, although all Shette saw was underwear. The owners of the luggage, however, looked a good deal more nervous than exposed underwear deserved. There was already a pair of merchants waiting behind them, enforced patience on their faces.

"What is it?" Shette asked, reaching for the coin he held. It was a ruddy gold, and very heavy. Probably worth more money than she'd ever held before.

"Therand gold," the youth said. He rubbed a thumb at the side of the mustache he was trying so hard to grow. "Worth a lot more than Solvan gold, at least here."

"Gold is gold," Shette said, but her tone was puzzled;

she passed her finger lightly over the crest stamped in the gold. "What's so special about it?"

"You never heard of Therand gold?" he asked, surprised. "In Solvany, only the Upper Level wizards can make tie spells into metal—but the clans have a way to stick their magic to the gold. Like mild curses and charms. I don't know the meaning of 'em, but the marks here under the crest are supposed to tell you what the charms are. Not that I'd trust 'em—who'd tell you outright they was cursing you?"

"Shouldn't you be careful with it, then?" Shette asked, quickly handing the coin back to him.

"Nah. I guess it takes some time for the spell to set in." He started a more detailed explanation, but Shette didn't quite listen, as interesting as the thought of clan-magicked Therand gold might be. For beyond the gate was Shaffron, and sitting on him was Ehren, whom she hadn't seen for two days. Drying sweat dulled Shaffron's normally fiery coat, and Ehren's hair, tied back and featherless, was even darker than usual with his own sweat. Who *wouldn't* get hot under that brigandine, Shette thought. In fact, he was wearing his greaves and gauntlets, too, and something around his neck, and had his helmet tucked under his arm.

She meandered over to the inspection area, an arch that came off the side of the station. Benlan—named after the recently murdered Solvan king, he'd told her, and called Ben—trailed her, not taking offense at her distraction. After all, he probably thought she was showing interest in his job.

"We have to stop them all," he told her, putting the gold in a small pile of belongings on the table at the side of the station. "Give 'em a quick search. Jiarna always finds 'em out if they got something—she knows right where to look, and how to make 'em nervous."

"What's Ehren been doing?" Shette asked. "He's been gone for days. And who are the two with him?" Now that she was closer, she could see two more guards off to the side, both mounted. Their ailettes looked more like Ehren's

than the Border Guards, though, and if anything, they and
their mounts were even more exhausted.

"More of the King's Guard," Ben answered readily enough.

More . . . ? "Ehren's in the King's Guard? Is that something
special?" Shette asked almost absently as she studied the woman
and man with him. The woman's broad face showed her fatigue
clearly. Her coloring was like Machara's, and her freckles were
visible from here—just barely out of earshot—and they matched
her kinky, coppery hair. Shette hadn't seen herself for months . . .
she wondered if she looked that grubby. The man was
nondescript, with brown hair and a nose that warred for
dominance with his chin, leaving his slightly narrow-set eyes
without much bid for attention. He didn't look quite as tired,
but there was something else on his face. Anger, she thought.
And though Ehren spoke quietly, the other man's reply was
almost emphatic enough for her to decipher from here.

"Is that something *special*?" Ben repeated. "You sure don't
know much about us, do you? It's as special as a guard can
get. And Ehren was the King's closest man. Jiarna told me
about him, after Ehren came through the first time. When
King Benlan died, Ehren spent a year looking for the killers.
I guess he found some of them . . . I don't know why he's
out *here*." Ben frowned. "I wonder if he's trailed someone
out here?" His voice grew eager. "Maybe I can help him,
you think?"

Shette wasn't really listening, she was creeping forward.
She glanced at Jiarna when she noticed the woman looking
at her, asking permission to cross with a hopeful expression.
Jiarna nodded curtly and went back to ripping the lining
out of the traveling cases.

Ben was giving her a brow-knotted look. "You don't know
much about us *or* the Therands. Where in the Levels are
you from?"

Shette hushed him with a wave. She wanted to hear what
the Guards were talking about, and Ben must have had
some curiosity about it too, for he silenced quick enough.
They settled in to listen.

"We should have caught the bastards," Algere said. He and Jada looked like different people than the gamboling youngsters who had taken Ehren on in the Guard practice room not so long ago. Older, now. Suddenly wiser. "Five minutes earlier—"

Ehren said sharply, "There's no point in that," but he felt just the same, and it was difficult to keep it from his face. In the moment that followed, with the three Guards simply sitting their tired horses and shifting as the animals stamped flies off their legs, he added quietly, "I ate with that couple on my way to the border. They were good people." *They didn't deserve to be slaughtered like that.* He recalled how wary they'd been when he'd arrived in their home, barely a week earlier. Kurtane might not know there was a serious problem here yet, but the people obviously did. The sooner he returned, the better.

"There's something going on here, and I don't understand why Rodar's not taking it more seriously," Jada said, an almost plaintive note in her voice. "These innocent people—*Solvan* people—are being robbed and killed. And what happened to that lout you caught, anyway? Do you really think it was his heart?" When Ehren merely gave a noncommittal if unconvinced-looking shrug—bad heart was a good guess for the sudden death of a man that stout, and he'd certainly had enough exertion—she forged onward. "We know from the men who tried to steal your horses that they're using phony ailettes—why doesn't Rodar send troops out here to take care of this?"

Algere backed her question with his own intent expression, one that verged on unspoken demand. Ehren remembered him as quiet and slower to trigger than his training partner, but he burned longer than Jada once his temper was engaged.

"I doubt he's fully aware of the problem," Ehren said dryly, keeping an eye on the younger man. "You yourself told me things had changed around Kurtane, Algere. The people making the decisions seem happy enough to let Rodar play. First and Second Level ministers, and—"

"Varien," Jada said, and scowled. "It was Varien who took you off your search for Benlan's killers, I'll bet."

"He intimated there were more hands than his involved," Ehren said. He gave the two younger Guards a hard look. "You came out here to give me a message rather than chancing it to courier. Concern about the gang running the border is admirable, Jada, but hardly under the jurisdiction of the King's Guard."

Algere gave a sudden quick grin. "Told you he'd know it was your idea, Jada."

Jada shrugged. "Bad feeling is all, Ehren. Things in Kurtane aren't being taken care of. Right after you left, the Kurtane Ready Troops lost half a unit of troopers—all mustered out, dishonorably, because of some prank they pulled. And it wasn't anything much, some kind of joke that got out of hand, is all. It got me to thinking about things. Gerhard's a good master, but even he can't supervise the training of understrength troops and give them the effectiveness of experienced ranks. We're losing people— retirement, accident—we lost a Second Level troop commander right before Algere and I left—dismissal, the normal things—and they're *not being replaced*. Border problems made a good excuse—a village Level Rep came with formal complaints right after you left—and I took it. Gerhard endorsed it as a training run, so the Levels let us come."

Ehren's silence was grim. Had things gone downhill that quickly? Or had he failed to spend enough time in Kurtane to see what was already there? Not that Varien had given him much of a choice. At last, he asked, "Do you consider the Guard able to fulfill its duties?"

Algere and Jada exchanged glances. "At this point, yes, sir. But we're a long way from the Guard you led under Benlan, and look what happened to *him*."

"That's not even taking into account the other parts of Solvany that could be put at risk," Algere said. "Border Guard was due to rotate a month ago; I checked."

"I don't know why you've come out this way, Ehren,"

Jada said, "but we really need you in Kurtane. No one else in the King's Guard has the experience to stand up to the Levels . . . and to Varien. We have to get things straightened out—we have to get Rodar to take interest, and take *charge*."

At Varien's name, Ehren felt his face grow hard. "I can't come back."

"But—"

"Jada, the answer is *no*."

They sat in silence a moment, broken only by the swish of the horses' tails. When Ehren spoke again, his voice was more forgiving, but just as firm, and devoid of the conflict within him. "You're a King's Guard, Jada. You have the right to an audience with the king. Take it. Use it well. If you impress him, he'll see you again. He's seventeen years old, and you're a woman. Keep that in mind."

"Ehren!" Jada protested, while Algere's expression said the same.

He regarded them patiently, one eyebrow slightly raised. "I'm not suggesting you seduce our king, Jada. I'm simply saying some approaches will get his attention better than others. Be impressed with him, even if he does have spots on his face. Be concerned for his welfare. What*ever* you do, don't make him feel like it's his fault that things are as they are—just that he has the power to fix it if he chooses."

"Is that the way you'd do it?" Jada asked, somewhat slyly, a little life showing on her face through the fatigue—and not a little bit of flirt.

That much of her, Ehren remembered well, and enjoyed. He smiled easily at her. "Probably not. Maybe that's why I'm staying and you're going. And try not to wear out too many horses on the journey, this time."

"It was the only way to try to catch up with you," Algere grumbled. "We rode none of them to the ground."

Ehren said, serious again, "See that you care as well for yourselves. And send a pigeon or courier next time, eh?"

Jada nodded. "We'll let you know what happens. But, Ehren—I hope you come back soon."

"As soon as I can," he promised.

"Ben!" Jiarna's voice broke the semblance of privacy the Guards had shared, and as one, they looked over at the woman. "Gonna earn your copper today, son? We got a backup here."

It was only then that Ehren saw the young Border Guard was on Solvan turf, and with him was Shette. In fact, they could have been doing nothing else but watching, and perhaps listening to, the Guards. They were both on their way back to the border station, now, where a group of harassed-looking travelers were hastily stuffing their luggage back together even as their cart moved away from the inspection arch. Ehren raised an eyebrow at Jada and Algere; his back had been to the border, but the two younger Guards had had a clear view of their eavesdroppers. They exchanged a glance and a guilt-ridden shrug, and he relented. They were all tired.

"No matter," he said. "There's nowhere for it to go, and I'll have a word with them both."

The last thing they needed was for the bandits to get word of Solvany's lack of readiness. If they didn't use the information themselves, it would sell well enough to someone else.

The young guard Ben first, then. Ehren lifted his reins, and Shaffron stirred beneath him. "Jada, Algere," he said, and hesitated, looking for the words that would mean as much as he wanted to convey. He settled for "Be careful," but he thought they understood.

Chapter 5

Shette hadn't really wanted to hear any more, anyway. The three Guards knew one another—it was obvious from their willingness to both argue and joke with each other. She envied their camaraderie, and didn't enjoy that feeling. Besides, she had enough to think about.

She would have liked to have slipped away unseen, though—and although she hadn't looked back, she was certain, after Jiarna's loud call, that the Guards had spotted them. Quietly, they'd returned to the Lorakan side of the border, and the little patch of neutral ground that the inspection area sat on.

Ben started talking as soon as they were back by the station. "Jiarna said there was something going on over the border," he told Shette, his words coming fast and excited. "She didn't really want to talk about it—said we had our duty here. But wouldn't it be great if we caught some of the bandits? Especially since they're using fake ailettes—no one'd be fooled for long, I bet, but it wouldn't *take* long, and then it'd be too late. I got a free day coming up here, soon, and I could—"

"Ben," Jiarna growled. The pair she'd been searching, relieved of their contraband, were just crossing into Solvany, looking much the worse for wear. Jiarna was already giving a cursory check of the two-wheeled cart that had been waiting behind them, conversing with the two men who pulled it as though they'd been going through this little ritual for years. Probably they had, Shette thought, giving the guardwoman's worn face another look as Ben hastened to help her. Shette was left standing alone by the side of the station, but she didn't mind. She had a lot to think about.

Who was this Varien, whose name seemed to leave such a bad taste in Ehren's mouth?

Sevita will know. The thought made her straighten, push away from the wall she'd been leaning on. She rolled her pants legs down and headed for the inn tavern at a brisk walk.

What Sevita didn't know, Dajania would. And there were others who usually spent the first part of the day in the inn, three more women who sold themselves, and who heard a lot in the process. If nothing else, Shette had learned that much on the caravan route—a whore had ears, and some men liked to be listened to.

She pulled open the heavy tavern door and peeked in; she'd never been inside without Laine before, and that had always been in the late afternoon or early evening, when there were plenty of rough looking characters in evidence, men and women both. Bracing them was not something she looked forward to.

But the tavern was nearly empty. Two men stood before the bar, leaning their elbows on the old, age-polished wood between themselves and the bartender with her kegs. The bartender herself was almost twice as big as Laine; in the evenings there were two of them, twins down to the hairy moles on their jaws. Their aprons were always stained and smeared, and they seldom looked clean themselves, but from what she'd heard the food—prepared by a small thing of a chef in the back kitchen—was as good as in any tavern of its size, and maybe just a little bit better.

It was certainly better than what Shette had eaten on the caravan. She just tried not to look at the bartenders while she was eating.

With sunlight streaming in through the open shutters, and the common room occupied by five women tallying their take and the tavern percentages—with no lack of competitively snide remarks, Shette gathered—it was almost like a different tavern altogether. No odor of crowded, unwashed men and women—although a certain amount of that was ingrained—and only one pipe in evidence. One of the whores, a middle-aged woman who stayed at the inn full time, was a cottage witchy as well, and seemed to be preparing for some sort of spell by the fireplace.

Dajania saw Shette first. Never quiet or demure, she called out, "Shette, girl! I do believe you've got up the nerve to come see us without your brother standing watch."

Every pair of eyes in the place riveted to her. If nothing intriguing, she was at least something new to look at. *Thanks, Dajania,* Shette thought sourly, pretending she didn't see the bartender's not entirely pleasant smile. As casually as possible, she threaded her way between the few tables to the women. "Laine's shoeing Spike," she said. "Figured I'd take the chance when I could get it."

"He's a mite overprotective, Laine is," Sevita said. Unlike Dajania's bold painted eyes and dark hair—which Shette half suspected was dyed, anyway—Sevita had a gentle appearance, soft brown hair and big hazel eyes that she painted with such subtlety they sweetened her features without looking painted at all. She was soft-spoken and pleasant . . . but she'd killed a man once, for his cruelty when they were together.

Shette gave an elaborate shrug, doing her best to dismiss Laine's influence. Once these women started talking about him, it was bound to go on for a while, and in some part of her mind she wished he would just go ahead and sleep with them, so he wouldn't represent such a challenge to them anymore. It wasn't like he'd never—but she wasn't supposed to know about that. She couldn't help a secretive little smile, and it was something the women recognized right off.

"Shette's had a thought, now, she has," Dajania declared,

casually recovering a copper that had strayed, somehow, too close to one of the tavern women's piles. "Shette, this here's Erlya, Sontra, and Heliga." Erlya was the cottage witchy, Sontra a dowdy and bleary-eyed woman who hadn't put on anything besides an old, patched dressing gown, and Heliga a small, pointy-faced girl with a barely perceptible harelip who, Shette realized, couldn't be much older than she was.

"Guides grant our acquaintance be a good one," she said, the politest greeting she knew, even if it was T'ieran. The girl snickered without bothering to hide it and Sevita gave her a low-key, even stare. The snicker stopped.

"Never mind, Shette," Sevita said. "Some of us haven't had the benefit of much polite company. Heliga, Shette here's the one who did the pretty stitching on my blouse."

"Ooh," the girl said. "It's wonderful, Shette. I want to learn it, someday." Her words were slurred by a severe lisp; it took Shette a moment to puzzle them out, simply because she wasn't expecting it, and by then the hopeful look on the girl's face had all but faded.

"Well," Shette said, shrugging again. "I'll probably be here a week or so. But you'd have to get the needle and threads; I used everything up but the mending thread."

Heliga nodded enthusiastically. "I know someone in the commonstall who carries it. He's got a liking for me, too. I can get it."

Inwardly, Shette winced. She thought she knew exactly how Heliga would buy the goods. *Stop thinking like that*, she told herself. She wouldn't make any friends like that, especially not if it showed on her face as clearly as Laine's thoughts tended to run across his own features.

From the fireplace, Erlya muttered an alarmed curse. She threw herself away from the hearth, right before the chimney made a muffled *whoomf*; a cloud of soot dropped onto the hearth, accompanied by large particles of creosote ticking their way down. Dowdy Sontra sniggered the same amusement that showed on all their faces—except for Erlya's, as she got to her feet and vigorously slapped soot off the one leg that hadn't quite gotten out of range.

"Maybe you ought to just do it like the rest of us," Dajania said through her smile.

"As if you knew anything about it," Erlya snapped.

Now that their attention wasn't on her, Shette grew suddenly bolder, and almost without thinking, she said, "Do you know who Varien is?"

As one, they turned their surprise her way, so that she wished she hadn't spoken at all. Then Sontra gave a lazy smile and said, "I know what he likes," and the strange tension was broken. The women picked up the conversation that centered around their accounting, and though Shette wasn't excluded, there was little she could add to it.

All except Erlya, who moved around the edge of the crowded table until she was next to Shette. "You mean Varien, the King's Wizard, don't you?" she asked in a low voice. "That's one best left unspoken of, even here over the border. They've never proved he's done anything wrong, and the court folk either worship him or fear him. But we know better, the lower levels of witchies do. He's got too much power, and too much inclination to use it. So even whilst you're among friends, it still does no harm to guard your tongue."

Shette kept her face blank. No one was that powerful, to hear her words in a worn little tavern at the border, but she didn't want to offend the woman. Erlya must have felt reasonably safe as well, for she dropped the furtive tone she'd been using and asked in a perfectly normal voice, "Why're you asking? You're Therand, aren't you, with talk of the Guides an' such . . . *that* one's Solvan politics."

"I'm not from Therand," Shette said. "I grew up in the Loraka border mountains. Folks believe whichever way they choose, there." Though, in fact, when she thought of it, she could only come up with one other family that followed the Therand belief of Guides for the Nine Levels. "I just heard the name, is all. I was wondering."

All the women exchanged glances of polite disbelief. "You *just heard* the name?" Sontra said. "No one banters that name around without reason. Skete, Bern, or Rikka—now those are all High Level mages you can trust, more or less. But not *that* one."

"Well," Shette said uncomfortably, not sure if she was betraying some kind of confidence, but increasingly aware that she wasn't going to get any information without giving it in return, "Whoever he is, Var—er, *that* one is the man who took Ehren away from finding who killed his king. He seemed pretty mad about it. I was just wondering."

"Ah, it's to do with Ehren, has it," Sevita said, as if that explained anything. "No doubt the Guard is angered if what you heard is true. He's a right good man, that Ehren. Trustworthy." The others nodded, as if this was the highest honor they could bestow him, but they were exchanging quick glances among themselves and finally broke into snickers.

"Damn good-looking chunk of trustworthy!" Dajania said, opening the door for the others to add their own earthy appraisals. Shette blushed bright red, and was very quiet until things settled down.

Finally, Heliga asked, "You sure he's off that search?" with doubt on her face. "I was with a fellow just last night, drunk he was. Talking about how glad he was to have finally gotten out of that country, Solvany, I mean. Made out as how he'd been in hiding for a year, creeping for the border, scared for his life the whole time."

"A year." Dajania repeated the words as though they had some special meaning, and at Shette's blank look, said, "It's been just that long that Benlan's been dead."

It hadn't been hard for Shette to learn the rest of what Heliga knew. The fellow she'd bedded had been on foot, and heading for Lake Everdawn. He'd left just that morning. And Heliga, though she couldn't quote the man, was convinced that he hadn't *done* anything; he merely *knew* something. "He's a little fellow, like me," she'd said, adding, somewhat empathetically, "He just wants to feel he's safe again."

He'd be safe enough under Ehren's wing, Shette was certain. If the man knew something that put his life in danger, he was surely running from conspiracy, and not from Guards like Ehren. And he was on foot . . .

She left the tavern, elaborately casual about her good-byes, and trotted across the road to the caravan encampment. Next to their wagon, Clang the mule eyed her with mild concern, a wisp of hay straggling out of his mouth.

Little did he know. Shette grinned at him. Clambering into the wagon, she opened the backmost compartment and pulled out a tangle of girth and bridle and blanket. There was nothing wrong with taking a little afternoon ride; Laine had never specifically said she shouldn't. And she *had* wanted to see more of the area, even if it was more road. At least there were people on *this* road.

She knew what the man looked like, what he was wearing . . . and if she happened to come upon him, and told him she knew someone who could guarantee his safety, as she was certain Ehren could . . . surely he'd come back with her. Shette's thoughts lingered on Ehren . . . she could well remember his expression at the thought of being taken off his search, just as she well remembered everything else about his features. The lines of his face were sculpted, and framed by a clean, strong jaw; his nose was equally strong and the whole effect was more than Shette would think to ask for. She tried to imagine the look on that face when Ehren realized she'd brought him a chance to discover who was behind his king's death.

Completely enthralled by her thoughts, Shette saddled and bridled the mule, who stood patiently albeit with mournful expression. She didn't realize how distracted she'd been until she tried to mount and the saddle slipped halfway down his side, dumping her on the ground. Clang craned his head around to look at her, his floppy ears perked at her as though he was surprised to find her there.

"Fine," she muttered, getting up and dusting herself off. She jerked the saddle back into place and tightened the girth again. Then she walked him in a circle around the wagon, stopped suddenly, and pulled the girth as tight as she could get it. After that, the saddle firmly resisted her hefty tug, and she gave the mule a satisfied smirk. "Gotcha," she told him, and climbed successfully, if not gracefully, into the saddle.

It was Laine's saddle, and too big for her. The stirrups were as high as they got, and her toes still barely touched the flats of them; she clutched the swell of the pommel as the mule lurched into motion, certain she was going to slide off to one side or the other. This was a far cry from her father's sturdy little mountain ponies, and she hadn't ever been all that interested in riding *them*.

She gritted her teeth and urged Clang onward, until he finally broke into a reluctant, shuffling trot. There was no telling when Laine would come out from behind the smithy's, and she wanted to be out of sight by then.

Not that you're doing anything wrong, she told herself. Just going for a ride, on a busy public road. What could be wrong with that?

But the road didn't stay busy. After a while, the travelers thinned out, and she rode alone for a good long stretch, starting to wonder just how fast one anxious man could walk. The road was boring, as well. It was hard and level, maintained by magic, and it followed along the Eredon River.

The river flowed off to her right, mostly a broad and majestic current of water that was occasionally cut by the ripple of shallow water over rocks. Sprawling willows hung over the banks, vying for root space with shrubby growth that sometimes hid the water from view entirely. The left side of the road was much the same, with more sycamore than anything else; not far from the edge of the road, the water-cut rock rose high again, covered with greenery anywhere there was a speck of dirt or a crack in the rock.

There were plenty of little animals scurrying through that growth, as well as the fast darting shadows of birds, all announcing her progress, but they somehow made the road seem all the more empty. Shette was beginning to regret her impulsive dash into Loraka, although Clang had settled happily enough into travel, perhaps grateful for the change.

Shette was considering a foray into canter when the lonely road got suddenly lonelier. Her escort of twitter and scurry had vanished.

What had Ehren said? Something about a gang running the border? Suddenly running seemed like a good idea, if she was the one doing it. *You're only scaring yourself.* Shette settled more firmly into the saddle, waiting for the flitter of nerves to pass.

They didn't.

"C'mon, Clang, let's move a little faster," she told him, working up to a good bold thump in his sides with her heels.

He stopped short.

"*Clang!* I mean it! Let's go!" Shette tried to assume the voice she'd heard Laine use, the *I'm about to have stringy mule soup for dinner* voice.

"Mule in't stupid," a lazy voice drawled from the brush beside her.

Shette jumped, startling Clang, who snorted and raised his head high. A man stepped out in the road ahead of her, a second fellow who looked as unsavory as the first one sounded. *Guides help me, there* is *a gang.* A third bandit, a short, stout woman, hopped down from the rock she'd been sitting on, ten feet up along the side of the lurching-up mountain.

"*C'mon*, Clang!" Shette said, setting her sights for the empty bit of road behind the man who blocked her way. She dug her heels into the mule's side, no more hesitation, and slapped his rump with the long reins.

He just stood there. His hooves grew roots into the ground, his head and neck, if anything, rose even higher, stubbed up in every inch of his body. He knew well enough that harm stood in his way.

She thought about throwing herself off the beast and running for it, back the way she'd come. But with a rustle of brush and the scritch of hard leather boot soles against a stray pebble on the hard road, that option vanished; she couldn't bring herself to look as the bandit who'd been hidden at the side of the road stepped up to her. A casual gloved hand, reeking of horse sweat and hard use, closed on the reins just below the bit. Shette was just daring to look down at the man when his other gloved hand curved around her waist and pulled her right out of the saddle, depositing her on the road without grace or gentility. She stumbled back a step and fell on her rump, staring up at him with her arms jutting back and the heels of her hands grinding painfully into the road.

"You're a sturdy one," the man said, much satisfaction on his face, a stubble-bearded face with lots of cheek and very little chin. "Ought to bring us a good price." He smiled unpleasantly.

A good price? *Guides, they're* worse *than bandits.* Shette stared up at him, aghast, as her arms trembled hard enough to shake her entire body. *Laine!* she wailed inside. *Laine, come find me!*

Laine had been trying to do just that, and for some time. The mule was gone, Shette was gone; Ben, the young guard who was trying to impress Shette, was on duty and therefore she wasn't off with him somewhere. . . .

"Damnation," he muttered, glaring at Spike as though it was all the mule's fault. Maybe it was. "If you hadn't taken so long, she wouldn't have had the chance for this," he told the creature. But no one had seen her ride out, and he didn't even know what direction she'd gone in.

What use was Sight if it didn't help at times like these? Laine scrubbed a hand across the back of his neck and squinted against the bright haziness of the hot afternoon. There were few others moving about the area; most of them were inside the commonstall, shopping or trading their wares. And while there'd been a handful of people passing the border station earlier, there were none, now.

Laine'd noticed that this year. People were traveling in unofficial caravans, as if it took a certain number of them to gather enough strength to break away from Everdawn. And in between, there were big gaps of empty road. Not that the road had ever streamed with people . . . but it seemed to him they moved with more caution and constraint than before.

Well, he wasn't going to find her by standing out in the hot sun. He headed for the tavern, thinking of a cool drink, hoping Erlya had managed to master the magic that cooled the barrel of sumac lemonade.

On the heels of that thought he had an image of dripping black sumac fingers reaching for his face, and grimaced. Cool water would do just as well, he decided.

The tavern was dim; what sun its small windows received had shifted away by this time of day. The bartender lifted an ambiguous hand of greeting, hardly looking up from the stain she was trying to scrape from the wooden bar. Laine wasn't sure which one of the twins it was—that was another thing Sight seemed to be useless for. He slouched into a chair at the table nearest the bar and waited for her to get tired of the stain before he asked for his water.

Heliga flittered into the chair opposite him, smiling at him, and apparently oblivious to his preoccupation about Shette. She carefully emptied the contents of her hands onto the scarred table top. Small skeins of fine, brightly colored thread. "Look," she said, lisping through her slight harelip. "Shette said she'd show me how to do the fancy stitches."

Laine gave her a blank look. "Shette did?" Shette had never been in the tavern without him, had never met the tavern whores, who were plenty busy in the evening and not given to spending time in idle chatter with other women.

Heliga nodded, and smiled almost shyly. "She's nice. She's not used to us, but she didn't act all haughty about it."

He wasn't sure he liked the idea of Shette messing around in the tavern without him. There were some pretty rough folks passing through, and Shette, who thought she knew plenty about everything, had no real concept of what some of the men were like. And she was certain, besides, that she had nothing that would interest them—thanks to her faith in Sevita and Dajania, who chattered on about dainties and ribbons and Solvan noblewomen, and her refusal to listen to Laine when he pointed out that there were plenty of fashions inspired by upper level military women, as well. Grumpily, he said, "I don't suppose she'll teach you anything if I can't find her. Or if I kill her when I do find her."

Heliga's delicate brows closed in on one another. "You can't find her? I thought . . . well, Sevita says she's been pretty sheltered. That she didn't stray much from your camp."

"Until today," Laine corrected her. "She's taken Clang and gone off somewhere, so if you run into anyone who has any idea where. . . ."

Heliga didn't say anything for a moment, but something in that silence alerted Laine. He straightened in the chair, watching her more intently. Eventually she said, "I might have an idea myself."

"Well, don't keep it to yourself!"

That earned a little frown. "Be civil, Laine, or learn nothing."

Most of the time she seemed like a slight young thing, hardly older than Shette, and twice as quiet. But every once in a while she did something to remind Laine she had been well-hardened all the same. "I'm sorry," he said. "Worried, I guess."

"Maybe with good reason," she admitted. "When we were all talking, earlier, she'd come in to ask us about Varien—who he was."

Laine frowned. He'd heard the name . . . *Varien. Solvany's wizard, that was it*. "Why'd she want to know?"

Heliga waved a dismissive hand. "Oh, she's all calf-eyed over Ehren, you know that—"

Well, yes, but—Laine stopped himself from asking what that had to do with anything and just nodded, *go on, go on*.

"—and she'd overheard some talk about Varien taking him off his search for King Benlan's killers."

She had? And Ehren, on a high-level assignment? Ansgare had said he was a King's Guard, but— "What does that have to do with where she is now?"

For the first time Heliga looked uncomfortable, and her gaze fell to the colored thread nestled between her hands. "I thought he was still searching. I thought he was here because of the man I was with last night. He babbled something about being on the run for a year." She looked up and shrugged. "We all know what happened a year ago."

Benlan had been killed, along with most of his Guards. It had been a slaughter, as Laine recalled the tales. How had Ehren survived it? "I still don't see what this has to do with Shette."

Impatience crossed her foxlike features. "She thought Ehren knew nothing of the man. If she's gone, Laine, she's probably gone to fetch him."

"Fetch Ehren?"

Heliga threw up her hands. "Fetch the *man*, you thick-headed country boy!"

Laine sat bolt upright. "You think Shette went after a *killer*? Ninth Level, Heliga, why didn't you come get me?"

"I could tear my hair out trying to talk to you," she said crossly. "I didn't know she was gone till now. I'm just guessing that's what she might have done. And the man wasn't any killer, no doubt of that. Little mouse-man, knew something he shouldn't have."

"That doesn't make any sense. Shette barely knows how to ride. She ought to have gone to Ehren with the news."

Heliga rolled her eyes and gathered up her thread, rising. "Just proves you ain't no fifteen-year-old girl, now, doesn't it?"

Laine simply stared after her, numb. Shette *did* talk an awful lot when Ehren was around. She'd been a little more tractable since they'd run into him, too. He sorted his memories and found images of Shette blushing, of her gazing off into the distance at nothing, of her watching Ehren when she thought no one was looking. But—to go after a fugitive just to impress the Guard? *Damn.*

He got a grip on his rising concern. Likely, Shette would never catch up with the fugitive before she got too saddle-sore to go on, nor recognize him when she saw him. Even were he a threat, Laine doubted it would come to that. No, he was thinking of the border and Trade Road bandits that had rumors flying. Even barring them, the Trade Road was no place for a young woman, alone. A naive young woman. *His sister*.

He stood so abruptly the chair tipped back before settling into place with all four legs on the floor. The bartender looked up from her scraping, a warning eyebrow raised. Laine barely noticed. Ehren. He had to find Ehren.

"What's my fault?" Ehren said, looking up from Shaffron's once-again glossy hide as the movement of his brush slowed. The light in the stable was dim, filtered through cracks and hazed with dust motes, but he could see the distress on Laine's face clearly enough. Shaffron shifted, rustling the hay before him, and the steady grinding of his teeth filled the silence.

"Maybe not your fault exactly," Laine said, standing well back from the stall and the reach of Shaffron's teeth, although the horse would bother no one who wasn't grabbing for his halter rope. "Heliga says there was a man here who knows something about Benlan, and that Shette went after him."

Ehren stiffened, so captured by the first of Laine's words that he didn't hear the rest. "Someone who knows of Benlan? Here?"

"Not any more—he's gone on to the lake. And so has Shette!" Laine hesitated, eyeing Ehren. "It's true. You knew Benlan, and you've been looking for his killer."

Ehren turned to face him, his dark eyes hard. "I knew Benlan from the time I was Shette's age. I knew every man and woman that died that day. I'll *never* stop looking."

"No matter what Varien says," Laine said. His expression, normally easygoing, was intense, his hound-sad eyes narrowed. "And now Shette's in trouble because of it."

"How the burning Hells do you know about Varien?" Ehren snapped. Next to him, Shaffron stopped chewing, and his head came up. Across the aisle, Ricasso snorted. For a moment the two men stared at one another, until Ehren finally processed the rest of Laine's words. "What do you mean, Shette's in trouble? Come at this head-on, Laine, will you?"

Laine took a deep breath. "Shette overheard you say Varien had taken you off your search. Don't ask me how or where—what little I know I got from Heliga at the tavern."

Ehren nodded, placing the woman in his memory. One of the whores, a little bit of a thing. He'd never spoken to her, but Ben of the Border Guard seemed to know her very well. "Let me see if I have this straight," he said tightly. "Heliga was with *some*one who knows *some*thing about Benlan. The man left this morning for Everdawn. Shette left sometime later to go after him and bring him back—"

"Because she's trying to impress you," Laine finished for him. "She's on Clang, and she doesn't know how to handle him."

"That's the least of her worries," Ehren muttered. He stuffed Shaffron's brush in the saddlebags that were hanging over the side of the stall, and just stood there a moment. He'd spent the morning riding hard on the trail of border bandits, and caught nothing but frustrated failure and a badly lamed, abandoned horse that they'd had to kill. Brushing the sweat out of Shaffron's coat had been nothing but an exercise in nursing his anger. Now it was time to put it aside, take a deep breath, and start all over again. "All right," he said, just as Laine's mouth opened again, impatience written all over that expressive face. "Shaffron would have been better for this, but he's done all he can for the day. I'll saddle Ricasso. I suggest you rent yourself a horse, one that's used to fast work. That mule of yours is steady enough, but I don't think he'll keep up."

Laine didn't even blink. "I've already done it. Did you

think I was just going to hang around here and wait if you weren't willing to come with me?"

Ehren gave him a wry smile. "Go on, then. I'll be right out."

Laine nodded, and walked swiftly out to the corrals. Ehren hoped the farrier had given him a good mount. He was going to need it, and it would be of more value than the absurdly ornate, too-short sword that the young man carried.

Ricasso proved fractious, unhappy at having been stalled while Shaffron went out, and well aware that something was up. "You'll be moving out soon enough," Ehren told him, settling the saddle on his back with no-nonsense efficiency of movement, tightening the girth in stages while he tied his water bota at the cantle and strapped his own sword on, hooking his plain, rounded helmet beside the saddle cantle. Ricasso mouthed the bit furiously when bridled, and was already dripping spit by the time Ehren led him outside.

"Save it," Ehren told him shortly, tightening the girth one last hole before he mounted. "You're going to need that energy."

Laine was waiting for him, astride a dark bay mare with long legs, short back and strong rump. Therand breeding— good. Something they could depend on to last through this ride.

Ricasso wanted to bolt out onto the Trade Road; from the look on his face, Laine wanted to do the same. "Steady," Ehren told them both, and allowed Ricasso an even canter. Laine surged ahead of him and then seemed to get a handle on his horse. By the time a mile had passed beneath them, both horses had relaxed and were willing to drop quietly into a walk.

Laine was not so complacent. "We won't catch up with her at this pace."

"We won't catch up with her if the horses give out halfway there, either," Ehren said, unruffled. "That was a warm-up. When they catch their breath we'll move out again."

Laine looked away, his jaw set. He *knew*, it was obvious,

and couldn't argue with what Ehren had said. Instead, unexpectedly, he asked, "What are you doing here, Ehren? What's a King's Guard doing on this side of the border, and not in Kurtane with the king?"

Ehren didn't say anything. He'd thought Laine wouldn't ask it, not after the first few days had gone by. "None of your concern seems like a fair answer," he said after a moment, although in fact, that was not strictly true. Not now that Shette had tangled herself in things.

"Depends which side of the question you're on," Laine told him.

Ehren gave him the faintest of smiles. "Maybe so. Let's say I'm tracking down a potential threat to the king, and leave it at that."

"But you'd rather be off looking for Benlan's killers. Shette had you right on that."

"Wouldn't you, in my position?"

Laine looked at him, and seemed to be giving the question honest consideration. "I don't know," he said. "I grew up in the Lorakan mountains just this side of the border. Loraka certainly never laid claim to us, nor Therand. I've never had a king, queen, nor T'ierand, that meant anything to me—or me to them. Sad enough, I guess, that Benlan was killed. But Solvany seems to be surviving."

"Is it?" Ehren said. "With bandits at the borders?" And its troops withering from within, if Jada and Algere had it right, never mind whatever was going on with Varien in the Upper Levels. Ehren looked away, over to the slow-moving water of the Eredon. "Maybe you had to know Benlan," he said. Maybe you had to have had the benefit of growing into a man in his court, and to see how many *wrong* decisions he could have made—and didn't. Or maybe it was simply the blind loyalty of a warrior following his leader. No matter. The result was Ehren, here and now. "I said it before. I'll never stop looking. Varien can't keep me away from Kurtane forever."

He made no attempt to hide the emotion behind his words, and Laine returned his gaze without judgment—

or true understanding. Ehren turned his back on the conversation and asked Ricasso to trot. The mare surged to keep up, catching Laine off-guard; he snatched the bay's dark mane and unself-consciously pulled himself back into balance.

"Shette doesn't even do this well," he told Ehren, speaking loudly enough to carry over the sounds of shod hooves on hard roads. "She might have gotten Clang to trot, but not like this."

"How much time does she have on us?" Ehren asked, automatically posting the trot when the bounce of Ricasso's powerful stride became too much trouble to sit. Laine followed suit—not gracefully, but well enough, despite his self-deprecating words.

"At least an hour, as best I can figure."

An hour on this empty road. She was probably no worse than bored to death. Ehren asked for another canter, anyway.

They rode on without much conversation after that, moving steadily, stopping once to detour to the river so the horses could drink. At last they met a small group of ill-matched travelers with handcarts going the opposite direction. Laine didn't hesitate.

"Have you seen a girl on a mule?" he asked them. "Sandy hair? Probably mad at the mule."

"Haven't seen anyone," one of them grumbled back without slacking pace. "Guides-forsaken road this year, it is. Too many soldiers about. Don't like it."

Ehren gave Ricasso's sweaty shoulder a pat and waited as Laine swung the mare around to stare after the travelers, his face a map of the emotions inside: realization that Shette was in trouble, fear at the prospect, and determination to find her.

"She may not have come this way at all," Ehren said.

Laine just stared at him. "Do you think I'm going to take that chance?"

"No. And neither am I. But we have to make a decision. If she was on this road, she's been taken off it. And there's no telling if that happened before us or behind us."

Laine took a resolute lungful of air, held it a moment, and let it out noisily. "Say it was an hour. Say she never got Clang beyond a jog. We'd have caught up to her by now, wouldn't we?"

"That would be my guess." Ehren watched the decision hesitate on Laine's face, and then said, "We could split up."

Laine shook his head with a rueful smile. "If she's in trouble, I'm not going to do her all that much good. Not unless there's only one of them, and he's not a whole lot bigger than me."

Ehren returned the expression. "That's better than thinking you're a whole lot tougher than you really are. Spend the entire first year of training pounding that into some of the new Guards. It's back we go, then."

Laine nodded, and pushed his horse into a trot.

"No," Ehren said, as Ricasso ambled forward. "For one thing, we want to have some horse left when we meet these people. For another, they weren't on the road. They couldn't have scaled the side of the mountain with Clang. That means they crossed the river, and left some sign of it that we missed on the way out. Single file, both sets of eyes on that side of the road. We'll find the spot."

They hadn't gone very far when Laine tensed. Ehren swept the side of the road with his gaze, finding stiff-stalked weeds that led to thick brush and a few stray sycamores. Beyond was the river, deep rushing water channeled between a series of large boulders. Not a place *he* would pick for a crossing. "There's nothing here."

"That's where you're wrong," Laine said grimly. "This is what I do for a living."

"It's spelled?" Ehren said in surprise.

"There's a clear path here, once you look through the magic. I didn't see it when we passed, before. Moving too fast."

"It seemed to be the thing to do at the time," Ehren said mildly.

"Follow me," Laine said, determined again. He led them through the brush and to the side of the river without hesitation, and more than once Ehren's knees pushed right through the edges of trees where they seemed too close to allow passage. Ehren didn't realize just how successful the illusion was until they were in the water, and Laine took the mare through one of the boulders before them—with no little protest on the mare's part. The younger man might not have finesse on horseback, but he could keep his seat when the occasion called for persuasive riding.

"Don't go around, unless you want to take a swim," Laine told him, emerging on the other side. "You can't see it, but there's a drop-off there."

"Wonderful," Ehren muttered. To Ricasso, he said, "Trust me, son." The big horse's ears swiveled around as he faced the rock, blatantly questioning Ehren. Ehren let him stand there a moment as he quietly gathered the ends of his reins, then, after a nudge produced no results, gave the horse a loud pop on the rump with them. Ricasso surged through the obstacle and into darkness, emerging from the other side with such momentum that he ran into the mare's rump. She squealed and kicked, and both horses plunged through the water, arriving annoyed and safe on the other side of the river.

"Let's hope they're not close," Ehren said dryly—the only part of him that *was* dry, after the cold shock of splashing river water. A welcome change, actually, from the sweat that had soaked him moments before. "Because if they are, that probably got their attention."

Laine was paying little heed; instead he scrutinized the brush in front of them, which to Ehren was just as impenetrable as the rock. For long moments, there was no conversation, just the swish of the horses' legs through the weedy grasses, the occasional clink as shod hoof hit stone, and the palpability of Laine's concentration.

Just as Laine's stiff back relaxed, Ehren realized he could see the path they rode on. It was narrow but definite, and bore the crumbling imprints of hooves from the last rain. Up until now, the path had pretty much followed the riverbank, but now it angled away, into a small stand of aspens and up a slope that foreshadowed the mountains to come.

"I didn't think they could keep it up for long," Laine said. "I imagine it takes a lot of effort to maintain an illusion that complete." He stopped his horse and moved her to the side of the path, looking expectantly back at Ehren. Ehren pushed Ricasso past her, engaging in a few moments of shove and jostle—and not a little knee-banging—as the mare laid back her ears and rolled her eyes at the gelding.

"Live with it," Laine grumbled at her, moving onto the path behind Ehren.

Ehren led them forward at a slower pace than Laine had set. Easy for him; it wasn't his sister. But he doubted they were far from her now. When he heard the snatch of a voice above the quiet sounds of their movement, he stopped and dismounted.

There were other horses ahead; Ricasso's raised head and widened nostrils told him that much. Horses—and a mule. The braying neigh of greeting told Ehren and Laine both that they'd found Shette.

Ehren dropped his reins and sprang for Laine's mare, reaching her just in time to cover her nose and startle her out of the reply she was about to launch. "You'd best dismount and keep close to her head," he said to Laine's surprised expression.

Laine dismounted and stood beside him, staring uphill into the aspens. "They're in there somewhere," Ehren said, though it was only the obvious. "I think it would be best if you stayed here with the horses and let me scout ahead."

"I won't argue with that." Laine stood resolutely by the mare's head, the reins grasped close to the bit. "But . . ." He trailed off, worried. Itching to take action.

"I'll be quick," Ehren said. He eased by Ricasso, giving the horse an absent pat and a murmured reminder to *stand*.

The ground beneath the aspens was layered with slightly damp leaves, and Ehren had no trouble keeping his silence as he moved between the trees and up the slope. He doubted the bandits were camping on a hillside, so he wasn't surprised when the ground leveled ahead of him. Slowly, he moved to the crest of the hill, flattening himself to the ground so only his head showed when he peeked over it.

It was a pleasant little spot for a camp, although worn from extended use. The faint odor of human waste drifted in with the breeze. They'd been here a while, then. The horses and mule were out of sight, around a bend to the right where the aspens thinned.

But the people were right in front of him. Rude lean-to shelters lined the edge of the camp, gathered around the central fire area. There was a man, sleeping in one of the shelters, and a woman, mending the sleeve of her shirt while she wore it. And there was Shette.

She sat by a campfire that was more wisps of smoke than actual fire, her elbows on her knees and her chin jammed into the heel of her hand. She looked sullen and uncooperative, and if she'd been scared, she'd had enough time to get over it. They hadn't treated her kindly, though— it showed in the amount of hair that had been pulled free from her tie-back, and the rip in her trouser knee.

Still, there were no obvious bruises, no bloodstains. That would help put Laine's mind at ease.

The short woman looked up as she brought her mended cuff up to her mouth and bit the thread off. "You might as well wipe that look off your snotty little face," she said. "When we get you to Everdawn, no one'll buy you but the sort you don't want to belong to, if you look like that."

"I don't want to belong to *anyone*," Shette said, glaring at the fire. She'd apparently decided it wasn't safe to glare at the woman herself.

"Then you shouldn'ta been traveling that road by yourself."

"I *wasn't* by myself, I was with my brother. Just got ahead of him, is all. Your puny little spells aren't going to fool him, either. You might as well just let me go—he'll get me back, anyway." She flipped the stray hair back out of her face, but her voice didn't carry the bluff her words needed. Poor Shette. Her quiet upbringing had surely never prepared her for *this*.

Ehren scanned the area again to make sure he hadn't missed anyone, and the sleeping man gave a great snort and rolled on his back, where he commenced to snore in earnest. Not an opportunity to be missed. Quickly, Ehren moved back down the hill. Laine was waiting impatiently, letting the mare browse on the branches around them to keep her mind off the animals above them. "What?" he demanded, as soon as Ehren was close enough that he could do it quietly. "Was she there?"

"She's there, all right," Ehren said, snagging his helmet from Ricasso. "And unhurt, as far as I can tell. There're only two others with her—a tough-looking woman and some fellow who's asleep in a shelter. He's snoring loud enough to deafen anyone within range."

"Then we ought to go *now*," Laine said decisively.

"Agreed. If you haven't had any practice moving quietly, you'd better learn damn fast. I want you to get uphill of that shelter. If you can bring it down on the man, he'll be out of the fight."

Laine nodded. "I'll do it." Ehren doubted he realized that his expression made it obvious he had no idea just *how* to move that quietly through the trees, but there was enough determination to make up for it.

He hoped.

"Tie your mare away from Ricasso—I don't want them fussing just as you're getting into position. And Laine—" Ehren broke off, his eyes hard, getting Laine's attention as he'd been about to turn away. "I don't know if you've ever killed a man. But you'd better be prepared to do it now, or I'm better off going up there alone."

Laine looked away, and when he looked back again, his face was just as hard as Ehren's. "I'll do it," he said. "You just be sure you get Shette out of there."

They went up the hill together; Laine was slow but quiet enough to suit Ehren. They crawled the last few feet to get a good look over the crest of the hill, and assessed the situation without comment. Things were pretty much as they had been, except the woman had put away her needle and was rummaging in a stack of goods with the cover tarp flipped back out of her way. Shette was ignoring her—had, in fact, turned her back on the woman. But her face, hidden from the enemy, showed clearly enough that she was feeling desperate. Her eyes darted from one edge of the camp to the other.

Looking for the best place to make a break, no doubt. Which meant no more delay. Ehren caught Laine's eye and nodded.

With the thin ground cover between the aspens, Laine would have to be more than quiet. He would have to be stealthy, and to choose the right steps to keep him as hidden as possible, should the woman happen to glance his way once he headed up the hill. For a moment, Ehren wondered if he hadn't made a mistake, if it would, after all, be easier to handle the woman and Shette than a sleeping man. But Laine had taken his cue and moved on with it, and there was no stopping him without calling out.

Nothing to do but wait. And waiting while someone else took action had never been Ehren's strong point. He eased his sword from its scabbard and followed Laine's progress as the young man circled the camp at a distance.

Shette was the one who saw him. She stiffened, and her mouth dropped open. For a moment Ehren thought she would give her brother away, for she half-rose from the rock she was sitting on, and the woman noticed immediately.

"Sit yerself back down again," she said gruffly. "Don't need to be worrying about you while I'm fixing supper."

Instead, Shette stood all the way up, walking to draw the woman's gaze away from Laine—and heading straight to where Ehren waited. He froze, knowing that the motion in ducking would draw her attention more surely than his unmoving head against the trees behind him. "I have to go to the bathroom," she told the woman, sounding sulky.

"You just went. Sit down."

"I can't help it. I'm scared. I have to go!" And this time she sounded scared, for she must have realized what Laine was going to do. Her brother was moving in above the shelter

now, although when he lifted his head and saw Shette looking
his way, he hesitated.

Just don't give him away, Ehren thought, and knew Laine
was thinking exactly the same thing.

She didn't. Apparently not trusting herself not to keep
her face schooled, she turned her back on the woman and
her brother, right in front of Ehren.

And she gasped when she saw him.

The woman's head rose sharply; Ehren didn't wait for
her to spot him, or for Laine to get into place. He surged
up from the trees and grabbed Shette on his way by, shoving
her back the way he'd come. She stumbled and fell as she
hit the slope, sliding down in the dirt.

Ehren didn't bother to check on her. "Run!" he told her,
a quick shout over his shoulder while he stood to block
the woman when she would have followed. On the other
side of the camp, the crack of splintering wood announced
Laine's arrival, but Ehren knew it hadn't been in time to
catch the man asleep. He hoped Laine could hold his own
anyway, for it looked like he was going to have his hands
full here.

"Just let her go," he warned the woman, standing ready
but with his sword to the side, point down. *I'm willing to
do this without a fight if you are.*

"King's Guard," she sneered, clearing her own sword of
the scabbard.

No hesitation, then. Ehren raised his sword to guard as
she rushed to meet him, quicker than he would have
merited. Quick enough so she probably felt she was good
enough to take him. The predatory grin on her face said
the same.

She took the initiative and went high, starting a flurry
of counterattacks, steel against steel and the distance much
closer than Ehren liked; he didn't push her. When they
broke apart she was still grinning.

She'd found a way, it seemed, to deal with her short
reach—come in so close he could barely cover himself,
and attack first so she had the initiative. It wasn't the first

time he'd encountered the strategy. When she moved in again he gave her no time for attack. His stop-thrust hit her just below her elbow, and she jumped back with a sound more of anger than dismay.

Behind Ehren, Shette screamed. *She was still here? Screaming at what?*

The woman seized his moment of distraction and lunged at him, closing the distance and following when he backed, parrying so close to his body he could barely move fast enough to keep her edge away from him. Shette continued screaming words he couldn't decipher; he couldn't even check to make sure there was no one coming up behind him, only continue to weave a pattern of parries that kept him whole.

Suddenly the woman dropped low, flashing down from fifth position to snap the blade at his thigh. He slashed a wild parry from first and found his opening, stepping into her lunge and bringing his elbow back from the parry and up into her face.

Her head snapped back; blood spurted from her nose and lips. He repeated the motion, jamming the stirrup basket of his hilt into her jaw, whipping the blade around to fourth position and slashing it down across her body from shoulder to opposite hip. Her sparsely studded cloth brigandine did nothing to stop his blade.

She fell back with a grunt of disbelief, staring down at herself. Ehren didn't pause to check her fate; he knew it well enough. And Shette was still screaming—

He could see why. Laine was caught in the fallen shelter, doing his best to avoid the knife his opponent jabbed at him while trying to disentangle himself at the same time. His sword was just up the hill—and out of reach. Ehren's victory seemed to have galvanized Shette—she bolted back up the hill toward her brother. Ehren intercepted her, not bothering to be gentle as he wrapped an arm around her waist and flung her back the way she'd come, using the motion to boost his own dash forward.

Laine's arm was bleeding, his expression that of pure

concentration rather than panic. Ehren could see, then, that they were both trapped in the wreckage of the shelter—and only one of them had the face of a man who wanted to kill, and the weapon to do it with. And then Laine lost his balance and fell, easily within reach of the knife.

Without slacking pace, Ehren took the man from behind, overshooting the shelter with his momentum and twisting himself back around as soon as he could.

But it was over. His slash, with all the power of his run behind it, had taken the man over the kidneys, and arterial blood gushed brightly across the ground as the man lay over the wreckage of his shelter. More panicked now than he'd seemed before, Laine fought to free the leg that had trapped him.

Quietly, laying his sword by his foot and keeping an eye on the dying man only an arm's length from them both, Ehren crouched down and moved the green-cut branch that had flexed around Laine's ankle and held him. Laine stumbled backwards, almost fell, and lurched into a tree, which he grabbed as though *it* had been the one to save his life—or was saving it now.

If he thought he was going to get a respite, he was wrong. Shette ran to him, connecting with full force and wrapping her arms around him. She seemed to have forgotten she was an independent young woman who knew all she needed to know, and settled for sobbing into Laine's shoulder.

Over her head, Laine watched the dying gasps of the man who would have killed him, his face pale, his expression aghast. When it shifted to Ehren, it was with a new awareness of just who this new acquaintance really was, and what he was capable of—and willing to do. "Did you have to—couldn't you have . . ." he said, but didn't finish the thought. He didn't need to.

Ehren didn't have time for it. He glanced around the aspens, anxious to get them away. This camp had been set up for more than two people. Without responding to Laine, he jogged around the bend of the hill to find a corral of slender, fresh-cut aspens lashed to standing trees. From within, Laine's mule regarded him with floppy ears pricked straight upright. There were two other horses in the corral, a small, round black mare and a hard-used grey gelding. All were loosely saddled, with their bridles tied to the saddles, and Ehren didn't bother with niceties. He brought his sword down against the lashing and kicked away the poles that fell, reaching for the lead rope that had been tied back up around Clang's throatlatch. These people kept themselves ready to move out quickly, that much was obvious.

Not that he'd learned anything else about them. Ehren felt a moment's regret for killing the man. Even in retrospect, Laine's peril demanded it—but dead men answered no questions. He gathered up the two horses as well, ignoring their distrustful snorts. The other bandits would no doubt be back, and would also no doubt move on before Ehren could report their position to either Lorakan or Solvan guards, but there was no point in leaving them extra mounts.

When he returned to the camp, Laine was guiding Shette away from the dead man, and just discovering that Ehren had disemboweled the woman. The strain around his eyes was a war of disbelief and horror.

Ehren didn't coddle him. "Let's get out of here," he said. "I don't really want to meet someone on the path out, and every moment we're here increases the chance that'll happen."

"Right," Laine muttered. He jammed his sword back in its sheath, and wrapped his arm tightly around Shette's shoulders. He reached his free hand to take Clang away from Ehren, and let Ehren lead the way.

Chapter 6

Laine concentrated on the little things as the trio returned to the road. The blood trickling down his arm to drip off his fingers, Shette's little sniffles, keeping Clang off his heels. No one said anything until they were back on the road. Then Shette, her voice still edged with tears, said, "I came out here for a reason. There's this guy—"

"We know about him," Laine all but snapped. He was still reeling inside, as much over what he'd seen Ehren do as the terror of being snagged in the wreckage of the shelter, unarmed, against a man with a ferally predatory eye and a knife. He thought he'd been prepared to do what had to be done. He'd *thought* he could be tough and hard if circumstances called for it. After all, he'd defended their cattle often enough. But he'd been wrong. "Don't you think you've run into enough trouble for one day? I know I have."

She blinked at him. They stood in the middle of the road, three people, four horses, and a mule. Ehren was tightening the girths on all the horses, moving efficiently to get them ready to move on. It might as well not have happened, to watch him.

"It's still a good reason," she said, finally, if a little unevenly. "And we can still catch up with him."

A drop of blood *splatted* onto the road. Ehren eyed Laine and said shortly, "We'll need to wrap that."

"He's on foot," Shette said, sounding a little desperate. "He can't be much further—I'd have caught up to him if I could've got Clang to go faster."

No one said anything. Ehren handed the loose horses to Shette and took a critical look at Laine's arm. "Not bad," he said. "But you're going to lose a shirt sleeve. They'll have better supplies at the border station once we get back."

"Don't you *care*?" Shette cried in frustration. "If I'd known you didn't, I wouldn't have come out here in the first place!"

Ehren whirled on her, and Laine winced, remembering the intensity of Ehren's reaction in the stable. But Ehren's words, when they finally came, were careful. "You shouldn't have come out here in any case, not alone. If you'd told me about it, I'd have the man by now."

She looked away. "I wanted to surprise you."

Ehren sighed. "I know." He looked down the road, considering. "We might catch up with him. But we wouldn't get back before nightfall."

"*Please* let's go after him. Otherwise I got caught by those egg suckers for nothing!"

"Shette," Laine said, his voice much less forgiving than Ehren's had been.

"Shut up, Laine!" she cried, turning on him with fury wobbling in her voice. "You don't know anything about it! I've got to make it worth something!" Her nose was red and her eyes watery, and suddenly as angry as he was, Laine wanted to have his arms around her shoulders again, making her feel safe. Except he wasn't sure anymore a mere embrace would do the job.

Ehren cleared his throat. "He knows enough," he said. "He was almost killed, getting you out of there."

Shette started sobbing, just standing in the middle of the road with her hands covering her face. Laine took an uncertain step toward her, but it was Ehren who put his arm around her and drew her in close to let her cry. Over the top of her head, he looked at Laine and said, "We can have that cut looked at at one of the inns as easily as at the border. She does have a point. I don't know who this man is, but I'd like to find out." Clearly an understatement.

Laine sighed. It was true, they were all safe now, and even if they stayed away a week, it wasn't likely to interfere with the caravan schedule. His desire to be back at his wagon *now* was more an attempt to get away from what had happened here than a need to return. And Ehren hadn't been obliged to come with him on this Shette hunt. He supposed he owed the man that much. So he shrugged, and nodded, and said only, "I hope you have coins on you."

Ehren gave him a slow smile, and nodded. After a moment, he brushed away the loose hair that had stuck to Shette's tear-wet face, and pointed her at the little black mare, suggesting they get acquainted. Then, while Laine held the rest of the mounts, Ehren cut Laine's sleeve off, tore it into strips, and wrapped it around the long, shallow slice down Laine's arm. Laine eyed Ehren's handiwork critically and said, "Well, it's a warm enough day. I don't guess I'll have another use for that sleeve before it ends."

"Is it bad, Laine?" Shette asked from atop the mare, her voice laced with trepidation. "Are you really hurt?"

"If I was really hurt I'd have made you carry me down that hill," Laine told her, some of the humor finally finding its way back to his voice. "Now let's get moving. After all this trouble, I guess I want to get a look at this fellow, too."

❦

They caught up with the man just as the early summer evening began to dim. Inns sprouted along the Trade Road, perched precariously along the river or jammed up against the steep rock of the other side, and the trio checked at two of them before stopping at the Goose and Gander. As before, Laine and Shette stayed out in front of the inn with their menagerie, while Ehren went to check the occupants.

He knew all that Shette could tell him. The man had been dressed in shabby clothes of an indeterminate brown color, was balding with what was left of his hair cut close in the new Kurtane style, and had a mole under his left eye. He was nervous and while he had a little money, he seemed to set more value on his satchel of papers than his purse.

In the dim light of the inn's common room, it was difficult to tell who was wearing indeterminate brown and who had on muddied blues and faded black. Ehren stood to the side of the doorway, letting his gaze wander the room with no hurry behind it. The diners and drinkers eyed him and ignored him, and a few who'd already had too much to drink scowled at him. One of them was within easy earshot, and muttered loudly, "King's Guard don't mean *nothin'* here."

Ehren paid him no attention—not once he'd seen the man carried no sword and his knife was skewed on his belt, making for an awkward reach. If the fellow got any sudden ideas, his movement would be easy to spot.

No, his attention narrowed down to exclude the thick smell of food and ale and sweat. His eyes, a grey so dark they were piercing black in this light, sorted the details before him and came up with—

There. There he was. In the corner, by himself and obviously wanting no part of company. He'd seen Ehren, and was studiously looking away, as if that meant Ehren wouldn't be able to see him, either. His eyes blinked rapidly, making the mole under his left eye twitch a little. On the table next to him was a small satchel; at his feet was a bundle of clothes in a blanket. All his worldly goods, no doubt.

Ehren eyed the number of tables between his quarry and the exit, and stepped back outside the inn.

Laine and Shette were waiting, both looking much the worse for wear. Shette was exhausted, and wrung out of tears or any other emotion. Her expression was dull, and it was time to coax some food into her and get her to bed. Laine's arm had swollen beneath its bandage, and he had his thumb hooked through his sword belt to keep it from hanging and, no doubt, throbbing. Other than that he seemed determined to put what he'd seen and experienced behind him. It wouldn't be behind him until he faced it head on, Ehren well knew, but there would be a better time to tell him so. "Stable 'em," Ehren told the two. "We're staying here."

Shette didn't even ask if that meant the man was here, but Ehren nodded at Laine's quick, questioning glance. "I'll take care of it," he added, and Laine shrugged and led the horses toward the riverbank corrals, with Shette still perched on the mare.

Ehren stood against the side of the inn, just beside the door hinges, and waited. The man was a runner, and there was no reason to think he'd change his ways now.

After a long moment, the door cracked open. It stayed cracked long enough for someone to get a good look around, and then, in the dimness, a small figure darted out.

Ehren's hand was faster. He clapped it down on the fellow's shoulder, stopping him in his tracks like a rabbit too scared to move. "I think we need to talk," Ehren said.

"I-I'm a Therand citizen, Clan Shahinian," the little man said, through teeth that were all but chattering. "I've committed no crime. You have no right to hold me."

Ehren raised an eyebrow, unseen in the darkness—not that the man had dared to turn around. "Did I say you'd committed a crime?"

"N-no."

"I don't recall saying I intended you any harm, either."

Silence. The fugitive wasn't about to believe that. With an iron grip, Ehren encouraged him to back a step or two, until his quiet voice was just above the man's ear. "Whether I intend you harm or not, you're well and good caught. I suggest you cooperate for a while, and see where it gets you."

After a hesitation, the man nodded stiffly, clutching his possessions tightly to himself.

The inn door creaked open again, and a woman came out, lantern in hand. She cast them a suspicious look and hung the lantern beside the door. "Trouble here?" she asked.

"Not that I know of," Ehren said easily. "Unless you're full for the night, in which case the trouble is ours."

"I thought he was staying in the common room."

"His luck has changed for the better," Ehren said. "I have two friends, and five horses being stabled. What about that room?"

She wasn't about to say no to someone who was spending on five horses. "Of course we have a room, sir," she said. "For a Guard like yourself, we would always find a room."

For a Guard with the money, she meant, but Ehren smiled at her anyway.

Shette sat on the small room's one bed, her shoes on the floor and her legs drawn up beneath her. She looked askance at the stained blanket again, deciding once and for all that she would sleep on top of it, although the innkeeper had assured them the beds were regularly spelled against fleas. She wasn't sure if she would ever be able to sleep again—or if she would be able to stay awake even one moment longer. The day was affecting her like that.

It seemed weeks ago that she had made the impulsive decision to come after this man. And had it only been this afternoon that she'd been in the clutches of bandits, and bound for slavery? No, not likely. Maybe it had never happened at all. The only thing she was certain of was the feel of Ehren's strong arm around her, and the leather smell of his brigandine.

The brigandine was off, now, and he'd changed to a worn linen shirt of a quality Shette had never owned. Ehren stood at the end of the bed, wrapping Laine's arm, while the fugitive who had started the whole thing was sitting on the floor with his back to the corner, looking miserable as his glance darted from the door to Ehren and back again.

"Ow," Laine muttered, looking like he would have preferred to say much more. Ehren's touch was sure and even, wrapping the salve-smeared arm with the hand of experience. He tied off the bandage and rested a brief hand on Laine's shoulder.

"It's not deep, and the edges are clean. It'll heal fine." Then he gave Laine a wry grin. "It'll just hurt like hell for a few days."

"Tell me something I don't already know," Laine said. He looked as tired as Shette felt. Neither of them were used to this sort of adventure. Ehren, she thought, must be. Despite the chase he'd undertaken that morning, and all the fighting he'd done at the bandit camp, he looked better than any of them.

The little man spoke from his corner, his words abrupt and clipped. "What do you want from me?"

They stared at him as one. They'd eaten with this man silent at their table, offering nothing by way of excuse or conversation, barely touching the ale they had ordered for him. He'd walked between Ehren and Laine with no objection, climbing the narrow stairs on the way to this room. He'd picked out his corner and he'd silently watched as Ehren tended Laine. And now, finally, he'd found his tongue.

"If you're going to kill me, do it now."

"If I was going to kill you," Ehren said dryly, "I wouldn't have brought along these two to help me."

"What do you want from me, then?"

"Why were you running?" Ehren countered.

The man laughed, a high-pitched and slightly panicked sort of sound. Shette felt sorry for him. "What's your name?" she asked.

He blinked at her.

"I'm Shette. That's Laine and Ehren."

"And what's a King's Guard doing with the likes of you?"

"Following me," Shette said. "Because I was following you."

"You? *You* were following me?"

Ehren grinned at the man. "You'll have to learn better than to spill your secrets to a whore." He nodded at Shette. "She asked your name."

Thoroughly puzzled, the man said, "Unai."

"Unai, a year ago, my king was killed. My friend. Heliga says you know something about it. I want to know what."

"Heliga?"

"The whore," Ehren said gently. "The one you shouldn't

have talked to." He left the bedside, and walked over to Unai's corner. No, Shette decided, it was more of an easy stalk, with Ehren's boot heels loud against the wood floor, and the buckles of his blood-spattered greaves jingling counterpoint. He crouched in front of Unai and said quietly, "I've been searching a year for Benlan's killers. I don't for a minute believe you had anything to do with it. But I *do* believe you know something about it, and the only thing that's going to get you in trouble now is if you *don't* tell me what it is."

Unai, skewered by that black gaze, couldn't seem to look away. At last he wrenched his head to the side and said, "I want to go to Everdawn."

"You can go anywhere you damn well please after you talk to me."

Unai shook his head, and then chanced a quick, sideways glance at Ehren. "No. I want an escort to Everdawn. If you want what I know, you'll keep me safe till then."

Ehren glanced over his shoulder at Shette and Laine, something indecipherable in his gaze. "All right," he said.

Shette blinked. "What about us?"

Ehren stood, turning his back on Unai, who looked as if he didn't quite believe what he'd heard. "That's your choice."

Laine gave him an uncertain look. "I thought you wanted to take the caravan back."

"I'll make it back in time."

"Ansgare won't wait for him, you know he won't," Shette said abruptly, not willing to say good-bye to Ehren—nor to travel back through that spot she was ambushed, without him. "We should go with him, Laine. Ansgare's not going anywhere until you get back."

She expected Laine's immediate protest. What she got was silence. He gave her a speculative look, as though he'd somehow heard her unspoken thoughts. And he looked at Ehren with that same expression. "We might just be in the way, Shette."

"I want them," the little man said suddenly. "I want them with us, or there's no deal. I'll yell so loud those louts in the common room will hear—there's no love lost for Guards down there, not when they're letting the borders grow so dangerous."

"Think it'll keep me in line to have her along, do you?" Ehren said, dry amusement in his voice. "It's fine with me."

All eyes were on Laine. "We owe you," Laine said to Ehren, and that was the end of it.

"Who owes who what is a little tangled at this point," Ehren said. "But I'm grateful all the same."

"Good," Laine said, then put a plaintive look on his face. "Now, can we get some sleep? I've had about all I can take out of this day."

Ehren slept by the door, after making sure the shutters to the small window were closed and latched. If Unai wanted to go out that way, he'd drop two stories straight down and clamber over Laine and Shette getting there, but the door was a different matter, and the little man had been eyeing it from the moment they got in the room.

He didn't expect to get much sleep, and he was right. Between Unai's restless squirming in the corner—for the bed was a small one, and barely big enough for Laine and Shette—and his own churning thoughts, there was plenty to keep him awake.

The ring was patently unhappy with him; even strung around his neck instead of on his finger, its mood was obvious. Instead of humming happily, it rested against his skin with a sort of soundless buzzing. He wasn't surprised. His orders had been explicit—drop the search for Benlan's killers and find Dannel's family instead. So here he was, following the wrong trail and moving steadily away from where he was supposed to find Dannel's family.

With no regret whatsoever.

In fact, for the first time since Benlan's death, he felt he'd found something that would lead further than the execution of another low-level henchman. And that was one bit he intended to take in his teeth and run with.

On the bed, Laine made a small noise; Ehren was instantly

alert. Not that it'd be unusual to have bad dreams after such a thorough introduction to mayhem and swordplay, but Ehren well remembered the last *dream* Laine had experienced. He sat up against the door and rested his forearms on his drawn-up knees, waiting.

There it was, that same soft sound a protest, almost a moan of frustration. He heard Shette shifting in the darkness. There was the sound of wood sliding on wood, and the shutters drifted open. Light drifted into the room along with cool night air, and Ehren could see the girl eyeing her brother with some concern.

Laine twitched, and jerked, and a chilling, raspy protest scraped through his throat. And that was enough for Ehren.

"Laine," he said, and his flat, loud voice made Shette jump.

"No, Ehren—" she said, as Ehren got to his feet and headed for the bed. She didn't try to stop him, though— instead she swiftly removed herself from the bed. "It's not safe, Ehren, don't wake him—"

"What's going on over there?" Unai asked, fear in his voice. Ehren ignored him; Laine twisted on the bed and enough was enough. He leaned over the low, narrow bed and took Laine firmly by the shoulders.

"Wake up, Laine," he said, his voice as firm as his grip. Neither had an effect, and he gave the young man a good shake. "That's enough, Laine—*wake up*."

Laine exploded into action, and the first Ehren knew of it was when Laine's fist connected solidly with the corner of Ehren's eye. Ehren rolled away, hitting the floor and coming to his feet in a crouch, ready to restrain this sudden adversary. But Laine was quiet again, on his hands and knees in the bed and slowly sinking to his haunches.

Ehren blinked rapidly, tears streaming out of both eyes as the one immediately swelled closed. His vision wavered, but he could still pick out the whites of Laine's unblinking eyes. Even in starlight those eyes looked blank. Slowly, he rose to full height, and blotted his good eye against his sleeve.

"I tried to tell you—" Shette started.

Unai demanded, "What's going *on*?"

"Be quiet," Ehren told him without sympathy. "Laine, wake up now. It was only a dream."

"It's never *only a dream*," Shette muttered.

Laine's voice was distant; Ehren's relief at his response quickly faded. "There was a man watching," he said. "A man . . . but he wasn't *there*."

Ehren turned to Shette, and she came to him from where she'd been standing against the door. He wondered if she realized it was probably all that had kept Unai from bolting. He nodded at Laine, who was murmuring something about being dead, and said, "What's this about, Shette? I know it's happened before."

"Are you all right? That was an awful solid hit he landed—"

Ehren didn't gentle the iron in his voice this time. "Shette."

In response he got a flare of righteously irked teenager. "Ask *him*," she said. "I'm not the one who does it, am I?"

He supposed it was better than being fawned on. "I will," he told her.

In fact, he didn't. The next morning found Laine in the sort of daze Ehren had observed when he'd had contact with Wilna's ring, and it wasn't easy to get his attention.

"I told you not to wake him," Shette observed acerbically, though she managed to say it only once. "You got a black eye and he's not worth a thing. It's best to let him sleep it out when they're that strong."

Ehren didn't tell her that he'd been afraid to let it get as bad as it had the last time.

They traveled without much incident. Unai spent the morning testing his limits; he rode the grey gelding and tried to get it to drift away from the group, but he was inexperienced at best and the gelding was a stubborn, herd-bound creature. Ehren let him think he hadn't been noticed and resolved to watch the man, although Unai seemed to settle into his new role well enough—half-captured, half-escorted, both by one of the best guards Solvany had to offer. Shette helped distract him from his plight; she seemed to have a sudden need to talk about the events of the day before.

She kept her little mare—a creature she had quickly adopted, and which now bore evidence of her affection in its fancily braided mane—next to Ricasso, which put her head far below Ehren's. And she chattered—she asked him if he'd ever killed anyone before, or rescued anyone from bandits before, and didn't seem to mind when he didn't give her more than one or two words as an answer. She wondered what sort of people bought the slaves, and she swore she'd never travel on this road alone again. Unai seemed to take it all in, and by the end of the morning, also seemed to have resigned himself to Ehren's company.

The road narrowed a little and climbed gradually but steadily; at intervals of the distance a man could comfortably travel each day on foot, a crop of inns showed up, occasionally accompanied by other amenities and a cluster of hutlike houses. The terrain allowed for nothing more.

Ehren rode the fine line of getting as many miles out of the horses as he could without wearing them out. Several days to Everdawn and the same number back, and he had no intention of taking it out of the horses' hides. Clang, of course, would look after himself, as all mules did.

They rode for two days. In the end, however, they didn't quite make it to Everdawn. As they ambled in to what Ehren figured would be the last stop before their goal, Shette asked, "Who're all those men in uniforms?"

He'd seen them. There were two by the barn, and three getting ready to ride out together. And he knew the uniform well enough, even if he'd only seen it in Guard manuals. "Lorakan army," he said quietly. He didn't mention that the army was generally inactive, except for the maintenance of its command structure. Like Solvany, Loraka had other branches of the service to take care of day-to-day peacekeeping duties.

But these men didn't seem to be doing anything in particular here. They were just . . . present.

Wearing his King's Guard identification was second nature to Ehren, but now he casually eased it off his arm. He slid Ricasso in behind Unai's grey and dismounted so he could shrug off his brigandine. He rolled it up lining side out and tied it behind his saddle with the gambeson, pulling his shirt from his saddlebag.

"Problems?" Laine asked. He seemed back to his old self now, but Ehren had not found the privacy to inquire about his dreams—nor had he completely decided that it was his business, after all. Even if his eye *was* still damnably sore, and splashed with the greenly dark colors of a hailstorm—or so Shette had informed him.

Ehren looked up at him. "Not that I know of." But he followed Laine's gaze to the two soldiers by the barn. "Just don't want to raise any interest. Being a Guard won't buy me any leeway here." He led Ricasso out in front of them and said, "Come on. Standing here looking at them isn't going to come across all that well, either."

Privately, he knew his feeble attempts at camouflage would do him little good if he happened across an experienced man. They would recognize it in one another, and if the Lorakan was looking for trouble, he would be able to make it.

Laine was still having trouble with his eyes. As they'd traveled, Shette had turned into that same vacant-eyed girl he'd first seen the evening he ran into Ehren, and Unai occasionally faded into a boy he hadn't seen until now, a youngster who was usually twirling himself in circles that dizzied Laine just to watch.

After several such incidents, Laine fell back into the old childhood habit of closing first one eye, and then the other, searching for some difference in the way his unmatched eyes perceived the world. If only he could find one, maybe he could figure out how to avoid these unbidden visions.

But he couldn't. And amongst it all, he had the feeling

there was someone looking over his shoulder. It was a man, he was certain, and he had cold, dark eyes with no mercy in them.

He knew he'd had another True Dream right after they found Unai, although he remembered none of it—that was the way of things when he was startled awake in the middle of them. He also knew he'd managed to thoroughly blacken Ehren's eye, and even when he didn't want to believe it, there was Ehren, sitting across the table from him and looking like he'd smeared soot on his fist and rubbed his eye with it.

They were in the common room of the last inn before Everdawn. Ehren had his back to the wall, scanning the room as ever. Unai was next to him, and Laine on the other side of that, trapping the little man between the two of them. But even Unai seemed to have no desire to create a scene, not with all the Lorakan soldiers around.

Ehren had said something, and Laine, thinking about that man's eyes, missed it. "What?" he asked, sounding a little dimwitted even to himself. He probably even deserved the disgusted-sibling look Shette threw at him.

"I don't think we should go in any further," Ehren said.

"You have to take me to Everdawn—that's the deal!" Unai's voice, which had lost its frightened edge over days of uneventful travel, grew tense again.

Ehren raised an eyebrow at him and picked up a chicken leg. Shette had just tried her first mouthful and had an incredulous look on her face; she snatched up the mug of watered wine in front of her and gulped it down. Hmmm. Laine was going to have to give it a try.

This inn—and its food—was a step above the others they'd stayed at—its proximity to Everdawn was probably a factor in that. In an inn of this quality, one expected the beds to be spelled against fleas, and the hall to have a glow-spell all night long; all the little amenities that were available in the cities.

But Shette had yet to get used to the food. Laine gave his little sister an affectionate, what-else-can-you-expect look she would have smacked him for if she hadn't been too busy blinking tears from her eyes.

When she'd caught her breath, giving the spiced chicken an incredulous look, Ehren finally responded to Unai. "You're close enough. Travel out with some of these soldiers tomorrow and you'll have an escort all the way in. I can't chance getting caught up in anything here."

"But you're not doing anything wrong," Shette protested.

"Only following a lead I'm not supposed to follow, and ignoring the orders I was given," Ehren said wryly. "Varien would love to see me in trouble here—and he'd probably laugh himself to sleep every night if he managed to get me stranded by denying my ties to the Guard."

"Why?" she demanded.

Ehren shook his head. "Tedious details, Shette. Let's just say the man doesn't like me, and that's reason enough."

"But I can't keep up with the soldiers," Unai said, his voice suspiciously close to a whine.

"The grey is yours," Ehren said without hesitation. "You might get a good price for him in Everdawn, if you bargain carefully. I wouldn't keep him. You don't have the funds to feed him on the road." He pinned the little man with his stare. "Don't squirm, Unai. Just talk. You've certainly learned enough about us by now to realize we're not going to kill you as you sleep tonight. For that matter, you can sleep where you choose, after I have what I want."

Unai pressed his lips together, a stubborn look entering his eyes. Ehren leaned forward, set his elbows against the table and said, his voice deliberate and quiet, "You're not going to get anything more out of me, Unai. But I'm perfectly willing to take you out behind the barn tonight and dunk you in the river until I get what I want out of *you.*"

Laine believed him, flashing back to the sight of a short swordswoman's ropy grey guts spilled out on the ground. Unai, too, seemed to take Ehren's words seriously, especially after looking at Laine's expression. He sunk down on his low, wide-seated stool and nodded. "But not here," he said.

Ehren didn't argue with him. They finished their meal in silence, and Shette, her eyes and nose still running from the hot spices, immediately announced she was going to immerse herself in the river. It wasn't as good as a bath and clean clothes, but better than living in the same sweat-stained garments for yet another day. Both because he thought it was a good idea, and because he didn't want Shette wandering around by herself, Laine went with her. Ehren dragged Unai to the stables when he went to check on the horses.

A strong moon made the riverbank clear despite full darkness, and a quarter mile from the inn, Laine found a calm spot carved out of the side of the bank. Beyond its edges the water rushed by, but he and Shette were able to immerse themselves and even get lost in a little sibling water war. They stayed longer than Laine had planned, and afterward, dripping and squishing, they made their way back to the road and walked slowly back to the inn, still lost in a mood of indulgence.

Ehren stood in front of the inn, looking down the road, back the way they'd come. That was the direction Laine and Shette had gone, and he'd expected them back long before. Now Unai was in their room, tied and gagged—for Ehren trusted him even less, now that the little man was close to what he considered safety. Ehren had no doubt Unai would be just as happy to draw the Lorakan soldiers' attention to Ehren's status. It'd be easy enough for him to slink away into Everdawn while Ehren untangled himself from Lorakan interest and vigilance.

Once he was in Everdawn, there was very little likelihood Ehren could find him. And this was one lead Ehren wasn't about to lose.

So Unai was tied, Laine and Shette were errant, and Ehren was about to set off to look for them. He started for the road with long strides, jingling slightly from boot buckles he could tighten if he wasn't actually enjoying the sound. The walk itself was pleasant, with an almost full moon and a number of enthusiastic insects chirping and humming to each other in the narrow track of woods between himself and the river.

When he saw a lone figure coming his way, he slowed. Not Laine—this was a tall, thin man sporting a beard and long hair that caught silver in the moonlight. He had a walking stick, and the stick . . . *glowed*. By the time he reached the man, Ehren realized he was seeing his first road wizard—one of the bevy of competent Lorakan magic users who patrolled and spelled the Trade Road in the off-use hours. There were spells to keep the roads from rutting and wearing away—those were the easy ones, from what Ehren understood. The hard part was keeping travelers on this road from falling prey to the same kind of wandering spells that made Laine's Sight so valuable to the caravan.

He lifted a hand in greeting as they were about to pass, but the other man stopped short with an obvious interest. "Now that's something," he said, though Ehren wasn't sure if the comment was directed to the air, or to him.

"Try that one again," Ehren suggested, hoping to find out.

"What is that you're wearing? The layers in it are masterful. May I see it?"

"Maybe," Ehren said, finding himself not a little amused. Whatever world this wizard spent most of his time in, it didn't seem to be Loraka. "Give me a hint. What are you looking at? Not my amazing personality, I'd guess."

"What?" Completely baffled, the man merely stared at him a moment. "Oh! Sorry." There was a sheepish grin behind his realization, easy enough to read in the moonlight. "You're wearing something around your neck. I was wondering if I could see it."

The ring. For the first time in this strange encounter, Ehren hesitated. "It's personal," he said.

"Oh, not to worry. I won't be able to read the spells themselves. I just want to examine the definition of the layers. It's rare to see such workmanship, I can tell that from here. It's a very new process, just out of Loraka the city, and can only be done with a certain class of spells."

Ehren lifted the ring over his head, but kept it closed within his hand. "Layers?"

"More than one spell. This object has two kinds—three spells that operate separately from one another, and a fourth that's nested in one of the others. Trigger that one spell, and the nested spell follows. One of the individual spells is operating right now, while the other two—including the one that will trigger the nested spell—is quiescent." The man sounded like he was lecturing an apprentice, and he must have realized it, for he broke off and gave another sheepish grin. "Sorry again. As I said, it's a fascinating piece."

Ehren hesitated no longer; he handed the man the ring. "Tell me what you can of it."

"Nice ring," the man said absently. "It seems to have a history behind it."

Ehren had seen Varien's sly works, and he'd seen cottage witchy work. He'd never come across a working wizard who was immersed in his craft on a daily basis, yet treated it so offhandedly. It was an opportunity he didn't intend to pass up, especially if there were layered spells on this ring. He knew of the finding spell; he knew of the spell that would identify Dannel's family. But what of the other two?

After a moment, the man sighed and handed the ring back. "Yes, indeed. I thank you. This has helped to clarify some questions I've had—"

Ehren didn't wait for the wizard to enumerate those questions. "What of the spells? What can you tell?"

The man blinked a little. "I said I wouldn't be able to read the spells; I can't. They've been laminated with energy. As I said, a very nice ring."

"Were they all set at the same time?" It *had* been Wilna's ring, after all—a spell of affection set on it when she gave it to Benlan wouldn't have been out of the ordinary for a royal budget.

"Oh, yes. They have to be, or the stone won't take them.

It's very tricky. There *was* a separate spell—on the metal instead of the stone—placed earlier in the ring's life, but it's mostly obliterated by the new ones. Those, I'd say, are but six months old."

"Six months?" Ehren repeated in surprise. Varien had this ring ready for him six months ago? Why, late winter had been filled with most of his successes in his search for Benlan's killers. It was a time when he firmly believed he was following the trail to its head, and would soon have all of the conspirators in hand. It was also the time of the first attempt against his life . . . although all of those could certainly be dismissed as criminal acts of attempted theft.

If the criminal was exceedingly stupid, and screened his victims on the basis of how well armed and horsed they were—and then chose the best of those instead of the worst.

"Six months, give or take a few weeks," the wizard said modestly. "I take it you know little of this ring's history."

"Some of it I know," Ehren mused darkly, "and some of it I obviously don't. Is there any way to find out?"

"Aside from triggering the spells? No. Though I could probably do that for you, if you don't know the trigger keys."

Ehren stared down the dark road, and thought it no darker than the road Varien had sent him on. "No," he said. "This is not the time or place for that to happen."

The man shrugged, obviously disappointed, and returned the ring. "Well, then, any good wizard could do the same, if you found one you felt you could trust. We're sort of like confidants, in that respect."

A murmur of conversation broke the silence that followed. Laine and Shette, still no more than vague shapes in the darkness as they walked up the road. Ehren nodded at them. "The friends I came in search of," he told the wizard. "I thank you for your help."

"Think nothing of it," the man said. "It was a pleasant diversion to the night's work."

"It may well end up being more than nothing to me," Ehren said. The wizard gave another shrug, one that looked embarrassed this time, and moved on down the road, his walking stick glowing softly as a hazy red counterpoint to the moonlight.

Ehren looped the braided grass around his neck and tucked the ring away as Shette and Laine reached him. No need for them to know anything about it.

Chapter 7

"My family's lived in Therand for many years," Unai said. "Long enough to be adopted into Clan Shahinian. But we came from Solvany. And there was a reason we left." It was the first time he'd strung more than two strong sentences together since they'd met, and he seemed a bit taken aback by the accomplishment; he stopped, and looked steadfastly at the finished wood of the rented room's wall.

"Don't keep it to yourself," Ehren suggested, although Laine heard steel backing his quiet tone.

There were two beds in this room; whether Ehren would be sharing his with Unai had yet to be resolved. Personally, Laine felt Unai would bolt from the room as soon as Ehren declared him free to go.

For the first time in far too many days, Laine felt clean and cool—since the camp where they'd found Shette, he decided. His shirt hung over the window sill, catching the breeze to dry, and the exposed cut on his arm was red-edged and angry, reminding him of that afternoon every time he caught a glimpse of it. He'd have to ask Shette to wrap it again, as soon as the bandages had dried.

No, he didn't want to think about that afternoon. It'd been days since his head was fully clear, and now that he'd found his wits again, he wanted to keep them.

Unai sat on one of the beds, his satchel clutched to his chest, apparently searching for words. Shette was curled up at the head of the other, Ehren sat at her feet—Laine wondered if he'd noticed how companionably those feet rested up against his leg—and Laine was sitting cross-legged on the floor by the end of the same bed.

Ehren grew more still, more focused. "Tell us what you know, and we can quit one another's company. You've made it plain that's what you want—why delay it?"

"I could be killed for what I know," Unai said.

Ehren stood, an abrupt and sudden teetering of his temper. "And *will* be, if you don't talk!" In the stunned silence that followed, Ehren, quiet but intense, said, "The sooner you stop being the *only* target to aim for, the safer you'll be." He towered over the man, seemed to realize the intimidation was only prolonging things, and sat down again with obvious effort.

"Once I give this to you," Unai said slowly, "I'm through with the matter. I'm going back to Grettlingdon to raise sheep with the rest of my family." He gave his satchel an odd look—one almost of respect—and slowly held it out to Ehren.

Laine had never thought of the man as having family. Maybe, he thought, Unai did better as a sheep farmer than an adventurer. The Guides knew he obviously wasn't cut out to take on the sorts of adventures that made heroes out of men—or warriors, like the man sitting next to his sister.

"Benlan's death," Ehren grated, ignoring Unai's offering. "Tell me about Benlan's death."

Unai's reaction was totally unexpected, and completely unfeigned. "Benlan's death?" he said. "Who said I knew anything about *that*? Other than the fact that it happened, of course, and thankfully before I met him and not *while* I was supposed to meet him. Finding Benlan's killers is up to you, Guard, and I'll be a lot better off myself once you do."

Utter silence fell over the room. Shette stopped combing

her fingers through her damp hair and simply stared, while Ehren went stiff—and, Laine thought, very dangerous. An assumption . . . they'd all made the same assumption.

"Just what *do* you know?" he asked, and that implacably hard edge was back in his voice.

"I had these words all practiced, once," Unai admitted. "I traveled the length of the Trade Road to tell the story. And then before I could, just moments before I could pass this story on, Benlan was killed." His gaze bounced off each of them in turn and settled somewhere between Laine and the door. "Two generations back, one of my ancestors was a servant at Keland's court."

Ehren waited.

"Her name was Hetna," Unai said, after an uneasy moment. "She was only there a little while—then she learned enough to frighten her into leaving. She was killed— supposedly an accident—shortly afterward. But she'd left her journal with the family, and no one knew she'd written it."

"*That's* what you've got," Shette said. "You've got the journal!"

"Yes."

Ehren seemed to need a moment to take it all in. "But you've been on the run for a year. That's no coincidence; you're tied into Benlan's death as well."

Unai didn't deny it; he shrugged. "I may well be. I don't know what the official story was, but the day he died, he was coming to meet me."

Ehren nodded slowly. "That makes sense. The official story was that he was on a pleasure ride, inspecting his favorite hunting lodge after winter. But it was never clear to those of us in the Guard if that was really true, even before the high number of escort assignments came through." He seemed to be lost in thought. After a moment he came back to the here and now, and said, "I want to hear more."

Unai gestured with the satchel again. "Take it. It's all in here."

This time Ehren accepted the book. He laid it on the bed beside Shette's feet, unopened. "After all this time, your family finally decided to let the Solvan monarch know what had happened."

Unai met his gaze, uncharacteristically forthright. "I'm the first to have reading and writing since Hetna died," he said simply. "The journal survived merely as a memorial to her, and not because anyone realized it held the key to her death—and to things awry in Solvany. It took me quite a long time to work up to bringing it here. Now I wish I hadn't. Hetna is long dead, Benlan is dead, and whatever the past problems, they're long done with."

"No," Ehren murmured. "They're not."

Shette moved to her knees, kneeling in front of the wrapped journal, and running her hand over it. "What do you mean?" she asked, not looking at Ehren now that she was this close to him.

"Benlan is dead, killed when he went to meet you." Ehren's voice was distant. "Unai, who knew about that meeting?"

"I have no idea," Unai said, shaking his head and waving Ehren's question away with his hands. "And I'm not getting into this any deeper by speculating. I paid a boy to approach him on one of the Days of Hearing, and to give him a note. Arrangements were made through the same boy. I told no one else, and the boy couldn't read."

Ehren took the journal out from under Shette's hands. "What's in here?" he asked. "What made you come so far, and risk so much?"

"Read it," Unai said bluntly. At the look on Ehren's face, he relented slightly. "Hetna was almost sure there was treachery in the court. She . . . did some prowling she shouldn't have. I don't understand the subtle things—the ruling structure is much different than Therand's, but there was, at the least, black market smuggling going on. Therand goods."

"That doesn't make sense," Laine said. "You're talking about the highest Levels, right? They've already got wealth—what's smuggling going to get them, besides in trouble?"

"Some people always want more," Ehren said.

Unai said sourly, "Don't ask *me* to justify it. All I can tell you is that someone was involved in it, and that Hetna was so frightened she wouldn't even write down a name, only dared to call the smuggled goods by two letters: *ML*. She left the court, and within a month, was killed by a supposedly runaway timber wagon. The documentation is in the journal, what there is of it. It wouldn't be half as convincing if Hetna had gone on to live a long and satisfying life."

Silence fell over the small room, flickering like the candlelight against the wall. Ehren stared at the journal in his hands, Shette stared at Ehren, and Laine, for whatever reason, found his thoughts drawn to the image of a man's watching eyes. Finally Unai said, "Is that enough, then? Can I go, and the grey with me?"

"That's it," Ehren said simply.

Shette said, "Can I read it?"

Unai snorted. "It'll make little sense to you."

"I can get as much from it as you did," she shot back at him, scowling.

"When I'm done, perhaps," Ehren said, cutting the argument short, for which Laine was relieved.

Unai seemed relieved, period, that the whole thing was over. "There *is* one thing in there that the clans have already begun to suspect on their own," he said, standing, his hand reaching for the small bundle of belongings that was all he traveled with. "A hundred years ago, a sect of the Upper Levels wanted to find a way to nullify the Barrenlands in order to wage war. To appease them, Coirra—she was the First Level Wizard, then, and Varien her apprentice— smuggled herself into Therand and put a curse on the firstborn of the ruling Therand clan. Hetna seems to think this was tied in with the smuggling somehow, but I don't know why. She was getting pretty cryptic by then. I do know that since the position of the T'ierand changes clans much more frequently than your monarchy, there have been quite a few blind children born in Therand in a hundred years."

Shette gasped. "That's horrible! How could anyone do that to *babies*?"

"How could anyone snatch a young girl off the road to sell her for slavery?" Ehren said briefly. Shette made a face and subsided.

Laine was thinking that if someone wanted the border kept closed, then perhaps they didn't want a war messing up their contraband smuggling operation—nor an open border that would eliminate the market. That would mean the smuggling was a long-standing tradition, going back to Coirra's time.

And Unai was making good his chance to quit their company. He stood, gave a stiff, slight nod, and left the room. Shette said acerbically, "Well, at least we can trust he won't try to take any of the other horses."

"That's why I tied them on the other side of Ricasso," Ehren murmured, still looking at the satchel-encased book. He said, more to himself than Laine and Shette, "If Benlan really *was* killed because he was about to get his hands on this book, then there may be more to this than just long-gone history."

"Be a lot simpler to have killed Unai, if someone just wanted to keep anyone from learning what was in the journal," Laine said, matter-of-factly.

Ehren looked at him, eyebrows raised. "That's true," he said. "So there must be more to it than that." His gaze went inward a moment, and darkened considerably. "Varien," he said. "There's one constant between the Kurtane court then and now. Varien."

"Just because you don't like him," Shette said, braving Ehren's annoyance.

Good point. But before Laine could express his agreement, he was suddenly taken by the feel of a blade against his throat, the splash of his own blood across his jaw—

"Laine!" Shette said, sharp concern in her voice. "Don't start doing it while you're *awake*, for Guides' sake!"

"Watch your mouth," Laine said mildly, automatically, glad to have those words to fall back on while he pulled himself back to the candlelit room and away from insidious dark memories that should have belonged to someone else.

It was bound to happen; Shette was half expecting it, and knew what was going on even before she got her eyes open. She took a few moments to register the fact that the candle on the box between the beds, although very low, was still burning, and that she was in the bed alone. Laine must have fallen asleep in the other one, while Ehren read.

But he wasn't asleep now, he was dreaming. Shette lay in the bed, staring up at the light flickering off the ceiling and listening to Laine twitch. Once she'd seen that look in his eye, earlier that evening, she'd expected this.

"Laine." That was Ehren, and hadn't he learned from the last time that he shouldn't interrupt? They didn't all get as bad as they had the night on the caravan that she'd thrown herself across Laine, scared by his thrashing. She sat up.

"You ought to just leave him alone," she said in a low voice, and winced at the thump from the next bed. She didn't look. "It's just a dream, I've told you that."

"I've seen men die from fits," Ehren said, though from his grim voice he understood why she didn't want him to wake her brother. "This is no simple dream, Shette."

As if on cue, Laine started thrashing. Shette covered her eyes, unable to look, unable to bring herself to stop him. Ehren had no such difficulty.

"Laine!" he snapped, his voice holding sharp command. At that Shette did open her eyes, and was surprised to see Ehren leap upon her brother, pinning him to the bed and shouting right in his face. "Laine, that's *enough*." Straddling Laine's bucking form, Ehren kept him there, shaking him with a merciless grip around his biceps. "Wake up, Laine, and do it *now!*"

And Laine's eyes flew open, staring right into Ehren's without comprehension. "They slit my throat," he panted. "Everyone's dead."

"Who's everyone?" Ehren demanded, not releasing his hold. "Where are you?"

"Hunting lodge . . ." Laine said, and frowned. "I don't know . . . it hurts."

Ehren tightened his grip on Laine's arms; Shette saw his knuckles go white, and winced, although Laine didn't seem to notice, even when Ehren gave him a little shake. "*What hunting lodge?*"

"No . . . I don't know—"

"You *do* know! Tell me! Who are you with? Go back and find it, Laine, it's still there!"

Shette couldn't stand it any more. She jumped out of bed and grabbed Ehren's arm. "Leave him alone! You're hurting him, and he can't tell you anything!"

Ehren turned on her, his intent gaze only inches from her own. She suddenly realized that those piercing black eyes, up close, were a clear, dark grey, and that, up close, she couldn't escape them. "He can," he said. "He has to. It's no longer just about *him*, Shette. There's more going on here."

"*What?*" she asked, incredulous. "He's done this all his life! Well, maybe not this bad, but—"

Ehren was ignoring her. He was back at Laine, recapturing the gaze that had gone unfocused while Ehren had been distracted. "Listen to me, Laine. It's right there in front of you, you had it a minute ago. Now *look* at it!" He shouted the last words right in Laine's face, but rather than flinching, Laine seemed to anchor on them.

"King's Guards," he said, clearly and calmly. "They're all dead. Someone had to know we were coming." He gritted his teeth then, and pressed his head back into the bed, clearly in pain. "Ahhh, Guides, right in the gut—no hope now. . . ."

"Benlan," Ehren whispered.

Laine's eyes flew open; his head jerked up from the bed and for an instant, he looked straight into Ehren's eyes. Then the life seemed to drain out of him and he slumped back, unmoving.

Shette had had enough. She gave Ehren a solid shove with all her sturdy self behind it, and knocked him off balance. "Leave him alone," she said again, meaning it.

Ehren looked at her, just looked at her; she couldn't tell what the expression was. Then he gave Laine's shoulder a pat and said, "It doesn't matter. I found out what I needed to know. And you might discover it did him no harm, after all." He swung his leg off Laine, like dismounting a horse, and stood by the bed.

Shette ignored him once he was out of the way. She knelt by the bed, putting a tentative hand on Laine's chest. "Laine?"

He blinked, and looked at her, and then looked at Ehren. "Did it again, huh?"

Shette hesitated. He seemed perfectly lucid, and she wasn't sure how to deal with that—she'd never seen it happen before, not when he'd been woken from a Dream. "Yes," she said. "Do you remember anything?"

He frowned. "Most of it, I think. But I'm not sure why my arms hurt."

"That was me," Ehren said, no apology in his voice. "Trying to get you back."

"That usually doesn't work very well," Laine said, almost apologetically.

"It worked well enough this time. You told me enough so I know exactly what you were seeing—though your Therand Guides take me if I know why."

Laine sat up and crossed his legs. "You do? What was it? Aside from an awful lot of people dying in front of me, I mean. And . . . me, too."

"Not you. Benlan."

"The same Benlan who used to be king?" Shette asked, skepticism clear in her voice. "Why would Laine see *that*?"

"Why would I see anything?" Laine asked back, looking far too reasonable for someone who had been in the throes of a True Dream only moments before. Shette felt like sticking her tongue out at him, but glanced sullenly at Ehren and refrained.

Ehren said, "That's a damn good question. You happen to have an answer?"

Unbothered, Laine shook his head. "It's just the way it's always been." Then he shuddered. "You should be glad you weren't there, Ehren. You'd have been killed like the others. They never had a chance."

"They might have, if I'd been there," Ehren said bluntly. Shette remembered being caught by that dark grey gaze, so close to hers, and believed him.

But Laine shook his head. "I doubt it. Anyway, I probably just dreamt about it because of that journal. That seems reasonable."

Ehren looked unconvinced. On the slat box between the beds, the candle guttered. It threw wild light against the walls and went out.

"No more reading," Shette said. "Did you find anything interesting?"

"Enough to make me want to read more." Ehren sat down on the end of Shette's bed and pulled his boots off; they thumped against the floor in the darkness. "Varien may be sorry he sent me out on this little quest after all."

Whatever that little quest might be, Shette thought. She was suddenly acutely aware that they had no idea what Ehren was truly looking for.

❧

Ansgare was as mad as Laine had ever seen him. When the trio arrived back at the Solvan border, the merchants who'd gone into Solvany had been back barely a day. Laine knew well enough that it would take another day or two to prepare them to take on the caravan route again, but Ansgare seemed little appeased when Laine pointed it out to him.

So while Ehren took the horses to the barn and Shette

was welcomed back at the tavern by Sevita and Dajania's open arms—all the tavern women were dying to hear about her adventures—Laine listened patiently to Ansgare's anger and finally cut him off cold by saying, cheerfully enough, "Face it, Ansgare, you were just worried about us. We're back and we're on time, and even if we'd been two days later it wouldn't have made a difference in the grand scheme of things." And because he was close enough to right on all counts, Ansgare merely *grumphed*, reminded Laine he had a contract to fulfill, and stomped off to see what Machara was doing.

In fact, the caravan was there for another three days. While Shette had stitchery to show Heliga, Laine found himself as bored as usual—until the day the Lorakan soldiers trotted into the border area with a bandit in tow.

Shette had been in front of the barn currying the little black mare, whom she'd named Nell and decided to keep. Despite the inconvenience of having the horse on the caravan, Laine didn't argue with her. Horse and girl suited one another perfectly. Nell was more a pony than a horse, and she was round and sturdy, with plenty of bone. She had a fancy little trot that looked as prancy as Shaffron when he was showing off, but was, underneath it, as steady as a horse could get. Shette adored her and it seemed to Laine that she deserved to come out of the adventure with something more than frightening memories and a week on the road. She had, after all, netted Ehren the journal, even if sending Ehren after it in the first place would have been much less trouble all around.

Laine was with Ehren by the wagon, getting his first official drills in swordsmanship when the Lorakans rode in.

"Listen up," Ehren had told him, before they even started. He'd gotten practice masks and an extra brigandine from the border station for Laine, but then hesitated, the mask tucked under the same arm that held his sword. "I don't want you to get the wrong idea about this. I just want to make sure you know how *not* to cut your own leg off. But if you get in a bad situation, your best bet is to run. When you lift this sword, you've got to be prepared to kill with it. Otherwise, keep it in the scabbard."

Laine leaned up against Clang, already hot in the brigandine; his healing arm itched. In his hand was the sword Ehren had bluntly told him was not only too short to do him much good, but had been designed with an eye to flamboyance rather than function. Ehren had muttered something about finding him another.

Fortunately, Laine had no problem with the idea of running away. It seemed a better thing than having someone die at his feet—and a *much* better thing than dying at someone else's feet. So he nodded, and said, "No, no, don't coddle me, Ehren. Tell me what you *really* think."

Ehren stared at him a moment and snorted, shaking his head. Then he slipped the mask over his face—it was a fine mesh of steel wire, strong but easy enough to see through—and gave Laine a quick salute with his sword. Laine hastened to do the same, decided it looked much better coming from Ehren, and copied the guard position Ehren had just showed him.

"Footwork is just as important as what you're doing with the sword," Ehren said. "That, and knowing your distance. But we'll start out with the parries, and just get you used to putting your sword where you want it to be."

"We've got a couple weeks to work on it," Laine said. "Unless I use up your patience before we get to the other endpoint of the caravan—that's a possibility, if I'm hopeless enough."

Ehren shook his head and, looking through both his and Ehren's mask, Laine couldn't quite decide if his expression was amused agreement or merely amused.

"There are various lines of attack, and corresponding parries," Ehren said, and then stopped, looking over Laine's shoulder and the wagon behind him to the road beyond. Laine twisted around, found himself looking mostly at the solid sidepiece of his mask, and pulled it off.

He'd never seen Lorakan soldiers at the border before—

he'd never seen them at all, until they'd overnighted near Everdawn—but here they were, riding up the road toward the border station. There were two of them, and between them was a third horse, a used-up-looking creature whose rider's hands were bound in front of him and then tied to his waist.

Shette, mounted bareback on the little mare, cantered from barn to wagon just after the soldiers passed her. Laine's raised eyebrows were more for her unusually bold riding than her precipitous arrival.

"That's him!" Shette said, her eyes wide.

Ehren came up beside Laine, the mask under his arm again. "That's who?"

"Which one?" Laine added, just to tweak her.

It worked; she would have stomped her foot if she hadn't been mounted. "The man they have! Look at him, he's the third bandit, of the ones who got me! He was their leader, I'm certain of it. Or else their older brother, the way he bossed them around," she added, giving her words a satisfied bite; she tossed her head so her hair flounced, and Laine turned to look at the Lorakans and their prisoner, movement designed to hide his smile.

But Ehren was on alert. He was at his most Guard-impressive today, with the battle-worn brigandine settled over his wide shoulders and his honor feather bright against his long black hair. Looking from Ehren to Shette, Laine suddenly realized that Shette's hair was tied exactly like the Guard's, with the hair on the side of her head drawn back away from her face.

"I think this bears checking into," Ehren murmured, and set the mask on top of Laine's wagon.

"The Border Guards might think that's their jurisdiction," Laine suggested, but he put his own mask next to Ehren's, wishing he could as easily shed the hot brigandine. Highly conscious of Ehren's comments about his sword, he left it on the wagon as well, and then tried to look inconspicuous as he followed Ehren's long strides toward the border station. If Ehren was out of jurisdiction, Laine was completely out of place, and not being noticed was the best way to get his curiosity satisfied.

As it happened, Jiarna was on duty alone, and her expression at Ehren's approach was more relieved than resentful. Competent and experienced as she was, the arrival of Lorakan military was not on the usual Border Guard roster.

"You seem a bit far afield, gentlemen," Ehren said to the Lorakans. "How can we help you?"

Laine thought it was a polite and restrained greeting, considering the Lorakans' attitudes, which hovered somewhere between disdain and arrogance. They were regular troops, if mounted, and Ehren was upper echelon military by virtue of his ailette alone.

"The question here seems to be, how can we help you?" the largest of the two men replied. He nodded at the prisoner. "Some of your riffraff, courtesy of Loraka."

"*Our* riffraff?" Ehren said, his tone flat. "The man has been operating on Lorakan soil."

"Yes," the man agreed, not sounding particularly agreeable. "It's getting irritating, the way you can't keep them on your side of the border."

"You found a brand on him, I take it," Jiarna broke in, her voice acrid.

The man shrugged, and nodded toward the bandit's arm. "See for yourself. Our people don't know your ailettes. This one's yours."

"Which is as much as saying no one in Loraka has the wits to think of this scheme on his own," she snarled at him.

The man's companion bristled back, and Ehren stepped up to take the bandit's horse. "If you would care to record the details of his capture, and the evidence against him, we'll handle him from here, no matter whose side he comes from. It suits me well to know he's in safe hands now."

Behind Laine, Shette moved up on Nell and muttered, "See? What'd I tell you about the guy who looked like he forgot to have a chin?"

He fit the description she'd given them, to be sure. But she'd somehow neglected to mention the cold look in those small eyes, and the impression that there was neither mercy nor scruple anywhere in the man's soul. "I don't care who got him," Laine said to her. "I'm glad he's *got*."

The exchange was not meant to be overheard; as far as Laine could tell, there was no hesitation in the cold sparks that flew between Lorakan and Solvan military.

"As a matter of interest," Ehren said, "what might you have been doing, scouting so close to the border? You're not the only soldiers I've seen, in recent days."

"We're in Lorakan territory," the smaller man said, abrupt and challenging words as he shifted forward on his horse. The animal, frothing excessively over a severe bit, responded by prancing a few steps closer to Ehren.

"As am I," Ehren agreed, without giving ground or appearing to notice he was being crowded. "But as a matter of course you don't extend your patrols this far. If there's been a change, the Solvan Border Guard would be pleased to accommodate you."

"The change is that you seem to need some help these days. Just get used to seeing us around. There're going to be a lot more of us, and we don't want to be tripping over you people. We'll get the job done; you just stay out of our way."

"No fear," Ehren said. "If you can't see where you're going, we'll be nimble enough to get out of your way." He looked at the rider whose horse pranced so close to his feet and said, "Or if you can't control where you're going," and stepped pointedly out of range of the jigging, steel-shod hooves.

Jiarna, smiling with an expression that threatened to turn into a smirk if it got out of control, spoke up before the Lorakans could come up with anything other than a glare in reply. "Gentle sirs, let me find someone to take your horses. We have some of your excellent steepberry tea, and would be glad to offer you refreshment while we take your evidence."

At her words, Ben finally arrived on the scene, flushed and trying to maintain his dignity; from the way he came around behind the commonstall building, Laine suspected he'd been at the tavern. He went straight to the soldiers and waited for them to dismount and haul their prisoner down, and then took the horses. Jiarna led the soldiers to the station, while Ehren watched them, pensive.

"Not going with them?" Laine asked.

Ehren said distantly, "They'll cause less trouble without me." He turned to gaze up the empty Trade Road to Loraka. "I wonder what's really going on here," he said. "It sure as Hells adds up to more than a few tactless soldiers rounding up leftover bandits."

Laine thought of the strong presence of soldiers around Everdawn and had to agree. It seemed all sorts of things were heating up along the border, and from Ehren's reaction, he didn't think Kurtane had a clue.

❦

Ehren would have preferred to stay at the border until the Lorakan soldiers left, but they seemed in no great hurry to do so—unlike Ansgare. The caravan leader wanted no part of the border station while the Lorakans were there, and Ehren's concerns held little sway with Ansgare.

Jiarna, at least, had been able to offer enlightenment about the Lorakans. The woman had been posted here for so long, she knew many of the Lorakan merchants by name, and they gossiped with her freely enough. What troubled her most, she'd told Ehren, were the reports of unrest in inner Loraka, beyond the mountains and into cultivated lands. Wizards, unrestricted by governmental controls, were so numerous as to crowd each other out of business, and they regarded both Therand and Solvany as sites for expansion—only neither neighboring country allowed the brash Lorakan wizards to immigrate.

There was a new political faction taking shape around these disgruntled wizards, Jiarna had told him darkly, and it was heavily represented in the free-trade atmosphere

Loraka cultivated. It promoted expansionism as patriotism, and as Lorakan destiny.

Ehren thought of the new Lorakan influence in the capitol, and of the concerns Jada and Algere had brought to him. Was there something going on in the Levels? Now that he'd read some of Hetna's suspicions of smuggling and collusion among the court of her generation, his need to finish this assignment and get back to Kurtane was stronger than ever.

Not to mention the increasingly strident feel of Wilna's ring against Ehren's chest, nagging him even more than Ansgare churried his merchants. Ehren was in no way inclined to ignore it. Not only did Dannel's family live south somewhere, but Laine was going that way, too.

After what he'd seen—and what Laine had *Seen*—Ehren was more interested in deciphering the anomalies surrounding Laine than appeasing a crabby ring; another True Dream or two might yield him more clues. Fortunately, staying with the caravan would serve both needs, for now—and since it had been his plan from the start, it didn't increase his guilt at being perfectly willing to use—and possibly misuse—the amiable young man he was growing to like and respect.

The first few days of the caravan seemed uneventful after the time with Unai and the tension provided by the Lorakan soldiers, despite the immediate presence of a strong spell Laine detected from several hundred yards away. Machara, Kaeral and Dimas, backed by Ehren, deliberately triggered it, but they were prepared for the unnatural tusk-toothed, razor-clawed giant boar that materialized, and dispatched it quickly.

It was what they found next that caused all the fuss, even if the threat was long-triggered and gone. Laine had been on point, as usual, but Shette, on the little mare and leading Spike, had been close on his heels. It was her dismayed and graphic reaction that Ehren had heard.

He was sitting on Shaffron, reins rested loosely on the horse's neck while he read over a passage of the journal he'd tried—and failed—to decipher by firelight the evening before. At Shette's cry, Shaffron's head came straight up, his nostrils wide while he drank the wind, searching for the threat.

"You never mind, son," Ehren told him, steadying the horse with the pressure of his thighs while he hastily stuffed the handbound journal back in its satchel. He tucked it securely in the back of the wagon as he rode by, threaded Shaffron through the narrow space between Laine's lead wagon and the rock of mountain rising to their right, and found Laine and Shette staring at a distorted corpse. *Magic.*

"Isn't this an interesting surprise," he said, deliberately casual.

Shette looked up at him, her nose wrinkled. "I'm going to get Ansgare."

"Good idea," Laine said. He crouched by the body, not touching it, but looking it over closely. The man was stiff, his arms rigidly held in front of his face as though trying to ward something off, his features contorted with fear. His eyes were dully glazed, and there was a clump of fly eggs in the corner of his open mouth. There wasn't a single visible mark on his body.

When Laine looked up at Ehren, it was with invitation in his expression. "I can't figure it out," he said. "Magic, I suppose, but I don't know just what."

"I'd say he's lucky to have made it this far." Ehren swung off Shaffron and left one rein dangling on the ground. Shaffron rolled a rattly snort through his nose; Ehren gave the gelding a hard look and a low reminder. "Stay put or you're monster bait."

When he looked back at Laine he discovered the younger man had that odd, distant look that meant he was trying to decipher magic. Ehren's hand moved to the hilt of his sword, his stance turning wary. This was only their second day of travel, and already they'd run into the boar spell— more than one of them would have been killed, if Laine hadn't warned them—and now this man, likewise killed by magic. If Laine was sniffing out yet another spell—

But no, Laine was pulling his attention back to the here and now; he looked at Ehren and shook his head. "I was just feeling a faint trace from the spell that got this fellow. It's like that boar . . . like the monster that nearly got Shette. It doesn't *taste* like the magic I've felt over the past two years. These are serious spells. Deadly ones."

Ehren heard Shette and Ansgare behind him, coming around Laine's wagon. They were both on foot, which was just as well. It was going to get crowded enough up here. Now that Laine had declared the area clear of further spells, he lifted his hand from his sword and moved in closer to the body.

"Found us some more trouble, ey?" Ansgare said, his voice a sour note.

Laine's mouth quirked in a wry grin. "That's what you pay me for."

"Maybe I need to pay you less, then." Ansgare moved up to where Ehren had been, while Shette hung back, making faces. He stared soberly at the body a moment, and then said, "This may be it, Laine. It's not that I don't trust you to detect the spells before we trip them, but there's going to come a point where we can't handle what you find."

Laine sat back on the rocky trail, one arm propped over his knee and the other hand raking his hair back. He looked distinctly unhappy, but he wasn't disagreeing. "Things have changed," he said. "The *spells* have changed. I think someone wants us out of here, Ansgare."

"This man was a fool to try the road on his own," Ehren said. "Ask someone who knows."

Laine gave him a quick grin, but shook his head. "You weren't here last year, Ehren, or the year before, to see the difference. Machara used to take it easy through here. The area was impossible to travel without Sight, but the spells were old and weak enough so that even if you triggered them, you had a chance to get out of the way. And if you didn't make it—well, I can't think of anything that would have killed as thoroughly as the things we've run into lately. As thoroughly as whatever *this* guy ran into."

"He's right," Ansgare said. "You might lose livestock, you might lose goods—you might even lose a limb. But such efficient death . . ." He shook his head.

"And you might want to come look at this fellow from over here," Laine added to Ehren. "Looks to me like this is a Lorakan device." He pointed at the man's collarbone, which from Ehren's perspective was a spot of folded shirt half-hidden by upraised arms.

"That *would* make things interesting," Ehren said, leaning over to straighten the shirt out. The device that was partially visible to Laine turned out to be the Lorakan version of an ailette, a pinned-on badge. This one, Ehren had seen before, and in Kurtane. It indicated a high-ranking Lorakan, comparable to his own position. Responsible only to the highest levels of the Lorakan government, they were investigators of a sort. And sometimes, instigators of a sort, as well. Ehren had never trusted them, never taken them at face value. They always had two plots behind their backs for every one they let you think you were seeing. And they were far too good at bluffing in card games.

"Well?" Ansgare said.

"Interesting, all right." Ignoring the stiff limbs in his way, Ehren unfastened the badge and handed it to Laine, and then proceeded to rifle through the dead man's pockets. He patted his hands over the man's body, looking for the crackle of paper, the solidity of a leather wallet.

Nothing. Nothing except a variety of disgusted noises from Shette. The inner calves of the man's trousers were stiff and grimy with dried horse sweat. If he'd been carrying any orders, any papers at all, they must have been with the horse.

Ehren straightened and stretched his back. "That's as much as we're going to get from this one. Might as well move him out of the way. Get some help up here, Ansgare, and we'll get this body covered all the sooner. There are plenty of rocks around here."

For a moment Ansgare looked like he was going to protest the loss of time, but he must have thought better of it. He merely nodded. When he came back, he had Machara and her men, and it was enough to make the job a quick one.

It was a somber one as well. No one said anything, and when they broke apart, preparing to start the caravan moving again, Machara put her hand on Laine's arm. "Be careful," she said. "For all of us."

Chapter 8

Laine made a strangled noise of alarm, and ducked away from the quick gleam of metal.

"Relax," Ehren said.

Laine responded with an incredulous snort. How could he relax, with Ehren's quick blade flashing in front of his head? Parry from first, draw back his blade, use some elusive, subtle motion to clear the point of Ehren's blade and guard, and come in at Ehren's head? It seemed simple enough when Ehren showed him, slowly and carefully. But when he tried to actually perform it . . . he stepped back, shaking his head. "I don't get it, I guess."

"No, you've got a good start on it," Ehren said, lowering his blade. "The whole idea of this exercise is to perform it with a relaxed shoulder. Tense up, and you've got a wild blade. Easy enough to parry that."

"I don't think you're going to get a good soldier out of me," Laine said ruefully, looking at his sword. It was a new one, bought with Ehren's guidance at the commonstall back at Solvany's border. Longer, infinitely plainer, it had a slight sweep in the blade, a leather-wrapped grip, and short, wide quillons. It was heavier than his first sword, too, and better balanced.

"I never thought I would," Ehren said. "But if you're going to be carrying that blade, you need to be able to use

143

it with some familiarity. You need automatic reactions—
and you need to be able to handle it without stiffening
up. When you can do this exercise, you'll be on your way."

Laine looked at Ehren, trying to see through the training
mask he wore, to read the expression beyond. "Maybe I
shouldn't carry it."

"That's an option," Ehren said. "But . . . all things
considered, I think it's best to be flexible. You can know
how to use it, and choose not to carry it. It doesn't work
as well the other way around." He tapped Laine's training
mask with the tip of his sword; it was a measure of Laine's
growing respect for Ehren's skill that he didn't flinch this
time. "I wouldn't have borrowed these from the border
station if I thought it was a bad idea."

A rock skipped down the slope beside them; Laine glanced
up to see Shette climbing down the steep trail from the
small, deep lake just up the hill. She said, "Aren't you worried
Machara will be annoyed? If anyone teaches Laine on this
caravan, she might think it should be her."

"I cleared it with her," Ehren said. "I've got no desire to
step on anyone's toes."

Laine pulled the training mask over his head, drinking
in the breeze that was shooting up the narrow valley. It
made the hot summer afternoon as pleasant as any day
would get, this time of year. They'd stopped the caravan
earlier than usual; they always put up for the night here,
in preparation for the rough spot ahead. Earlier, Laine had
scouted the lake and declared it free of magic, but it was
about time to repeat the precaution. He glanced at Ehren,
who seemed to have divined his thoughts, for he shrugged
and sheathed his sword. Laine slipped his sword into its
scabbard and struggled out of the brigandine, laying them
both next to the wagon to walk bare-chested to the lake.

The steep, rocky trail to the lake edged along the hillside,
far too narrow for Laine's wide feet. Of course, he could
have taken the easy way up, even if it *was* longer . . . but
no, going this way left him hot and sweaty, and just ripe
for plunging into the lake. It was a barren little thing,

contained by rock and edged by nothing more than scraggly grasses—but it was spring-fed and wonderfully cool. Even so, considering the children playing around the area, he didn't stay in the water long before walking the perimeter, spiraling outward to catch any sign of dangerous magic.

Nothing. Another quick splash in the water—never mind wet clothes, they'd dry tonight—and he headed back down the path. Once he had a good view of their camp, he stopped and watched. It was a tranquil scene. The mules were in front of the wagon; Ehren's horses and Nell were behind. *The boys*, Ehren called them, although that certainly wasn't how Laine thought of them, after Ricasso had gone after first himself and then Shette.

By the wagon, Ehren seemed to be showing Shette how to throw a good punch, and spent some time demonstrating how she should hold her hand and fingers. He folded her fingers and removed her thumb from beneath them; as Ehren held up his hand and had Shette punch it, Laine wondered how much Shette wanted to learn and how much was an excuse to be with Ehren. Equal parts, he decided, and figured Shette's newly enhanced punches would be aimed his way. After a few hits, Ehren nodded, said something that made her blush, and glanced up at Laine.

Probably knew I was here all along. So much for his quiet contemplation of their new companion. Laine descended to the wagon and dripped on the ground next to them. "All clear," he announced, unnecessarily. "How about it, Ehren, should she train for the Guard?"

"No more than you should," Ehren told him, and gave Shette a grin.

"Ha," she said to Laine. Then, without preamble, she asked Ehren, "Why do you always wear that feather?" and then blushed at her own abruptness.

Ehren didn't seem to take offense. "It's an honor feather. Awarded by consensus of the King's Guard."

"If you got too many of them, you'd look like a goose," Shette said, and then reddened a shade brighter. "I mean—"

He smiled. "I know what you mean, Shette. You're just too used to talking to your brother." Laine snorted. "You only get the one feather. It's spelled; it won't break. After that they give out the beads. Different colors and numbers, different ranks of honor."

Laine'd noticed those beads, several strings of them attached to the feather, mostly hidden in Ehren's hair. Despite himself, Laine was impressed. But then, since the bandits' hideout, there'd never been any question in his mind that Ehren was a capable warrior. More capable than Laine thought he'd want to be.

"Do you know this area pretty well?" Ehren asked him without preamble.

"Depends on what you mean by *this area*," Laine said, suddenly wary, without really knowing why—the reminder of just who Ehren was, he decided, and then hoped that was all there was to it.

"The route." Ehren gestured ahead and behind the wagon. "The territory around it."

"The route itself, I know pretty well. The surrounding areas . . . well, when we originally scouted we saw a lot of it. That's how I knew about the lake. But I haven't seen much of it recently, if you were looking for a guide."

"Not a guide," Ehren said, and didn't clarify the comment for a few moments. Instead his thoughts seemed to take him further inside himself for a moment. Shette met Laine's eyes, and raised her eyebrows in question, but he didn't have any answers and shrugged back. When Ehren looked at Laine again, he said, "I've been reading Hetna's journal. She seemed to think the smuggling was linked to a pass she found described in pre-Barrenlands records—its east end is a cavern, and would be right near the Solvany-Therand border in the Barrenlands, now. A wizard—a good one—could get to it." His expression grew momentarily dark. "That's what it all comes down to, isn't it—wizards. Where else but in a wizard's records would Hetna find mention of Coirra's curse on the T'ierand while she was poking into the smuggling? Who else but a wizard could negotiate a pass in the Barrenlands?"

Laine exchanged a quick glance with Shette, but Ehren didn't say what they were both expecting. Varien's name. But then, Varien could hardly be gallivanting around the pass with so many court duties to attend to.

Ehren shook his head, took a deep breath, and moved on. "I wondered if you'd seen any sign of such a thing coming out in the mountains. You've certainly had more access to this area than anyone else since the inception of the Barrenlands."

Ehren's open expression was one Laine didn't think he'd seen before; it seemed the man was always thinking behind his dark grey eyes, and not merely waiting for a response— certainly never waiting for help of any sort. And Laine found himself wanting to provide the answers, but—

He thought of the dream memories he had. His parents had come from Solvany and Therand, and reached the folded southern mountains of Loraka *some*how, without bracing border guards.

And then he looked at Ehren and shook his head.

Maybe his parents knew the pass, maybe not. But that was too private, and Laine had never questioned his dreams, only accepted what little he was given to know. The dreams didn't give him facts about his parents; they showed him two people meeting and growing to love, and then struggling to find a place that would nurture that love. Now that they had it, and their peace, Laine would do nothing to disturb it. "I've never seen any signs of a pass," he said truthfully. "There's no break in the mountains anywhere along here."

Ehren gave him a rueful grin. "I didn't think it would be that easy," he said. "I guess I'll just have to keep working on it."

And that, Laine suddenly realized, was what he was afraid of.

⚓─────⚓─────⚓

Ehren was bareback on Ricasso, watching Laine move back and forth on Nell's round sturdy back, his legs absurdly long against the mare's black barrel. Too hot today for saddles, though Ehren might have wished for a blanket between himself and Ricasso's sweaty back.

Shette was in the wagon, not feeling well and not talking about it. Laine, tired and footsore after almost an entire day of walking on rocks, had appropriated the little mare.

They were almost through what Laine called the roughest leg of the route. The wagons lurched over rocky ground, perpetually tilted down on the left, up on the right, as they traveled the least-sloped part of a valley so narrow it didn't even hesitate at the bottom before heading back up the mountain ridge on the other side. To their right was the main ridge, the one they'd followed all the way down, but it no longer even looked faintly hospitable. It was full of shale and chunks of sedimentary rock that loomed beside them and sometimes over them; as they traveled, bits of loose rock skittered down the hill to clog the trickle of the creek winding through the bottom.

Not a friendly place at all. Ehren could well see why Ansgare chose to stop the caravan early the day before, instead of trying to camp in this stretch.

But they were almost through it; Laine had said as much just moments earlier. And for whatever reason, it was an area that seldom held any hint of magic—just as well, Ehren decided. It would be Hells trying to handle a tricky situation in this terrain.

Which is why he was taken completely by surprise when Nell stopped short in front of him. Laine had stiffened to attention; when Ehren came up beside him he discovered the younger man had a puzzled expression, his head slightly cocked as though listening instead of looking. One eye closed, he scanned the area around them, while behind them, an assortment of equine snorts and shouted commands indicated the entire caravan was coming to a halt.

"Something?" Ehren said, suddenly realizing he'd come to take Laine's response to impending magic as seriously as he would take a warning from one of his own Guards.

"As strong as I've ever felt it," Laine said, still looking puzzled. "But I can't *See* it." He looked back at Shette, who'd come off the wagon to stand by Spike's head.

"What?" she called to him.

"I'm not sure. Stay put—and holler back to get Machara up here."

She nodded, a broad gesture for the distance, and looked warily around, apparently just as cognizant as Ehren and Laine that this was a bad place to have trouble. As she passed Laine's request back down the wagon line, Ehren watched Laine, feeling Ricasso's impatience beneath him. Even the horse knew something was up. "Let's find out," Ehren said.

Laine nodded; Nell moved out at a slow walk. Ehren had to check Ricasso a few times until the horse accepted the pace, and then, while Laine moved ahead with that not-quite-there look on his face, Ehren's gaze was moving over the foreboding landscape, watching for things more mundane—things that his more limited sight could perceive.

Rock trickled down the slope below them, the only sound besides shod hooves on stone and the impatient, occasional huff from Ricasso. Ehren attributed the sense of menace to the fact that responding to any threat on this footing was going to be difficult, more than to anything he actually saw—until Laine stopped again, his sad-dog eyes narrowed in a baffled frown.

"It's so strong," he said. "But there's nothing—"

But Ehren had seen what they needed to know. "There is," he said, his voice low. "Look with your normal sight, Laine. There, just underneath that overhang ahead."

It was a man, crouched at the edge of the protection and squinting at the rocks up the steep mountainside.

"What—" Laine started, his voice at almost full strength. He cut himself short and said, more quietly, "What in the Guides' eyes is he doing?"

"Casting a spell, unless I'm mistaken," Ehren said, frustrated by the distance between them. He had no doubt it was another one of the hostile spells, and it grated on him to be too far away to make out the details that might tell him who the man was—or at least who he worked for. Clothing, hairstyle, weaponry . . . all nothing more than one man-shaped figure.

A figure who abruptly looked their way, starting in alarm.

"It was bound to happen," Ehren said, and closed his legs around Ricasso. The horse surged forward, his big hooves scrabbling slightly on the uneven footing; then he found his balance and was moving in a powerful canter, straight for the wizard.

The man didn't hesitate an instant. He whirled back to his spell casting, waved a complicated gesture, and ran back under the overhang. As Ehren closed on the spot, he saw the flick of a tail beyond it. The man was mounted, then— but Ehren was willing to bet he had the better horse, and he urged Ricasso forward, riding as quietly as he could to keep the dark bay's slippage on the shaley footing from turning into a dangerous stumble.

But Ricasso, who took great heart from such a chase, was suddenly slowing, his steps turning high and prancey instead of reaching out in ground-eating strides. And there was a rumble in the air, something that reverberated deep inside Ehren's lungs and made him want to cough . . . *what the Hells*?

A stone pinged off his thigh and another off Ricasso's neck, and above the growing noise he heard Laine's shout of warning—"Run, Ehren!"—and something jumbled that, as a larger rock bounced off his shoulder, drawing blood, Ehren suddenly knew was, *He spelled an avalanche!* A quick glance behind showed him Laine galloping back to the wagon, where Shette frantically pushed at the alarmed and uncooperative mules.

An avalanche, and he was directly in its path.

Ehren gathered the reins and slapped them across Ricasso's rump, across the lathering flesh of a horse so willing he'd never felt that sting before. Ricasso's abrupt burst of speed nearly unseated Ehren, and then the horse was racing flat out across the uneven path, stumbling and slipping and running ever faster each time another rock hit his sweat-dark coat. When they reached the overhang, Ricasso was in all-out panic, and Ehren threw himself down beside the bay's neck. He clutched desperately at the black mane, feeling his legs slip against Ricasso's wet hide as rock scraped along his shoulder and dug into his thigh.

It would have been better to stop beneath the relative safety of the overhang, but Ehren was no longer in control. They cleared the dank cool length of protection, and he barely had time to raise his head before the horse plunged up and over a giant chunk of skidding rock. Ehren's face slammed against Ricasso's crest, leaving him so stunned he could only cling to the runaway animal, his body moving with the lunging gallop of its own accord.

When the horse finally began to slow, Ehren became aware of his fingers, tangled painfully tight in the mane of the horse. The burn of his shoulder and thigh plucked at him, and the warm flow of blood down his leg echoed Ricasso's scalding body between his legs.

Before him, two tightly pricked horse ears sat atop a tense, arched neck. Ricasso trembled beneath him, trotting in jerky, high-stepping movements, the ears swiveling this way and that, searching for the threat that had chased him here. Wherever here was.

"Easy, son," Ehren said, disentangling one cramped hand to slide his hand along the horse's neck, sluicing away the foam there. Still more than a little dazed himself, he gingerly straightened to look around.

The valley had widened out, its features grown gentler and more inviting. While not abundant, there was plenty of greenery evident, especially along the little creek. As Ricasso finally slowed to a walk on his own, Ehren rearranged the knot of fingers, mane, and reins into something that made sense, and rotated the shoulder that must have taken more than one blow. In fact, the whole right side of his body was a shout of bruises, and he had to check his sudden impulse to get down and inspect Ricasso. Once down, he wasn't at all sure he would make it back up again, and he didn't think it was time for that yet.

Ricasso snorted, loud and hard enough to rock Ehren with movement of his body. He snorted again, ducked his head down, and gave the bit a quick cross-jawed chew. "Good boy," Ehren told him softly, offering him another pat and letting the reins slide through his fingers. As far as the horse was concerned, the run was officially over.

It was Ehren who straightened to attention at what he was finally focused enough to see. Just ahead of them, down below the trail and half in the creek, was a man. Even from a distance Ehren could see the bright splash of blood soaking the ground around the man's head, almost obscuring the rock there.

Whoever and whatever the man was, Ehren's only clues would be what he could glean from the body. Even the horse was gone, taking its brands and breeding with it. Painfully, Ehren slid from Ricasso's back, clutching the snarled mane when his legs threatened to give way. He glanced back at the settling finality of dust-hazed rocks behind him, and went to do his job.

* * *

"Get back, get back!" Shette screamed at the mules as the first stone missiles shot past them. The muted roar of moving rock swelled, and the mules did nothing but make frustrated, short-lived attempts to back the awkward wagon. Their efforts were fast edging into panic—Laine threw himself off Nell and jerked Shette away from the mules as Spike reared, plunging in the harness and triggering Clang's fear. They fought one another, the harness, and the weight of the wagon as Laine grappled with Shette.

"Let them be!" he hollered in her ear. "You can't do anything for them—now *run!*" He pressed Nell's reins in her hands and gave her a shove. A massive chunk of rock slid into the side of the wagon, and it lurched toward them— Shette suddenly seemed to realize their danger, and lit out for the back of the caravan.

Laine ran for Shaffron, who was tied to the back of the

wagon. The horse struck at him, wild with fear, and it took several tries before Laine was able to dart in and jerk the lead rope free. Shaffron wheeled around and galloped away at top speed. Laine wasted another instant for a regretful glance at his mules, but when he saw Clang go down under a wave of stone, he ran.

His whole being was centered on the roar of tumbling stone and the unsteady ground beneath his feet; he raced by another abandoned wagon and its panicking team, and a third wagon whose occupants were still trying to back it. At the fourth wagon he dared to turn around and stopped short, overcome by awe at the mass of stone tumbling so inexorably down the hill where his wagon had been. A pebble pinged off his forehead; he scarcely felt it. He just watched, stunned.

Eventually the rock stopped moving and the rumble died away, replaced by several wailing children and an array of horses and mules calling anxiously to one another. The sounds came to him as though through a filter of cloth, and still all he could do was look at the spot where he'd been. Where Ehren had been, and where there was now nothing but jumbled stone, some as big as the mules there were now no sign of.

"Laine." It was Machara's voice, and it sounded far away. He just blinked. Her hand came down on his arm and squeezed it, painfully. "Laine, what the Hells happened?"

"Avalanche," Ansgare said, puffing up on foot behind them and stopping on the other side of Laine from Machara. "This spot has always made me nervous. But surely nothing we did triggered . . . where's Shette, Laine?"

"Back a ways," Machara said shortly. "With Sevita, crying her eyes out. Better to ask, where's Ehren?"

At that, Laine gathered his wits. "I don't know," he said. "He was on Ricasso. He was trying to outrun it."

"If he didn't, I doubt we'll ever find him." Machara's voice was grim, and her grip on Laine's arm had turned into something less urgent, and more consoling.

"We *didn't* cause this, Ansgare," Laine said suddenly,

turning away from the avalanche for the first time. Another large stone ricocheted down the hill before them, triggering a trickle of tiny slides at its impact points. "There was someone here, working magic. We surprised him, and he started the avalanche. I'll bet it was the spell he was setting up in the first place." He met the shorter man's gaze, settling his odd-colored eyes on Ansgare's suddenly flinty blue ones.

Ansgare took a slow, deep breath, controlling everything but the flare of his nostrils. "That's it, then. We're a caravan of merchants, not warriors and magic users. We can't fight this sort of thing. We'll stick to Therand for a while. That Sherran of Grannor keeps her country safe for the likes of us."

"But there's got to be a reason for all this!" Laine burst out. "No one would go to all this trouble for *nothing*— there *has* to be something going on here."

"Son, I don't *care* what's going on here. It's obvious enough that we're stepping on someone's toes. The old wandering spells didn't keep us out, so someone's upped the stakes. If we'd triggered this in the middle of that section, we'd have lost more than—" He stopped short, looking ahead to assess just what they *had* lost.

"My mules," Laine said, really realizing it for the first time. Hardly lovable, they were still companions of a sort. And they'd spent their last few moments in terror, anchored to a wagon in the path of several tons of deadly rock. "And . . ." And maybe Ehren. But he wasn't going to say that out loud yet.

His feelings about Ehren sometimes ran up against one another—admiration for the man bumping into the realization of what he was capable of. *In self defense*, he told himself. He'd ever been aware they didn't really know Ehren's business here—and had never shaken the menace of the threatening aura he'd seen at Ehren's chest. He'd caught the occasional stray expression on Ehren's face aimed his way, as well. Not calculating, but . . . considering.

But undeniably, despite or perhaps because of it all, he'd

begun to think of the man as *friend*. A friend who didn't deserve to die like this.

As if any one does, even mules. He closed his eyes, took a deep breath, and looked at Ansgare. "Keep Shette here. I'm going to see . . . what's left."

"It's probably not safe," Machara said, though her voice made it clear she knew he wouldn't listen.

"Probably not."

They walked with him to Bessney's tinker's outfit, the new leading wagon of the caravan. Bessney was just daring to return to the spot herself. There was a pile-up of smaller rocks on the uphill side of her square, enclosed wagon; its right wheels were tilted off the ground ever so slightly. The two stout ponies that drew it were tangled in the broken wagon tongue and their traces; they stood together and trembled, and the offside pony was bleeding freely from a dozen cuts. The nearside pony had a serious gash in its leg from the broken tongue, and at first glance, Laine wasn't sure it could be saved.

"Have Shette run back for the blacksmith," Ansgare said to the tinker sharply. "She's at Sevita's wagon. And Kaeral and Dimas will help you. I'll be back in a moment. We'll get you squared away."

Bessney was pale, and trembling as hard as her horses. She nodded mutely and trotted unsteadily back down the line.

"Give them both something to do," Ansgare said, as they stepped over the first of the rocks in their path. A few more steps and there *was* no path, just rocks, scrunching, sliding over one another, squirting out from beneath their feet and blocking their way. Ansgare went a few more steps and stopped.

"I think it would be better to wait. We've got repairs and people to see to. Let's make sure it's stable before we walk here."

Laine shook his head. "*You* see to things, Ansgare. I've got to find the mules. I want to make sure they're . . . not suffering. And I want to look ahead . . . see if Ehren's there."

"I'll stay with him," Machara said. Laine gave her a sharp look, and she shrugged. "No one should have to do this alone."

He hadn't expected it of her. Efficient, good at her job, kept to herself . . . as if she read the thoughts in his expression, Machara shrugged again, and walked out onto the scree of the avalanche.

She was the one to find the smashed remnant of the wagon. Most of the goods within it had been strewn through the rocks; Laine picked up a bent plate, turning it over in his hands as he made his way to where Machara stood.

"You can probably salvage some of it," she said.

Laine didn't respond. He was looking at the twisted body of Clang. Machara moved onward, sliding downhill while Laine resolutely turned his back on the mule and pried loose one of the slats of the wagon, reaching into the storage area to see what was left.

When he looked up, Machara was straightening from a crouch, her knife by her side and her expression grim. She said nothing when she joined him again, and he didn't ask. Some things, he could live without knowing.

He stood, dropping Spike's riding bridle back into the wagon. "I can get these things later," he said. "Let's find Ehren." *If we can.*

Walking any distance across the rocky detritus was tiring; they slipped constantly, and were bombarded at random by loose stones from above. The overhang at which Ehren had spotted the wizard had collapsed over the path in several giant pieces; Laine could only hope Ehren hadn't stopped here. They struggled on, and were out of sight of the caravan, sweating from heat and effort, when Laine spotted Ricasso's dark form standing out against the rocky greenery of the widening valley bottom.

"There's one of them," he said. Even if it was only Ehren's horse, Laine felt real hope for the first time.

"Two of them," Machara responded, wiping the sweat out of her eyes and pointing next to the horse with the same hand. "Or is it . . . three?"

Laine couldn't tell. There was a figure on the ground, all right, not moving much, and it could be that the dark blob beside it was a body as well . . . panting, he increased his pace; they were almost out of the rocks and the going was easier. Soon enough he was jogging, Machara beside him—though it had turned to more of a stagger by the time he reached Ehren.

For Ehren it was, kneeling stiffly beside another man with a little pile of belongings on the ground next to them both. Ehren's leg was stretched before him, his pants soaked with blood; his shirt was torn and the skin beneath deeply scraped. He gave Laine a wry sort of grin and said, "Glad to see you made it in one piece."

"I'd say the same about you, if I was convinced it was true," Laine retorted, staring uneasily at the blood on the ground and wondering how much was Ehren's. "What happened to this fellow?"

"Looks like his horse tossed him." Ehren shifted so Laine and Machara could see the man's smashed head.

Laine made a face. "Can't say he didn't deserve it."

"He deserved it all right. I'd have preferred that he received it *after* I questioned the Hells out of him, but I've found some odds and ends here that tell us more than he probably would have, anyway." Ehren poked at the items beside his bloody leg.

Machara crouched by the things and sifted through them. "Lorakan dagger," she commented. "A badly drawn map . . . looks like the route. But what's this?" She held up a tightly stoppered, thick glass vial, turning it in the sunlight. The liquid within left a viscous coating inside the glass, staining it an odd light blue.

At least, that's what Laine saw at first. Then his Sight took over unbidden, blurring the vial with an intense blue light. He winced, and looked away. Machara wasn't slow to notice. "Magic, I take it," she said, hefting the vial thoughtfully. "But nothing I've seen before." When Ehren shrugged, she handed it back to him, and turned back to the one item she still held. "And isn't *this* interesting."

"What is it?" Laine said, shifting so he could get a closer look without bringing the man's head into his field of view.

"Part of a letter," Ehren said. "Pretty cryptic; I doubt we'll decipher it. But I can tell you one thing about it—this paper is damned expensive. It's meant for the largest type of courier bird . . . the ones that no one has unless they're Upper Level."

Machara looked sharply at him. "Upper Level—that's Solvany's structure, not Loraka's."

"That's right," Ehren said evenly. "And it's Solvany's paper, too. I've seen Lorakan missives. They use a different bleaching process."

Laine just stared at the paper Machara was holding. Solvany and Loraka, tied together in this one man who'd just tried to kill them all. Who, for all they knew, had been setting all the dangerous new spells they'd encountered. When Laine met Ehren's grim eye, he saw the same conclusion echoed there.

Lorakan soldiers at the Solvan border, Lorakan wizards setting deathly spells in the mountains . . . and someone in Solvany tied to it all.

Chapter 9

With Laine's help, Ehren managed to get up on Ricasso's tender back, although he hated to ride the battered horse. They'd towed the wizard out of the stream—no use in letting him foul the water—and deposited him behind a grouping of rocks on the other side of the valley from the caravan trail. Then Machara had sliced up half the man's shirt, and used it to pad and wrap Ehren's leg. By the time they were ready to go, Ehren was in a light-headed sweat of pain.

Ricasso recovered enough to snap at Machara when she reached for his trailing reins; without comment, Laine swept them up and offered them to Ehren. Ehren shook his head tightly; he was going to have enough trouble staying a-horse. Machara took the lead, picking them a slow path through the rocks, past the remains of the overhang and to the spot where Laine's wagon should have been. Laine spent a long moment looking down the hill, and then they were back on undamaged trail again, such as it was.

Machara hesitated beside the tipped tinker's wagon. Bessney and the blacksmith were examining one of Bessney's ponies, expressions grim. The other was tied to the back of the wagon, still trembling. "I think we should just go straight to Sevita's wagon," Machara said to Laine, glancing up at Ehren but no longer including him in the conversation.

"It's where he'll probably have to travel, and Dajania's going to have to look at that leg anyway."

"Shaffron," Ehren said, suddenly struck by the realization that his horse had been tied to Laine's crushed wagon.

Laine looked back up at him. "I got him loose," he said. "I don't know where he is now."

Relief. "He'll be back," Ehren said, more of a mumble. "He'll find Ricasso. Thank you." Laine merely shrugged, but Ehren knew the feat couldn't have been easy to accomplish. Fear-maddened, trained not to let anyone but Ehren handle him . . . no, it wouldn't have been easy.

They moved on, and Ehren lost track of things for a few moments, until he suddenly realized Ricasso had stopped. Laine was by his side, looking up at him and waiting. "C'mon, Ehren. Dajania's going to take a look at you." Machara appeared, too, lending her wiry strength to the process of getting Ehren down. Laine took Ehren's weight with ease. "I'll see to Ricasso," Laine said with a grunt, pulling Ehren onward in a world that was suddenly turning grey. "Whoops, whoops—*he's going out*—"

Not quite. Vaguely aware of the grunt of Laine's efforts, of being handed from person to person, his head bobbing, of Shette's gasp in the background, Ehren still had a small, crystal clear awareness in the back of his thoughts, one that was coldly observing he must have lost more blood than he'd thought. Then he was settled on a soft bed, and the small spot of awareness drifted away with the rest of him.

Until someone prodded his leg, and brought him up spitting an oath of pain.

"Lay back," Machara said. Beside her was Dajania, looking a little pale in the bright air of the wagon. They'd thrown open the back and side panels to let in the afternoon light, but the ceiling was undeniably low and oppressive, the wagon crowded. Laine sat at the back of it, leaning against its wall and looking extraordinarily tired. There was dried blood smeared on his face and shirt; Ehren didn't remember it being there before.

"You're supposed to know better," Machara said briskly, nodding at Dajania, who returned to the task of cutting Ehren's pants with a knife. "You should have told us you'd lost so much blood. Hells, you should have bound it yourself before we got there."

He just stared at her a moment, clearing his head, thinking over the run and knowing he could have bled to death without noting a thing, just trying to stay a-horse. "I was too busy, just then, to pay attention."

"Huh," she grunted at him, looking unconvinced.

Dajania finished with his pants and, biting her lip, cut carefully at the makeshift bandage. She pulled it off with an expression of great distaste and tossed the sodden thing out the side of the wagon. Then she looked at him and made a sound of dismay.

"Nasty," Machara agreed. "You did this how?"

Ehren didn't answer, instead propping himself up on his elbows to see for himself—at which he promptly swore a heartfelt oath. The leg would be weeks in healing, and probably cause him trouble for some time after that. "Must have been something sticking out under that overhang."

"Lovely," Dajania muttered, some of her usual self-confident bite returning to her words. "Those overhangs are wonderful, damp places, great for slime."

Ehren snorted. He was clear-headed again, more than he preferred to be while Dajania cleaned the leg. Mercifully, no one required conversation of him until she was through. She finished up with a sigh of relief, and then gave him a thoughtful, suddenly wicked look.

"Here," she said, and bent over him to kiss him most thoroughly, after which he hiked his eyebrows up and just looked at her. "That's my own special medicine."

"Is it," he said, trying for a straight face.

"Better'n most you'll get. It'll last you until I can get some of Ansgare's wine dosed for you. You're lucky I've got so much of the pain-slip mix with me. I only picked it up at the border because of that monster we ran into on the last leg." She backed out of the wagon.

Machara put a hand on his shoulder and rested it there a moment. "She'll take care of you," she said, and then thought about her words and grinned. "Any way she can." She turned to Laine. "Come to Ansgare's wagon as soon as you're through here. We've got a lot of talking to do."

The wagon shifted as she jumped out and Laine moved further in, sitting on the narrow bed along the other side of the wagon. After a moment, he said, "Sorry you got caught up in this. It's caravan trouble, not yours."

Ehren shook his head. "It's got Loraka and Solvany written all over it," he said. "Loraka's everywhere, Solvany's suddenly underdefended . . . and there's that mysterious pass. . . ."

Laine looked skeptical. "And it could simply be an unofficial protest to our presence here."

It suddenly struck Ehren how well-spoken Laine was, that he only heard the younger man speaking slang and dialect if he was joking around with someone with coarser speech. And why that should seem significant to him now, with Dajania's kiss lingering on his lips and his leg pulsing with a fire that made it feel bigger than the entire rest of his body, he didn't know. But it was, or he wouldn't have thought of it at all.

And then it occurred to him that Laine had been talking to him, but had trailed off, and was now simply watching him.

"What?" Ehren said.

"Shette wants to come in and sit with you a while," Laine said. "She's worried. And frankly, she needs something to do. I don't want her around the mules' bodies while I'm salvaging the wagon."

"There's nothing to worry about," Ehren said. "It hurts like hell and then it'll heal." And he really wanted to be alone right now, while it was in the hurting-like-hell phase. But all he said was, "Have her wait a while after Dajania brings that wine, will you?"

"Sure," Laine said, and got up, at least as far up as he could get inside the wagon. He grinned at Ehren and said,

"You'll have some fun, now—Dajania's put you on her list of challenges."

"I imagine I can handle it," Ehren said, but his crooked grin was half-hearted and distracted. Laine grinned back at him and left the wagon.

Ehren never knew when Shette came in. He drank the wine Dajania gave him, and when he woke again, the wagon was in the morning shadow of the mountain beside them. Dajania, Ansgare, and Laine were talking, at the head of the wagon by the sound of it.

"I really don't think he should travel yet," Dajania was saying. "And neither does Machara—she's got more experience with big wounds like this. He's lost enough blood already."

"It's going to take us another day to clear a path down to the creek," Ansgare said, irritated. "And then, we won't have much choice. We don't have the fodder to delay any longer, and we won't have any grazing to speak of until we go another day's distance. After that we might as well go all the way—it's only one more day to the Trade Road, and smooth travel after that."

"What about Bessney's wagon?" Laine asked, a reasonable voice that nonetheless held worry. "Her pony'll live, but even if we could replace the wagon tongue, the pony won't be up to pulling for a while."

"We're leaving it," Ansgare said, coming down harshly on the words, and Ehren had come to know him well enough to recognize it as regret. "We'll take her goods, somehow. And maybe we can come back for the wagon another time. That reminds me, Laine—somehow, we've got to get Ehren's pack on that crazy chestnut of his. It's a miracle you salvaged as much as you did from that wagon, but we're not going to have a place to put it all."

So Shaffron was back. Ehren released an anxiety he didn't know he'd had. But there wouldn't be much chance that anyone else could tack up the spirited horse—he doubted they'd even actually caught the gelding. Laine could have worked with Ricasso, assuming they'd rescued that saddle as well, but Ricasso was bruised and cut, and Ehren wouldn't allow it.

He reached over his head to the front panel of the wagon and knocked on it, lightly. After a moment, Laine appeared at the side of the open wagon, about level with Ehren's own head. "Are you back with us, then? I think Dajania gave you a little too much of that wine."

"I did not," Dajania's voice said in the background, and Laine winked at Ehren.

Stiffly, Ehren propped himself up on his elbows. "Don't hold us back for me," he said. "I'm not saying I'll enjoy it, but I'll certainly live through a little travel."

Laine nodded. "I don't think we'll have much choice," he said. "Ansgare's right about our fodder." He nodded back over his shoulder, downhill. "We're going to try to travel along the creek until we get past the avalanche. The bottom seems solid enough; I've walked it twice."

"You know," Ehren said thoughtfully—or as thoughtful as he could get right now, "whoever sent that wizard is likely to know about his death. They tend to keep in touch. That's another reason for not waiting around here."

Laine grimaced. "I don't think I'll mention it to Ansgare. Machara, though . . ."

"Tell her," Ehren confirmed. He ran his tongue around the inside of his mouth; it was dry and tasted odd. Drugged.

Laine wasn't slow to notice. "Dajania," he said, over his shoulder, "I think some water would be appreciated here. And food?" he added, questioning Ehren with his gaze.

Ehren shook his head. "Not hungry." Feeling sick was more like it. "I heard what Ansgare said about Shaffron. Don't try to handle him, Laine."

"You didn't hear me volunteer, did you?" Laine asked, humor in his voice. "He's wandering around here loose, and everyone's been warned off him. Mostly he sticks by Ricasso—who's going to be fine, by the way. Much less banged up than you."

"When you're ready to load him, I'll whistle him up,"

Ehren said. "I'll hold him. It might still be a little tricky, but I think the two of us can make it work."

"All right," Laine said. "We'll give it a try."

Dajania appeared at the end of the wagon, bearing a leather water sack and some bread; it was fresh, Ehren could smell it from there. It turned his stomach.

"You probably have nature's call to answer, too," Dajania said cheerfully. "Well, we'll get it all taken care of. And I brought you some more wine. By the time I'm through with you, you'll probably want it."

"You give me something to look forward to," Ehren said.

"Not really . . . but I *can*, if you'd like." She winked, outrageously saucy.

Laine laughed out loud. "Told you," he said.

Laine couldn't believe how fast things had gone bad. He sat on the empty bed in Sevita's wagon, watching Ehren while he waited for Shette to return with Dajania.

First the loss of his wagon and mules—Laine hadn't realized he'd gotten so attached to the creatures. They were self-serving and difficult, and didn't show the obvious affection Ehren's two horses gave him, or that Nell was already starting to bestow on Shette. But they were honest, and they had worked well for him. After two years they'd seemed like part of his life.

He didn't have the money to replace them, but it didn't seem like that would be necessary. He agreed whole-heartedly with Ansgare—unless something changed, it was no longer worth the risk to take their shortcut. Which meant Ansgare had no need of Laine's Sight. Since Laine had little of a merchant's wile and none of a caravan guard's skills, he was thinking hard about the small shaggy beef cattle his parents raised.

He'd miss this part of his life, though, and wasn't eager to let it go so easily.

He slumped over on the bed, elbows on knees, tired to the bone. They'd done it; every single person on the caravan had worked to clear a wagon's width of ground down to the creek, and to mend wagon damage. All of Laine's recovered belongings had been distributed among the merchants, and Ehren's things lay beneath his pack tarp, waiting for Shaffron in the morning. They'd been so busy they'd done nothing more than peek in on Ehren now and then, satisfied to find him sleeping off the drugged wine and never guessing until too late that he was fighting—and losing—to a wicked infection.

Laine studied the guard a moment. He was fevered, and a shiver swept through his lean frame as Laine watched. In the afternoon sunlight, the bandage, wet with serum as much as blood, was biting into the leg that had swelled beneath it. Laine wasn't surprised at the red streaks that stretched down toward Ehren's foot; he viewed them with what dismay his exhaustion left him.

There was no real recognition in Ehren's dark gaze, just a sort of dull wariness, and a reflection of the pain the infected leg was causing him.

Laine didn't know much beyond the practical, everyday parts of the healing arts. But he did know you didn't get this kind of infection and expect to live through it, not unless you took the affected limb off, and fast. This infection was so high on Ehren's leg, Laine didn't even know if it could *come* off.

He heard Shette's anxious voice, worrying Dajania along. Sevita was with them, too; she said something soothing to Shette, and was right behind Dajania as the darker woman climbed into the wagon.

"Oh, Hells," Dajania said, first thing upon seeing the leg. Then she noticed Ehren's gaze, and said, if a trifle too cheerily, "You've got yourself in a spot of trouble over this one, handsome." Then, shortly, to Laine, "Make yourself useful. There's a quilt under the bed you're on. There's no reason he has to take chill."

Laine, who had sweated copiously all day and was only now cooling down, gave a guilty start and hopped up to search under the bed. When he turned back with the quilt, he found Dajania and Sevita in consultation and in his way, so he sat on the bed, his legs drawn up out of the way, and watched. They murmured to one another, removing the bandage and staring at the leg with grim expressions. Sevita touched it once, gently, to feel the heat of it, and Ehren hissed a curse of pain.

At that, the two women stood up—as straight as they could get under the low ceiling—and came to some sort of tacit agreement.

"What do you think?" Laine asked.

"What you probably already know," Sevita said. "There's nothing ordinary healing can do for him. Not that we wouldn't try, but . . . I've never heard of an infection this bad just getting better. It's come on so strong, and so fast. . . ."

"I should have cleaned it better," Dajania said. "I thought it bled clean, but it's deeper than it looks, and there might have been something caught in there. We'll never find it, now."

"Aren't you even going to try?" Laine asked incredulously. "You can't just let him . . . die. Not like this."

"You *can't*," Shette said, from the foot of the wagon, strident in her distress after holding it in for so long.

"Oh, we don't intend to," Sevita said. "We've got one last thing to try. But it's not something we're qualified to do, you should know that."

"At this point, what does it matter?" Laine said. "What can go wrong that's worse than having him die?"

"Not much," Dajania said bluntly. "But it should be Ehren's decision, if we can get it out of him. And Ansgare needs to know."

Laine gave them a suddenly suspicious look. "Just what do you have in mind here?"

Sevita met his eyes squarely. "Black market magic, Laine."

Laine's eyes widened despite himself. "Sevita, you can't trust a bought spell, not an unauthorized one! There's no telling what it actually *is*."

She didn't back off an inch, not in expression or tone. "I got this from someone I happen to trust. Not all qualified

magic users have the crown seal of approval, you know—
just the ones who grew up in the right part of town, and learned
through the expensive schools. You just think of all the good
that could be done if people were allowed to buy such spells,
instead of punished for it. That's the way they do it in Loraka
proper, and it was a Lorakan wizard sold us this."

"All a wizard has to do is sell one dud spell, and we hear
about it," Dajania added. "Some of them don't work as well
as others, but this should do no harm."

"It's a spell to kill infection?" Laine asked warily, more
of Sevita's temper than any answer she might give.

Sevita pressed her lips together and shook her head. "We
couldn't afford to buy something that specific. It's just a
generalized healing spell, something to enhance what the
body does anyway. We'll back it up with drawing compresses
and the pain-slip in wine."

Laine gave her a skeptical look. If he'd been from a Solvan
city, he knew, he might feel differently—they were certainly
accustomed to the Upper Levels' long-held practice of
spelling finely crafted precious metals and stones, such as
the ring Ehren no longer seemed to wear. But an ordinary
rock? Spelled by an ordinary market wizard?

Dajania frowned at him. "I'll see about finding the spell,"
she said, moving lithely past Sevita in the narrow space
and disappearing behind the curtained partition in the front
of the wagon.

"Fine. I'll talk to Ansgare. Once you've found the spell,
stir up the fire and get some of that comfrey boiling. I
want both of us to be here to trigger the spell, and we'll
need the comfrey, anyway." Sevita glanced down at Ehren
as she turned to leave the wagon, but stopped; Laine
followed her gaze and discovered Ehren was staring at her,
his eyes as clear and piercing as they ever were.

"I'm dead without that spell," Ehren said. "You use it,
and if it doesn't work, I'll still thank you for trying."

"All right, Ehren," Sevita said quietly. She leaned forward
and placed her hand against his cheek. "We'll do our best
for you."

He closed his eyes, and Sevita brushed her hand along his hair a few times, then straightened, giving Laine a hard look. "I'll be back. You keep your notions of boughten magic to yourself, and get that quilt over him."

"Yes, ma'am," Laine said, responding automatically to that maternal command.

As soon as Sevita went out, Shette came in, and did a fine job of hovering while Laine flipped the quilt out its full length and let it settle on Ehren.

"You've got to tuck it in," she said, and proceeded to do so, being very careful around his leg. "What's this?" She stopped at his shoulder and fished around on the pillow, bringing up a ring on a long braided length of grasses. When she spoke again, her voice was curiously neutral. "A woman's ring."

"What?" Laine said, and bent to look over her shoulder. "Wilna's ring," he murmured, though the words might as well have been coming from someone else's mouth. Shette frowned at him, and was about to tuck the ring back inside Ehren's shirt when Laine reached for it, prodded by some inner need. He brushed his fingers across it.

The fear of ambush, the flash of metal, and eyes . . . a man's eyes, cold and satisfied.

"What are you doing?" Dajania asked sharply, and Laine blinked up at her from the floor. Shette stared with her mouth dropped open, her gaze going from Laine to the ring and back.

The ring. Every time he touched it, it plunged him into the world of Dreams. Deep, detailed Dreams, where he could almost turn around and *see* the person who, there and yet not there, watched Benlan die. The ring practically called to him, the same itch he felt when there was magic to be Seen.

If he dared, he could answer that call. If he dared.

"Laine!"

"Uh . . ." Laine said, finally, realizing his grip on reality was going tenuous. *No. Not this time.* Ehren was what mattered now. "I fell," he said. "Tripped over Shette's feet."

"*That*, I believe," Dajania said. "It's too crowded in here. You can still see from outside the wagon, if you're bound to watch this. And afterward you can sit with him, Shette." Her voice changed from businesslike to blatant slyness. "Just remember, *I* have first go with him."

Laine snorted, and pulled himself to his feet, herding Shette out of the wagon before she could think of a reply. "We'll just get out of your way," he said. "I'm going to find a place to put my blanket for the night. I'll be back when you're through, to check on things."

"But," Shette said, trying to turn around as Laine descended from the wagon behind her. He put his hands on her shoulders and kept her moving forward. "But Laine, I want to—"

"They'll do better without an audience, Shette," Laine said, though not without understanding. "They're going to try something difficult, and we don't want anything to distract them. Right?"

"I suppose not," she mumbled, reluctantly convinced. "I'll . . . I'll go brush Nell."

He took his hands off her shoulders. "Don't go back there without me, all right? I'll be at Machara's wagon. She offered me a place for the night, though I doubt it'll rain." Nothing from Shette, who was rapidly outpacing him, her steps annoyed and hurried. He knew better than to let her go without acquiescence. "*Shette*."

"All *right*," she snapped.

That, he supposed, was as good as he was going to get. Laine started for Machara's wagon, near the back of the caravan, but stopped, and then headed downhill instead. He needed time to think about that ring.

Ehren didn't remember anything past agreeing to try the black market spell. Not clearly, anyway. Now, waking later, he had only dim memories of the intervening hours. He remembered the pain, and his whole body a-throb with fever and infection. He knew he'd protested the misery with chesty groans and the occasional curse. There'd been gentle hands at his head, holding him down if he moved too much, soothing him when he was quiet . . . and a voice, murmuring in his ear. Something to hold on to.

Now, though . . . now there seemed to be more form to this world. The bed beneath him, the thick quilt over him; his leg still hurt like all Nine Hells but the ache was confined to his thigh, and didn't spread itself up to his hip and loins, nor down to his very toes.

And there were quiet voices within the wagon. Shette, he realized suddenly, and her throat sounded thick with tears recently shed.

"I don't understand it," she said. "Why has everything *changed* all of a sudden? It was good, being on the caravan, and having Ehren with us, and being able to follow you in the wagon. Now there's no wagon, and the mules are dead, and . . . and Eh—Eh—" She made a little choking noise and gave a great sniffle.

"Shette," Laine said, nothing more than her name in a big brother's comforting voice. The noise of cloth against cloth gave Ehren an image of Laine's arm around her shoulder.

"And your dreams, they're so scary now." Still ragged, Shette persevered. "You can't believe what it's like to watch—it didn't used to be like this!"

"Shhh," Laine said, and paused. "No, he's still asleep. Good. You're right. It didn't used to be like this. The dreams . . . used to be something I could look forward to."

"Tell me about them, the old kind of dreams," Shette said. It was the request of a child who knows a story by heart, but wants it again, anyway.

"The old kind of dreams," Laine repeated, and snorted softly. "They sure have changed, at that. All right. I used to see . . . Mum and Da when they met. He loved her almost right away—though he was in big trouble at the time, and should have had getting *out* of it on his mind instead. He was tall, like Ehren, and she looked a lot like you. And sometimes I see the way he sneaked across the Barrenlands to court her."

Sluggish as his thoughts were, Ehren knew this was wrong.

No one could cross the Barrenlands. Its effect on human senses was devastating, and not far from the state he'd spent these last, interminable hours in. No one but those with spelled dispensation, which only the countries' rulers could give out. Or royal blood itself . . .

"They went on night rides together. He brought her gifts of exotic flowers, and a pair of the small-eared rabbits that she still breeds at home. Knew just how to get through to her."

"He still does," Shette said, somewhat dreamily. "And then they ran away together."

"Ran away from both their countries. To the noble end of raising cattle—and raising us. And Da doesn't chase those grasslands stags anymore. He says he caught what he was looking for on that chase that took him across the Barrenlands."

Ehren couldn't help the small noise that escaped his throat. *Dannel and Jenorah.* Dannel had chased a stag across the Barrenlands, stumbling into Therand just outside the borders of the Clan Grannor T'ierand's summer home. Stumbling into Jenorah as well. *No wonder Laine's so sensitive to that ring.*

There was instant silence from the other side of the wagon. After a moment, Shette said softly, "Ehren?"

But Ehren was drifting away again. And this time he had plenty to think about.

~~~~~⌘~~~~~

"I hope you've got a good hold on him," Laine said fervently as Shaffron skittered away from him and up against Sevita's wagon. Despite the matter-of-fact air he tried to project, Laine knew Ehren was far from strong. And holding a fractious horse through the open panels of the wagon was an awkward task at the best of times.

"I've got him," Ehren reassured Laine. "Shaffron, son . . . ease up a bit. It's your very own blanket, not some monster."

"Then again," Laine said, more cheerfully as he got the blanket settled on the chestnut's back, "on this road, you never can be sure."

Ehren snorted. So did Shaffron, sticking his nose just inside the wagon to do it. "Thank you very much," Ehren said dryly. Or, as dryly as possible under the suddenly damp circumstances. Laine took advantage of the horse's distraction to lower Shaffron's saddle to his back. The horse promptly turned to snap at him, his teeth clicking shut just inches from Laine's arm as the lead rope brought him up short.

"Whoops," Laine said, skipping back out of range. "I hope this gets easier—we've got quite a few days left on this road."

"Sorry," Ehren said. "I can't really correct him for it . . . considering I'm the one who taught him to do it."

"You did?" Laine said incredulously, warily reaching under Shaffron's belly to grab the girth and bring it up around. "You taught him to be vicious?"

"I taught them both to accept no hand but mine," Ehren corrected him. "They won't bother anyone who doesn't reach for them."

"I don't suppose you thought about this situation when you did it," Laine said, tightening the girth a careful notch by notch.

"Nope," Ehren said. "But I don't regret it, all the same. It's gotten me out of trouble before, and I suspect it will again. Ricasso accepts you now; I wouldn't try to ride him, though."

"No fear of that," Laine said. He settled the canvas pack base over the saddle, and began securing it, crupper, breast band and all. Shaffron seemed to have decided he would put up with the process, and settled for thinking very hard about biting, his lips twitching sporadically along with little Laine-aimed jerks of his head.

As Laine stepped back to survey the goods that he had to load on the horse, Ehren said, "You and Shette were in the wagon last night."

Laine looked over at him. Still abed in the wagon, propped on one elbow but looking like he'd really be better off lying down, Ehren was just about on eye level. "We sat with you a while," Laine said. "Shette . . . needed to do it." He said nothing of his own concern, but gave a little shrug. "We weren't sure until well after dark that you were really going to make it."

"Dajania had a spell," Ehren said, frowning a little. "I seem to remember . . . don't I?"

Laine grinned. "You do. I'm surprised, though. Between the pain-slip they keep giving you and that infection, I'm surprised you remember anything of yesterday." He thought, briefly, of the family stories he'd told Shette. They were the sorts of dreams that had upset his parents, and therefore things that were for no one's ears but Shette's. He'd been sure, at least for a moment, that Ehren had been awake.

Ehren grimaced. "I remember far too much," he said. "I know how lucky I am the women had that spell."

"It's a new thing, Dajania says." Laine tied a sack of grain and mentally balanced it off with the leather bag holding horseshoes and nails. Soften it with the brigandine beneath . . . the foodstuffs would go well in the center, over the saddle. "Something out of Loraka that Solvany and Therand haven't sanctioned yet. Some of the, umm, less official local wizards are setting spells into stones and crystals. Dajania said the structure of the stones are supposed to help preserve the structure of the spell just as well as the fancy rings the High Level wizards charge so much for. And then anyone who knows how can trigger it."

Ehren lifted an eyebrow. "That's going to make those High Level wizards pretty unhappy. They prefer being exclusive."

"Whatever it makes the other wizards, it saved your life yesterday," Laine said soberly. "I don't have any doubt about that." He'd seen the sudden glow around the wagon from downhill in the creek bed; even from there he could tell it was a good thing, although spells of that sort didn't have precise visual clues.

"I agree."

Laine looked up from his packing at the stress he heard

in Ehren's voice, and returned to the task with purpose. Ehren, he was sure, wouldn't complain, but it was obvious enough he'd already used up his strength.

Besides, the sooner he could climb into the front wagon with Machara, the sooner he could quit watching out for those teeth. At least the horse hadn't shown any inclination to kick. Yet. He bent to completing the job with deliberate speed.

"Almost done?"

Laine didn't look up from the knot he was tying to answer Dajania. "I hope so."

"Ansgare wants to get moving. If we push it hard, we can make the Trade Road early morning, tomorrow."

Cued by the displeasure in her voice, Laine checked the tightness of the rope and stepped back from the horse to look at her. She gave Ehren a quick glance and said in a low voice, "It'd be better if he weren't traveling at all."

"No doubt," Ehren said, ignoring the fact that he wasn't supposed to be listening. "But if I lived through yesterday, I'll live through today."

She made an exasperated noise. "All right, then. You'll drink down this wine with no more said about it, won't you."

"You might as well," Laine said. "I'm done here."

Ehren spent a few obviously exhausting moments with the awkward business of tying the frayed lead rope through the throatlatch of the halter and around Shaffron's neck so he couldn't step on it. "All right, Dajania. I'm all yours."

"Don't I wish," she said smartly, and winked at Laine as she went around to the back of the wagon.

Ansgare was waiting at the head wagon, along with Machara. The wagon itself belonged to Vitia, who sold cloth goods and could whip up a quick alteration as well. Hers was a big, sturdy wagon, an emblem of her success over the years. At the Solvan end of the run she'd finally earned the last coin needed to buy the little shop she'd had her eye on, something well within the borders of Therand. And she'd readily agreed to let Machara drive her team while

Laine concentrated on the road ahead. Machara, she said, was much better equipped to handle further trouble than her own aging body.

She was one more reason Laine was determined to make sure nothing else happened to this caravan.

"I don't think we'll have any trouble," he told Ansgare, trying to ease the tension gathered between the merchant leader's light blue eyes. "With any luck, we caught up to that wizard, instead of running smack into him as he came out from the Trade Road. That means we've sprung everything he set this time out."

"You said as much yesterday," Ansgare grunted. He looked over at Machara. "You be careful. Don't get into anything stupid."

"You say the sweetest things," Machara replied, and then gave him a slow wink. Laine looked at Ansgare in surprise, a grin spreading across his face. The end of the caravan meant the end of Ansgare's casual association with Machara. He'd never had to state his interest before; she was always there. In order to keep her company now, he'd have had to speak up—and it seemed he had.

"You wipe that look off your face," Ansgare told Laine. "I'm still your boss, at least for the next few days. Show some respect."

Laine sketched a quick and careless bow, and Ansgare dismissed him with a wave of his hand and a grunt. "Smart-ass youngster," he said, and walked away, adding over his shoulder, "You keep your eyes open, both the black and the blue!"

"That's my job," Laine said, and climbed up into the wagon, settling himself beside Machara, where the grin sneaked back onto his face.

"Unlike Ansgare, I can whip you silly," she said. "Even if Ehren *has* been giving you lessons."

"True enough," Laine said, and promptly turned his attention frontward.

Machara gathered the reins and clucked to the team, a pair of mules very much like Clang and Spike, only bred from draft stock. Big enough to handle this wagon with little trouble, they were confident creatures, and when Machara asked them to turn downhill from the trail, they did it without hesitation, their neat mule hooves treading carefully in the uneven footing, controlling their descent speed as opposed to actually pulling the wagon. They hit the creek and turned into it, lurching. Laine clutched the side of the seat to keep from being thrown into Machara, and bounced off her anyway.

They'd traveled along the creek without problem, following the slightly bowed course caused by the fill of the avalanche, before Laine looked back. The rest of the wagons were following without incident, leaving Bessney's forlorn-looking and damaged equipment behind. Her wagon suddenly seemed to represent the entire caravan and its way of life.

Laine looked away, blinking his eyes so they were clear enough to scan the path ahead.

Chapter 10

Ehren was just as glad he couldn't remember the trip along the creek bed. The pain-slip hadn't taken effect until after Dajania's wagon negotiated the downhill journey from the blocked path, and just the memory of those moments was enough to last him several years. His leg oozed almost constantly, but not copiously. After three days on the smoother Trade Road it was much improved.

He was overwhelmingly aware that because he'd lost flesh as opposed to merely cutting it, it was going to take far too long to heal. He wanted this mission over, and he wanted to be back in Solvany, figuring out what was behind the strange things going on in Kurtane—and beyond. But Sevita cheerfully gave him a month before she thought he'd be moving around with ease. He figured he'd be riding as soon as it didn't open the wound to do so, and he was counting on that to be considerably less than a month.

He was sitting up on the bed, watching, one foot on the floor and the injured leg stretched out before him, when they entered the edges of the Therand border town. Even from the outskirts he could see that the town was far more significant than the station by Solvany's border; here, merchant services had more room to spread out, for just outside the pass were lush green pastures dotted with cattle and sheep. The mountains ended abruptly on Therand's eastern edge just as on Solvany's, but to the south they gradually faded away, rippling into hills that spread into Therand.

Ehren hadn't realized it would be so different from Solvany. It was beautiful, and it made him wonder what the rest of this country, cut off so long from his own, had to offer.

It took him a few moments to notice the wagon had stopped. Dajania had weakened the draft she was giving him, but his mind still had a distinct tendency to wander. The wagon shifted as the women disembarked, and Ehren was left alone with his wandering thoughts and a view of the wagon that had been behind them and was now parking beside them.

He had decisions to make, he realized, whether or not he was in the right state to make them. For the first time in weeks, he took the ring off his neck and fitted it on his finger, leaving the loop of braided grass in place. He always had a sense of it against his chest, but the impressions lacked clarity. Now that it was on his finger, he could tell the thing emphatically wanted him to return to Loraka. Damn. He supposed if he'd been wearing it all along, he would know exactly when he'd passed the spot where the ring stopped wanting him to move forward, and began prompting him elsewhere.

The delicate silver band began broadcasting sudden new excitement, and Ehren frowned at it, pulling it off with a decisive movement. Laine showed up at the back of the wagon a moment later.

"Hey," Laine said, by way of greeting. "How're you feeling?"

"Like I have the brains of a turnip," Ehren said promptly. "We've crossed the border?"

"Almost. We're just on the outskirts of T'ieranguard. We'll have one of the inspectors come here and go through the wagons; it's easier that way. There's a lot of business to be had in town, not like the border on your side. Our stopover here is usually twice as long as the other one." He grimaced, and said, "Usually. I don't know what's going to happen this time. There's a big meeting tonight."

Ehren eased his leg into a different position. "What will you do?"

"Same thing I came to ask you. Me, I usually break off from the road a ways back; my family lives a couple of days away, and I always spend the stopover time with them." He sighed, looking away from Ehren and down the street into town. "Ansgare's going to buy me a pack saddle—he wants to give me the price of the mules, at least—though it wasn't written into the contract that way."

Ehren was not surprised to discover Laine could read. Not after what he'd heard the other night—information he still had to come to terms with. "Generous," he said, not really thinking about Ansgare at all. After all he'd been through with Laine, after he'd grown to look upon him as a friend in this world where Ehren now had so few he could trust . . . he suddenly had a terrible choice to make. Completing this assignment would no doubt mean betraying Laine.

But if he didn't, if he walked away . . . he'd be betraying Benlan.

"Ansgare *is* generous, when he doesn't stop to think about it," Laine said. "I'll load what's left of our stuff on Nell and take Shette home. Then I guess I'll have to do some thinking about the future. Depends on what the merchants decide tonight." He gave Ehren a direct look and said, "What about you?"

"What about me?" Ehren asked, with the feeling that he should have been able to follow that, if only his brain wasn't so thick. A turnip. Definitely a turnip.

"I thought you might want to find a surgeon, if you have the money. That leg's going to take an awful long time to heal."

A complete healing would cost more than he had. Much more. Ehren shook his head. "Maybe Sevita can get her hands on another one of those healing stones."

"Ansgare's asked her to look," Laine nodded. "He wants

to do that for you . . . I just wanted to make sure you didn't need help finding something a little stronger."

"Ansgare's an honorable man," Ehren said.

Laine leaned against the raised tailgate of the wagon, resting his arms along it and settling his chin on his fist in a contemplative air. "What then, Ehren? What are you looking for?"

You and your family. The sudden clear thought sprang up in the midst of Ehren's fog. He couldn't turn away from this, not yet. When after he found Dannel, he didn't have to trigger the ring right away. He could think about it.

"Ehren," Laine said, sounding amused.

Right. He'd been asked a question . . . but not one he wanted to answer out loud. If only he weren't so foggy—but then again, maybe that was the answer. "Even with a healing stone, it's going to be a while before I can go wandering around on my own again. I need to find a place to hole up . . . and I wondered if I might come with you."

"Home?" Laine said, raising his head as wariness infused his face and posture; he closed a doubtful eye.

"Not if it's a problem," Ehren said, sensing that to push would only increase resistance. "Maybe Dajania and Sevita will let me stay here a while—do they work out of a hotel while they wait?"

"I'm not sure," Laine said. "I've never stayed around to find out." He added, grinning, "I'm sure they'd love to have you stay, no matter what their working arrangements are. I have to tell you, life got a lot easier for me once they had you to work on."

Ehren looked around the interior of the wagon. It was a comfortable place, with small homey touches that had initially surprised him. "They're not as tough as they make you think," he said, although it was true Dajania had a most disconcerting habit of walking up behind him unannounced and tracing her fingers over the back of his neck, playing with the hair there. "I think if you agreed to pay for a night with one of them, you'd ruin all their fun."

"That's what I figured. All the same . . ." Laine shook his head. He gave his head a decisive shake. "Leave you with them? I'm not sure I could do that to you. Unless you want me to, of course," he added, raising an eyebrow with a leer that made Ehren laugh.

"They're lovely ladies," Ehren told him. "But I'd rather save my energy." He had, in fact, been far too focused on finding Benlan's killers to think much about such entertainment over the last year, although Jada would have tendered an invitation, he thought, if he'd spent a day or two more in Kurtane the last time through. And before Benlan's death, there'd been another Guard—

Of course, just like all the others, she had been killed with Benlan. And now he had work to do.

"By the way," Laine said, "Ansgare said someone was asking about you, up at Vitia's wagon. You know Ansgare— he told them to ask questions somewhere else until we got the caravan straightened out. But I thought you'd want to know."

Ehren's eyes narrowed. No one knew he was here. Or, no one should. It was, he thought, possible for a wizard to track someone down, given the general area and a personal acquaintance—or at least a belonging—with which to narrow the search. But who would bother? Did Varien really distrust him that much?

If so, there was no doubt just as much reason to distrust Varien.

"Ehren," Laine said, his voice both patient and amused, for the second time. Ehren looked at him, slightly surprised, wondering just how long he'd wandered off, this time. Laine was shaking his head. "We're not used to visitors, Ehren. We keep to ourselves, and that's what my parents like. It'll take a bit for them to get used to the idea that you're there. But . . . it's a good place to heal. A safe place."

Ehren thought the words *a safe place* held more significance to him—for Dannel and Jenorah—than Laine would have liked, had he known.

But he didn't. And Ehren was about to find himself at the end of his search, at the very homestead of Dannel and Jenorah. He looked at Laine's open, honest face and then turned away, feeling a pain that had nothing to do with his leg.

Laine set a significantly slower pace than usual, trying to accommodate Ehren. Although Sevita had indeed come up with another generalized healing spell—from where, she would not say—and its effects had enabled Ehren to ride without reopening the wound, it had left him far from whole. Sevita had given Laine a generous amount of the pain-slip powder, and showed him the correct amounts for both moderate and light doses. Ehren drank it without comment when it was offered, and that alone told Laine how much healing he had yet to do.

Shette was in glory. She walked by Ricasso, never repeating her mistake of reaching for the horse's head, but never far away, either. Laine was frankly glad for her presence; while he went about the process of setting up for the evening, it was Shette who made sure Ehren had what he needed—and furthermore, she managed to do it without an excessive amount of chatter. The avalanche seemed to have sobered her somehow. She had grieved for their mules, and for Ehren—first for the death she thought was imminent, and then for his hurt. She had watched Laine facing the loss of his life as a guide, and for once, *she* had reached out to comfort *him*, completely aware of how much he had enjoyed the traveling and the challenge of spying out the magics.

The fate of the caravan was yet uncertain. No one would commit to another run within the summer traveling season, but no one wanted to sever their connections to the lucrative route, either. Finally, Ansgare had said he'd get word to Laine before the summer was over. He seemed to think it was time to do another run on their own, rechecking the route to see if more traps had indeed been set. There was some hope that the wizard's death meant the end of trouble.

Laine tried not to think of it as he led Shette and Ehren down the road back into Loraka. The first day, they traversed the pass, a zigzagging trail that climbed sharply, peaked, and then dropped off nearly as sharply. Ehren was in clear disbelief that he'd missed noticing this the day before, and eyed the pain-slip askance, with exaggerated skepticism that made Shette laugh.

They reached the turnoff at the end of the first day, and spent the night on a steep wooded hill, unable to do so much as stand with their feet level, never mind sleeping level. At least, Laine commented the next morning, none of them had slid to the bottom of the slope during the night.

That day's travel saw the landscape gentling. Valleydwell, the small town closest to their destination, had grown in a wide, hilly valley between two steep ridges. The homesteads were carved out of the highly mounded hills of the transition from valley to mountain, and Laine's family had settled in the farmost end of the valley, in the cleft where the two ridges joined.

At the end of the second day, they were nearly into the valley, and Laine assured Ehren, straight-faced, that the journey was all downhill from there.

Midway through the third day, they walked into the small town with much anticipation of good food and drink. There was only one place to eat, a small tavern whose customers were mostly area farmers come into town on business. They were occasionally rough, and their table manners weren't to be envied, but never had Laine worried about Shette eating there alone, like he did on the Solvan border.

Of course, the drawback was that everyone tended to think they knew your business, or else thought they had a right to know, even when they weren't all that familiar with you in the first place. Laine fended off quite a few questions about Ehren—in Ehren's amused if slightly wine-fuddled presence—with the kind of evasions he'd learned over the years. Short, and given with a smile. Tell them nothing and make them think you want to tell them all. It had worked when people started asking about his Sight, and it worked now.

Another proprietor put them up for the night. The woman's house was an unofficial inn—the real thing wasn't to be found in the little town of Valleydwell—and when the tab ran high enough to warrant it, Laine brought her out fresh meat from their pastures. Their room was merely a small nook off the back of the house; Nell and the horses stayed at the blacksmith's for the night. Once Laine had Ehren settled, he went to spend the rest of the day checking the merchants his parents habitually patronized, to see if there was anything waiting to be picked up or paid for. They didn't travel into town unless absolutely necessary, and he and Shette had done most of the buying and selling for years now.

He came back with a round of goat cheese, but had to leave the two restaved barrels. Upon arrival at their rented room, he discovered Ehren asleep in the bed and Shette wrapped in a blanket on the floor next to him, though it was yet early evening. He felt a brief moment of brotherly affection; though Shette was clearly worn out, she'd really done well on the trip as a whole, and despite her fifteen-year-old's fits of cantankerousness, he might just take her out again some time.

If there was another trip to take her on, that was.

Laine left the cheese and went back out to the tavern, ready to enjoy their mediocre ale and a good round of catch-up with whoever might be there tonight. He definitely wasn't going to think about the caravan.

Ehren forbore to take a noon dose of the pain-slip. Laine told him they'd be home before late afternoon, and he wanted all his sense about him when he first met Dannel and Jenorah. The path they were following was nothing more than that—a narrow trail no doubt more often used by creature than human. Laine led the way, followed by Ehren on Ricasso—the horse's deliberate and powerful movements were easier to sit than Shaffron's brio under saddle, and even that was hard enough, healing spells or no—and trailed by Shette, who led Nell.

The small copses of trees they traveled in and out of spoke of what this land would be like had it not been tamed and turned to pasture and slanted fields, and there was always something skittering out of their path, some small creature not used to the intrusion. The sun was still high in the long summer day, and shone strongly on them, unhazed, creating sharp shadows that rippled over the grassy ground and disappeared when they moved through trees. Ehren thought he should simply be enjoying the countryside—Laine obviously was—but he was hot and exhausted by pain, and irritated at his weakness to boot.

Laine finally looked back at him and said, "Just over this rise, Ehren—you look terrible."

"Thank you." Ehren didn't bother to hide his general irritation.

"Well, you do. Don't worry. A few more minutes and we'll have you off that horse and drinking something cool." His words were meant to be reassuring, but beneath them, there was worry—and not, Ehren sensed, about him. Or, not exactly.

"Your family won't be that happy to see me, will they?" he asked, brushing away a deerfly that had settled on Ricasso's shoulder.

"Well-l-l . . ." Laine dropped back to talk more easily, and admitted, "Probably not." He rubbed the heel of his hand above each eye, wiping off sweat, and said, "Don't be surprised if it takes them a minute to get used to the idea. They're just private people."

Ehren looked pointedly around the remote area. "You're kidding."

"Don't worry about it. I wouldn't have brought you if I didn't think it would be all right. They'll like you . . . it just may take them a moment to realize it."

At this point, Ehren didn't care if Dannel and Jenorah hated him on sight, as long as arrival at the farm meant getting off Ricasso and having some place cool and soft to prop his leg and close his eyes.

They crested the rise Laine had pointed out, and Laine stopped before him. Ricasso stopped with no cue from Ehren, having grown used to the ways of their own little caravan, and it was only Shette who was taken by surprise. Ehren heard her muffled comment—a word she wasn't supposed to use, he was sure—and after a moment she joined Laine in the widened path.

"Home," he said to her. "Always gotta take a minute to look at it, Shette."

"I've seen you," she said, as they both looked down at the yard and the little house fenced within it. The fence was stacked split rails, the house made of logs, and built into the side of the hill. It wasn't a structure Ehren was familiar with; it had two stories in the front, and the entrance seemed to be on the second floor, by means of a full front porch on stilts. The lower floor had a big solid door, securely barred from the outside.

There was little extra decor—no flower plots, no ornamentation—just a large vegetable garden to the side, and an air of neatness and care. Ehren looked back the way they'd come, for the first time taking in the waist-high field flowers that had lined the path for some time. There was, he decided, a certain larger beauty to just letting it happen as it would.

Laine looked back at him, and seemed to see the appreciation on Ehren's face, for he grinned. Then he started them moving again, down the hill and into the yard. They hadn't reached the weighted gate when Ehren heard the distant, commanding bark of a herding dog, and the rustle of a horse moving in the trees behind the house. About the time a tall man on a small, Nell-like horse emerged from the trees, traveling a little recklessly for the sharp pitch of the slope, the door on the upper level of the house opened, and a woman ran out.

"We're home!" Laine called unnecessarily, and winked at Shette, who had dropped Nell's halter rope and burst through the gate to meet the woman as she came down the stairs. They embraced in a solid hug as the man's pony scrambled to a stop in front of Laine. "Da," Laine said, and though Ehren couldn't see him, the grin still showed in his voice.

Ehren could only stare at the man. There was no doubt it was Dannel, for it was like seeing Benlan alive again. Dannel dismounted, and met his son with a crushing hug that was more brief than the one Shette had bestowed upon her mother. "You're late," he said, as they parted. But he was looking at Ehren.

"We had some trouble," Laine told him. "You're not going to believe some of it . . . but let me tell you now, for once, Shette won't be exaggerating."

Ehren still held the man's gaze, sitting atop Ricasso and feeling like a wart on a pretty girl's face. Laine turned to introduce him, but Ehren didn't wait. "My name is Ehren," he said. "I met Laine on the caravan route."

"*On* the route?" Dannel said, his voice even but his expression unwelcoming; he glanced at his son.

"Like I said, we had some trouble. Ehren was badly hurt in the last of it—in fact, we thought we'd lost him. He needs someplace to heal for a while." Laine's voice was pitched as a request, and an acknowledgment that he'd known his decision to bring Ehren here might not be appreciated.

"If he is your friend, and he's hurt, of course he may stay until he's able to travel easily." The words were formal, and if they were grudging, it didn't show. But Dannel's eyes never left Ehren's, while Laine cast his gaze back and forth between the two of them, his expression growing puzzled.

Dannel, it was clear, knew he'd been found.

It took two of them to get Ehren dismounted; he wasn't yet able to lift his leg over Ricasso's haunches without help. Jenorah came down, then, her arm still over Shette's shoulder— looking like an older version of Shette, though age had done little but pad her frame and turn her black hair silver. Dannel introduced her as Jenny and himself as Dan; no doubt they were the only names the two had used since their flight.

But Ehren didn't have long to think about it, for his feet weren't exactly firmly on the ground. He held Shaffron while Laine pulled the packs off, and then, too much in the sun and too long in the saddle without the pain-slip, he wavered. Laine caught him, and Dannel took up his other side, careful, at Laine's warning, of the healing bruises there.

Between the two of them, they got Ehren up the porch stairs and through the house, into a room that was cool and shaded and smelling of spicy wood. Ehren was so grateful for the respite, he fell instantly asleep, with Shette's voice in his ear urging him to drink the drugged wine he wasn't willing to wait for.

It was waiting there for him on the small bedside table when he woke. A table carefully crafted, rubbed with an oil that brought out the beauty of the grain, and made with the same painstaking skill that characterized the rest of the room . . . it was something to let his eyes wander over in the shadowed room. Ehren stared at it, and didn't think of much else for a while.

He had found Benlan's older brother, and it didn't yet seem real. The table, on the other hand, was definitely real. And so was the sweat dried on his body, and the smell of the clothes he'd worn since he was hurt. A good washing, himself included, would not be amiss.

A sound alerted him he was no longer alone; he found the door, but the figure within its rectangle of light was shadowed to obscurity.

All the same, it had to be Dannel. Too tall and rangy to be Laine, too familiar to be anyone but Benlan's brother. Briefly, Ehren rested his hand over the ring on his chest; a touch was all he needed to know the thing was beside itself with excitement.

Without saying anything, Dannel came in the room, up

to the bed; he leaned over Ehren and opened the shutters at the small, unglazed window there; quiet light flooded the room. Then he retreated to sit on the chest on the short wall opposite the foot of the bed. From there he watched Ehren, and said nothing for a time; in his hand was Ehren's honor feather. At last, he said, "My son trusts you." What he didn't say was, *Are you about to betray that trust?*

Ehren didn't answer the unspoken question. He held his own silence for a moment, and then said, "Your brother Benlan was my liege . . . and my friend."

"I see. But Benlan didn't send you here."

"No." Ehren drew himself up in the bed, carefully dragging his leg with him. He sat against the wall and brought his good knee up, resting his elbow on it. He had no intention of talking to Dannel while flat on his back. "Benlan . . ."

"Is dead. Yes, I know. And his son rules in his stead."

"More or less," Ehren said, his mouth crooked in a humorless smile. "He didn't send me, either."

"Who did?" Dannel said. Blunt words, untempered.

"Varien."

Dannel straightened, raising an eyebrow at Ehren. "Since when does Varien order the king's men about at his own pleasure?"

"Since recently, it seems." Ehren watched Dannel a moment. The man's features were quieter than Benlan had been wont to be, more contemplative; he seemed less apt to jump into action before considering all the alternatives. His hair was greying brown, and his eyes a slightly lighter blue than Laine's left eye. Ehren thought he saw the strong texture of Laine's hair, and perhaps the slant of jaw, but it was no wonder he hadn't immediately recognized Laine as being born of Benlan's line; all his other features belonged to Jenorah. "Laine doesn't know, does he?"

"Neither of them have been told. There was no point; nothing could come of it but trouble. Jenny and I had no wish to be found."

"And you've done well with that, for good and long."

"But no longer," Dannel said heavily. "Isn't that right?"

Ehren shook his head once, for some reason not ready to answer that—though three days before he'd thought his answer was an inevitable *yes*. "I don't understand how no one ever realized . . . surely they heard tales . . ."

"You think someone should have put Dan and Jenny together with the lost royal lovers?" Dannel asked, somehow seeing humor in the question. "Ehren, the people in this valley are here because they don't fit in anywhere else. Half of us have escaped our past in this place. We all respect that. It's certainly possible that someone knows who we are, although we traveled the Trade Road for years before we settled down here. But you see—if anyone *does* know, they simply don't care. I raise quality cattle and provide half the meat and leather the valley uses. *That's* what they care about."

"I'm still surprised Laine never put it together for himself."

"What makes you think he's ever heard about Dannel and Jenorah in the first place?" Dannel asked. "He's only been outside this valley for the last three years. He may have heard references, but as far as I know, never the whole story."

"He knows you ran away together through the Barrenlands. He knows your families were against your pairing," Ehren countered.

Dannel blinked. After a moment, he nodded. "The dreams," he said. "I'm surprised he told you those things."

"He didn't. He thought I was unconscious." Ehren's mouth quirked. "For all I know, he thought I was dead. It was close enough."

"So I understand. Laine's told me about your meeting, and some of your adventures. However I feel about your presence *here*, I'm glad you were there when Shette needed help."

"Did he tell you how bad the dreams have been, this last year?"

"No." It was Laine's voice that answered; his form blocked

the doorway. "Da," he said, "did I ever mention to you that the sound from this room carries downstairs to the dairy?"

Dannel winced. "I should have thought to check it," he said. He rubbed his hand over his face, and sighed. "Well, son, perhaps it was time you knew some of this."

Ehren didn't have to see Laine's face to know the anger it held; his voice held it plainly enough. "Long past it," he said. "Was it something you intended to hide from me forever?"

"Only until the time was right," Dannel said, sounding tired. "It wasn't an easy decision, Laine. But . . . your mother and I never wanted anything but to be together. We didn't care for the trappings that went with the lives we used to lead . . . we didn't care for the people we used to be. We made a life here . . . had you and your sister . . . and as the years passed, we just couldn't seem to make ourselves give that up."

"Give that up?" Laine said. "We're talking about sharing a heritage, not giving anything up!"

"It was *our* past, Laine! It had nothing to do with your life, or ours, anymore. If it hadn't been for those dreams of yours, I doubt we'd have even considered telling you at all." Dannel's voice had gone sharp; he stood to face his son. "Once we told you, we *would* give something up— the illusion of who we were trying to be. And what if you'd wanted to do something about it? What if you'd wanted to go to Therand, or Solvany, and explore the life you might have led? In Therand, with their floating monarchy, it wouldn't have made that much difference—perhaps they'd scrape up some land for you, or let you spend the summer in the high clan home. But in Solvany, I expect it would be a different story." He gave Ehren a sudden, piercing look; his voice dropped low, almost a whisper. "That's why you're here," he said. "I know the way the court thinks. I know the way *Varien* thinks. You're afraid I'm a threat, or that my children are going to cause trouble."

Ehren said nothing. He didn't have the opportunity, in

any case; Laine had moved into the room, right up to the bed. "That's what this has been about, all along? You were here because of *me*, and you never told me? You acted like a friend all this time, and let me believe it?"

"Laine," Ehren said, and his voice was hard, deliberately punching through the anger he saw growing in the younger man. He took up Laine's gaze with his own, looking into the odd-colored eyes that simply looked black from this distance. "I didn't know you were Dannel's son until the night you and Shette stayed up with me. I'm surprised I even remember it, between the drugs and the fever, but I do. Anybody from Kurtane, hearing what you told Shette, would have known just who your parents were."

"You didn't say anything. You asked to come here—you knew you were the last person that would be welcome!"

"I did at that. I'm a King's Guard."

"The question," Dannel broke in, "is what you're going to do *now*."

Ehren knew what he was supposed to do. He had his orders, and once he triggered the ring, whatever its various spells, he was free to return to Kurtane and untangle what was happening there. To face Varien.

But suddenly, somehow, it didn't seem that clear-cut. He had new alliances here, people who didn't deserve to be caught up in Solvany's problems. His eyes still on Laine's, Ehren slowly shook his head. "I don't know."

~ ~~~✣~~~ ~

Their small barn was just around the sharp curve of the hill from the house, and that's where Laine was taking himself, his feet leaving a clear trail through the heavy silver of the early morning dew. He'd almost wished for some of Ehren's wine the night before; he certainly hadn't gotten much sleep. The whole house was in an uproar, more than his father could have anticipated when Laine showed up in the doorway to Shette's little room. For Laine hadn't been alone in that dairy, stowing the cheese he'd brought and counting up their storage.

Shette had been there with him, her face showing pale

in the dim light of the dairy as their father's conversation had filtered clearly down to them. If only they'd been out at the barn . . . or if Laine had told Dannel of the time he'd discovered how easy it was to hear from directly below Shette's room. But he'd found it when he'd accidentally overheard their mother explaining certain aspects of womanhood to Shette, and somehow he wanted to make sure his sister *never* discovered that fact.

Yesterday afternoon, he'd left her in the dairy, too stunned to move as fast as he, or to protest being left out. If the truth were known, he suspected that this was one fight she preferred to be left out of—especially when she could hear just as well from where she was.

But last evening, while Ehren slept again, Shette had burst into question. Hard questions, and tearful ones. From them he gathered she felt just the same as he—she couldn't care less about their heritage. The betrayal was in the lack of trust. Laine kept his silence, and this time, let her ask—and protest—for the both of them.

Not that the answers had turned out to be any more satisfying than what he'd already heard. It was their life, their mum had said—*Jenorah* had said—and had nothing to do with Laine or Shette. It had been their decision to make, and it wasn't necessary that either child approve.

Jenorah. Laine kicked a small stone in his path, and it skipped through the grass in its way, a bright green snake of a trail in the dew. He'd heard that name before, dropped now and again, right along with Dannel's. He wondered how he'd been so thick, and if he *had* actually heard the whole story, would he have managed to put it together anyway?

Probably not. His parents were Mum and Da, Jenny and Dan. Cattle farmers, private people who were obviously still deeply in love. They had nothing to do with the disembodied names of two royal runaways, not even when he had inner knowledge that told him differently.

Deep down, Laine could accept that, although Shette was having a harder time. She and their mum were close;

they shared many things, including their tempers . . . and
how deeply they felt things. Laine wasn't surprised she
was angry and hurt, and feeling left out. He winced at the
thought of the tempestuous days to come, grateful that
she didn't fully understand that Ehren was poised to betray
them, as well.

No, in Laine's mind, the questions and thoughts that had
driven him early from sleep dealt with the present—and
the future. What, exactly, would Ehren's presence here mean
to Laine's family? Was he going to take Dannel and Jenorah's
hospitality, heal, and return to Solvany's capital to announce
the location of the lost branch of the royal family? And if
he did, were Laine's parents in danger?

He smiled grimly, wondering, too, if Ehren himself would
create the very situation in which Laine was willing to test
his new swordplay . . . swordplay Ehren had taught him
over the course of their travel together, still new to Laine
but a solid foundation. Ehren had said Laine should avoid
putting himself in that situation . . . but perhaps Ehren
would be the one to plunge him into it.

The barn stood before him, small, tidy and familiar. One
of their two goats stood in front of it, staring at him like
he was an intruder. It gave a sporadic chew at the weed
that was hanging out of its mouth, and bounded away like
a manic, deformed deer. "Good morning to you, too," Laine
grumbled. He loitered outside the barn for a moment,
pulling out the shoot of the scratch vine that stubbornly
refused to give up its spot there, and idly wondered if this
would be the time he finally reacted to the stuff.

There weren't any chores waiting for him; the cattle were
out in their summer fields, and it wasn't quite time to
prepare for the second hay-cutting. There was a calf in
the barn, an injured youngster who'd been taken away from
his mother and was fast being spoiled rotten. Maybe he'd
check in on the creature, and then throw a saddle on his
father's sturdy little horse, Nimble. Or maybe he'd just stand
around and think, which was what he came out here to
do.

The barn was built like the house, into the hillside. Below was a stone-walled cellar that held the forge and anvil, for Dannel had long been trying to teach himself the rudiments of smithing. It was too damp there to store much else; grain and hay molded almost immediately. And while there was an indoor-outdoor pigsty built in to the side of it, the pig was out, flat on its side in the sun, making happy little snorting noises.

So what, then, had made the little scuffle he'd just heard, inside the barn?

Laine suddenly wished he'd brought his sword out here with him. Just as abruptly, he scoffed at himself—he was *home*, now, and not on some grand adventure. Still, when he moved to the double doors and found one ajar, he hesitated before slowly opening it the rest of the way.

"Ehren!" He could hardly have been more surprised if he'd discovered a magicked monster there. "How the Hells did you get down those steps?" And how long had he been here, that there was no sign in the dew?

"Slowly," Ehren said, then shook his head and added a grin. "*Very* slowly."

"But why—"

"Let's just say I needed a place to think." He was sitting beside the anvil in an old slat-bottomed chair with half the slats broken out; doubtless it was here waiting to be fixed. As he looked up at Laine, his hand closed into a fist. *Holding something*, Laine realized.

"You and me both," Laine said, eyeing that hand. "My head's still spinning, and I didn't even get any of your wine."

"Wine's no help when there're decisions to be made." Ehren rubbed the bridge of his nose and looked at Laine, his expression one of speculation. "I've made mine . . . but I can see I'm going to need help to act on it." His eyes flicked down to his closed fist. Laine couldn't help it; he looked again, too. But it was still nothing but a fist. A fist suddenly dark with aura.

Startled, Laine looked at Ehren, looking for that same aura. Nothing. What . . . ? He made an impatient noise—

impatience with himself—and asked, "What do you need?" He hoped it was something good and distracting, something that would keep his mind busy with practical matters.

"I need this forge fired up, if you've charcoal to do it with. Or I need you to take me into town."

Laine snorted. "No town today, or the next, either. Now that we've got you here, you're stuck until you heal. And by then maybe you'll know us well enough to suffer over the trouble you're going to cause us."

Ehren's open expression shuttered down and became hard, but for some reason, Laine didn't necessarily believe it was aimed at him. After a long, stony moment, Ehren said, "Do you have charcoal?"

"I'm not sure. What do you need it for?"

"Does it matter?" Ehren asked.

"Everything you do matters, now."

Laine thought he saw a flash of temper rise to the surface of that hard expression, but Ehren seemed to swallow it. "This was never something I wanted to do," he said, his voice low and strained. He closed his eyes, and the struggle was clear on his face. After a moment, he uncurled his fist and held it out to Laine. "I need to destroy this."

The ring. "Destroy it?" Laine asked, the protest clear in his voice. He took a step back, surprised by the depth of his feelings. *Wilna's ring*. The ring that could send him off into True Dreams, that had brought him closer and closer to understanding the bits and pieces he'd seen all these years. *But I'm not there yet*. All the times he had felt sharp metal bite into Benlan's flesh . . . the ring had the power to plunge him into those dreams, far enough in that he might just discover the unknown presence that was always watching.

But he'd been getting closer and closer, as well, to some sort of boundary. Shette's hushed description of the fits he'd had while dreaming had made him shy away when he could. That last time in the wagon, when he'd almost touched the ring . . . he could have stayed down, then . . . but it hadn't been the time or place, not with Ehren fighting for his life next to him. It was then that he'd truly realized what the ring could do for him—or *to* him—but it hadn't occurred to Laine then that it might be his last opportunity. Nor that it had been the ring creating the darkness he occasionally saw around Ehren.

"Ehren," Laine said with difficulty, holding his vigorous protest back to a strained question, "just what *is* this ring?"

To his surprise, Ehren answered readily enough, holding the silver and emerald ring up to catch what light was coming in the door Laine held open. "You said it once. Wilna's ring. Benlan was wearing it when he died. Varien said that gave it a sort of power . . . made it easier to use in conjunction with spells. And because it came from Dannel's brother, it was easier yet to use in locating Dannel. It was pretty happy about you, too—which took me a while to figure out."

"But not Shette?"

Ehren shook his head. "It was hard to tell. I took it off when I saw it bothered you, and when my course was set to the caravan route anyway. But I'd have to say no. I'd finally decided it reacted to you because of your Sight. Now I know it's because you're firstborn."

"But . . ." Laine said, groping for some logical protest, "why destroy it now?"

Ehren gave him a sharply probing look. "Why not?"

Laine frowned in frustration, but he'd had enough of riddles. He crossed his arms, leaned back against the door, and said, "I asked first."

Ehren laughed. "I should have expected that," he said, shaking his head, though he soon grew serious again. "Listen, Laine. I don't think the thing is safe. Varien sent me on this mission, I told you that. You saw your father's reaction— the man isn't supposed to have the authority to send the King's Guard anywhere. But he not only sent me, he as much as said I'd be killed if I stayed, and that success on this venture was the only way to appease the factions who felt I was no longer an asset."

"You've spent too much time at court to think straight,"

Laine said bluntly. "No longer an asset, my lost Guides. That's no reason to kill a man."

"Depends on how much he's getting in your way. Don't get hung up on that. Think instead about new magic in the mountains, and of generations of smuggling. Think about border bandits and Lorakan military presence. Now think about this ring—and who gave it to me. Do you really want it around?"

Laine felt a stubborn reluctance to let go of his claim. "I do," he said.

Ehren sat back against the chair with a sigh; it creaked its protest and for an instant both men hesitated, waiting to see if it would hold. When it did, Laine shrugged at the wounded Guard, feeling a victory of sorts. "Yes, I want the ring around," he repeated.

"Listen," Ehren said, and his voice had regained some of its strained quality. "I've been thinking about this all night . . . about . . . what's important to me. I was supposed to use this ring to find your family. When I did, I was supposed to trigger it. That spell would confirm your identity—and it would tell Varien of my success. Only then am I allowed to return."

Laine understood. He understood the strength of Ehren's need to return to Kurtane and find Benlan's killer . . . and that Ehren was weighing that need against the needs of Dannel and Jenorah—and of the son who had trusted Ehren enough to bring him here.

"I didn't know what I'd find here . . . but I do know your family is no threat to Rodar. That's enough for me. It probably won't be enough for Varien . . . but I'm willing to destroy the ring and take my chances."

When Laine only continued to regard him steadily, Ehren went on, his voice inexorable. "While we were in Loraka, I met a wizard who told me this ring has layered spells on it—two more than I know about. One of them, he says, will be triggered simply when the other is. I only know of one spell I can trigger—I have to assume the second layer is tied to it. That means if I trigger the spell, something else is going to happen, too. Something of Varien's doing. I'm not willing to trust that, are you?"

Now *that* Laine was sure of, just as sure as the fact that he wanted to keep the ring. "No," he said decisively. "But that doesn't mean we have to destroy it."

"Nine Hells!" Ehren snapped in exasperation. "When will you understand its danger? When it rises up to consume you?"

Laine shrugged, deliberately insouciant. "I would've thought you wanted to know who killed Benlan."

Ehren froze, as Laine'd known he would; it almost wasn't fair, dangling that out in front of the Guard, not when the struggle of this decision still showed so clearly on his face. "Of course I want to know," he grated, and after a moment, and with some skepticism, he said, "Are you telling me you can do that?"

"I think my dreams might, and that ring always takes me straight to them. At least, the dreams *would*, if I could get all the way through one of them. Lately, everyone's been waking me up."

"There's a reason for that, Laine," Ehren said heavily. "Did you know you stopped breathing once? Shette told me that. It was the first night I was with you. She was terrified."

Laine's inner eye flashed to the vision of Guards falling around him, blood everywhere. He remembered the death blows, and the way he'd felt dragged down with them. For the first time, he hesitated. "I . . . knew she was frightened. I didn't know . . . Sometimes it's hard to break away. Sometimes I think, when they die . . . that maybe I'm too close to escape their death, too."

"It wouldn't do you much good to discover who killed Benlan if you were too dead to tell us," Ehren said flatly.

"It wouldn't come to that." Laine tried to muster his confidence again.

Ehren raised an eyebrow. "You think not?"

Laine didn't answer, this time. He just held Ehren's gaze, and it wasn't an easy thing. Those grey eyes seemed to see

everything sometimes. Finally Ehren sighed, and closed
his hand back around the ring. "All right," he said. "For
now, we'll keep it at hand."

"I don't think you'll regret it," Laine said, and hoped he
would be able to say the same of himself.

Chapter 11

"What I don't understand," Shette said, taking a swipe at the strawberry juice that dripped down her chin, "is why Laine has any wits at all." She gave him a sideways glance and amended, "Well, not that there's much wit there, anyway, of course."

"Of course," Laine said, making an exaggerated face at her. They sat on the porch with their legs dangling over the edge, picking late-season strawberries from the pail Shette had gathered early that afternoon. Dannel sat at the top of the stairs, and Ehren was in the chair usually reserved for Jenorah, feeling a little guilty even though she'd urged him to take it. Instead she sat on the second step, nestled between Dannel's knees and letting him feed her strawberries. Beneath the steps, their two sturdy little herding dogs slept in shallow hollows of cool dirt, their paws twitching.

It was the way they often ended their summer days, Laine had told him, with the bugs starting to rise and the crickets and cicadas growing loud in the background. It left Ehren somewhat bemused with its bucolic tranquillity, though it was his third evening with the family and he ought to be used to it by now. But not so bemused he didn't take his share of the berries, when Shette offered.

Every time he reached for one, the ring moved gently against his skin, beneath his shirt. It made him think about the obligations associated with it . . . obligations that Varien would no doubt consider unfulfilled. After all, despite Varien's orders to ensure that the self-exiled royal family would pose no problem to Rodar, *no matter what it took*, Dannel and his family still lived.

But Dannel's family had no designs on a throne or anything else—except perhaps their own privacy.

And a few quiet moments with strawberries, on a cool summer evening.

"After all," Shette continued, oblivious, when no one seemed inclined to ask her what she was talking about in regards to Laine's wits, "Unai's journal—or Hetna's journal, I mean—said that there was a curse put on all the firstborn of the Therand ruling line. And when Laine was born, wouldn't Mum have been in the ruling line?"

"What are you talking about?" Jenorah asked, while Ehren gave Shette a sharp look.

"That's right," Ehren said. "Jenorah's mother, Clan Grannor—then, and Clan Grannor now, for that matter."

"Sherran," Dannel said. "A strong woman." He twisted around to frown at them all, and Jenorah looked around his torso to do the same. "What's that to do with anything?"

"You didn't tell them about the journal?" Ehren asked Laine.

Laine shrugged. "There were so many other things that came first."

"The man Shette went after in Loraka," Ehren started, then cocked an eyebrow at Laine. "You *did* tell them about that?"

"I started to. We never got any further than the part where we went into that camp after Shette."

"All right. She'd heard of a man who had information—it turned out to be this journal—about the king's death; after we freed her, we continued on his trail." Ehren gave them a quick rundown on the events of the journey, and the results of it. "I've still got the journal, if you'd care to look at it. You've got as much interest in it as anyone." He wondered if Dannel would see the same significance he did in Hetna's comments, although she shrank from naming names and places. Early in her palace residence, she noted the penchant of certain ministers for meeting people, from other ministers to common couriers, in odd places. Hetna's duties as linen mistress took her to all corners of the palace, and eventually she realized that no matter what she was up to, all she had to do was carry an impressive stack of towels, hangings, or bedsheets along with her, and she was as good as invisible. A non-entity. Shortly after she learned that little trick, she started using the initials *ML* in conjunction with her suspicions of smuggling.

And shortly after that, she was dead.

"Yes," Dannel said, drawing Ehren's thoughts back to the here and now. "I believe I'd like to see that journal. But from what you say . . . Shette is right. Laine *should* be affected by the curse."

"Even before we left, the Clans T'ieran suspected there was a problem," Jenorah said. She rested her arm on Dannel's leg, sitting sideways on the step so she could look back onto the porch without twisting. "With our system of rule by acclamation, the position of the T'ierand can change clans once every several years—or sometimes not for two generations. So we have many more *firstborn of the ruling line* than Solvany would have." She fingered the ends of her long hair, which was drawn back at the nape of her neck, like Ehren's. But where Ehren's hair was slightly wavy, Jenorah's fell straight, black as Laine's if it hadn't been silvered by age. She brushed the end of the thick fall against her cheek, staring contemplatively at her oldest child. "The pattern has been, overwhelmingly, of blindness."

Dannel laughed. "That's one thing our Laine is *not*," he said. "Two different colored eyes; two different kinds of sight. Maybe you're making up for the rest of them, son."

Laine shrugged, but the vision under question seemed turned more inward than anything else. Then he reached around Shette to steal the berry bucket, and asked, abruptly, "Do you know of another pass, Da? A . . . secret sort of thing."

Dannel's expression closed up. "What makes you ask?"

"Different things coming together." Laine popped a berry in his mouth and seemed to be putting his thoughts together, but Ehren got there first.

"The journal was written sixty years ago by a young woman, a servant, who discovered someone in court was smuggling something in from Therand, something she refers to only by the letters *ML*. She also found a reference to a hidden and dangerous pass. Its Solvany-Therand end has been in the Barrenlands for so long, and was known by so few to begin with . . ."

"We thought," Laine said, "that maybe it was tied up with the new hostile spells that have been showing up this year. Ansgare's certainly taking them plain enough to mean we shouldn't continue using the route. If someone was trying to scare us away from the pass . . . well, that's certainly one way to do it."

"I'd like to know who sent that wizard," Ehren said, thinking of Varien, and of the possibility of other, generation-spanning treachery in the Levels.

"Ooh, he was disgusting," Shette said. "You should have seen him, Da—lying on the rocks like this—" And she assumed the contorted posture of the dead man they'd found shortly before the avalanche.

"Shette," Jenorah remonstrated quietly.

"Well, he *was*." But she slumped forward against the porch rails, hanging her arms over the second tier.

"There are so many loose pieces floating around," Ehren mused, rubbing his hand over the front of his leg, trying to soothe the ache without actually daring to get close to the wound. "It'd be nice if I could get just *some* of them to make sense." He gave Laine a wry smile. "Not that anyone wants me to."

"What they want is for you to mind your own business," Laine agreed.

"There *is* a pass," Dannel said suddenly, resting his hand on Jenorah's shoulder. "I stumbled on it the summer before I met your mother—I was always out wandering where I shouldn't have been. It opens in the Barrenlands, all right—

only someone of ruling blood or a damn good wizard could
get to it in the first place. Even then, it's a very difficult
journey, some of it underground. You won't have seen it
from the caravan route you've described to me, but it's
not far. Certainly close enough to make someone nervous,
if they were using the pass to smuggle contraband. Oh—
but I'm losing track of your pieces, Ehren. The smuggling
happened many years ago."

Ehren just looked at him, steadily rubbing his sore leg.
"Maybe not."

Ehren was up early again the next morning. He was taking
only light doses of the addictive pain-slip, and they didn't
last long enough to get him through the night. He dressed
in darkness, in the cleaned, torn pants that accommodated
his leg, and a borrowed shirt to replace the avalanche-tattered
remnants of his own. His shoulder, which had benefited as
much as his leg from the two healing spells, was merely
stiff and sore, and no longer hampered him in any way.

Getting out of the house was a little more difficult. Ehren
was, he'd discovered early, in Shette's bed; Laine had given
her his own tiny room and was sleeping on an old feather
tick in the middle of the main room. There was a kitchen
alcove off the back of the house, and a solid wood stove
between the main room and alcove. It was far from the
ornamental Kurtane court, but it suited Dannel well.

Despite his uneven gait, Ehren got by Laine without
waking him—fortunately, when not dreaming, Laine was
a mighty heavy sleeper. The stairs were slow, and he broke
a sweat on them, even though the dawning morning was
still cool. *Damn leg.* He had things to accomplish, and
accommodating the leg was a growing irritation.

*It could have been worse. It could have been avalanche-
flattened King's Guard instead.* The thought did nothing for
his mood, however. He walked through dewless grass to the
barn, absently aware of that portent of rain, and retrieved
his grooming brushes from the packs stowed in the barn.

The boys were in the corral behind the barn; Laine said

he'd been able to lead Ricasso there, and Shaffron followed. They greeted him with the kind of snorting and snuffling that seemed to imply they hadn't been fed or watered in days, and Ehren stood between them, intercepting the jealous nips they aimed at one another and trying to keep his balance amidst their nudges of affection. When Shaffron wandered away to see what was left of the hay they'd received the previous evening, Ehren retrieved the brushes and set to work on Ricasso.

This was when he could think best. No one around but the two horses, his hands busy with the rhythmic work of grooming, his mind free to wander.

He'd been told to trigger the ring upon discovery of Dannel and his family; he'd chosen not to. He'd been told to ensure the family would cause no trouble; he'd decided they wouldn't, and planned to leave as quietly as he'd come. Varien, he knew, would prefer—had all but *ordered*—Ehren to slaughter the family in their sleep.

But Ehren was a Guard. Utterly loyal to his king—if not the king's wizard—and with enough beads on his honor feather for any two men. And being a Guard meant doing what was right, not just what was convenient for those in power. Or doing what was right, and not necessarily what he'd been told to do—despite the little-veiled threats behind those orders. If he hadn't cared about living up to what that meant, he wouldn't have irritated the odd Upper Level minister in the first place.

In this case, *right* meant returning to Kurtane and trying to unravel the tangle of events he'd discovered—trying to see how they tied together, where Varien fit, and if things were as bad for Solvany as Ehren thought they were. New goals, to replace the ones he struggled to walk away from.

Ricasso swung his head around in a tight arc and nudged Ehren's unmoving hand, and Ehren gave him a pat, and a rueful shake of his head. "Sorry, son," he said. "Deep thoughts. You really don't want to know. It's bound to cause trouble for both of us."

He wondered if Jada and Algere had stumbled into

anything in Kurtane, if they'd sent messages to the border
station—and if they were waiting for his help. He hoped
not. He felt a chill down his back, realizing they might go
to Gerhard—he *was* their master, after all—and that
Gerhard had been a Lorakan import.

Hells, the trip back promised to be a long one. The caravan
route was no longer an option, and every mile he went on
the long Trade Road would be one during which he could
do nothing with what he'd learned.

He finished brushing out Ricasso and moved on to
Shaffron, whose long mane was a tangle. "You've been
rolling," Ehren accused him.

The flame-colored horse ignored him; his small, neat ears
were pricked at the barn. Ehren's first impulse was to draw
his sword—which he had not brought with him. *Damn
stupid. Anyone could have followed us here—*

It was Laine. "Breakfast's on," he called.

Anyone could have followed us here—and hadn't there
been men asking about him in T'ieranguard? *Damn.* Ehren
took a resolute breath and gave Laine a wave with the hand
that held the brush; he made a quick job of untangling
the chestnut-tinged flaxen hair of Shaffron's mane, and left
the horses.

He and Laine walked back to the house together, but
neither of them made conversation. It wasn't until they
were sitting at the smooth wood table in the kitchen alcove
and Jenorah had greeted him with, "Guides grant you a
good day," that Ehren spoke.

"We've got to leave," he said.

Shette looked up from the seasoned potato chunks she
was serving, her hair still loose and her eyes sleepy—though
at his statement it seemed she was waking fast. "Why?"
she demanded.

"We?" Dannel said, pointedly, as Jenorah fastened a
concerned look on Ehren. Laine just met Ehren's gaze
evenly. Waiting.

"Laine, Shette and I," he said, answering Dannel's
question. "It's a . . . feeling."

"A *feeling*," Dannel repeated. And Laine waited.

Well, he'd certainly gotten their undivided attention . . . even scrutiny. Then Shette shook her head. "That's just the pain-slip, I'll bet, Ehren. It's affecting you more than you know."

"Do you think I haven't had pain-slip before? I haven't had it this morning, in any event. No, I'm serious about this. If we stay here, we're putting your parents in danger."

"You're not ready to go back out on the road. It must be a mighty strong feeling," Laine said quietly—and Ehren heard no indication that Laine disbelieved him. In fact, he thought he saw hidden alarm in Laine's face, far more notable for the fact that he'd bothered to hide it, when his expressions usually mirrored his thoughts whether he meant them to or not.

"The Lorakan agent," Ehren said, his words clipped as memory suddenly added this man to the equation. "We have no indication what he was doing there. I started out on that road before, Laine, when I first ran into you. Plenty of people knew I was going. What if he found out, and followed me in—not knowing I'd returned and was on the Trade Road with you, going after Shette?"

"The timing would be pretty tricky," Laine said. "But it could have happened. If you don't mind me saying so, why would anyone care where you were going? You're a Guard, not a member of the royal family." He gave a sudden grin. "Guess I can't say that about *us* anymore."

"There have been several attempts on my life within the year," Ehren told him. "It'd be mighty convenient for Varien—or for those who killed Benlan—if I met an *accident* on the road. And there're plenty of ways to get messages from the Solvan border station to T'ieranguard, to alert someone on this end. Most of them are faster than your caravan route, even without the delays we had."

"Birds, for one," Dannel said. "Or magic."

Ehren nodded, feeling grim. "How hard do you think it would be to track me down? And what about those men who asked about me?" They'd asked Ansgare to play dumb should the men ask again, but— "Do you suppose it's occurred to Sevita or Dajania that discussing me with the other women might be dangerous for me—for *us*?"

"They'd never do anything to get you in trouble," Shette said, all confidence. She returned the iron skillet to the small cookstove and cracked a handful of eggs into it.

"Not on purpose," Ehren agreed. "But anyone who really wanted to find me could eventually discover I'd gone off with you and Laine. I should have thought about it right away, but it seems I wasn't doing much thinking at all. The only way to keep them from coming *here* is to make ourselves known at T'ieranguard again."

Jenorah said, "Don't let the eggs burn, Shette," and turned back to Ehren. Her hair was loose, hanging down to her waist, and she gathered up a hank of it and fiddled, worried. "That agent may have had nothing to do with you. As you've said, there seems to be plenty going on at the border right now."

"Then going to T'ieranguard poses nothing but an inconvenience. Jenorah, I'm trying to protect what you and Dannel have built here. If we get people in this valley looking for me, they're going to be asking questions. It may not take them very long to figure out who you really are."

"I don't think you're ready to travel again," she told him. Ehren noticed she wasn't arguing his point.

"And I don't think we have any choice. I may not have any magical Sight, but I've got experience to spare— experience I lived to acquire because I knew when to heed my feelings."

"Mum, Da . . ." Laine started, then hesitated. He took a deep breath and said, "I think he's right. I think I've caused more trouble than I ever thought by bringing him here."

No, it never would have come to this if Ehren hadn't wrangled an invitation out of Laine. But now that he was here, now that his decision to spurn Varien's orders was made, he had no intention of making Dannel and Jenorah casualties of whatever strange play was going on. His voice held an anger he hadn't intended when he said, "The people that cause the trouble, Laine, are the ones that try to bend the world to their personal whims."

"In the end, it doesn't matter," Dannel said, and his voice was just as hard. "Life doesn't come with directions, Laine. But sometimes you can come out ahead, anyway." He looked at Jenorah. "We'll manage. We've done it before."

"Once we arrive in T'ieranguard, we'll spend a day or two being visible," Ehren said. "And then we'll make some very public good-byes, and I'll head back up the Trade Road."

"I really don't think you should head out on your own," Laine said, the doubt clear on his face.

"There may be another way," Dannel said, realization crossing his face. "There may be . . ." He gave a sudden, unexpected grin, looking at Jenorah. "It's been done before."

Shette was scowling, looking like a kid left out of a secret. She scraped well-cooked eggs into everyone's plate, added the strips of beef that had been frying, and plunked the skillet down loudly on the table. "Give us a clue," she said, sitting down in the empty chair. "And eat before it gets too cold."

Jenorah lifted an eyebrow at her, and after a moment, Shette wiggled. That seemed to be enough; Jenorah took up the tined spoon beside her plate and calmly began to eat. "She does have a point. And it might be good for everyone to have a chance to think before this conversation goes any further. Eat."

They ate in silence, but not for very long. Dannel was the one who broke it. "It's a good idea, I think," he said. "Listen, Ehren. You want to get back home as soon as possible. I want my children in a safer place than T'ieranguard."

"Ehren taught me how to watch out for myself," Shette said, stung.

Laine shook his head. "And now I know how to hold a sword correctly. But it doesn't mean we'll be up to the sorts of people who might be bumping around T'ieranguard, especially if they're looking for information about Ehren. Do you honestly think, Shette, that if the bandits ambushed you today, things would turn out any differently?"

She looked down at her plate, and after a moment, mumbled, "No."

But Ehren's attention was fully on Dannel. "What have you got in mind?"

"The summer clan house for Grannor is practically on the border of the Barrenlands. That *is* how I found Jenny, after all. They'd probably be delighted to take Shette in for a while—and you, Shette, would probably have the time of your life there. Laine'll chafe, I suppose, but he'll survive a month or two of it." He looked at Ehren and grinned. "And, as I mentioned before, Grannor *is* the T'ierand clan again."

"They can give dispensation for traveling the Barrenlands," Ehren said, finally catching where Dannel's thoughts were taking them all.

"They'd probably be glad to, after you act as escort for Laine and Shette," Jenorah said, a smile breaking over her face as well. "I knew Sherran, when I was younger. She'll do this for me."

"Wait a minute," Laine said. "You want me to hole up in Therand, too, and leave you two here alone?"

"Your parents' best chance is to *be* alone," Ehren said. "And to be very quiet. If we three went to T'ieranguard and then Shette and I left for Therand without you, I wouldn't vouch for your safety there alone. Not if I trust my feelings about this whole situation, and believe me, I do."

"I could come back here . . ." Laine said, but trailed off, evidently realizing they were back to the argument that was taking them away from this farm in the first place. He was associated with Ehren, now. "I just don't like it much," he said unhappily.

"We'll be fine." Jenorah gestured with her spoon for emphasis. "We're the parents and that means we know what we're talking about."

Ehren ducked his head, which didn't go far in hiding his amusement. Laine rolled his eyes, and said, "It's true, Ehren. That's a rule they made up when I asked *why* one too many times. It's been a long while since they dragged it out on me, though."

"In this case, a good rule," Ehren said, still smiling. "And it helps settle things. I want to leave tomorrow."

Jenorah rose and picked up her plate. "Then I'd best be finding that ring my mother gave me—the Clan Grannor crest with my birthstone. And some paper and a pen. My, I hope I remember how to write."

Dannel smiled at his wife's back, and gave Laine a wink. "It'll be all right, son. And it's about time you saw something of *one* of your countries."

But it was Ehren that Laine looked to for final reassurance; Shette, as well, was giving him a worried eye. He nodded at them. "It's a good plan. It'll work." *We'll make it work.*

Ehren limped through the open market of T'ieranguard, feeling very little like a Solvan King's Guard. He no longer wore his ailette, for this wasn't the place to advertise his affiliation. He certainly didn't look like a Guard—with pounds lost in recovery, pants ripped and tied, and a borrowed old shirt—and he definitely didn't look like the kind of man who could defend himself against all comers.

Time to change some of that. In appearance, at least. There was no reason a loose pair of cloth trousers couldn't fit over the thin bandage he now wore, and a shirt that fit, period, would be a good start, even if he got them both from the used clothing booths.

Laine and Shette were off looking for open traveling parties, to hook up with for at least part of the journey. They were playing up Ehren's ability to protect them— not too much, Ehren hoped. At the same time, if that's what it took . . . he definitely didn't want the three of them out on the open road alone, easy to identify.

He smiled at the old woman on the other side of the table of clothes from him. She sat beneath a tarp spread on staked poles, and there was a wagon piled with more goods behind her. She smiled back, a toothless expression, and her eyes, permanently narrowed from years of squinting into the sun, brightened as they traveled up and down his frame. "I can fit you well, I'm sure, lad," she said. "Not the fancy things for you, am I right? Just something broad enough for those shoulders, eh?"

Ehren moved his shoulders inside the too-small shirt. "It'd be a welcome change," he replied, shifting his smile into something rakish that flirted back at her. "And no, not the fancy things. Well-made, well-mended, that's good enough."

"Pair of trous, too, I can see," she said, nodding at his leg. "I can take the shirt in trade, but not those pants. The sewing, I can do. But those bloodstains'll not come out! Been in a bit of trouble, have you?"

"A bit," Ehren said. "Odds are, a bit more, before I'm done." He said it lightly, but meant it well. Back to Solvany, and through the Barrenlands to do it. Back to Kurtane, without triggering the ring. He doubted he could come up with another combination of events to make the Levels more annoyed with him.

And, of course, Varien.

"Been in the city long?" the woman asked him, pulling a shirt from the wagon behind her. She shook it out and leaned over the table, stretching her bowed, shortened frame to hold it in front of Ehren. She shook her head. "Not your color. A man like you should have a shirt that shows him off."

Ehren grinned at her. "I like your sales pitch. No, not long. A week or so." Two days was more like it, but he wanted to lay a confusing trail, one that would hide the fact that he'd been out of T'ieranguard. If anyone was looking, he wanted them looking here, and not for the home where he'd spent several days.

"Long enough to pick up some friends, then." The look she shot him was unreadable; he raised his eyebrows at it. "Ah," she said, pulling something out from the bottom of a pile. "I was saving this one. See if you like it. Color'll look mighty fine on you."

It had been a deep scarlet, he guessed; now it was

something milder. But it was a thick, tough weave, and the fit looked right. He held it up against himself and said, "I bow to your judgment."

"In that case, take it! Though I'll see you in it before you go. Part of my price." And she winked at him.

He laughed, and pulled off Dannel's shirt right there. "Here's the trade. It needs a washing."

"As all my goods are washed before I sell them," she said in a scolding tone. "Something for the other half, then . . ." Her age-crooked hands prowled through the mounded clothing, making Ehren wonder how she could possibly know where each item was. He shrugged himself into the faded scarlet and tugged it into place. She glanced up at him and nodded. "That's just the thing for you, young man. Now then, tell me: you aren't planning to spoil it right off with more of your precious blood, are you?"

Ehren snorted, more surprised than anything else. "Not if I can help it."

"That's a good thing. Couldn't help but wonder, you see, the way those two have been keeping an eye on you."

Ehren stiffened; he forced himself to relax. He'd seen two men at the inn this morning who looked a little too familiar; they'd left the building while he was still finishing a breakfast of thick porridge with Laine and Shette.

She glanced up at him, and her gaze hesitated at his face; the banter was gone from it. "Here, now," she said. "You just turn all the way around so I can make certain that shirt fits." She gestured the circle with her finger, and then repeated it when he didn't respond immediately. "Go on, then. You don't get to keep it until I've judged the set of it across your back."

Holding his arms away from his sides slightly, he did as she requested. Yes, the same men.

"Was that enough?" she asked. "Or do you need another go at them?"

He grinned at her again, only this one was tight. "I saw them, thank you."

"Good. Will these do you?" She handed him a pair of

black pants with a line of grey piping down the sides, a
soldier's wear. "I judge they'll go the length of your legs,
which says something for them."

"Considering how well you did with the shirt, I'll have
faith in that." He paid her the few coppers she asked of him,
and another besides. "Thank you for your help. All of it."

"Oh, my pleasure," she told him. "I like to have a man
undress before me now and then. It does my soul good."

"Glad to oblige," he said, giving her the deliberately rakish
grin again as he took the pants and turned away; it faded
quickly. He hoped those men were as unfamiliar with this
market as he was, for if he didn't lose them, he was going
to have to discourage them.

◆━◆◆◆━◆

Laine tightened the cinch on his father's pony Nimble
and made sure the packs on his new mule were fastened
securely, trying to take stock of the situation he'd found
himself in.

Ansgare was still in town, still undecided about his future.
He'd convinced Laine to make a run of the route when he
returned, just the two of them, hopeful that the wizard's
death during the avalanche would mean their troubles were
over—although deep inside, Laine knew better. In the
meanwhile, Ansgare was staying here, feeling out new
connections in case the route was still unmanageable. And
he was willing—or, more accurately, eager—to spread
misinformation about Ehren's whereabouts.

Shette led Nell up beside Laine, both of them nothing
but dim figures in the early morning darkness. "Are you
sure we should let Ehren talk to these guys alone?" she
asked, her voice hushed.

Laine hesitated. "He knows what he's doing. But . . . I'm
not sure we should let him do this *alone*." He sighed, testing
one last knot and letting the stiff rope fall to the side of
the pack with a *thwap*. "Of course, I'm not sure he's any
better off with me there, either."

"But Laine, his leg . . ." Shette said.

He could hear her struggle to keep the words from turning

childish, and he gave her a nod. Besides, she had a point. "All right," he said. "I'll go see." *And I'll try not to interfere too much* . . . He handed her the pony's reins and the mule's lead, and headed for the entrance to the stable, as uneasy about it all as he'd been the night before, when Ehren had told them about the men over dinner.

"You were followed?" Laine'd asked numbly. The fine venison in his mouth had suddenly turned dry, and hard to swallow. Ehren's concerns about staying at the farm had been justified, then. And the danger to his parents . . . Laine longed to return to them, to make sure everything was all right. But that would only make things worse, now. He gritted his teeth, then deliberately unclenched them to take a long draught of watered wine. After a moment, he said, "I take it you lost them."

"I did," Ehren nodded. "But it was only an exercise. I saw them here this morning, as well."

"But—" Shette started, her light brown eyes wide with worry, "what're we gonna do?"

"Discourage them, I suspect," Ehren said. "And leave, tomorrow."

"I found a small group of travelers," Laine said. "They're willing to have us along—in fact, I think they'd be glad for us. They were just visiting family, and don't seem too confident about being on the road—I guess there's been some trouble here, too. But . . . they're not leaving for another several days."

"It's more important for us to get out of here. Those men we're here, now," Ehren said. "They've undoubtedly gotten conflicting information on just how long we've been here—we've got enough people convinced we were here the entire time that I doubt they're going to look too hard in your folks' direction. It's time to lose them and move on, before they decide to do more than just keep track of us." He took a generous gulp of his wine, and nudged away the drop at the corner of his mouth with his knuckle. "We can always wait, a few days down the road, for the people you've found."

Laine said, "I think we should. They're going right to the town beside the Grannor summer home."

"Discourage those men . . . how?" Shette asked faintly, pushing a strip of venison around on her plate.

"With whatever it takes," Ehren told her.

With whatever it takes, Laine repeated to himself, feeling grim as he headed out into darkness. Ehren had turned the tables on the two men who'd been following him—not only had he lost them in the market, he'd then followed them back to their own rooms in a rougher inn nearby. And now he was there, discussing the situation. Discouraging them. Alone.

Laine navigated the dark, close streets of the inn and tavern quarter of the city, and found the Trader's Choice with little trouble. The thick door was heavy but well oiled, and when he entered, full of trepidation and uncertainty, he was glad to discover a smoking candle lamp sitting on the end of the bar. Light from a back room meant someone was up, probably the cook.

Laine drew his sword, his hand sweaty on the grip—and quietly found the steep, enclosed stairs to the second story, leaving the sleepers in the common room none the wiser.

One step at a time, he traveled the length of the hall at the top of the stairs. Another flickering candle sent dancing light from the end of the hall, picking out the edges of each doorway. No magic light glows in *this* inn. He stopped at each door, listening, wondering if he'd found the wrong inn after all and knowing there was no way to explain himself if he was caught.

He'd just about decided he'd completely misunderstood Ehren's intentions when he caught a murmured word from the doorway he was about to leave; he held his breath and moved up closer, straining his ears—and finally caught the familiar timbre of Ehren's smooth voice. There was nothing in that voice to suggest trouble, but Laine cracked the door and looked inside anyway.

Ehren was sitting on the bed with two men, who were both lying down; he cast a quick, alarmed look over his shoulder at the door, saw Laine, and jerked his head in a silent *Get in here*.

By then Laine realized Ehren wasn't sitting *with* the two men, but *on* one of them, straddling the man's stomach. The other lay crowded up against the wall; Ehren's sword was against his throat, while his dagger pushed into the notch between the first man's collarbones.

"Shette was worried," Laine said, uncomfortable with the tension that permeated the room, and the rank smell of fear.

"No need for it," Ehren said. "These two drink too heavily, and sleep too heavily as well. We were just discussing their orders. Who gave them, their specific intent . . . that sort of thing." His voice, deliberately casual, held an edge of danger.

Laine just nodded uneasily, knowing he shouldn't have come. Hindsight was such a wonderful thing. His sword felt awkward in his hand, but he left it there. As near as he could tell, Ehren had simply entered the room and put his blades against both throats. Waking both men would have been a tricky moment—but there Ehren sat, testimony to his success. And now he shifted both sword and dagger— combined with his expression, a not-so-subtle suggestion that someone start talking.

"There's no use to ask," the inner man said; his partner seemed to be having enough trouble just breathing with Ehren sitting on his stomach, not to mention talking. "We can't tell you anything."

"Make an effort," Ehren said. "Because if you can't convince me you're going to stop following me, I'll just kill you right here."

Laine winced. "Ehren, do you have to—"

"Stay out of this, Laine." Ehren's voice was pleasant on the surface and steel underneath.

"You wouldn't," the man said. "All we done is follow you. There ain't no great harm in that!"

"That's my call, " Ehren said, intensity filling his voice with threat. "Why don't you ask my friend if he thinks I would." Ehren gestured at Laine with a nod, never taking his eyes from his captive's. "And keep your voice down while you're at it. I can cut your throat and still get my answers from your partner."

Laine was still trying to get control of his face, which was, he was certain, showing his horror. Ehren was hard, an experienced warrior who knew how to kill . . . who'd disemboweled a woman and attacked a man from behind— *to save my life*, he reminded himself—and then walked away from the bodies without looking back.

The man *did* look at Laine, as though to ask—but saw the answer in Laine's face and swallowed hard instead. He tried to wiggle back away, but the wall stopped him.

"We can work something out—" His voice had gotten hoarse at the edges. A thin trickle of blood ran down the man's neck, black in the grey dawn light that was brightening the window.

Ehren leaned over the man, bringing their faces only inches apart. His expression and voice were equally hard. "Don't waste my time."

Laine found himself suddenly sweating.

"Your orders," Ehren said, pinning the man with his piercing gaze, still only inches away. "And who's paying you."

"You don't understand," croaked the man Ehren was sitting on.

Ehren snapped a quick, meaningful, "Shut up!" never turning away from the man against the wall, never turning down the intensity of his gaze. "I'm waiting. But I don't have long. Make your choice."

"We don't know—I mean, we're only to follow—"

"No, Brent!" his partner gasped. Ehren didn't even look at him, but snapped the ridge of his knuckles, weighted by the dagger, against the man's throat in a quick, decisive motion. While his partner choked, the fellow he'd called Brent talked, and talked fast.

"We're only following you, until the boss is satisfied. We make our reports to—" His voice cut off, stopped from within as though by force. His eyes widened, frightened and imploring.

"I told you not to say!" his partner managed to choke out. "I told you—!"

Brent's mouth was moving—useless, aborted attempts at speech; Ehren quickly lifted his sword away from the man's neck. And Laine, suddenly aware that his Sight was tickling him, made the effort to See the three men. Coalescing around the stricken man's chest was a roiling red ugliness. "Magic, Ehren!"

Ehren threw himself away from the man, dragging his other prisoner to the floor with him. "Watch him," he snapped at Laine, springing back to his feet with a speed that belied his still-healing injury.

Laine blinked, startled, but managed to get his sword into a position that would do the man some damage if he tried to move. There was no need. They all three had only one thing on their minds. While Ehren stared, narrow-eyed, Brent managed one last croaking gasp, something that sounded like a plea for help. Then he choked up a stream of unending red foam, and seemed to collapse in upon himself, his chest sinking and his eyes bugged out and staring.

"Guides preserve us," the other man whispered, his hand at his nicked throat, and one creeping toward his groin, where Laine's sword pointed.

"I think it's too late for that," Ehren said. He shook his head, expression grim, and handed his knife pommel first to Laine. "Cut up his pants and tie him with the scraps. It'll slow him down at least."

Stunned, hardly able to tear his eyes from the fading magic, Laine did what he was told. Fortunately his captive no longer seemed interested in any kind of struggle. He lay on the floor, expression dulled and hopeless, while Laine divested him of his pants and cut them into long strips.

Ehren was running his hands over the dead man, performing a quick but efficient search. He came up with two daggers and a small purse, and he took them all. Then, when Laine was done, he repeated the process with the securely tied captive. When he stood up, he said, "We're leaving. Don't bother trying to follow. None of our friends know where we're going; no one's up early enough to see us. And now that I know you can't tell us anything, next time I see you, I'll just kill you right off."

The man shook his head. "You ain't gonna see me. I got too much stake in being alive." But his fearful glance was on his dead partner as much as on Ehren.

"Gag him," Ehren said, and moved to the door. "And then let's go. It's time we left this city."

Chapter 12

"What happened?" Shette had asked, again and again. Laine just looked at Ehren and shook his head, and it was finally up to Ehren to tell her they wouldn't be bothered by those men any more.

But Ehren wasn't at all certain there wouldn't be others. There was magic involved here . . . powerful magic. Varien had the magic, but he was also much too smart to waste effort and power for no purpose. Which surely meant Ehren was more than just a nuisance . . . more like a threat.

But ironically, given the history between his country and the one he now traveled in, he'd felt safer as soon as he'd entered Therand. Unlike Solvany, Therand was a land of subtle magics, where the lore was woven into everyday life. In Solvany, the low-level cottage witches like Erlya were the only sporadic signs of magic outside the colorful displays and dramatic healings of the higher levels. Here, Varien's magic would draw intense scrutiny, and he was unlikely to use it.

A few days into the quiet green pastures, they stopped outside a small village and waited for the family Laine had arranged to travel with. The pace Ehren had set was slowed by the newcomers, for they had no mounts, and only a small donkey to carry their goods. They, too, were avoiding the inns, if only because of the cost. Shette and Laine traded off their ponies so all the travelers would have a turn to ride, and no one questioned why Ricasso and Shaffron weren't included in the offer. Ehren walked his share, too, in an effort to keep his leg in good working order while it healed.

They traveled through country that was slightly rolling, going north and then west, and roughly paralleling the Barrenlands; it was woods and pastures, with small farmhouses along the road and sheep and shepherds in the fields. Several times they passed breeding farms, and Ehren discovered horses that looked much like Shaffron; they had his fire, too, and snorted their challenges from behind fenced paddocks, prancing back and forth as the travelers walked by. It was quiet travel, and they passed only a handful of people a day unless they were skirting a village. Being with the friendly family seemed to set Shette at ease, and even Laine relaxed a little; his dreams were gentle, and when Shette asked, he would say only that they were brief pieces of Dannel and Jenorah's courtship.

But Ehren, wearing a ring that vibrated its unhappiness against his chest, was ever reminded of the task he had left undone, and of the puzzle pieces he was yet unable to put into place.

Two days before they closed in on the summer lands of Clan Grannor, the family broke away from Ehren's party. Laine, Shette and Ehren traveled faster, then, and stayed their last night on the road in an inn. The next day, they passed between two standing rocks, several stories high apiece, that marked the borders of Grannor land. They were deeply incised with words in the old T'ieran alphabet, which Ehren knew only enough to recognize. After they'd passed, Laine turned and stared, with the expression Ehren had grown used to.

"What do you see?" he asked, but Laine only shook his head.

"I'm not sure. Something we *didn't* trigger, I think." He stared a moment longer, then abruptly shrugged, turning his pony back to the road. "I'd like to know what happens if someone unfriendly goes through there."

"So we passed inspection, did we?" Ehren gave Shaffron's damp neck a pat. At midday, the heat was still oppressive, but high summer had passed them by, and the evenings were cool and comfortable. He glanced back at the stones himself, and said, "I doubt it'll be the last inspection we have to pass."

They rode in silence for a while, until Shette looked around with a dreamy expression and said, "This is where they met, Laine. This is where Mum and Da met, and where they fell in love. Isn't it perfect?"

Ehren thought it was just another stretch of hayfields and wood strips; from the look on Laine's face, he felt the same. Both were too wise to say so. Off to the south was a stand of trees that went as far as they could see, east and west. The road continued to parallel it, dipping slightly between the hummocks of the rolling ground. It was a good road, and suddenly put Ehren in the mood for a canter.

Laine must have picked up on the feeling, for he gave Ehren a glance and sent his small horse ahead, the mule trailing a few steps with its neck stretched out. Shaffron picked up the gait right away, Ricasso behind him, and behind that came Shette's startled, "Hey!" as she broke out of her dreamy staring and realized she'd been left behind.

Shaffron was ready to run; he put all his extra energy into high-stepping movement. When Laine suddenly pulled his pony up, Ehren rode past him—and when he saw the three mounted figures coming to meet them, he continued on, leaving Laine and Shette behind and cantering right up to the three.

They were nose to nose, then, with all four horses chewing their bits and moving restlessly beneath their riders, and Ricasso fidgeting behind. The figures turned out to be two men and a woman, and they all wore the red and black colors of Grannor. Their matching swords hung at precisely the same spot on each hip, and the riding gear was as clean as black leather could get. Impressive.

"Clan Grannor was not expecting visitors today," the woman said. Sandwiched between the men, she was without insignia on her collar, but was clearly in charge.

"Clan Grannor has visitors, nonetheless," Ehren said, glancing back to see Shette and Laine moving up on them at a sedate walk.

She raised a fine eyebrow; she was petite between the men, hale specimens, both. "Visitors from afar, from your speech," she said.

"But visitors who are very close to you, as well." Ehren reined Shaffron back a step as the woman's mount laid back its ears and stretched its neck to snap.

The woman murmured a chastisement to her horse. "Visitors," she said dryly, "who like to play games."

"I'm good at it." Ehren shrugged. "We'd be grateful for your escort to the keep."

"I'm sure," she said, in that same dry tone. "Much more grateful than an escort to the stones, no doubt."

"Much," Ehren said, and grinned at her.

She shook her head, allowing a smile, uninfluenced by her two disapproving comrades. "Son of Solvany," she said, "did you think to go unrecognized here?"

"I didn't bother to try," Ehren said. "Important news is still important, no matter what its source. And my companions will be more to your liking, I think."

She was looking beyond him, then, her chin raised and her dark eyes narrowed. Ehren didn't have to turn around to know that Laine and Shette were right behind him, their horses' hooves quiet on the spongy turf of the road. Shette's black mare gave a little whicker of greeting.

"These are Grannor's children," the woman said.

"More or less," Laine said, directly behind Ehren. "It's . . . a little complicated."

"Considering your accent, I would say so." She afforded Ehren another long glance and lifted her reins. "Follow us, then. I'll know the answers to the questions you raise in me, and I expect they'll be easier to get if we ply you with tea than demand them from your hard Solvan friend."

"With all due respect—" started one of the men, but she hushed him with a wave of her hand.

The summer home turned out to be a keep designed more for convenience than defense; Ehren doubted anyone had ever actually tried to hold these walls against invasion. The wall meandered in a leisurely fashion, inscribing a rough circle around the low wood and stone keep and leaving a generous gap at the road. Its sole purpose seemed to be marking where the general populace and grounds workers could build their own small homes. And, of course, it also held sheep.

There were plenty of children scattered around, and a few harried-looking women trying to make sure those children stayed out of the road; their escort waved at both women and youngsters as they rode past. Beyond the inner walls, there were no children, but there was plenty of activity anyway; as far as Ehren could tell, they were gearing up for the final cutting of hay.

The woman stopped her horse to the side of the keep entrance, a tall, narrow stone doorway, and gave her reins to one of the men. "Torre, see that their beasts are cared for, and then escort them into the hall."

"Yes, ma'am," the man said, taking the reins of the other man's horse as well when the fellow, still rather stiffly at attention, followed the woman into the keep.

Their remaining escort said little to them as he led them to a long, low three-sided shelter with paddocks down its length. Behind it was a small building, and it was there they stowed their packs, although Ehren kept his saddlebags. "We can put them on grass or in paddock," the man said, nodding at the horses.

"Grass," said Laine immediately, but Ehren hesitated.

"Mine aren't safe to approach," he cautioned. The man made no comment, merely returned to the building and came out with strips of red cloth.

"Tie these to their manes and tails," he said. "Even the children will stay away from them, then."

Thus decorated, Shaffron and Ricasso celebrated their

freedom by cantering into the green grounds of the keep, tails flagged and heels kicking. Ehren looked after them and shook his head. "Ridiculous," he murmured, and turned to follow their escort into the keep.

Laine had never been in any building as solid as the Grannor summer keep. The walls were thick stone, the timber framework for the tiled roof was massive, and the building as a whole was huge, and could have held his own home over and over . . . and over.

Shette was enchanted, and they moved through the hallway at a pace that was obviously too fast to suit her—there were windows to look out of, and tapestries to gaze upon, and myriad bits of color to catch her eye. Laine finally hooked his arm through hers to stop her hesitations; they were a good distance behind Ehren and their escort by then, anyway, despite the hitch in Ehren's gait.

"Laine, I want to see—" she protested.

"Shh!" he hissed at her. "If we behave ourselves, you'll get plenty of opportunity." She subsided then, and moved right along with him, so that by the time Ehren stopped at the huge archway before them, they'd almost caught up.

The hall sprawled before them, with a line of empty tables down the center and a roomwide dais at the end, flanked with intensely colorful tapestries.

At the far end of the tables, sitting casually in a wooden, high-armed chair with a drink before her, was the woman who'd met them on the road.

Their escort turned, and with some satisfaction, said, "The T'ierand Clan Grannor, Sherran."

Ehren looked back long enough to catch Laine's eye and give him a quirk of eyebrow and mouth before striding out into the hall. Laine hesitated, remembering the somewhat tart exchange between Ehren and the T'ierand on the road. Shette gave him a puzzled look and he realized he still had her arm, but he wasn't quick enough; she got in a poke to his ribs before he managed to move out.

"Tea?" the T'ierand was asking Ehren, her voice as implacable as ever, "or would ale be more to your liking?"

"There's a Therand tea we occasionally import to Kurtane," Ehren said. "It's called Ariel's Spice. If you don't have any, ale would be fine."

"Oh, we have it," she assured him, and although she'd made no signal, there was suddenly a young woman approaching the table. She gave a quick gesture of obeisance, and waited. "Ariel's Spice, for all of us," Sherran said, looking at Laine and Shette and getting two quick nods, although Laine had no idea what Ariel's Spice tea tasted like. "Cooled, please."

When the girl had left, Sherran gestured to the chairs on either side of her. "Have a seat. You, for one, look like you need to get off that leg."

"There's truth to that," Ehren said, and Laine wondered why it sounded like sparring, when the words were so bland and polite. He took one of the chairs, and Shette another, while Ehren went around to the T'ierand's other side, dropping his saddle bags on the floor.

Laine decided not to wait for Ehren to start more trouble, no matter how subtle. "My name is Laine," he said. "This is my sister, Shette. My parents sent us here; they were hoping we'd be safe here, and that we could stay for a while."

"Were they, now?" the T'ierand asked, though her voice wasn't unfriendly.

"You'll know the names, I think," Ehren said, and he clearly enjoyed the taste of surprising her. "Jenorah of Clan Grannor, and Dannel—another of Solvan's sons."

Her eyes narrowed, as her sharp gaze went to Laine and Shette—and then went right through them, from the feel of it. They were like Ehren's eyes, dark and penetrating, and they were set in an oval face whose strong expression almost disguised the fact that her features were actually delicate. She was, Laine realized with a shock, not as old as he'd expected, but was perhaps just a few years younger than Ehren.

"This is unexpected," she said evenly, and then brought that sharp gaze back to Ehren, waiting for more.

He shrugged. "It was unexpected when we found Therand's T'ierand riding out with her road guards," he said, leaning back so the young girl, returning with a tray of pitcher and mugs, could set them on the table and serve her commander.

"I enjoy a good ride," Sherran said, as the girl took away whatever she'd been drinking and replaced it with the tea. She held Ehren's gaze a moment, and then turned back to Laine. "Well, there's no denying it, you've the stamp of Grannor in your faces. But there are plenty of us to be had in Therand."

"My mother wrote a letter," Laine said, pulling it out from where it had been tucked in his sword belt—the scabbard empty now, along with Ehren's—at the small of his back. It was, of course, a little the worse for wear, but several weeks in his saddlebags had done most of that. He fanned the air with it, hoping it wasn't too damp with his sweat, then gave up and handed it to the T'ierand.

She took it without remarking on its condition, broke the seal, and neatly caught the ring that fell out. She scanned the letter quickly, glanced up at Laine, and read it again. "Do you know what this says?"

"I haven't read it," Laine said, suddenly wondering if he should have done so before his mother sealed it. "I know it's safer for my parents right now if we're away from . . . where we live. I also know they'll worry less if they think we're staying here."

She raised an eyebrow at him, then looked at Ehren; they exchanged what looked like a knowing glance. Laine felt a prickle of irritation, but before he could put words to it, she asked, "And what would *you* like?"

"I'd like them not to worry," Laine said, feeling unaccountably stubborn.

Sherran looked at him for another long moment, then abruptly put the letter on the table, and held out the ring to him. "All right," she said. "We won't push that for now.

I can send a message to Jenorah, to let her know you've reached us safely, if you'd like."

Carefully, Laine took the ring. "Does that mean we can stay?"

"Of course you can. The day when Grannor cannot take in two of its own will be a sad one. Other things . . . will require some discussion." She gave Ehren another glance; he tipped his raised mug at her. "Now, how about that message?"

"That'd be wonderful," Shette started, cutting off when Laine shook his head.

"It'd be better if their location doesn't get out."

"No fear," said Sherran. "We have some rather special courier birds here. I'll have my handler take care of it; all you'll need to do is provide a good image of the area from your thoughts, both large and small scale."

"It'd be a good idea if I looked at a map, first."

"He'll bring his own, the ones the birds are used to working with. We even have some of Solvany—" she gave Ehren a sly look, "—so you can take them all, and never give us a clue to where your parents are." She hesitated, and leaned forward, elbows on the table. "Just tell me this. Are they happy? Did they make the right choice?"

"No one who sees them would ever question it," Ehren told her, answering in Laine's stead. "Love doesn't answer to politics."

"No," she said, giving him a thoughtful look. "It never has."

"What about Ehren?" Shette asked, a thought without introduction; it made them all blink, and the T'ierand seemed positively taken aback. Shette said, "He needs to get home."

"Of course." She gave a small nod and took a deliberate sip of tea. "Jenorah mentioned it. Dannel's idea, she said—and not the first time he's had it." She smiled to herself, but quickly turned her attention back to Ehren. "She says you'd like passage through the Barrenlands."

"I was prepared to ask for myself," Ehren said, "and not entirely without something to offer in return."

"Passage is not something we give lightly," Sherran told him. "In fact, aside from Dannel, I can only name a handful of people within the last century who've crossed on their own."

"It's not something I ask for lightly."

She didn't respond immediately, and Laine decided it was a good moment to try the tea, busying his hands and his tongue. From the corner of his eye, he spotted several young men and women walk into the hall from the kitchen entrance, stop short at the sight of their T'ierand sharing tea with strangers, and then hover uncertainly. Sherran lifted a hand to gesture them in.

"This is no longer the place or time to talk," she said. "They need to prepare for dinner, which you are welcome to join. Come at the first bell; the second is for the servants and yardmen. I'm afraid I'll be tied up for the rest of the evening, but we'll talk again tomorrow. My bird handler will be with you shortly."

"There's one more thing," Ehren said, just as Laine leaned forward to get up. Surprised, he settled back again, unable to guess what Ehren was up to this time. Ehren didn't make him wait; he dipped his hand into his saddlebags and came out with the small thick vial he'd found on the dead wizard after the avalanche. Laine had forgotten about it, but not about its magical properties. Piercing blue-white light seemed to glow right through Ehren's fingers, burning Laine's eyes. He quickly looked away, catching Sherran's gaze in the process.

Her expression was unhappy, a quickly disguised flinch. "Where did you get that?"

"From someone who couldn't tell us what it was," Ehren said. "It may have come from this country. I hoped you would recognize it."

Laine suddenly realized that Sherran, too, was averting her gaze from the vial. Ehren must have noticed, as well, for he took it back down below the level of the table. Laine heaved a sigh of relief, and Sherran gave him a quick, perceptive glance. But her full attention was on Ehren. "I

have an idea what it might be," she said. "But I'd prefer
not to say anything until I have Marcail, my resident magic
user, take a look at it. Are you willing to let me take it?"

"If you're willing to give it back, no matter what it might
be," Ehren said without hesitation.

After a moment, she gave the slightest of nods. Ehren
reached for one of the thick cloth napkins piled in the center
of the table and, holding the vial below the edge of the
table, wrapped it up. He then presented it to Sherran,
holding it in the palm of his hand. Her nose wrinkled in
distaste she was obviously trying to suppress, Sherran
carefully took it from him. "I'll get back to you as soon as
Marcail has an answer for me," she said. "And at that point,
perhaps you'll be willing to share some of its history with
me."

"Perhaps," Ehren said, with no promise in the words at
all. He rose from his chair, and Laine hastened to follow,
with some vague realization that remaining seated when
the T'ierand was about to rise was not the thing to do. Ehren
went one further, and offered his hand to Sherran.

Laine didn't really expect her to take it. But she did.

❦

The events of the evening filled Laine's thoughts, and
as tired as he was, they refused to let him sleep. The evening
meal had been a lengthy and sometimes boisterous affair,
and even after the second bell rang for the servants' meal,
many of the participants of the first sitting merely moved
into an adjoining room. There were several musicians with
a variety of string and wind instruments, informally
combining for duets and one memorable quartet; their
constant background noise made the room seem much more
crowded and lively than it had actually been.

Other than Shette, Laine and Ehren, there were a large
number of various Grannor relatives—some on a brief visit,
and some who obviously lived wherever the T'ierand lived,
although aside from one brother of Laine's age, there didn't
seem to be any immediate family members. There were,
of course, a number of suitors for the T'ierand's hand, but

there was very little true rivalry to be found among them. None of them seemed to be trying very hard; it was almost like they were playing out roles in a game.

Shette had found several girls her own age, and they were already filling her with ideas of what true T'ieran ways meant as far as fashion and deportment were concerned. Laine was relieved to find her chatting so amiably among them, especially when he realized the topics never had anything to do with where Shette had come from, and exactly who her family was. He'd walked by once when they were asking about Ehren, breaking into fits of giggles, and gave the slightest shake of his head when Shette glanced over at him. She changed the subject without hesitation.

Well, no doubt she figured she'd have plenty of opportunity to tell them what she knew of the enigmatic Guard. And there was also no doubt in Laine's mind that she could make herself comfortable here for the rest of the summer.

As for himself . . . he was less sure. It wasn't so much the thought of staying here, on Clan Grannor grounds in Therand, as it was the feeling that his time here would be useless. He'd be fighting his dreams—which he had no doubt would return to nag at him—while Ehren was off fighting battles on his own.

They're battles Ehren knows how to fight and you don't, he told himself, flopping over to lie on his stomach. The bed was too big, maybe that was the problem. Or too comfortable. He had been assigned here with Ehren, who was still out and about, while Shette was already sound asleep in an adjoining room; there was a door, but at the moment only a heavy curtain was drawn between the rooms. It had been Shette's decision, and Laine didn't have to think hard to know that despite her excitement, she was uneasy at the thought of being completely alone in this huge keep.

He wasn't sure he blamed her. But they'd both have plenty of time to get used to it. Awash in comfort, with a cool breeze blowing in through the wide, unshuttered window, Laine fell asleep, and straight into True Dreaming.

He skimmed through the visions with a slight curve at the corner of his mouth, for these were the dreams of old, the dreams of Dannel and Jenorah, and their growing love. Triggered by Laine's presence in this keep where the couple had first realized the potential of their feelings, the dreams showed him things he had never seen before—or perhaps never noticed, without the background of the story to make sense of them. The black and red colors of Grannor, the obvious importance and status of Jenorah's family . . . The struggles that Laine saw were made sweeter by his inner knowledge that in the end, the lovers won their battle to be together.

And then the dreams took him deeper, past the place where he could *watch* and into the place where he simply *was*, then spitting him out to live Benlan's death anew, into a yard full of desperate Guards who were first fighting for their lives, and then laying them down to protect their king.

Ehren! Ehren, I need you!

Benlan, watching his men and women die before him and knowing they were lives given in vain. His arm ran warm with slick blood, and his sword slipped in his weakening grip. *Ambush, who knew, who'd had the magic to overcome Varien's protections?* And then, *Don't think, idiot king— fight!* But it was too late, and the smell of blood was all around him; he took another cut to his belly and suddenly had no strength. *Gut wound . . . no hope for that. Ehren!*

The sword tipped out of his hand as Benlan/Laine stumbled to his knees. Someone grabbed his hair from behind, and pulled his head back, arching his neck for the final cut. Death touched him, ran its cold fire through the fatal wounds he felt as much as Benlan had. His world was already fading, but his awareness of something else was growing. Someone was watching. Someone making sure of his death, from afar. Laine *knew* he'd be able to see who it was, if only he could turn around somehow—

No, someone was screaming. Not the hoarse cries of men in pain, but a shriller, frightened sound. Familiar . . . and even annoying.

Shette.

Laine suddenly became aware that there was a hard, cold floor at his back, and that Shette was screaming right in his face, shaking his shoulders so hard his head went bump-bump-bump against the floor. "Stop that," he gasped at her, as best he could when his teeth were clacking together.

She released him immediately, and threw herself on his chest, sobbing.

"Shette," he said, dazed, lifting one arm to pat her back, "What's wrong?" She only held him tighter, unable to speak. There was some commotion outside the room, but not enough to latch on to, now that Shette had let him go. Without something in this world to grab his attention, something shouting at him nose to nose, Laine couldn't fight the fugue that so often snared him at the interruption of a True Dream.

Shette seemed to sense it; she raised herself and said, "Laine, no—come back!" And then, when the disturbance at the doorway increased, "Ehren! Ehren, help me, I can't get him back!"

There was no denying Ehren, who was suddenly there. "Laine." The voice was sharp but calm, if not compelling enough. But when Ehren lifted him up by the front of his shirt and slapped his face, not once but several times, shouting at him the whole while, it was enough to cut through that quicksand of hazy reality. Laine blinked, and opened his mouth—

And suddenly things erupted into chaos again. Ehren disappeared, ripped away from him, and Laine thunked back to the floor, this time making a half-hearted attempt to soften the landing. Shette screamed again, a background to the punctuation of hard blows against flesh. Only this time, she was screaming Ehren's name.

Laine rolled over to his knees, shaking his head, surprised to find it was actually clearing. Then someone landed on him and he sprawled face-first. If only people would stop *dropping* him—

"Hold!"

The T'ierand's crystal clear command brought instant silence. Even Laine froze in the midst of shaking the weight off his back.

For a long moment, there was silence, broken only by Shette's great sniffle. When Sherran spoke again, her voice was unyielding and hard. "Sem, get off of Laine and see how badly Sandy's hurt. Ehren, I hope you have an explanation for this."

Finally, Laine was able to turn around, and if he wasn't on his feet, he was at least sitting up. Shette was cringing against the doorway between their rooms, dressed in nightgown and tears, her frightened gaze fixed on the T'ierand. Ehren, standing tightly erect and looking nothing but dangerous, had a red-and-black dressed form crumpled at his feet, and a smear of blood from a small cut on his cheek. Sem, the man who'd been on Laine, was staggering over to check his injured partner.

"I'm waiting," Sherran said tightly. "You're a guest here, Ehren, but if it pleases you to think about your answers in detention, I would be glad to oblige you."

"It wasn't his fault!" Shette blurted. "They attacked him from behind—what was he supposed to *do*?"

Ehren raised an eyebrow at the T'ierand. Laine read it as defiance and didn't understand why Ehren didn't just tell her what had happened—what*ever* that had been. He, for one, wanted to know.

Sherran gave Ehren a long look and turned to her guard. "Sem?"

Sem was prodding Sandy's shoulder. "Dislocated, I think, ma'am."

She took a deep breath, gave Ehren another sharp look. "It could have been worse, I'm sure. Unless someone tells me exactly what happened here, it *will* get worse." She zeroed in on Shette. "Your brother looks like he just fell on his head, your friend Ehren doesn't feel cooperative— and *you* look like you saw it all. Talk."

Shette wiped her wrist under her nose, looking nervously from Ehren to the T'ierand. "It was one of his Dreams.

Ehren, you should have seen him, I thought he was dying, and he wasn't *breathing* and I got him back, but then I couldn't keep him the way you can, and then when you got him, those two jumped you from behind—"

Sherran shook her head, making an abrupt cutting motion with both hands. "That makes remarkably little sense. I don't suppose I should be surprised. Sem, report!"

Sem blinked, still looking as dazed as Laine felt. "You told us to protect these two as if they were high-ranked Grannor. We heard the young lady screaming, and when we got here, this fellow was on top of her brother. Of course we moved to protect him."

"Ehren was *helping* Laine!" Shette broke in.

Sherran rolled her eyes, and the corners of Ehren's mouth broke a smile. Laine grumbled, "I'm confused, and *I* was here."

"Ma'am, I swear to you we only acted to protect him," Sem started anxiously, and Sherran cut him off with a short shake of her head.

"Be at ease, Sem. You acted in honor. If Sandy can walk, take him to the surgeon. If not, get some help up here for him."

Sem nodded, prodding Sandy to his feet with a spate of grunts and murmured encouragements. When they'd limped out the door together, Sherran crossed her arms and leaned back against the door frame. "No lack of excitement with you folks around, I can see. Now, since it seems the immediate crisis is over, do you think you can explain this so a simple T'ierand can understand?"

Ehren said dryly, "I expect we'll manage," but there was a touch of humor in his eyes. "It'll be difficult to top Shette's version, though."

Gingerly, Laine climbed to his feet. "What time is it? What are you doing up, Ehren? Are Shette and I the only ones who actually went to sleep tonight?"

"It seems that way," Sherran said. "Though it shouldn't surprise you to hear a T'ierand's duties often keep her working until the small hours of the morning." She looked at Ehren.

He shrugged. "I was out with the boys. Just on my way up."

Sherran looked at Laine. "And you were sleeping in your clothes, and you had a Dream." She managed to put the correct amount of emphasis on the word, although she clearly had no idea what it was all about. "Fine. Shette, you of all of us are properly dressed for bed. I suggest you get back into it. And you two—since you've managed to chase away the thoughts of sleep I had so carefully cultivated, you may accompany me to the study, where we'll have some wine and you'll make clear what happened here. I suspect it has more relevance to your sudden appearance in Therand than you've told me."

"I don't know that that's true," Ehren said. "I would classify it as an unrelated bonus."

"Nonetheless," Sherran told him, and left it at that, the command implicit. Laine exchanged a glance with Ehren, who gave him a sudden and totally unexpected grin before following the T'ierand out the door.

Sherran slowly turned the wine glass in her hand, resting it thoughtfully against her full lower lip. If Ehren had been forced to guess, he would have classified her expression as slightly embarrassed.

"I may have an answer of sorts for you," she said, and downed the last swallow of sweet red wine, reaching for the bottle. Ehren moved it closer to her, across the short, round table between them, and settled back into his well-stuffed chair, resting his ankle over his knee. Laine, the third of the trio, looked less relaxed; his attention was riveted on Sherran.

"*You* know why I didn't fall to Solvany's curse?" Laine asked.

She'd listened attentively while Ehren and Laine—but mostly Ehren—told her about Laine's Sight and Dreams. Ehren told her they tended to hold to him too tightly, but deliberately omitted the details of those dangerous Dreams—for Benlan's death was not Therand's business.

Neither of them had expected Sherran not only to accept the fact of the Solvan curse so quickly, but to come up with answers they didn't have. Not that she was making it easy for Laine; she seemed to be weighing how much she, too, wanted to reveal. She wiped her finger up the side of the glass to catch a sliding drop of spilled wine, and absently licked the wine from her finger. Then she looked squarely at Laine and said, "We cursed the Solvans, you see."

Ehren got it first, and snorted, shaking his head. *Therand's ruling line, cursed. Solvany's ruling line, cursed. And Laine a son of both of them.*

Sherran looked at him and shrugged. "It was the fashionable thing to do at the time."

Ehren couldn't help it; he laughed out loud.

Sherran kept her reaction to a smile, though it looked like it would much rather be an undignified and wholehearted grin. After a minute, she said, "A hundred years ago, things were pretty tense. There were factions in both countries that wanted to remove the Barrenlands so we could change our cold war into an active one. Wiser heads prevailed . . . and apparently came up with the same way to help appease the warmongers."

Was the smuggling older than Varien's Upper Level appointment? If so, an open border a century ago would hardly be desirable—no more so than a year ago. Any wizard involved would lose the control of the black market goods. *Whatever they were.* Curses, to appease the Levels and keep the Barrenlands whole.

Laine had clearly missed their exchange; he was staring blankly at nothing. "The Solvan children I keep seeing," he said. "The ones who always seem so oblivious to the world around them, like their minds were trapped somewhere else . . ." Shette and Unai had turned into those eerie children, time after time.

Sherran nodded. "Some have been stillborn; some simply seem to have no wit at all. I'm not surprised they haven't figured it out yet," she said to Ehren. "They've only had a couple generations, and since the affected children are in the family line, it's natural they'd think it was in the blood. Which it is, I suppose, in a way. But *we* knew there was something going on a long time ago—to have so many firstborn turn out blind? It didn't affect the T'ierands who'd already started their families before they took office, of course . . . and you'll notice the rest of us now avoid starting our families while in office. Why do you think there are so few of the eligible Grannor here? At the moment, they're simply not interested in me."

Ehren raised an eyebrow at her and let it go unaccompanied by comment. He'd not let such a thing discourage him.

Laine still seemed to be chewing it over. "So from my father's side I should be witless, and from my mother's I should be blind. And instead I have Sight and get chased by Dreams."

"It makes sense, in a strange sort of way," Sherran said. "Mind you, Laine, I think you came out lucky. There's no predicting how those curses could have resonated off of one another."

"Are you going to give Ehren passage through the Barrenlands?" Laine asked abruptly. His dazed look had vanished, and turned intent. Ehren wasn't sure that boded well.

Sherran, too, regarded him somewhat warily. "Why?"

"Because I want to go with him."

"Laine—" Ehren started immediately, while Sherran's fine eyebrows rose. Laine cut off both their protests.

"Shette can stay here," he said. "But Ehren . . . the ring . . . you remember what I said about triggering the Dream—"

"That's too dangerous," Ehren said, doing his own share of interrupting. Sherran instantly went still, like a stalking cat who doesn't want to be seen.

"Maybe you wouldn't think so if *you* were the one being chased by these Dreams, and never able to see who's killed you, over and over again! I've got to get through them, and using your ring is the only way I can think of to do it. Besides, after what I saw tonight, I think I *can* lead you to whoever killed Benlan."

Instantly, Ehren forgot the other complications of this trip—the increasing border trouble, the military activity in Loraka, the unusual interest in his activities—and especially the trouble that waited for him in Kurtane. He stiffened, dropping his foot to the ground to shift forward and gift Laine with his most intent stare.

He had not a moment's doubt that if Laine saw something in his Dreams, it was accurate. There was no way the young man could have fabricated the facts of Benlan's death, which he'd related to Ehren outside Everdawn. "Tell me," he said. He sensed more than saw Sherran's acute interest in his reaction, but ignored her for Laine.

But Laine shook his head. "I can't," he said. "I . . . didn't quite see it yet. And even if I had, I couldn't give you enough of a description to make a difference. But I'd recognize him. *If* I went all the way with the Dream."

Sharp disappointment flooded Ehren. "Do you think Shette was frightened out of her senses for nothing, Laine? Will it do either of us any good if you see something, and then die without passing it on?"

Sherran cleared her throat. It was a deliberate noise. When Ehren looked at her, it was with his priorities sharply established—he was a Solvan King's Guard, with his own agenda—and she reacted accordingly, with more than a touch of the formality that had gone by the wayside for this late night discussion. "No one is cleared for passage through the Barrenlands yet," she said. "No one has given me a reason to make that decision yet."

"What suffices as reason?" Ehren shot back at her.

She didn't miss a beat. "Who *are* you?" she said. "Why are you in my lands? What do you want?"

"My name is Ehren," he said, though he knew well enough what she meant, and raised a hand to forestall the anger that flooded her face at his sidestepping answer. "I'm more than just Solvan's Son. I'm a King's Guard, and I was in Benlan's closest ranks. Others in Solvany want to put Benlan's death behind them, but I'm not prepared to do that yet. To stop me from causing trouble, I was sent to find some people. I found them. I've found some other things, too, and now I need to return to Solvany as quickly as possible. This was the best way to do that. Now *you* tell me if I'm wasting my time, because if I am, I'll leave immediately and head for the long road. There's too much happening to spend my evenings drinking wine instead of on my way to Kurtane."

"I see," Sherran said, taking it all in stride. She took a measured sip of wine, sat back in her chair, and watched him, looking for the world like she had taken in his burst of information, processed it, and was merely taking her time to respond—because she was the T'ierand, and it was her time to take. "Well, this explains what happened to Sandy and Sem—although a little time in personal combat would seem to be in order. Even a King's Guard should have trouble with two of my own."

"Depends what they're expecting," Ehren said, stepping on his growing irritation. He hadn't judged her as a woman who would toy with a man, not when she knew what was at stake for him.

She saw it in him anyway, and smiled quiet sympathy at him, a genuine and guileless expression that made him take a deep breath and reestablish his temper. She said, "I need to know if what you've found—if what you're involved in—affects my country."

Did it? Ehren thought about the border trouble—there'd been evidence it was increased on this end of the Trade Road, as well. And if there was a pass on Laine's caravan route, and Lorakan wizards were protecting it, it meant Therand as well as Solvany was at risk. He shook his head, more to himself than anything else. It was ten percent fact and ninety percent feeling.

But, as he'd told Laine, he'd been a Guard so long precisely because he trusted those feelings. Did what he'd found affect Therand? "It might," he said. "There seems to be some serious unrest and warmongering in Loraka. You probably know about the problems at your border—you may not know that the same thing, only to a greater extent, is happening at the Solvany-Loraka border as well. And it's possible—*possible*—that there's a tricky pass that the existence of the Barrenlands has pushed from our minds. Both our countries could be at risk if the Lorakans learn of it, and I have reason to believe at least *some* of them have. Imagine soldiers keeping us busy at the Lorakan borders—while the bulk of their army comes at us from the Barrenlands."

She nodded, and considered him over her wine glass, drinking in the intensity of his stare and not showing any signs of unease. Merely . . . a measuring. Laine only watched, as he'd been doing, obviously out of his element here as well as behind a sword. Finally, she said, "In that case, I had best let you go. It would profit Therand nothing if Solvany is threatened even as we are. And if there's nothing to it . . . well, you're the one taking the risk of the crossing."

"The risk?" Laine asked.

She looked at him, something of pity in her eyes. "Didn't you know? The Barrenlands are kind to no man, royal dispensation or no."

Ehren wasn't surprised when Laine, tired and fighting renewed haziness from his dream, bid good night while there was still plenty of wine to be had. And he wasn't the least disappointed to find himself alone with the T'ierand, although it was past midnight and there was fatigue starting to show in her eyes, as well.

She was looking at him somewhat pensively, as if she'd forgotten the conversation they'd just had and was thinking of going on to something new. Ehren watched her, letting his eyes rove over her and thinking back to the moment they'd met. Amazing how it'd only taken a few words to drink in the quality of her. Amazing how much he wanted more. He didn't even care about the folly of it, a Solvan King's Guard and the Therand T'ierand, Clan Grannor in all its glory—but he *did* care about justice for Benlan, and not even a woman like this could slow him down.

The glory of Grannor did not miss his examination. She

was small but solid, with precise features nearly dominated by her large eyes. Her lips, he decided, looked like they needed a good kiss or two—maybe even three—although at the moment she had the edge of her lower lip caught between her teeth. Not a happy expression.

It was not, he thought, his frank admiration causing that expression. She was too strong a woman to let that bother her. In fact, she was too strong a woman to let anything of insignificance bother her, so he asked, "What is it?"

She released her lip. "You're going to let him come with you? To trigger those dreams? From what I've heard . . . it doesn't seem like a very good idea. Dangerous, one might say."

One might. "Yes," he said, answering both question and observation. Then he hesitated, took a long, slow breath, shifting through his thoughts to find the best words to make her understand. "Sherran, Laine's a grown man. He knows what he wants, and he knows the risks. And he knew what he was doing, dangling Benlan's killer in front of me like that. I'm Benlan's man, and he's dead. What lengths do you think your people would go to, if you had been similarly slaughtered?"

After a moment, she said quietly, "I would hope to have at least one with the same loyalty Benlan has in you."

"If you don't, your people are fools," Ehren said with feeling, and then cleared his throat. "Besides, unless you deny him, there's nothing I can say that will stop Laine. Sometimes I think his Sight directs him as much as he directs it."

"Yes," Sherran said. "Magic can be like that."

Ehren gave her a sharp look. *She knows*, he thought. Never mind that little charade of handing the blue vial over to her wizard—Ehren would bet anything that Sherran had more than a passing acquaintance with magic, herself. "Was that vial what you thought it was, then?" he asked, making no attempt to segue into the question.

She hesitated another moment, and then dipped her hand in the pocket at the side of her long, casual tunic. It was a well-worn, comfortable piece of clothing, something that told him she'd really rather be off-duty. On the small, round table between them, she set a tightly wrapped cylinder. Quietly, she said, "I'd like to know where you got this."

He raised an eyebrow. "Without telling me what it is? I don't think so."

A frown drew her brows together, though he didn't think it was anger at him. Concern, then, and frustration. Which meant there was something in that vial worth it all.

"Sherran," he said, and nothing more.

She threw herself back in her chair and with one practiced motion freed her hair of the thong that held it back and scratched her scalp at the freedom. She looked at him another moment, considering. "It's contraband of the highest order. I'd thought we'd put a stop to its production several years ago. Obviously I was mistaken—this batch is fresh enough." She made a face, complete exasperation. "Damn them, anyway."

"Damn who?" Ehren said, under the strong impression she didn't mean whoever had made the substance.

"The young magic users who think it won't happen to them. The ones who think they can get away with using it." She shook her head, her gaze going inward. "Damn them," she whispered to herself.

Ehren picked the vial up, and turned it over in his hands. "It's magic, I know that much. Laine can hardly glance at it. Nor can you." Ehren gave her a pointed look.

She sighed. "It's deadly. Taken in minute doses, it enhances a wizard's ability to channel magic, and enhances it significantly."

"And?"

"And, over time, its side effects kill."

Ehren merely raised his eyebrow at her.

"It gets worse," she said. "It's almost instantly addictive. That's why it's so important we destroy the production sites. Far too many Therand youth have succumbed to its lure— that's what it's called, mage lure. It's the rare individual who can escape after using it."

Mage lure. Hetna's *ML*.

"This," Ehren said, hefting the heavy glass, "was not found in Therand."

She frowned at him, slowly sitting up straight in the chair. "It has to have been. There are detection spells at the border, and only Therand grows the raw material."

"Loraka," he told her. "In the mountains." *Near Dannel's pass.* If a wizard was going to smuggle something, wouldn't he make it profitable in more ways than one? Who better to have access to young magic users? And how many apprentices had Varien been through in his position as First Level Wizard? A perfect way to control who lived to support him . . . and who died if they refused to. Ehren did a quick tally of Varien's successful apprentices, the ones who had moved on. There was Bevis, to whom Varien sent many of his own subtly unsatisfactory apprentices, and Thayer, who was so reclusive, and Farica, who lived closest to the border. Any one of them could be involved in this.

Ehren thought of the young woman who had greeted him upon his entry to Varien's rooms, and felt the pleasure of being in this room with the T'ierand grow distant, pushed aside by cold anger. She was not the sort Varien would approve of.

"Ehren," Sherran said, and the warmth in her voice reached through his wrath. He looked up at her, almost startled. She was leaning back in the chair again, slouching more than anything, and fiddling with a tangle in her thick dark hair, her fingers moving gently, absently. "I don't know who you were thinking of just then, but I hope it wasn't me."

He was startled a moment, but then shook his head, smiling. "No."

She just looked at him. He very much felt the tables were being turned, and that her open appraisal amused her as much as pleased her. He cleared his throat. "If you recall the pass I mentioned a while ago, I think you'll see there *is* a way for the mage lure to get into Loraka without triggering your detection spells."

"You know more than that," she said without hesitation, surprising him.

"I do," he told her, and opened his mouth to say more—demurral—but she held up her hand.

"No," she said. "It's all right. Or rather, it's not. If you were anybody else, I wouldn't let it stop with that. But you . . ." she smiled at him. "Insisting won't do me any good. And knowing that, I'd rather leave you with the best possible memories of this place."

He stood up. It was one fluid motion—until he hit the hitch in his hip. She noticed, of course, and he gave a rueful grin. "The wizard I got that drug from brought an avalanche down on me first. If Shette stays here long enough, I'm sure you'll hear about it. Believe about half of it, if you want the truth."

"I know how to listen to a teenage girl," Sherran said. "I was one, once, a very long time ago. And I even had my share of crushes on dashing warriors."

He stood in front of her, looking down at her; he could see in her eyes she knew exactly what she'd said. "I have to go," he told her.

"And I have to stay." She stood up to meet him, and her head only came to his chest. A foot away, close enough to touch, and neither of them did it. For a moment, they just stood there. Breathing. Aware. She looked up at him and said, "But perhaps it won't always be that way."

Chapter 13

Sherran and a handful of her guards rode to the border with Laine and Ehren. Shette was along on Nell, her face uncommonly pinched and unhappy. Her bid to join them on this journey had been brief. Her attempt to keep Laine from going was not played out yet, and Ehren wished she'd get it over with. There was no stopping Laine unless Sherran refused him passage, and she was not the kind who made other people's decisions for them. That didn't mean, Ehren told himself, that Laine would end up getting his hands on the ring. But the lure of it was strong for both of them.

It was a breezy morning, and the Grannor pennant carried by one of Sherran's men lifted with the play of air, as did the long black tail of hair down Sherran's back. Though they'd started before dawn, half the morning had passed in the travel, and it was coming on the heat of the day when the Barrenlands showed up on the edge of the horizon. Against the rolling hills of grass, dotted with clumpy tussocks of weed and briar and well-beaten by the cloven hooves of the sheep that wandered these hills, the stark, ochre-brown edge of the Barrenlands was unmistakable.

Ehren had seen the Barrenlands from the Solvan side, a more level section of land with less green and more shrub, and it hadn't struck him as such a blight at the time. From here, it seemed a travesty.

A travesty of half a day's fast travel and a lifetime of madness, if you weren't properly protected.

Ehren realized that the entire party had eased to a halt, and were all silently considering the sickened land before them. Shette's expression was that of mild horror as she looked from the border to her brother and back, but Sherran's face was composed—although she, more than anyone here, knew of the dangers of the land.

"Dannel might not have thought of it," she'd told Ehren, over the last of the wine the evening before. "He came through on a lark, and well-protected. As you should be, given my sanction. But others have risked passage, and not been so lucky."

Ehren had been inclined to say little. The wine was good, the T'ierand was enough to grab any man's attention, and his decision was already made.

Sherran exchanged a glance with Ehren now, and seemed to read something of his determination in his face, for she gave a small smile and lifted her reins, and the group started moving again. Within half an hour they stood at the border, a land-defiling demarcation of green to barren brown, and the guards withdrew while Sherran dismounted and Ehren and Laine followed suit.

Laine went to Nell and looked up at Shette. "I'll be back," he said. "There's no need to let Mum and Da know I'm gone—they've been told I'm safe with the Grannor and that's good enough."

"I don't understand why you think you have to do this," Shette said, biting her lip and sounding only the tiniest bit petulant—which, Ehren thought, was probably a major victory for her. "He's not going to let you use the ring."

"Maybe not," Laine said. "But things change. And I'm not ready to let go of this yet. You only traveled the caravan route once, Shette—but it was what I *did*. Whatever's going on has a part in my life, and not just because I keep Seeing things."

She looked at the foreboding land before them and nodded without saying anything, staring into it for a long, moody moment. Almost without warning, she turned to her brother and threw her arms around his shoulders, bending down to reach him from Nell's back and making the little mare step to the side to keep her balance. Shette's hug was strong and long, and when she broke away she gave Ehren a quick, red-eyed look and said quickly, "Be careful," before she whirled Nell around and cantered away from the border.

Sherran lifted her chin at one of the guards and he followed at a more sedate—and discreet—pace.

"Well, that was easier than it might have been," Laine said, sighing.

"We had a talk yesterday," Sherran said, and was rewarded with a look of surprise from Laine. "I have the impression she's done a lot of growing up this summer, Laine."

He nodded, looking at Shette's diminishing figure. "I expect she has. I did, my first summer out."

She shifted into efficiency; Ehren was glad. It would be easier for them all. "Generally, this is the only magic a T'ierand knows, but we do know it well, gentlemen. It'll get you through the Barrenlands if you don't disturb it— and back, if you decided to turn around immediately. It lasts a full day, but no more." She fished into a pocket along the bottom edge of her tunic—for she was dressed formally again, red tunic belted with black leather, over black trousers; the scabbard at her side was black, and her black, knee-high riding boots were trimmed with red. Very official, Ehren thought, as she opened her hand to Laine and showed him a smooth flat oval of rock. Black, of course. "This will get you home, Laine, if you should decide to come this way. We'll welcome you if you do."

Laine regarded her with some surprise, but it changed to gratitude quickly enough. He took the proffered stone and said, "But what do I do with it?"

She smiled. "I forget that sometimes it takes a while for new things to spread to the more remote areas. It's a spellstone. Trigger it, and it'll release the spell I've placed within it."

Laine glanced at Ehren, who was remembering that Sherran had said, *Generally, this is the only magic a T'ierand knows*. Laine said, "Like Dajania used for you. She seemed to think it wouldn't work unless you triggered it just right."

"It might not work the first time," Sherran agreed. "It's more or less a matter of holding it with the proper intent and making a firm inner command. You'll know when it works—you'll recognize the feeling." She put a hand on his arm, and wove the other into the crook of Ehren's elbow as he held Shaffron's reins. She closed her eyes and Ehren watched her face, studied it, almost, as she concentrated. It was serene, and the only sign of effort was the tiny hold her teeth had on her lower lip. He barely noticed the cool wash of magic through his veins, and was still watching her when she opened her eyes. "That's what you'll be looking for," she said. "Don't lose the stone, Laine, or you'll be going home the long way around."

"I might, anyway, if I can't get it to work," Laine said, but the good-natured expression that generally found a place on his features was back where it belonged, and he turned back to his horse and tucked the stone away in the bottom of his saddlebag.

Ehren looked down at Sherran's hand, still resting firmly on his arm. Glancing at her guards, she moved up close to him, and dipped into her pocket again, taking his hand to press another stone into it. "And *you* don't lose this. In case you should ever find a reason to return."

Ehren turned the stone over in his hand, and ran his thumb across the smooth surface. She was standing very close to him, the T'ierand and the King's Guard, and she had to tilt her head back to meet his eyes. He looked down at her, and though his mouth gave the merest of quirks on one side, his eyes crinkled at the corners in a quiet smile. "I won't lose it," he told her.

They stood that way for a moment, until Ehren looked up to find Laine watching him with some surprise, and perhaps a little suspicion that he'd been left out of something important. Sherran released the hand that held the stone, and stepped away so he could gather his reins and mount.

When Laine had done the same, she looked up at them both and said, "The spell holds as long as you don't do anything to negate it. That's where most people get into trouble. For men of lesser spirit, it would have been best not to mention it at all, but . . ." she smiled at them, and lifted one shoulder in a shrug. "Even so, 'tis best not to give you time to ponder on it. We all have some small bit of magic, some more than others. And while the Barrenlands don't bother beasts, even those travelers who are spelled against the Barrenlands feel the oppression of it. To counter that, they often bring into play, all unthinking, what little bit of magic they might have." She put her hands on her hips and stared at them. "Don't," she said, and it was to Laine she looked longest. "You will feel the lack of your own magic, Laine, but don't reach for it. My protection for you will withstand all from without. It cannot stand what comes from within. And now that you know, it would be better if you forgot, and simply set yourselves to crossing this hellish strip. Guides grant you safe journey."

"Encouraging words," Ehren told her, but reserved the slightest quirk of a smile for her, the last good-bye. He turned Shaffron to the Barrenlands while Laine was still trying to form his questions. No use in giving him time to wonder exactly what Sherran was talking about.

Shaffron, while not affected by the Barrenlands as a whole, had some serious reservations about placing his feet on ground that changed color and texture so abruptly. They danced more than walked into the life-leached land, while Shaffron blew rolling snorts high in his nose and Ricasso alternately crowded their quarters and hung back. "Boys," Ehren muttered at them, "you're not making a good impression."

Ehren heard Sherran laugh, and then he was in the Barrenlands and the sound cut off. The wind against his cheek died down, and looking at the ground, Ehren would have sworn he saw the hoof prints from the last man to ride this way—and he somehow knew the signs of their own passage would remain until the next traveler obliterated them.

"Ehren?" said Laine from behind him, and Ehren twisted in the saddle to find Laine had crossed the border as well.

He wasn't taking it well. Pale and practically reeling in the saddle, he clutched at his horse's mane, taking deep gulps of air. Ehren stopped Shaffron and let Laine's horse draw up alongside before moving again; as they walked, he leaned down and wrapped his hand around Laine's upper arm, digging his fingers in. "Ignore it," he said, his voice harsh and without sympathy. "Ride on and ignore it." To punctuate his command, he sent Shaffron into a fast trot, something that Laine would have to concentrate on if he didn't want to bruise his bottom.

The horses exchanged repeated snorts of comment, little sneezelike exclamations that told Ehren he'd gotten their attention as well. He kept them all moving, and when he looked back again—for Laine's smaller horse quickly lost ground—Laine was looking less bereft and more just plain annoyed.

"All right, you got me," he said, the second time Ehren looked back. "Can we stop now? That or canter!"

Ehren laughed and touched Shaffron's sides; the horse moved into a relaxed canter and from behind Laine said, *"Thank* you," making it clear that all his sarcasm was still intact, if not his magics. They cantered through the desolate, oppressive land, and what dust was stirred by their passage settled quickly and heavily to the ground.

Ehren took them down to a walk before Laine's Nimble grew too tired; they had a long day of traveling through this place, and the last thing he wanted was to extend it because the pony pushed too hard, trying to keep up with Shaffron and Ricasso.

"This must be what the Hells are like," Laine muttered, coming alongside Shaffron.

"From the tales I've heard, I wouldn't doubt it," Ehren said. "Those who stumble in here without protection don't come out again. Foolish of me not to realize there was danger even with the T'ieran's sanction. Although," he looked sharply at Laine, "I take it you've got yourself under control? Not fighting this place any longer?"

Laine made a face. "I'm trying," he said. "It's . . . not easy."

"Try hard," Ehren said sharply. "There's a reason the Barrenlands have managed to keep Solvany and Therand apart for centuries, even though it takes less than a day to cross it. Without protection, the Barrenlands will take more than your magic away. They'll take your sight, your hearing, the feel of your feet against the ground and the air against your face. It's like being blind in every sense you have, and even if you're only two steps over the border, there's very little chance you'll find your way out again."

Laine, already pale, closed his eyes. "Sherran might have mentioned it."

"Would knowing have changed your mind?"

It only took an instant's thought. "No," Laine said. "I guess not. And there's no way she could have *described* to me what it feels like to be without whatever magic my Sight brings to me. It's one of those things . . . I just couldn't have comprehended, not without feeling it myself. But . . . I take it you don't feel any different."

That wasn't quite true. He felt . . . dulled. He thought that here, he wouldn't be able to count on the leaps of intuition and occasional preternaturally quick reaction that had, in the past, saved his life. But to Laine he said, "Nothing significant. And I take it that you *do*."

Laine's expression answered the question for him; after a moment, he said, "I'm getting used to it. I was dizzy, there at first. And everything looks different. Not that I could tell you just *how*—Hells, this place makes *every*thing look a little brown, you and me included."

That was true. Even Shaffron's fire-chestnut coat was drab. "The less time we spend in here, the better," Ehren said by way of agreement, and took up a gentle trot again.

They'd gone another two hours before Ehren dared to give them any kind of extensive break, but the horses were ready for it, and so was his leg. Pulling back to eye Laine, he eased Shaffron down into a walk.

Laine's face, he thought, still showed the tension of the Barrenlands pressing in on him. But his eyes were distracted, and . . . elsewhere. "You all right?"

"Fine," Laine said, not taking any time to think about it. After another moment, he finally noticed Ehren's close scrutiny. "What?"

"I'm not sure I believe you."

Laine shrugged. "I'm not comfortable, but I'm all right. There's a difference. Besides, I was just thinking . . ."

"What?" Ehren asked, not sure he really wanted to know.

"This. The Barrenlands. They're behind it all, you know. Without them, there wouldn't be any smuggling—or at least, it wouldn't be solely under the control of some wizard somewhere. There wouldn't have been a need for my parents to run to Loraka, or the curse that I got from both lines. I wouldn't have been needed to guide Ansgare's caravan . . . and I wouldn't have met you in the mountains, caught in that spell."

"Stop," Ehren said. "You'll drive yourself crazy that way. And me, too, if I listen to you."

"But I'm right."

Ehren sent a glance heavensward. "Without the Barrenlands, our two countries would have fought one another to oblivion, back when we barely preferred iron to bronze. Whatever they set into motion, they did it a long time ago."

"Still," Laine said. He looked around the featureless terrain, varied only slightly by barely rolling land. Ochre sky met brown earth so subtly it was hard to tell where one stopped and the other began. "It's a more powerful place than just the magic that goes into it."

"That it is."

Laine sighed and patted Nimble's neck. "And I've got to come back through it. Alone. If I can get up the nerve, I suppose." He considered Ehren a moment. "You've got a stone, too, right from Sherran's hand. And it looked to me like you'd be welcome back. Very welcome. Just how late did you two stay up together the other night?"

Ehren gave him a look meant to quell all such questions. "Late enough to make sure you children were sleeping all right." He would have stayed with her all night in that study, listening to her inquire about Shaffron's breeding and Guard training, and even about the details of Benlan's death—a matter he'd found astonishingly easy to brace with her, even when her next question had them sparring like a sword fight. But she'd been tired, and they'd reluctantly parted ways.

"Ouch," Laine said, physically ducking both Ehren's words and his glare, but sneaking a grin in there as well. "Well, at least you discovered Therand had something worth your attention, although I saw you looking pretty closely at the horses, too."

Ehren cantered away from him, and pretended he didn't hear Laine's laughter following.

What slight humor they'd shared quickly faded, and the oppression of the Barrenlands bore down on them. Laine was grim and worn by the time they saw Solvany on the horizon, and his expression was set, a man enduring what he had to and making it through on strength of will alone. When he didn't react at seeing the end of their passage so near, Ehren pushed the horses back into a trot. The sooner Laine was out of here, the better.

The edge of the Barrenlands was just as distinct on the way out as it had been on the way in. Not quite as aggressively green as Therand, Solvany was nonetheless a jewel against the dull, dead swath of land Ehren and Laine traveled through. Trees and undergrowth—the thick secondary growth of land that had been cleared and then abandoned within recent years—came up right against the sterile dirt and stopped short. When the two men rode into it, they were assaulted by the sounds of birds and the breeze in the trees and blinded by the sunshine, as clouded as it was in the late afternoon. By tacit agreement, they stopped, blinking, and simply sat their horses, breathing in the odor of the foliage they'd just crushed.

"Much better," Laine said after a moment and a huge sigh of relief. "I thought I understood about the Barrenlands, before . . . but now I *know* why that border has worked so well all these years."

"Even if you're protected, it's no easy obstacle," Ehren said, admiring the glint of flame that reclaimed its proper place in Shaffron's coat. "And unprotected . . ."

Laine shuddered. "I'll just take your word on it."

Ehren dismounted; they hadn't stopped to rest since they'd entered the Barrenlands, and the horses deserved a good forage. He stripped Shaffron's bridle off, and the horse quickly took advantage of the chance to wipe his sweat-itchy head against Ehren's shoulder, knocking him off balance.

"Quit," Ehren said sharply. "Your head is too bony for that." He slipped the halter on and left the lead rope trailing as he loosened the girth a notch. Ricasso was already browsing on the leaves within his reach. By the time Laine finished haltering his own horse, Ehren was staring pensively back the way they'd come.

"What?" asked Laine, in a voice that said he wasn't really sure he wanted to know.

"She said we'd be able to go back in there." Ehren was still holding Shaffron's bridle, and he hefted it thoughtfully.

Laine said pointedly, "If we *wanted* to."

"It'd be nice to know." Ehren walked up to the very edge of the green and brown border, with Laine following, trailing his horse.

"But the spell doesn't hold, you said it yourself, you can be lost forever, just two steps from the border!"

Ehren turned to look at him, and grinned at Laine's worried expression. "Let's pretend I have more sense than that." He held out the bridle reins. "Take the ends. You can haul me out if I look stupefied. I only want to go in long enough to be sure it's safe."

Looking distinctly doubtful, Laine accepted the reins, and

held them tightly as Ehren turned back to the Barrenlands and, without any ado, walked right in.

It took him a moment to realize he'd held his breath in the process, and by then it was obvious he was just as capable of perceiving his surroundings as he'd been a moment earlier, even if those surroundings were hardly worth noting. He walked to the end of his impromptu tether, circled, and joined Laine in Solvany again. "I take it I never looked quite stupefied enough to alarm you," he said, as Laine handed the reins back to him.

Laine cracked a grin at him, although there was real relief in his unmatched eyes. "It was close."

Ehren merely harumphed at him. With the bridle jingling against his leg, he made his way back to Shaffron. He tied the bridle atop the saddlebags and scouted ahead, looking for any sign of a trail. It would have been easier if he'd had a clear notion of what part of Solvany they'd emerged in, but he didn't; he had only a general idea.

"What now?" Laine said, when Ehren returned, rubbing the leg that hadn't quite been up to all those hours of riding.

"Now give the horses a break. It's too close to nightfall to go far, but we'll ride another mile or so and try to find some water. Starting tomorrow, we're going to be riding to Kurtane as fast as I can get us there." Ehren lowered himself to the ground and kneaded his upper thigh. *Damn thing.* After a moment, he eased back on the ground and stared up at the wispy layer of thin clouds. *Mares' tails. That means rain.* He hoped they found a good road before then.

Meanwhile, he closed his eyes, intent on taking rest when *he* could get it, too.

Shaffron's snort sounded far away; Ehren's eyes snapped open and he knew instantly he'd been asleep for at least an hour. A short distance away, he heard Laine stretching noisily, so he hadn't been the only one.

"What's up?" Laine's voice was groggy still, but as Shaffron snorted again, and Ricasso called out, Ehren found himself completely alert.

"Get up. Get your sword out, and mount up. If we get into trouble, drop your mule. You can pick him up later, and you can't use him if you're dead, anyway."

"What're you *talking* about?" Laine asked, though Ehren heard him rising as he followed his own advice, and turned his attention to finding his horses.

"Nothing, if we're lucky." With his sword against his leg to avoid catching the brush, Ehren followed the trail the boys had left. "Don't follow too close."

He could practically feel Laine's disgruntlement, but the other did as he said, and that was all that mattered. He found a path before he found the horses—game trail, most likely, no sign of shod hooves aside from those of the boys. Once he knew which way they traveled he didn't bother to check the ground; the horses would stick to the easy way. Within a furlong or two he'd picked up Ricasso, and then, soon after, Shaffron.

Although the chestnut was edgy and had his attention riveted down the trail, Ehren bridled him with no-nonsense efficiency and tightened the girth. Laine was just in sight behind him when he mounted up, and he gestured the younger man forward.

"Something ahead of us," he said quietly. "If they hadn't called out, I'd say boar or bear, but I suspect it's horse."

"And man," Laine added, sighing. "Well, that doesn't mean it's a problem. There's no way anyone could know where we were. We could have come out of the Barrenlands anywhere, if someone even happened to know we went into them in the first place."

Ehren gave him a grin, one that bordered on the predatory. "The way things have gone for us, Laine, we'll assume it's a problem."

"When you put it that way, I have to agree," Laine said ruefully. "Are we . . . just going to sit here and wait?"

Unruffled, Ehren said, "We can hear them moving better if we're not. Let them come to us—until I decide otherwise."

It didn't take long. The path was narrow and the trees were small and thick, and although they heard the sounds of several horses approaching, the newcomers were only thirty-odd yards away when Ehren finally got a good look at them.

King's Guards. Two of them. And although Ehren's first instinct was to relax, his second was *not* to. "Hold there," he called, and they stopped, but not before gaining another several yards.

"That's him, all right," one of the Guards said, and though his face looked vaguely familiar, Ehren couldn't put a name to it. The other man, he knew not at all.

"I'm surprised to see you here," Ehren said, not at all welcoming, "but it seems you expected *me*."

"You, if not him," the man replied with a nod. "And you're to come with us."

"Is something wrong?" Laine asked. He was crowding Ehren from behind, concerned, and had obviously recognized the ailettes and general style of brigandine as those that Ehren had worn when they'd met.

"Back off," Ehren said between his teeth, aiming the words over his shoulder but not turning his head so far that he couldn't keep an eye on the men in front of him.

"What?" Laine at least had the discretion to keep his own voice low. "What's wrong?"

Ehren didn't answer; he backed Shaffron a few measured steps, and Ricasso followed suit behind him. When Laine caught sight of the big sturdy rump heading his way, he turned Nimble right around and circled, yanking the unhappy mule behind him, so they ended up with several horses' lengths between them.

"Oh," Laine muttered loudly. "I get the idea now, thank you."

Ehren ignored him. "We're on our own business," he said. "We'll make our own way."

"We've got orders," the man said, and nodded back at his partner. "We're to bring you back to Kurtane."

"It's a long trip for you, just to ensure I get where I already intend to go," Ehren said. "And unless you can show me signed orders, I won't be needing your company." His voice was flat and final, and he shifted his grip on his sword. Shaffron knew it was unsheathed, and knew just as well what that meant. The chestnut was the horse for tight quarters like this; already he was drawing under himself, ready to respond to the slightest shift of Ehren's weight. *Not the time to sneeze.*

The man hesitated, and then gave what struck Ehren as a particularly forced grin. "Never thought I'd see the day when a Guard would distrust his own like this."

"I don't know you," Ehren said. "I've seen you, but not as a Guard. And I've never seen your friend. If you're King's Guards, they're cycling you through too damned fast." He paused, and added, "Which probably means you're no damned good."

"Ehren!" Behind him, Laine gulped out the word, aghast. But Ehren's attention was on the opposition, for both men had reacted, giving up their pretense of congeniality with one quick exchanged glance. They rushed him, one crowding the flanks of the other but unable to draw up aside in the narrow trail.

Ehren dropped Ricasso's lead as he raised his sword; Shaffron broke into a fast canter from standstill, only a few strides from collision point. Ehren closed the reins and tightened his legs; the chestnut surged forward and up, leaping over an invisible obstacle. When Ehren's sword flashed down from this new, unexpected angle, the leading man fell beneath it, while his horse staggered beneath Shaffron's momentum. Branches raked Ehren's side, momentarily blinding him with leaves as Shaffron was forced off the trail; the noise of whipping foliage, pounding hooves, and grunting horses made up his world until Shaffron broke into the clear.

Blinking his leaf-whipped eyes, Ehren pivoted Shaffron on his hindquarters, facing the men. One hung over his horse's neck, no longer a threat; the other hesitated just beyond disgruntled Ricasso, his horse dancing—and then chose to turn on Laine—much to Laine's obvious astonishment.

"The Barrenlands!" Ehren bellowed over the distance.

Laine instantly dropped the line to his mule and whirled the handy little horse around, disappearing into the woods. The Guard followed—and so did Ehren.

They were out of sight the whole time, but Ehren knew well enough where they were going—and had no doubt that Laine would get there first, considering the advantage he had with his quick-footed mount.

Unless, of course, he fell off.

Ehren ignored the pain shooting through his limb-whipped leg and sent Shaffron after them, but kept him to a high-stepping jig once they turned off the path. If the man was smarter than he looked, he'd stop his pursuit, pull off to the side, and attack Ehren as he rushed by. Ehren did not intend to rush.

But he met no one coming through the trees, and when the Barrenlands were within sight, he stopped altogether, although Shaffron continued to jig in place. Through the brush, he saw Laine, cantering a wide circle within the Barrenlands, one that would bring him back to his point of entry. He seemed to be missing one stirrup entirely, but other than that looked unaffected by his mad dash through the woods. The guard who'd pursued him hesitated at the border, his horse fighting the bit, clearly weighing the idea of following. Ehren could almost read his mind, the tentative conclusion that it *must* be safe if Laine could do it . . .

Ehren grinned. *Why don't you find out?* A shift of his seat, and Shaffron was galloping all out. He reached the Guard just as the man turned to see what was happening, and Shaffron hit the other horse squarely in the shoulder, sending him staggering into the Barrenlands.

The man had started to clutch his horse's mane; instead his hands kept right on going, and he tumbled to the ground, screaming—or, at least, his mouth was open, his face contorted, although Ehren heard nothing from within the ochre lands. The man stopped screaming only when he started retching; by then Laine had circled around and was dismounting. He dropped his reins to the ground and kicked aside the sword the Guard had lost. Then, through the slightly blurring air of the Barrenlands, he gave Ehren a shrug and reached down to grab the man's booted ankles, dragging him toward the border.

Ehren dismounted and met him at the border, taking an ankle for his own. The man's screams broke the air as his head crossed the border, then abruptly cut off. "Guides have mercy," he babbled repetitively, until Ehren grew tired of it and rested his sword tip firmly on the man's chest. Then the babbling cut off, too, replaced by gasping, which Ehren could hardly fault him for.

"I've got him," Ehren said. "Get your horse. See if you can get his, too."

It wasn't much of a task; the Guard's horse was cantering aimlessly in the same circle Laine had taken, and seemed more than pleased to find a human that might give it guidance. While he was gone, Ehren gave a sharp whistle. With any luck, the mule would follow Ricasso, and they wouldn't lose any of their supplies. Without the grain and foodstuffs they had packed, the trip would take a lot longer.

When Laine emerged from the Barrenlands and Ehren heard Ricasso making his way back to them, he turned his full attention back to their captive. "Now," he said. "Suppose you tell me what this is all about."

"No," the man said, but it came out as a moan, and without any defiance at all. He lay on his back on the ground, looking wrung out. Unresisting.

"No?" Ehren said, leaning on the sword, taking the weight from his leg.

"Guides, Ehren, not another one," Laine said, sounding a little desperate. When Ehren glanced at him, he looked immediately abashed. "I mean—"

"Never mind." Ehren cut him off sharply, his thoughts, as Laine's, going back to that night at the T'ieranguard inn, when the man had died under questioning. "*Is* it, Laine? *Is* it another one?"

Laine blinked, and then caught on. He looked down at the man again, his face suddenly gone distracted; when he winced, it was all the answer Ehren needed. "Don't say anything," he ordered the Guard, taking all his weight off the sword, which had only cut through the first layer of the man's stained brigandine.

Ehren stared pensively at the man a moment, his inner sight seeing again the gruesome death of the last man he'd questioned. He'd not be part of *that* again, not if he could help it. But he needed to know what he was walking into . . .

The ochre-smeared brown of Barrenlands, just feet away, caught his eye. No man's magic worked in there, not even personal things that were otherwise part of him. Nothing but the dispensation spell.

"What do you suppose would happen if we were to go back in there," he nodded at the border, "with this one between us? Would our protection extend to him?"

Laine looked startled. "I don't have any idea. It didn't work when we dragged him out. Maybe flesh to flesh—"

Ehren looked again at the Barrenlands, and gave a decisive nod. "Let's find out. Give me a hand." Without removing his sword, he reached down and caught his knife in a fold of the man's sleeve, slicing it open. He closed his hand around the spot and straightened. After a moment's hesitation, Laine did the same at the other side; it was only when they'd dragged him a step that the man came out of his dazed state and realized what was going on. Ehren's sword was no deterrent.

With a howl, he twisted in their grip, fighting to stay out of the Barrenlands. He cursed and gibbered and even tried to bite, but they were only steps away, and although the man twice came close to tearing free, the Barrenlands closed around them before he was successful.

As soon as he realized they'd crossed over, he froze, his face screwed up in anticipation of the utter disorientation he'd experienced last time. Ehren and Laine exchanged a glance and gently lowered him to the ground, kneeling so they could maintain contact. After a moment, one of the man's eyes opened slightly, then closed just as quickly.

"You're all right," Ehren told him. "And you'll stay all right, as long as we're holding on to you like this. So I wouldn't try to get away if I were you."

"No," the man said, his eyes still closed. "I'm not gonna move—just don't—don't let go!"

"I don't have any plans to," Ehren said. "Unless, of course, you don't feel like talking to us."

The man struggled with this a moment, and then the words burst out in a rush. "I can't! Don't let go!"

"Relax," Ehren told him. "You're under some kind of spell, am I right? Something that will kill you if you talk about your orders?"

This time the man opened his eyes, and they held surprise. "Yes, and it's no bluff. I know of one man who already died."

"So do we." Ehren shifted his weight so he could straighten his sore leg, causing the man to stiffen in alarm. "Stop it. I said I wouldn't let go yet, and I won't. But I need you to talk to me."

"We think you're safe in here," Laine added. "Nothing works in this place, no magic but the dispensation spell."

"You *think*?" the man asked incredulously.

Ehren's grip tightened on his arm. "You were the one who came after me—and you're the one who lost the fight. We're doing our best to protect you, but make no mistake— I *will* walk away and leave you here if you don't start talking to me, and I'm not planning on waiting much longer."

Their captive paled a few shades lighter, and his skin looked a sickening yellow in the reflective light. Laine wasn't looking all that much better, and he watched Ehren with a question in his eyes. *Would you really?*

Yes. Ehren met that question evenly, and turned back to the erstwhile Guard. "I want to know who sent you, how you found us, and exactly what you were supposed to do with us."

The man closed his eyes, swallowed with effort, and said carefully, "It's *you* we were looking for." He paused, and took a deep breath, trembling beneath Ehren's grip. And nothing happened. Ehren gave him the time, and after a moment, the man looked up again. "It . . . it was the ring," he said tentatively, and paused again. The next time he spoke, his voice was stronger. "We have a ring that's been keyed to yours. Adlin has it . . . is he dead?"

"He wasn't when I left him," Ehren said. "Keep talking and you might have a chance to find out."

"We . . . we've been at the border for more than a week. He knew you were in Therand, and *where* . . . he must have guessed you'd try to go through the Barrenlands . . . we were supposed to bring you in, in disgrace—if you lived through the taking."

"*He?*" Ehren stabbed the word at their captive like a knife point, and the man winced as though it had struck home.

Hesitantly, in a voice barely loud enough to call a whisper, he said, "Varien."

Ehren nodded. *Varien.* He looked down at the man and his renewed trembling and said, "You're still alive," in a dry voice.

"I—I don't know how long it would take—"

"We do," Ehren assured him flatly. "And it's not going to happen. Are you truly a Guard?"

"Adlin is . . . was. He went through half the training and was mustered out for his temper. Varien got in touch with him, offered him an assignment, and then a sweeter deal if he could round up some others to help—that's where I came in. I think . . . he didn't say so, but I'm almost certain—he already had people placed in Therand."

"He used to." Ehren wiped his sword on the man's leg, sheathed it, and rubbed his eyes with his free hand. "All right," he said. "We've got Varien annoyed at me, no big surprise. I *am* surprised he kept such close tabs on me, and that he'd bother to send anyone for me—if he can track me through the ring, he'd have seen I was heading for Kurtane, anyway. There's got to be something else going on here. There's *got* to be more to this than a failed assignment."

Laine just shrugged at him, sympathetic and unhelpful. Ehren shook his head, mostly to himself. Varien wanted him dead, and there was no reason for it. He frowned. "He can't have any idea what we know . . ."

Someone in Kurtane is smuggling mage lure through a Barrenlands pass only a magic user can withstand.

Varien, of course—Ehren was well convinced of that. But Varien couldn't know what they'd discovered. No one could. As far as anyone knew, Ehren was looking for Dannel, an exile of sorts himself—though he'd been sent before he'd been back in Kurtane long enough to step on anyone's toes. If he'd been as disagreeable as all that to the ministers, why not simply discharge him? Or, as Varien had strongly hinted they might, have him killed?

You don't get killed for stepping on toes. You get killed for being a genuine threat.

If the current smuggling was left over from Hetna's days, who knew how many years earlier than that it had been established? One hundred years ago, Coirra, Varien's mentor, had cursed the T'ierands in a last-ditch effort to keep the Barrenlands intact. *To protect mage lure smuggling even then?*

One year ago, Benlan had been on the verge of renewing diplomatic ties to Therand; he'd been on the verge of learning about the smuggling. Now Ehren was after Benlan's murderers. And Varien wanted him dead. *You get killed for being a genuine threat.*

It was a long leap, a thought-skipping jump from one conclusion to another. *Varien, protecting his interests. Benlan, murdered.* Ehren clamped down on the cold rage growling in his throat, and cleared it, instead. He'd find out, by the Guides he'd find out! But right now . . . he met Laine's questioning look without offering any answers, and turned to their captive. "You'll leave your ailettes, brigandines, and weapons with me," he told the man. "If your friend's still alive, you can take him to the closest surgeon. And if I see you again, I'll kill you first, ask questions later. Understood?"

Mutely, the man nodded, his gaze darting between Ehren's no-nonsense finality and Laine's belief in it.

"All right, then. On your feet. I have no intention of dragging you back out of here when you can walk." Stiffly, Ehren gained his own feet, careful not to lose his hold on the man. Slowly, they walked the few feet to Solvany, where Ehren released his grip and stood, waiting pointedly.

Awkwardly, the man unlaced his brigandine and struggled out of it, left with his shapeless, quilted gambeson. His sword was on the ground by the border; he made no move to pick it up. His horse was tied loosely by the reins to a springy limb it had stripped of leaves; the man took a hesitant step toward it and looked at Ehren, who nodded. He wasted no time mounting up and riding out.

Laine went to fetch his mule, which had indeed followed Ricasso back to them, but hadn't felt obliged to stay close. When he returned, Ehren was checking Ricasso's girth, and thinking about how much distance they could make in what remained of the day—as well as mulling over what they'd learned. What in the Hells was Varien up to? And why was Laine closing his deep blue eye to look at him like that?

Ehren stopped in mid-thought to look at Laine, *really* look at him, and see the hesitancy that had sprouted there. "What?" he asked, wondering if he should check behind himself, to see if he had grown a tail or some other astounding thing. "Spit it out, Laine."

After some hesitation, Laine said, "Would you have? Left him in there, I mean. If he didn't answer your questions."

Ehren snorted. "I'd have given him a taste of it, no doubt about that." He looked at Laine again, saw the sincerity of the question, and raised his eyebrows. "Did you really think it of me? I'd give him the mercy stroke before leaving him to blunder in that senseless wasteland."

"But . . ." Laine said, and stopped, then tried again. "After that man in T'ieranguard . . ."

"The one who died from magic?"

Mutely, Laine nodded. He was serious, and looked younger than his twenty years. Sometimes Ehren felt he could have been Laine's father, for the differences in their life experiences.

"Would I have killed him, you mean? Followed up on my threat, if he hadn't talked?" Ehren shook his head. "All it takes is convincing them you mean it." He gave Laine a sudden, crooked grin. "*You* believed it—that's what made it work so well. I didn't know talking would kill him . . ." He shook his head again, and when he looked over at Laine, his face had turned hard. "People aren't all decent, Laine. They don't all respond to 'thank you' and 'pretty please.' Sometimes it doesn't matter. But when they're a threat, you do what you have to to get the results you need."

Laine didn't say anything. He didn't completely agree, that was obvious. But he was out of his element in some parts of Ehren's world, and that was obvious, too. Sherran, Ehren thought, would have understood.

Chapter 14

Laine held on to the mule's frayed lead rope, fingering the fringe of it. After a moment, he tied a knot in it to keep it from fraying further, then fingered that. Ehren was off in his own thoughts again, looking unapproachable, being the quintessential Guard as he cleaned his blooded sword so they could ride.

But Laine didn't want to ride. He was tired—tired from traveling half the day in the blasted Barrenlands, where he'd felt like a flat ghost of his normal self—and unexpectedly wearied from their encounter with the two men. And, as Ehren pulled the ring from around his neck and gave it a contemplative stare, Laine knew he had one more battle yet to fight.

"Ehren," he said, and couldn't keep some of that fatigue from his voice.

Ehren looked up, surprised. "Almost ready," he said. "With any luck, we'll find a clear path before it gets dark."

"I was hoping we could stay here," Laine said. "I need to talk to you about that ring."

"I know." Ehren's hand closed around the ring; he gave it a jerk that broke the braided grass he'd been using as a chain, and hefted it in his hand. "It gave us away—it'll only continue to do so. I'm getting rid of it."

"No!" Laine blurted, suddenly afraid Ehren was about

to haul back and pitch it into the Barrenlands. When Ehren looked at him, mildly surprised, Laine felt the blush on his face. "I meant . . . I know. We can't keep it with us. But before we go on . . . I want to—"

"No," Ehren said.

If Ehren thought that Shette was the only stubborn one in the family, he was about to find out differently. Laine's jaw set. "This is my decision."

"That may be," Ehren said evenly. "But I have the ring."

For a moment they faced off against one another, two boys vying for the high ground in King of the Hill. Ehren was the one who relented; for a moment, he looked as tired as Laine felt. "How can I hand this ring to you, knowing what will probably happen? It's hard enough to live with the nights when they hold the memory of enemies dead by my hand—or of good people like that border couple, who'd be alive if I'd gotten there ten damn minutes earlier. What would I do with the sight of *you*, dying because I simply didn't have the wits to keep this ring from you?"

"You'd know it was my own choice," Laine said. "And I wouldn't choose it if I didn't think I'd be all right. You've always been able to bring me out of it—*Shette's* always been able to bring me out of it. Maybe I'm hazy for a couple days, but that'd be well worth it."

"Well worth it for *what*?" Ehren asked. He backed away from Ricasso and sat, his leg stretched out. His hair was free of its binding—that'd happened in the recent fuss— and he scraped it back from his face with one hand. "What do you think you're going to find that'll be worth the possible price?"

Laine blotted his face with the hem of his shirt and said, "Answers." And an end to the interminable itch, the feeling that he could just turn around and *see* who'd killed him— killed *Benlan*. Not the hand that'd wielded the weapon, but the one behind the ambush. Sometimes he caught himself checking behind without thinking, very quickly, as though he could see that person even in his waking hours. As though he was being watched, even now. "Ehren, every time I go to sleep, I wonder if this Dream is going to grab me. I wonder if there'll be someone to wake me if it goes too far. If I can only get it *over* with, follow it to the end, then maybe it'll let me go, once and for all."

Ehren looked at him, his face somber. "I hadn't thought of it like that. I didn't realize—"

"Well then, *do* think of it like that! It may be through other men's eyes, Ehren, but every time they die, so do I."

"What if seeing it to the end doesn't stop the Dreams?"

Laine went over to Ehren, sat heavily down beside him, and said, "Then at least I've tried. Would *you* settle for any less?"

Slowly, Ehren shook his head. He looked down at the ring in his hand; the ivy design was imprinted in his skin from the intensity of his grip. "Varien is up to his neck in machinations and intrigue; I'll have a hell of a time proving any of it. But he wouldn't try to kill me without a reason. The *only* thing I was doing in Kurtane was hunting Benlan's killer. If . . . If you happen to find that he had something to do with Benlan's death . . ." His hand closed, the knuckles going white. "I won't need any more proof than that. I'll kill him myself, and face the consequences."

Laine winced. This time, he knew Ehren meant it.

They unsaddled the horses and mule and hobbled them all, having learned long ago to three-hobble the wily mule. Without much conversation, they pulled out cheese, and bread that had been baked late the night before. There were strawberry preserves for the bread, and Laine ran into some raspberries on his way back from nature's call. Added to some of Sherran's fine wine, it wasn't a bad meal for the road, and it didn't take a campfire.

Of course, Ehren was of the opinion that if someone was near, they'd manage to find the two men simply because of the ring, fire or no. He was satisfied enough with the probability that Varien wouldn't have enough men to spread them thickly, and Laine decided not to worry about it. He sat cross-legged in the area they'd tromped down, and ate.

After they'd eaten and the horses had been grained and watered—not enough water, but it would hold them—Ehren leaned back against the stacked bundles of his pack, gave Laine a long and searching look, and held out the ring, dangling from the loop of grass. "Guides grant you a good journey."

As far as Laine knew, Ehren followed the Solvan custom of Guideless Levels, but he appreciated the sentiment. He took a deep breath, looked into the dark grey implacability of Ehren's eyes, and said, "See you later."

And Ehren dropped the ring into his hand.

Laine fell straight to confusion. He knew he was Benlan; the feel of that older body had become as familiar as putting on a pair of well-used gloves. But where? Doing what? His vision was distorted, a fine pattern of mesh. A training mask. His own arm wielded an expert blade against another, though Benlan's eyes were fixed only on the center of his opponent's chest. There was no fear, no tension, just a big bellow of laughter that rolled up when a killing blow whistled in through his guard and at his chest, checked just in time to become a mere tap.

And then his sparring partner pulled his own mask off to reveal an easy grin, an almost carefree expression. Long, dark hair tied back from a face younger than the one Laine was used to seeing. Ehren. *They were friends. They were truly friends.* Had he ever seen Ehren look that happy, that at ease with anyone? Or with himself, for that matter?

What kind of a Dream was this? His hand, Benlan's hand, clapped down on Ehren's shoulder with true affection, the air cool on skin just released from a heavy leather glove. Wilna's ring sparkled there.

Laine stared into the depth of that emerald, and it widened to swallow him, sucking him through dim scenes etched green upon green. Wilna, giving the ring to Benlan, a mild spell reflecting her affection set within it. And then another set of hands, removing the emerald from Benlan's dead finger, tucking it away somewhere dark.

Finally, someone brought the ring into daylight, and worked over it. It had to be Varien, though Laine saw nothing but the hands. They were neat and manicured, and the movements precise. And the spells . . . Laine felt them go in, and knew exactly what they were—the spell of finding, keying in on the tiny remnants of Benlan's blood, and of his very self that the spell of affection had touched. The spell of location, that told Varien where the ring was. The spell to confirm Dannel's identification, which would tell Varien Ehren's mission had been completed.

And then, tied tightly to that final spell, there was yet another, one that would trigger itself when the confirmation was used. Laine saw the horror of a slow, painful death for them all—including Ehren. *He was never meant to return from this journey.*

But the Dream didn't give him time to reflect on the unexpected revelation. It took his green visions and turned them into bare branches, thick woods with the faintest signs of buds turning to spring leaves. Benlan's body again. Taller than Laine's, with a longer stride, a confident, swinging walk despite his padded surcoat; he was sweating slightly in the spring chill. He wished all the Guards weren't with him, but they'd sensed something was up, and insisted on full Guard coverage. He'd managed to leave half of them with the horses, milling outside the modest stable.

Laine rode the waves of Benlan's thoughts, taking them in, trying to gather them up so he'd still have them, even when—

The first cry hit his ears—unmistakably a death cry, plunging down into a gurgling moan. Benlan whirled, drawing his sword.

It still took Laine by surprise when Benlan's arm was cut, when he looked into a grinning woman's eyes as she slipped past his guard to slice through the padded layers of cloth and into his belly. Laine wanted to wrench himself free as Benlan fell to his knees—*Ehren, get me out of here!* It was a dual thought from both their minds, as sharp steel slid across his throat, moving so smoothly, slicing so cleanly, Laine hardly felt it.

But he *did* feel the eyes. He remembered there was something else yet to do. *Turn around. Someone's watching you*— His body was falling, his eyes were half closed, no longer seeing. But it was his inner Sight that turned, the gift that had brought him here in the first place. He turned, and through the darkness that engulfed him, picked out the lone figure standing, watching. Erect, but hooded and cloaked, the man watched the slaughter, nodding to himself. And though he seemed at a distance and in shadow, somehow Laine could see the aloof cruelty in his eyes. And the cool victory.

It was enough. It was someone he would know again. Satisfied, Laine turned to go—

And couldn't. Twist as he might, he was trapped by Benlan's body—and by his death.

Laine dropped like a stone. Ehren watched him with no little trepidation, every muscle tense. After a moment, when Laine did no more than twitch, he forced himself to relax. Muscle by muscle, leaning against the pack, thinking of the amazingly loud buzz of late summer insects around them, the chomping of equine jaws, the clumsy, hobbled movement in the brush. The thumping of his own heart, for that matter.

Laine was doing this for his own reasons. But Ehren knew who he'd blame, if something happened. Himself. The man who'd given Laine the means to do this thing.

Laine jerked, a small contraction that seemed to sweep through every muscle in his body. He'd fallen in an awkward position, Ehren thought, and resisted the temptation to interfere by arranging him more comfortably. No doubt it made little difference to Laine, wherever he was now.

A bead of sweat wound its way down along Ehren's temple, though the temperature was comfortable, if too humid, and cooling for the evening. He swatted the first of the evening's mosquitos and wondered if there was any ground nearby that was damp enough to grow jewelweed, the tender, juicy leaves of which eased the itch of insect bites.

You're a seasoned Guard, he told himself, abruptly recognizing the equivalent of mental babbling. *Get hold of yourself.*

All the same, when Laine grunted, Ehren jerked, startled, snapped his gaze back to the younger man. *It's inevitable. He's going to do this; he always does. So long as he's breathing* . . . Ehren winced—*there he goes*—body arched, straining, fighting battles it was never meant to fight; blood dribbling down the side of his face from a badly bitten lip; sounds of protest forced from laboring lungs—

And sudden collapse. The air left his lungs in an audible whoosh, and rigid, jerking muscles turned flaccid.

"Laine?" Ehren's hushed voice sounded startlingly loud, even against the backdrop of cicadas and katydids. He moved closer. "Laine? Are you . . . there?"

A careful hand on Laine's shoulder met no resistance, got no reaction, not even after Ehren pried the ring from his hand and shoved it onto his own finger. "Damn," Ehren muttered. "Here we go." He didn't waste any effort with gentle handling, but knelt over Laine and slapped him hard several times. Laine's head rolled with the blows without a flicker of reaction. Was he even breathing?

No. Of course not.

"Come *back*, Laine," Ehren said under his breath, the words jerky with his efforts as he took Laine's arms and shook him; it'd worked once before but failed now. "Laine!" he shouted, right into Laine's ear. "Guides damn you, Laine, come *back*!" Panting, he stopped the physical assault and put his palm over Laine's mouth and nose, watching his chest in the diffuse late evening light. How long could a man go without breathing before there was no coming back?

Ehren flipped his head back, scraping the hair out of his eyes and away from his sweat-damp face. He caught a flicker of brown in the corner of his eye, and froze. *No magic in the Barrenlands.*

It was worth a try. Grunting with the effort, he worked

his arms underneath Laine and hauled the younger man up over his shoulder. Then, limping badly under the strain, he crashed through the undergrowth to the border, tripping right in front of it. He and Laine both went sprawling into the Barrenlands—him flat on his face, and Laine rolling a few feet before his flopping arms slowed him down.

Ehren didn't even bother to get up. He crawled over to Laine and shoved him roughly over on his back, prepared to slap some life into him once more.

But Laine's eyes flickered, and he gave a little cough, then a deep breath. Ehren sank back down, flooded with relief.

"Ow," Laine said. "Why's my face hurt?"

Ehren heard the frustration in Laine's voice as his friend secured the packs on the mule. "All I have to do is see his eyes again, or even the way he's standing. I *saw* the man behind Benlan's death—I just can't describe him—"

"It doesn't matter," Ehren said, though of course it did. "You saw the dream to its end, and now maybe it'll leave you alone. I already know Varien was tracking me, that the orders went out *dead or alive*. Now I know about that killing spell on the ring . . . and I'm Guides-damn sure I can tie him to the mage lure smuggling if not to the Lorakan trouble. That gives him motive. If Varien was involved in Benlan's death, I'll find that, too. If he wasn't . . . well, I'll have an easier time finding the traitor, without Varien in my way."

"I'd know him if I saw him again," Laine insisted.

Ehren prowled the young woods, searching out rocks. The area was obviously poor pastureland let go, and suitable rocks were few. No doubt already gathered and dumped somewhere—*ah, there's one*—

Out loud, Ehren said, "What makes you think you'll get the chance?"

Laine didn't answer directly. "I'd tell you what he looked like if I could, but I can't. Would you really stop me from coming to Kurtane? As if I couldn't follow on my own," he added meaningfully.

Ehren shook his head. "There're people out there trying to kill me." *So what's new?* "They've already shown they're willing to go after anyone with me. Why take that risk? I can do this on my own." All he had to do was make it to the Guard barracks. Once they learned the lies and treachery Varien had instigated against one of their own, once they got a look at the journal and the questions it raised, they'd use Guard prerogative and go straight to the king.

Assuming Gerhard, the only one who could deny them Guard right, wasn't part of the problem.

Laine said, "You may be able to bring Varien down for smuggling. But that doesn't guarantee you'll prove he's at the bottom of the conspiracy that killed Benlan. I *can* make a difference, and you know it."

Laine was sure of himself—and he had reason to be. Ehren scowled at him, and had the satisfaction of seeing the uncertainty it brought to Laine's face, as momentary as it was. Then he turned silently back to his task. Laine was right, of course. He'd already made a difference, had guided Ehren's thinking with his Sight, giving Ehren the openings that led him this far. Even now, he was popping up with the odd pieces that helped to make this puzzle whole.

The ring, for instance. It gave Ehren chills to think he'd carried the deadly token over so many miles, and that he'd come so close to unwittingly killing them all, just by invoking the confirmation. It was long past time to get rid of it, and even Laine didn't have a reason to argue it anymore—not that Ehren gave him a chance.

But Ehren's options were limited. He had no means to destroy the thing, and he wasn't about to leave it lying around, waiting to be found. Burial wasn't good enough, either. What he needed was a way to keep it out of the picture until he was able to return here with someone who could handle it. In the end, the Barrenlands came to the rescue once more.

Now, with the pile of rocks he'd managed to gather as a marker, Ehren buried the ring just over the border of the hard yellow-brown Barrenlands soil.

Working carefully, so only his hands crossed that line, Ehren used his knife to dig the hole, and then firmly pushed the ring into the dirt. It was a task made more difficult by the fact that Sherran's spell of the day before had lost its efficacy, and he could no longer feel what he was doing. Laine watched patiently, and without comment—and then, when Ehren had finished, wiped his hands and his knife, and mounted up, Laine did the same. He looked at Ehren without challenge, but his expression was implacable all the same. He meant to see this to the end, that was clear—to find the killer that fit into his Dream.

Ehren regarded Laine with a sour look. "The question is, will you get in more trouble with me, or without me?"

"Without you, I expect," Laine said, far too cheerfully. Ehren just grunted, and turned Ricasso for the deer trail they'd found the day before.

Before the end of the day, they'd run across a definite path, and then a road. Ever bearing north, Ehren kept a low profile. He packed away his ailette, honor feather, and even the brigandine—although he fully intended to unpack that last as they grew closer to Kurtane. To all appearances they were two men on a long journey, and if Laine's speech patterns were a little out of the ordinary, it only made sense. Ehren told all who asked that they were going to visit long-lost family, and it amused some small, hard part of him that for Laine, the story was true.

Kurtane was as far from its southern border as from the eastern pass, and Ehren could have easily stretched the trip out to two weeks to spare the horses. Instead he bought extra grain and hay when they passed crossroad villages, and pushed them all, as well as his dwindling purse. Even solidly muscular Laine was beginning to look worn around the edges after a week. By then they were on the Offcoast Highway, and Ehren knew well just where they were and how to get where they were going.

Getting there quietly was another matter altogether. People seemed to be in a mood for trouble, and Ehren already had ducked out of two tavern fights where he'd have been just as pleased to show the troublemakers what *real* trouble was. His restraint seemed to impress the gravity of their situation on Laine as nothing else had.

Ehren estimated them five days away from Kurtane, riding at a slogging trot through a day-long rain, when he looked up and saw another Guard riding toward them. The Guard was obvious in an emblazoned grey slicker, although the hood was drawn up so far Ehren had no chance to see who it was.

Damn. Ehren's Guard patch was long gone from his own slicker, but any other Guard was bound to recognize the grey, service-issued slicker. He wanted to warn Laine, but instead kept Shaffron moving, nudging him forward when the horse, feeling Ehren's own hesitation, faltered.

Oddly enough, the other Guard seemed to display the same aloofness, staring straight ahead within the slicker hood, only glancing sideways as they passed, and then just for the merest instant. Ehren had ridden another fifty feet before those heavily shadowed features came together in his mind and turned into something familiar. He stopped, and half-turned Shaffron in the deserted wet road.

He wasn't surprised to discover the other Guard had done the same. Laine, ensconced in his own slicker, made a noise that could have been the beginning of a question, but broke it off and watched cautiously instead.

Ehren let the other Guard approach, his hand a notable distance from his sword hilt but not all that far from the knife in his boot. Heat from Shaffron steamed the air before him and scented it with warm horse, and the steady rain slicked the reins and dripped water over the bony curve of Shaffron's eye. Slowly, the other Guard reached up and pushed the slicker hood off his—no, *her* head.

"Jada," Ehren said, through a sigh that released his tension.

Her face was strained, her expression uncertain, and her

horse worn. "I've been looking for you," she said. "Ehren, you won't believe—" She stopped, looked him up and down and then checked Laine out as well. "Well, maybe you would. But let's find a dry place to talk about it." Her voice held a note of pleading. Though the last thing Ehren wanted to do was lose an afternoon of travel, he nodded. "I passed a place a little ways back," she said. "It looked abandoned— ought to be all right."

She flipped her hood back up and moved her horse abreast of Shaffron. Silently, they walked to Jada's dry place, which turned out to be an old farmstead. The house was burned and fallen in, but half the barn remained, and if it creaked alarmingly now and then, it still kept most of the rain out. Ehren put the hobbled horses in a half-fenced, overgrown paddock, trusting the combination of restraints to keep them out of trouble. Then the three of them, plenty wet despite rain gear, found an old stall to hunker in.

Food came first. Ehren waited until Jada's freckled face lost its pinched look, and until she stopped giving Laine sideways glances—although Ehren had introduced his companion as simply that, and made no effort to explain. Then he set aside the ham and bread they'd picked up at the last village and trained his gaze on Jada.

She was quick enough to notice, and to realize he wasn't going to wait any longer. Her usually cheerful face was sober, and without preamble she said, "They told us you'd killed a Guard. One of *us*."

"Who is *they*?"

She blinked. "I don't know, exactly. Gerhard is the one who told us, but he seemed very upset by it all . . . like he didn't want to be passing the news on—but it was part of our orders, and he didn't have a choice."

"And what were your orders?" Ehren held her light blue eyes, reading them.

Jada didn't flinch. "That you were to be arrested at the first opportunity. Killed, if that's what it took to detain you. That any of us who helped you would be under the same punishments. It wasn't clear just what those are, but they're dire enough, I'm sure." Some of her confidence returned, enough to lend her voice its wry note.

"And who," Ehren said quietly, "am I supposed to have killed?"

She frowned. "I'm not sure. Gerhard said it was someone who'd been on remote duty—away even longer than you've been. Someone watching our interests in Therand and Loraka."

Up until this point, Laine had been slouching in the corner, tired enough from the constant travel to offer no protest at his obvious exclusion in the conversation. But now he raised his head, and said, "Then they don't know—" *The men by the border* . . .

Ehren's sharp look cut him off. It didn't go unnoticed; Ehren had had little hope of that. Jada was inexperienced, but if she had the chance to gain a few years' work, she'd rank with the best of them—and being a Guard meant more than using muscle.

"How about it, Ehren?" she said, her eyes narrowed. "You been going around killing Guards? Did Algere waste his life trying to warn you?"

"*What?*" Ehren said, his voice just as sharp as his silent admonishment to Laine. "What happened, Jada?"

"You first." She crossed her arms and looked at him, clearly willing to wait in silence until she was satisfied.

Ehren rubbed the back of his neck, watching her wariness. He couldn't blame her. But how to explain . . . "A man is dead," he said. "He wasn't a Guard—he was Varien's man. And I didn't kill him—Varien's magic did. It happened in T'ieranguard."

"Varien," she said, and although her face didn't change, her voice sounded resigned. She took a deep breath and said, "He's kept a very low profile in Kurtane. We felt something was going on, that someone was orchestrating changes, but I never would have pinned it all on him."

"Changes?" Ehren said instantly.

Jada combined a frown and a shrug. "Little things . . odd decisions that all seem to have the same flavor. The

Levels sent Reds out to deal with the border bandits, but they were mostly foot soldiers." When Ehren responded with a disbelieving stare, she insisted, "Guide's truth, Ehren. Some cavalry went, but the bulk were foot. The justification I heard was that we couldn't afford to send away more cav when we're so short-handed here, and that the mere presence of the soldiers ought to send the bandits packing."

His voice expressionless, Ehren asked, "What else?"

"How about the orders to step up the cavalry breeding program? We're short on horses—an amazing number of them have colicked to death this summer—so instead of hunting up new ones, we're *breeding* them."

In five years, it might even make a difference.

Jada waited for him to take it in, and said, "There are a number of new people working the diplomatic levels. Seems like they're everywhere, sticking their noses in everybody's business. It's not that I've seen any one of them acting inappropriately, but . . ."

"It feels wrong," Ehren finished for her. She nodded. Ehren drew a hand over one eye, a gesture of fatigue, and kept both of them closed while he considered what he'd heard. "It may not all be Varien's doing. But we have evidence that he's been involved in subterfuge for quite some while. In some respects, since the beginning of his office in Kurtane. It's possible he had a part in Benlan's death. That's something I'm still trying to discover."

Laine was conspicuously quiet. That didn't stop Jada's gaze from going to him, her eyes still narrowed from her reaction to Ehren's statement about Varien. She looked at Ehren and then pointedly back to Laine, and said, "I'm already in trouble for you. It looks like I may get myself in a lot more. I want to know exactly what's going on."

Ehren nodded. "That's fair. Jada, meet Dannel's firstborn. Laine."

Her eyes widened in a moment of astonishment, and then her gaze snapped back over to Laine, fairly daring him to confirm it. He shrugged at her.

"This is it in a nutshell, Jada. While I was riding the coast this last year, there were several attempts on my life. I have to say I didn't take them very seriously—any year a king dies, there's unrest, and any lone rider on the road is bound to run into trouble now and then, even a King's Guard." He rubbed his leg, trying to sum things up as simply as possible. "When I returned to Kurtane, Varien sent for me. He told me the Upper Levels weren't too happy with me, for a variety of reasons, and that he was therefore sending me away on a mission of his own." Ehren gave a wry grin. "He did, of course, offer me the chance to resign."

Jada's expression indicated her opinion of *that* option. In the background, Laine snorted. "Right," Ehren said. "So I went. And I wasn't supposed to come back without success."

"That's why you wouldn't return with us at the border," Jada said.

"If I had, I wouldn't have been able to help you at all," Ehren said. "I would have been discharged—assuming I lived that long." He paused, trying to order his words. "Varien sent me to find Dannel. Along the way, I discovered interesting things going on along the border. Loraka's soldiers are everywhere there, and there's new magic being set at the borders—not to mention the bandits we ran into. You know the man who died? They thought it was his heart?"

She nodded, frowning. "You think differently?"

"I think it just as well could have been magic. The man who died in T'ieranguard did so because he was about to talk. There was another we ran into about a week ago; he was under the same spell. It's all tied together, and it all leads to Varien."

"It seems to," she said. "But where does it go then? What's he up to? He has to have a *reason* for being involved in all these things."

"Why does a man do anything?" Ehren asked. "For love—or hate, which is close enough to being the same thing—for power, or for greed. In Varien's case I suspect it's the last two, in mixed doses."

She shook her head. Several strands of her kinky red

hair had come loose from her braid, and they fell over her forehead to dangle at her nose. She rubbed it, vigorously, and tucked the hair away. "I don't really understand," she said, and the hair fell back down. Jada made a growling noise and said, "Damp weather. I hate damp weather."

"Just wait until you've got some bones that hate it, too," Ehren told her. He drank one of the last few swallows of the wine Sherran had given him, and offered the rest to Jada.

Jada downed it, raised an appreciative eyebrow, and said, "There's more, Ehren. There's got to be more."

"There is," he admitted. "There's documentation that years ago—two generations, at least—someone at the Highest Levels was involved in smuggling contraband drugs from Therand. Mage lure."

"How?" she said, her eyes wide.

"There's a pass somewhere in the Barrenlands." He paused a moment, shook his head; his anger was growing again just thinking about it. "I'm certain it's Varien's doing. It's a dangerous drug, Jada, and one that would give him way too much power over other wizards."

"This is . . ." Jada searched for the word and gave up. "So much!"

"The ironic thing is, I wouldn't have found any of it, if Varien hadn't sent me away." Ehren mused over his words, looking for the missing pieces. "He did, of course, plan to kill me, along with Dannel's family, and I'm not certain he's through trying."

"After today, *nothing's* going to surprise me again," Jada said, sneaking the wayward hair back behind her ear again.

Ehren wondered what she'd think if she knew exactly how he gained much of his information. It'd have to come out eventually, he realized, looking at Laine. Maybe it was a good thing Laine was coming along, after all. His presence, and his obvious abilities, would lend credence to the tale. Few would gainsay Dannel's son—and Laine still had his mother's ring to prove his identity. "There's still more," he told Jada, and she made an incredulous face. "Think it through," he said. "Notice all the new Lorakan influence in Kurtane? It might not have been obvious to you; you haven't been there that long. I learned an earful from our border guards, too, things our Upper Levels should know but certainly aren't acting on. There's a lot of unrest in inner Loraka these days—they're working up to one of those ugly rallies around patriotism that provides people with an excuse to go stomping on borders."

Jada opened her mouth to comment, but Ehren raised a hand, cutting her off. "Now we know Loraka, through Varien, may have access to that hidden pass. Put that together with the depleted state of Solvany's defenses, and it's not a reassuring picture."

Laine's eyebrow went up, a gesture almost missed in the dimming light. "When did you come up with all *this*?"

"I've been doing a lot of thinking," Ehren said. "Here and there."

"So it seems. I wouldn't be surprised if you come up with a way to mend the political gap between Therand and Solvany while you're at it." Laine obviously wasn't serious, but Ehren gave him a grin.

"I've come up with a good place to start," he said, and lifted Sherran's empty wine bota with its black and red dyed leather. It wasn't a reference to the wine.

Laine grinned back. "The nicest kind of diplomacy."

Jada scowled at them both. "I won't even pretend to know what you're talking about. Is that it? Are there any more surprises?"

"There might be," Ehren said, sobering fast. "We know that right before Benlan was killed, he became aware of the smuggling, and was considering working with Therand to stop it. He'd been looking for an excuse to get through the Barrenlands, maybe even eliminate them. Losing the Barrenlands would make a mess of that smuggling. And if Varien truly is a traitor as well, involved in the changes we've seen in Loraka's behavior—" He stopped, checked to see if she was following him, found she hadn't quite made the connection. "Solvany's been weakened from within in many ways. Exchanging a weak king like Rodar for Benlan's strength may have been part of it."

"Where'd you *get* this information? How the Hells did you put all this together, stuck out in the Lorakan mountains?" Jada's stray lock of hair wrapped tightly about her finger, one twist short of being a snarled knot.

"Unusual places," Ehren said. "But very good sources. Couldn't have done better if Benlan had told me himself."

Laine snorted. "Let's just say it runs in the royal blood."

"Oh, Ehren, no wonder he wanted you out of Kurtane," Jada breathed. "He'd never have hidden all this from you, not with changes that have taken place since you left. No wonder he wants you dead, now!"

Ehren shook his head, once but firmly. "He always wanted me dead. As far as I can tell, all he knows is that I went to where I was sent—but I took some side trips on the way, and gave myself a chance to see what's happening in Loraka. He knows I was in Therand, too, and may guess I was at the Grannor summer home. After all, we *did* come through the Barrenlands, and we couldn't have done that without help."

"That's enough to make you a problem, as far as he's concerned," she declared.

Ehren smiled, a feral grin. "I was always a *problem*," he said. "Now, I'm going to be more trouble than he ever imagined."

Chapter 15

Laine rode behind Jada and in front of Ehren, in the cool morning air. The rain had stopped, and though the path was still damp and the fields and woods they passed sparkled with a surfeit of moisture, the sky was clear. The sun was hot against Laine's side, and he was sure they'd be searching for shade before they hit noon—despite several days of cool and gloomy weather, it was still, after all, fully summer.

Jada and Ehren weren't saying much. Perhaps that was just as well, for they'd certainly had enough to say the evening before. Laine still winced at the recollection of Ehren's face when Jada told them again her partner Algere was dead, and how it'd happened.

"We've had some men and women pulled into the Guards from the Reds," she'd told Ehren. *Kurtane Ready Troops*, they explained to Laine. "We need the numbers, all right, but most of these people have some sort of chip on their shoulders—think they already know all they need to know, that Guarding is just some glorified version of what they've already been doing."

And Ehren had snorted, a derisive sound.

"Right," Jada said. "So when Gerhard came in with one of the Upper Level flunkies and told us you'd killed a Guard, we weren't really surprised when he pulled out a group of the booted-up Reds to look for you. Even though only a few of us trained with you, the rest of us have heard about you . . ." her voice broke slightly, but she gathered herself quickly enough. "—and looked up to you, like Algere. Gerhard probably thought he was doing us a favor, sending the others out. But I felt he was doing it all wrong. I thought those Reds would as soon put a crossbow bolt through you from a distance than try to talk you in, and risk facing you." She smiled grimly. "They've heard some about you too, you see."

"Comforting," Ehren grunted. "Gerhard may have known *exactly* what he was doing."

"Algere agreed with me, and well . . . you know what he can—could—be like. All quiet, till he finally loses his temper. He talked to Gerhard, argued with him . . . and Gerhard understood, you know . . . he didn't come down on Algere like you probably would've. Like he ought to have . . ." She took a deep breath and looked resolutely at an unoccupied and shadowed corner of the creaky little barn. Laine was instantly grateful he hadn't known Algere. Whatever had happened to the man, it was bad enough to shake this woman, and even on short acquaintance he doubted that was easy.

"What happened," Ehren growled, a demand more than a question.

She shook her head, slowly. "Gerhard was trying to reassure Algere, I think. He told him that Varien had a good idea where you were, and that this road was the only logical way to come into the capital; he said the other Guards—if you could call them that—would find you quickly, and bring you in safely, and that we'd get this all settled soon. But as soon as Algere and I knew where you'd be coming in . . ." She shrugged. "We decided to beat them to you."

Ehren nodded, but his face was grim, and he looked at the bota in such a way that Laine knew he was wishing there was more wine. "And?"

She scowled; Laine thought it was a vengeful expression.

"We also decided to delay the others. We saddled up our horses and then turned the rest of them loose—and we made sure the city-ward gate was open for them."

Ehren smiled at that, though he obviously tried to suppress it. "Good idea," was all he said.

"We thought so. But we didn't count on so many of the Reds being gathered at the tavern south of the palace."

"The Crippled Swan," Ehren said. "Not a nice place."

Jada swallowed, and looked away. "The Reds frequent it, lately. All our new Guards were there, and they had plenty of friends. One or two of the loose horses came that way, and then when we came by, all packed for a trip . . . it didn't take them long to figure out what we were up to. We just weren't expecting their reaction. . . ."

"No," Ehren said. "They were still Reds, where it counted."

She nodded. Her eyes filled, spilling a tear or two down her cheek, but her voice remained reasonably steady. "There were some Guards in the barracks who had a good idea what we were up to, but they were all for it. We're a *unit*, and they didn't like what they'd heard any more than we did. But the Reds . . ." She took a deep breath. "They came swarming out of that tavern, and we should have run. We should have *known* we couldn't trust them like Guards."

"But you didn't, and they tried to take you." Ehren finished it for her, since she was obviously reluctant to. "Are you sure Algere is dead?"

She nodded. "Pretty damn sure. If it hadn't been for my horse . . ." She sighed, soft and sad. "They outnumbered us ten to one, but they never even gave him a chance. They came at us with live steel."

Ehren ran a hand over his face, let it rest there a moment. His eyes, when they reappeared, were as watery as hers— but his face was hard, the clean lines of his jaw resolute. "Then," he said, "we'll have to make sure his death isn't wasted."

And that's how the travelers—two rogue Guards and the son of a Solvan prince—had ended up on this little side ride, wandering over small plank bridges and jumping the occasional downed tree that no one had bothered to move. They were riding the tracks that went through the woods, and skirted hayfields, and meandered from farmhouse to farmhouse. Laine knew he rode in the middle position because he was their weak spot, and it bothered him not a bit. There was no place for ego in a reality this dangerous.

He tried to keep that in mind throughout the day, as Ehren and Jada traded places, their wariness making him constantly aware that they were riding straight toward people who wanted Ehren, if not dead, then out of commission. Jada was undoubtedly in no better graces. And here he was, Dannel's son, a member of the family Varien had sent Ehren to kill. Laine decided to hum drinking songs instead of thinking. It seemed the wiser option.

Drinking songs got him through the day, and then through the next, when they repeated their off-road travels. But by the end of the day, Laine had noticed even the paths had gotten substantial, and the villages closer together—and larger. Definitely larger. After some discussion, they stopped at one of the villages and found a place to stay the night. It was one of the grubbier inns Laine had seen, and by the time they'd stabled the horses, he was seriously considering staying with them for the evening.

"No," Ehren said, as he finished brushing down Ricasso. "We need to talk. And it's best done in the common room. If we slink up to our room, that'll draw as much notice as huddling secretively in a corner. It's nothing but an overnight, Laine, and a normal conversation."

"I hadn't really thought of it otherwise until now," Laine said with some dignity. But when he followed them into the inn, and sat down in the crowded common room—where he was about to wait far too long for his meal—he was a little intimidated all the same. The other customers were rough-looking, and none of them seemed to be in a very good mood. In fact, it reminded him very much of the inn in T'ieranguard where Ehren had braced Varien's men.

Laine hoped no one died tonight.

After they'd ordered their meals—one choice on the menu, no big decisions there—Ehren plunked his elbows on the table and said, "Things change tomorrow."

"How?" Laine asked.

"This is the last of the smaller villages before Kurtane," Jada said. "If we keep going in this direction, we'll hit the outskirts of Kurtane tomorrow evening."

Laine rested his chin in the heel of his hand. "Do you think they're still looking for you?"

"Undoubtedly," Ehren said, a touch of amusement in his voice. "With any luck, they'll figure Jada warned me off, and they'll spread their search outward—but sooner or later they'll pick up some trace of us, and realize that we're actually headed into the city."

"They might even get the rest of the Reds in on the search," Jada murmured. She leaned out of the way so the boy bringing their ale could set it in front of her, then drank half of it down before Laine even got his. "Bring another," she told the boy shortly.

"Yes'm," the boy nodded. His face, Laine thought, aside from being dirty, held an uncommonly vigilant expression; his eyes were wary and moved constantly over the crowd.

"Nice place you picked here," he muttered to Ehren.

"Isn't it?" Ehren said, his expression turning far too cheerful. "So much lowlife through here, what's to notice in us? We're a bit too travel-worn to blend in anywhere nicer."

Laine gave himself a rueful onceover and decided there was truth to that. He tried to remember why he'd been so adamant in coming to Solvany with Ehren in the first place. A desire to put the final element of his Dreams—absent these past several weeks—behind him? The need to be part of this thing that was so tangled with his heritage? Or the simple—and naive—reluctance to watch a friend walk away?

"They probably *will* get the Reds going," Ehren said, a response to Jada. "They—whoever's behind this, whether it's Varien alone or whether he has company—won't want this to get out of hand. Fortunately, I have other plans."

Jada's expression determined. "So do I. Look, Ehren, we've got to do two things. We've got to stop Varien, and we've got to get through to Rodar. At the least, he's got this smuggling to look into, and at the worse, the smuggling ties into his father's death, and there're more than just Varien involved. Rodar needs to learn this *privately*, so he can investigate quietly enough not to warn anyone off—or endanger himself." She shrugged, and added simply, "I think we're more likely to live to stop Varien if we make getting to Rodar our priority—*but*—it'd be nice to get an idea of what Varien's up to, first."

Ehren gave her a skeptical look. "Of course it would," he said. "But unless you intend to walk into the palace and ask—" he stopped short. "No," he said. "We're not going to do it."

"I'm not stupid," Jada said, wrinkling her nose at him. "You're far too recognizable to pull that off. But Laine and I could."

Ehren reached over the small table and tugged the bright copper braid that fell over her shoulder. "And you're *not*?"

Laine noticed no one bothered to ask if he was even remotely interested in trotting into Varien's turf. On the other hand . . . if he could get a glimpse of the man, he'd know for sure if Varien was the man from his Dream. And of the three of them, he was the one who hadn't been outlawed.

"Hair can be covered or dyed," Jada said. "No one's going to question us, not unless we do something stupid. Rodar's got so many work gangs on renovations that it's hardly surprising to run across an unfamiliar face. That's what I want Laine for—he can do the talking, and draw the attention. That accent'll do it."

"You can't count on him in a fight," Ehren said promptly. "You'd be responsible for both your safety." He gave Laine an apologetic glance. "Sorry to be so blunt. I know you'd do your best."

Laine, who had indeed been a bit taken aback, ruefully

shook his head. "No, you're right. I can hold my own in a scuffle, but not against someone who knows what they're doing. But—I do want to go. I want to see Varien, even from a distance."

"If it comes to a fight," Jada said, "we're both in trouble. I can hardly carry my sword inside and claim to be from a work crew. The point is *not* to get caught."

Ehren rubbed a hand across his face, looking tired. "I rank you, you know. You really should listen to me."

"You're outlawed," Jada replied promptly. "That doesn't leave you much of a rank." She flipped her braid behind her back and said, "Look, Ehren, if it was a *terrible* idea, you wouldn't still be talking about it. All I want to do is get in, pick up on the current gossip, and get out again. It's going to be tough enough to get through to Rodar—we might as well make informed decisions instead of wild guesses."

He raised an eyebrow at her. "In and out again?"

"I swear it on my honor feather."

Ehren snorted. "You don't have an honor feather."

Laine snuck in a suggestion, but not with much hope. "Any chance we could just . . . write it all down? That might at least get Rodar's attention. Maybe then we could go in as invited guests . . ."

Ehren shook his head, a decisive movement. "It was just such a note that got Benlan killed. It's a good idea, Laine—but not until we know who to trust."

Jada shrugged, unfazed by any of it. "Which is it to be, Ehren? Do you want to charge the palace and fight our way through to Rodar, or will you let me take a little risk now so we can avoid it later?"

"There *isn't* any way to avoid risk," Ehren said, his expression dark. "Not as long as we're intent on seeing Rodar—and right now, as poor a king as he makes, he's the only one I trust *not* to have a hidden motive in seeing us dead."

No, there wasn't any way to avoid risk. But Laine knew they were going in, anyway.

I swear it on my honor feather. Laine recalled Jada's words and snorted softly to himself. "He should have made you swear on something you *did* have," he muttered to Jada.

She turned around just long enough to give him a beatific smile. "Yes, he should have."

"Wonderful," Laine grumbled, shifting the heavy sack of mortar on his shoulder. Jada carried one, too, and it spit tiny puffs of dust on her back from a weak seam as she walked. Her hair was dyed dark brown—a strange-looking color, with the odd glint of copper showing through. Her face had been darkened as well, making her copious freckles more difficult to see—though frankly, Laine thought her broad and mischievous features were obvious enough, freckled or not.

Together, they'd come in through the temporary workers' entrance, and when questioned by the bored guard there, Jada had spouted off an equally bored recitation of name and location assignment, and they'd been waved through.

Since then, Laine was certain, they had walked all the public areas of the palace, shifting the heavy bags from one shoulder to the other, pausing for gossip and looking busy when it was necessary. He had no idea where they were going, now, nor—since they'd heard Varien was out of the palace, and Laine wouldn't have a chance to see him—did he think they'd learned anything of any use. Unless you counted the fact that mortar dust was quick to stick to sweat.

Jada touched his arm, guided him to a hall entrance and pulled him aside. "That's it for these," she said, glancing around as she eased her burden to the floor. "Put it down."

"What are we doing?" Laine asked warily, glancing down the airy hallway. It had freshly painted plastered walls and some perfectly garish gilded crownwork. "There's no work going on here—we can't exactly blend in."

"We're not likely to run into anyone," Jada said. "And if we do, you lay that accent on them. Tell them we're new, we went out to use the commons, and now we're looking for the north baths."

"If we're not going to run into anyone, how are we going to learn anything?" Laine asked. It was, he thought, a reasonable question.

"That's exactly *how* we're going to learn something," Jada hissed, growing impatient with him. "You wanted to come, didn't you?"

"To see Varien! And he's not here." But Laine set his bag next to Jada's.

"Neither is Rodar," Jada said. "That means security's not half as tight."

Laine blinked at her. "Rodar's not here? Who told you that?"

"No one. But I saw some painters coming out of the private wing. They wouldn't have been there if Rodar was in the palace." Jada glanced around the small area where they'd paused, a place where two hallways intersected, enlarged enough to serve as a small room, with large, open windows that let in the breeze and the fragrance of the garden below. "We'd better get moving before someone *does* come through," she said. "It won't be as easy to explain our presence if it doesn't look like we're at least *trying* to find our way to the north baths."

"Oh, yes it will," Laine muttered. "I'll just say we were arguing."

She ignored him, brushing past him to take the gilded hall. "C'mon."

What was he going to do, *stand* there? As Laine gave chase, he also gave a fervent wish that it was Ehren he was skulking about with, for Ehren's judgment, he could trust. As it was, he was growing more than a little irritated that Jada felt free to drag him hither and yon without bothering to explain what she was up to. Just how long had she known Rodar wasn't here, anyway?

Ahead of him, she put up a hand, cautioning silence; her step grew light and wary. Laine frowned at her as she stopped in front of a tall, heavy door and put her hand on the latch, briefly listening for signs of occupation within.

What are you doing? he wanted to demand, and didn't

dare. She opened the door, stuck her head in, and removed it long enough to look at him and jerk her chin at the room within. When he hesitated, she grabbed his arm and yanked him in.

Laine found himself in a small anteroom, with a desk that filled one wall, and glass-faced cabinets of dried herbs lining the others. There was a petite scale and weight set neatly lined up along the back of the desk, and a tidy sheaf of papers off to one side. "Where *are* we?" he hissed at Jada, afraid to raise his voice to the level he'd have preferred to use.

"Varien's rooms," Jada said as she scanned the contents of the room, and he could have sworn he heard a smug note in her voice.

"*What?*" he yelped.

She turned on him with a mighty frown. "*Quiet!*"

But it was too late. Someone had heard them, someone on the other side of the door that barred the way to the inner rooms—there was a muffled noise from within. Jada lost her annoyance for alarm. "He's not supposed to be here—"

"Let's go," Laine said, already turning to suit action to word.

Jada's hand landed heavily on his arm. "No—listen."

Listen? What he wanted to do was *run*. But . . . Ehren trusted her. Laine clenched his teeth, took a deep breath, and listened. Within seconds, he heard what had caught her attention. Faint, muffled by at least one door, it was an unmistakable cry of distress. He exchanged a frown with Jada, and when she put her hand on the inner door's latch and looked at him again, he nodded. At least she bothered to *ask* this time.

They padded silently into the next room, a much larger chamber with thick curtains walling off tall windows, shutting out the light that would have brightened the place. Instead it was dark and foreboding—filled with heavy furniture, carpeted with a thick, luxurious rug, and overwhelmed by the centerpiece table.

"Yuck," Jada said softly. "Rodar could have decorated this room better than this, and that's not saying much."

"It's all for show," Laine said. "I'll bet he's never even sat down at that desk." He nodded at the far wall, which was divided by two more doors. "His real workroom is back there, I'll bet."

"I'm not going to take you up on that one," Jada said, rounding the table to regard the doors close up. She looked from one to the other and chose, apparently at random, closing her hand around the latch on the left hand door. As soon as she touched it, a whimpering cry filled the air, trailing off into a weak sob. Jada snatched her hand back and stared suspiciously at the door.

"No," Laine said impatiently. "It came from behind the other one."

"I knew that," she said, and didn't wait for further comment before grabbing the latch to the right-hand door and yanking it down. The door opened without resistance, and in she went, leaving Laine on the other side of the table. "Oh, Hells," she said, her voice filled with dismay and loathing. "Damn that man, damn him to the Lowest Level."

Laine scrambled around the table to hesitate at the doorway and peer in. It was a small room, windowless and unadorned. Jada was at the far end, blocking most of his view of the cot that fit snugly between opposite walls. A small trunk, a tiny dressing table, and a pungent smell sufficed to fill the rest of the room. "What is it?" he asked cautiously. He wasn't sure he wanted to know, not from the smell—which seemed to be equal parts unwashed body and ripening body waste.

"Come see for yourself," Jada said grimly. Before her, something whimpered. She bent over, murmured something soothing, and looked back over her shoulder. "Come, Laine. I'm not sure we have much time with her."

Laine came, hesitant and dreading what he might see. And when he got there, he realized his imagination had fallen far short of actuality. Jada was kneeling by that time, murmuring a soothing something, and he had an unimpeded view of the young woman on the bed. She wore only a thin shift, stained with copious body waste, and the mottled bruising on her torso was perfectly clear through the material. Her legs, tangled in sheets, were marked with lightning strikes of blotchy purple bruises that snaked down her ankles and fanned across her feet. Her eyes bulged sightlessly at Jada, and fresh blood marked her lips; she cried in a soft, constant whimper of pain and fear.

"Who . . . who is she?" Laine asked. "What the Hells happened to her?"

"Varien's apprentice, Ileen," Jada said shortly. "And I have no idea what's wrong with her—except I bet it's Varien's doing."

"Yes," Ileen said, softly keening the word. Tears streamed down her cheeks. "Varien . . . I'm going to dieeee—" A strained sob seized the word and carried it away, and Jada glanced back at Laine, nodding—as if he needed confirmation to know that the girl was right.

"Ileen," Jada said, carefully stroking the girl's limp, dirty hair, "tell us. Tell us what Varien has done. We're here for justice, and we'll see that he pays."

"Then you know," the girl gasped.

"We know he's done wrong. We need to be able to prove it. Help us."

"What did he do to you?" Laine asked, and his voice came out in a horrified whisper.

The girl's face contorted in sudden fear. "Who is it? I don't know you, I know I've never heard that accent before—*who*—"

"It's Jada," the Guard said quickly. "I've been serving King Rodar. And Laine—he's a friend, Ileen. He's here to help stop Varien. But we need *details*."

"I don't have details," Ileen said, almost too faintly to hear. "He . . . he's been using a drug on his apprentices. He didn't tell me, he doesn't tell any of us, and now he controls so many wizards, so many of us. . . . Because if he takes it away, it kills. When I found out . . ." She had to stop, her breath coming in shallow pants. When she continued, they both had to lean in close to hear her. Laine covered his nose with his hand, trying to mask the smell. "I found out . . . I was so mad, so frightened . . . I snooped, I wanted a way out. I discovered there was so much more going on . . . Loraka, the other ministers . . ." She stopped and took a slow deep breath, the effort obvious. "He found out I knew more than I should. He took the drug away, and spelled me so I couldn't get out of bed . . . not until it was too late. And then he left."

"Mage lure," Laine whispered.

"We knew that," Jada said. "Ileen, what did you find out about Loraka and the other ministers? What about Benlan?"

"Benlan?" Ileen repeated without comprehension.

Laine shook his head. "It's too much for her. Go slow, Jada."

"I can't go slow," Jada said, biting off the words with frustration. "She doesn't have that much time. Look at all that bruising—she must be bleeding inside, too. I don't know why she's even still alive—"

"The drug goes through Loraka," Ileen said. "Typhean takes some of it as payment."

"Typhean?" Jada repeated. "Who is—"

"In Everdawn. He's working with Varien . . . there are others—" She cut herself off with a gasp of pain that turned into a thin wail. "Oh, Guides save me!" she cried. "Take me—"

Laine made a strangled noise as the young woman clutched the sheets, rocking her head back and crying out between agonized gasps for air. Blood trickled from her nose, spilling down the side of her face and dripping to the soiled bedsheets.

"Jada . . ." Laine said helplessly. "Jada, we can't just watch—"

"No." Jada's shoulders squared, and she looked down at Ileen. "I'm sorry," she whispered, and then she moved too fast for Laine to follow, striking with precision—and then stopping, still cradling Ileen's head as it lolled on a broken neck. Silently, she moved back and stood up, and then turned around, facing Laine's astonishment as if daring him to say something.

"No," he said. "You . . . you *had* to." He glanced down at the girl, and turned to stumble out of the room, drawing a deep breath of untainted air.

Behind him, Jada laid a hand on his shoulder. "Let's go," she said. "We didn't get much, but we know more than we did. Now we have to get out of here and take it to Ehren."

Laine wasn't even sure how they made it out of the palace. He remembered blurting out their prepared excuse of needing to use the commons—there was a constant trickle of such activity, and no one looked twice at them—while Jada contrived to look inconspicuous, hanging behind him. Other than that, their retreat was purely in Jada's hands, and she moved them swiftly to safety, from the palace itself to the grounds, to the broad streets of the city near the grounds . . . and then to a day stable where the horses were tied, and finally to the same small tavern where they'd spent the night—and Ehren.

Ehren took one look at them and secured two mugs of uncut ale. Laine had never had such strong drink so early in the day, but he didn't hesitate to take a gulp. He let Jada tell the tale, and dispense the pitifully little actual information they'd acquired. No one looked very happy when she was done.

Ehren sat back in the creaky wooden chair he occupied, disregarding the way it sagged under his weight. "Damn," he said. "She was so young." He shook his head. "And she didn't even live long enough to pass on the information she died for knowing. *Damn*," he said again, with more feeling. "We needed that information. And now we'll have to lurk around here until Rodar returns."

"We tried to find out where he was," Laine offered miserably, dimly remembering Jada's questions of the other workers in line for the commons. "No one knew and no one cared."

But Jada was watching them both with a gleam in her eye. "Waiting around wasn't what I had in mind."

Ehren raised an eyebrow. "Do tell."

Jada grinned at him; she looked pleased with herself, and her broad face was, Laine discovered, infectiously appealing when she had a gleam in her eye. "When Algere and I came after you at the border, you told me to use my position as a guard to get closer to King Rodar."

"You did it?" Ehren said, hope lighting his eyes so they looked less black and more grey, less piercing and more . . . approachable.

She nodded. "I've been in all his hunting parties since then, and after a few of those, he started asking for me to stand by him at those feasts he likes to throw so much." She looked at Laine's impressed expression and said, "It's much more boring than guarding the hunt. On duty, we're not allowed to drink anything but water, and no eating. But it's a way to keep track of who's who in the court, and who wants to be who."

"Information I'm certain we'll end up using, before this is all straightened out," Ehren said. "There's no telling just how deep Varien's rot goes."

"We can use some of it right now," she said. "I should have realized this before—I'll bet anything the king is out hunting. He'd been talking about it. He's got a taste for young deer, and the foresters can't convince him of the folly of thinning the year's crop of them. He wants a last go at them before we get into fall rutting season."

"The *lodge*?" Laine asked, looking at Ehren. *The lodge where Benlan died?*

Ehren nodded, holding his eye. "Yes. It won't cause trouble, will it?"

Laine shook his head. "I don't know. But I get the feeling we're going to find out."

"What about Varien?" Jada said. "There's no telling where *he* is."

"If he's smuggling mage lure, and has something started with Loraka, he's got other fronts to mind," Ehren said. "It's not surprising that he's off dealing with them. Unexpected fortune, I'd call it."

"Unless he's with the king," Laine said. *Some*one needed to point that out.

Ehren looked at him, his dark grey gaze even. "Then," he said, "I guess you'll get the chance to see if he's the man you saw in your Dream."

They spent the next day skirting the edges of Kurtane, east and north, heading for the hunting lodge. They found a farmer who was willing to keep Laine's mule and packs, and left half of Ehren's pack there as well, taking only what they needed to keep the horses going. Jada claimed Guard privilege for food and lodging that evening, and after that, they moved through a thickly wooded area with wide, maintained trails—although Ehren quickly shunted them off to game trails. They traveled slowly, impeded by branches. Laine, on the smallest horse and behind Ehren on the largest, didn't always duck in time when the branches Ehren bent aside sprang back into place. Inevitably, they whipped into his face, and he thought wistfully of his former role as caravan guide and front-runner.

Jada rode behind Laine, and Shaffron followed them all, his head free. From Jada's occasional cursing at the chestnut, Laine got the impression Shaffron was crowding her, trying to pass on the narrow trail so he could get closer to his buddy. Jada's comments were punctuated by intermittent squeals from the mare she rode; no matter how hard they tried to keep their progress quiet, noise was inevitable.

"We're half a day from the lodge," Ehren told Laine when he stopped in a wide spot in the trail so Laine could ride up alongside him, bumping his knee on the swell of Ricasso's belly. Ehren was rubbing his leg absently, and there was a little gathering of wrinkles between his eyes that said he wasn't sure he was happy about their situation.

Laine moved ahead another couple of steps and understood why. Their trail was about to dead-end on a wide path, and it didn't appear to pick up again on the other side. "There's probably another one a little ways down."

"There probably is," Ehren agreed. "But with the king

here, and two rogue Guards running around, there's also bound to be a lot of traffic on any of these main paths."

"If *I* was in charge, there would be," Jada agreed from behind them. "Shaffron, get *back* before I take the ends of my reins to your nose!"

Ehren smiled without turning to check on his wayward horse. "Now you see why I don't worry about losing him. Laine, I hate to say it, but I think you're the best one to send out there. Even if you stumble into someone, you can play the poor confused traveler."

"Wouldn't be far from the truth, either," Laine muttered. Then he stiffened, for both Ricasso and Nimble had perked their ears and brought their heads up in attention.

"Riders," Ehren said. "Back it up, Jada!"

Laine moved his smaller mount off the trail and into the thicker brush. When the horse remained riveted on the sounds of approaching riders, he pulled Nimble's head around with the rein, bringing the surprised creature's nose right to his boot and thoroughly distracting him from any thought of calling out. The riders were only visible in snatches of movement through the leaves, and in the color of white and chestnut horseflesh moving through the greens and browns of the woods.

A glance back as the riders passed in front of them showed Laine that Ehren had managed to move back a reasonable distance from the edge of the road; if they were still, and quiet—

Jada's mare gave an unmistakably irritated squeal, and Shaffron grunted as her back hoof hit home. Laine froze, his eyes widening, knowing discovery was imminent no matter how still he sat. The riders stopped, their voices raised and somewhat contentious—and then Laine heard a low rustle behind him and looked back just in time to see Ehren was dismounted and heading his way, knife in one hand and the long springy wand of a cut sapling in the other. "What—" he hissed, as Ehren reached him.

Ehren's answer was action. Quick and quiet, he brought the improvised whip down across Nimble's quarters, and the astonished animal jerked the rein out of Laine's hand, straightened himself out and bolted right through the trees. Instantly, Laine threw himself down over the gelding's neck, shielding his face and praying Nimble didn't run him up against a tree.

Nimble didn't. Nimble burst onto the path and ran him up against a sweating horse butt.

His arrival was accompanied by a chorus of cursing, and the three horses bumped and jostled, ears back and tails clamped, until the riders finally got them sorted out. That left two young Guards looking down at Laine, swords out and horses angled across the road ahead and behind him.

He looked up at them, one after the other, and tried hard to assume the innocent expression Shette always railed about, the one that she said made him look like a big, sad and earnest goofy hound dog who's just unwittingly bumbled into trouble.

"This is a restricted area," one of the men growled at him. "King's grounds."

It wasn't hard to look properly impressed. *I hope you have a plan if they don't buy this*, he thought at Ehren, with no little annoyance. "I got lost," he said. The Guard behind him snorted. "I'm trying to reach my sister's husband's family. They're in Southgate, have you heard of it?" He ended his query on a hopeful note and tried to forget the fact that he'd always been a terrible liar.

"You're lost all right," the first man said, the one in front of him. "We're west of the city. Southgate is *south*." He gestured south with his sword. "This was a bad place to get lost, stranger."

"I see that," Laine said, fingering the reins and thinking about how Nimble could probably outpace the larger horses on a game trail. But this time, there would be no Barrenlands to run to.

The man behind him grunted. "He's not who we're looking for, Kail."

The other man shook his head. "You want to take a chance on making Varien mad?"

Kail scowled. "Gerhard's the one that should matter. We don't answer to Varien, and I'm damned sick of hearing his name."

Laine stayed very quiet, trying to look like a man who knew his fate was in the Guards' hands, and that he would accept whatever decision they made.

"So'm I," the first man said, and he frowned down at Laine. "Where're you from?"

"Just over the border," Laine said. "I've ridden an awful long way. Probably did pretty well not to get lost until now." He offered the last with a self-deprecating little grin. "I knew I'd gone wrong but these paths twist every which way . . . if you'd point me the way out, I'd be *glad* to get out of your way."

"I'll bet," the first man said.

"Look," Kail said, "if we waste time taking him in to the lodge, we'll end up missing Ehren—assuming he's here. It's my bet he and Jada slipped through the Reds and're long gone."

"Probably. Don't know why Varien's so concerned about the king's safety, anyway—there's no way any Guard's gone *that* bad. Even if he had, he's not going to get through Varien to reach the king."

Laine said tentatively, pretending the entire byplay had gone over his head, "May I go, then? South? Out of the woods?"

Behind him, Kail reined his horse out of the way. "Go," he said. "But if you happen to find yourself twisted around again, don't expect it to be so easy."

Laine definitely didn't. Burbling with enough gratitude to annoy even himself, he turned Nimble south and put him into an immediate canter, prompting an outbreak of laughter behind him. He wondered if Ehren knew the Guards, and if he'd been able to hear what was said.

Varien was here.

Varien was here. Ehren left Ricasso tied in the woods with Jada and scouted south along the path, moving through the trees. Damned hard to outsmart a wizard, when the man was powerful enough to call Seeings. He probably had a very good notion that Ehren was in these woods, even if the Guards were less confident. Not many of them had worked with a wizard before joining the Guards, and none of them had been Guards for long. Ehren had over ten years of working at Benlan's side, and had more than enough exposure to what, with a mental snarl, he called the magical arts.

Art that was nothing but ugly when wielded by the brush of Varien's hand.

And just how far had Laine gone? Ehren was beginning to doubt the split-second decision that had sent Laine bursting into the Guards, when he could only hope Laine would pick up on their previous discussion and play the naive and blundering visitor. For a moment there, he'd thought he'd have to interfere, but the fact that the rest of the Guards were as unhappy about Varien's influence as Ehren was had saved the situation.

Finally, he caught a glimpse of Nimble through the screen of trees he'd put between himself and the road, and he gave a low whistle. Laine stopped, clearly uncertain, warily watching the spot where Ehren eventually emerged. When he saw it was Ehren, relief washed across his features—and then outraged indignance. "If I thought I could whip you in a fair fight . . ." he said with a scowl, and then shook his head.

"How about if I consider it done?" Ehren offered.

"Including a big fat black eye that'll remind you not to *ever* do that to me again?"

Ehren grinned. He'd figured Laine's normal good humor would win out over the anger, faced with an offer like that. "A black eye, a loose tooth, and a fat lip."

"Deal," Laine said. "Want a ride?"

"Two of us on Nimble? He's a sturdy little fellow, but I'd feel guilty. I'll walk." Ehren fell in beside the horse. For all his deliberately light conversation, he scanned the road ahead, looking for any glimpse of movement, listening for a stray hoof fall.

"One good thing," Laine said. "I found a couple of game trails to pick up."

Ehren nodded, but he wasn't sure they needed trails any more. He'd gotten oriented, and knew where they were going; Jada would, too.

"Did you hear what they said?"

Another nod. "That I did. Complicates things. Rodar would have been a lot easier to reach without Varien around."

He was silent a moment, thinking, and Laine looked at him, and asked warily, "What?"

Ehren didn't answer right away. When he did, his thoughts were still far away. "Just wondering when Varien turned into such a problem. I've never liked the man—but there are plenty of people working for Solvany's good who I don't like personally. Sometime along the way, Varien quit working for Solvany's good, and started working mainly for his own. I just wonder . . . how I missed it."

"Probably off doing your job," Laine said, as if it was obvious.

Ehren gave him a raised eyebrow. "Watching out for people like Varien *is* my job, Laine."

"Oh. I didn't realize you were the only King's Guard Solvany had." Laine's words were light, but his meaning clear. Ehren didn't respond. There wasn't any point; it wasn't an argument Laine would win, or that he would ever win with himself.

They hadn't quite gotten back to the spot where they'd encountered the Guards when Jada's voice came from the trees on the other side of the woods. "Over here. I've got an idea, Ehren."

Ehren nodded for Laine to go ahead and join the other Guard, and retrieved Ricasso and Shaffron from their original stopping point. When he returned, Laine was concluding his version of the conversation between the Guards, and the critical information it had revealed.

"Varien," Jada said in disgust. "He keeps cropping up in this mess even if we *don't* go looking to lay blame on him."

"There's got to be someone—or some*ones*—Upper Level on his side," Ehren said. "Someone's backing him—and protecting him."

"Upper Level this, Upper Level that," Laine complained. "At first I thought you were just talking Upper Level Hells, like most people. But you're not, are you?"

Jada gave him an amused glance. "Know a lot of Solvany, do you? We *do* have a government, you know."

"The king," Laine said. "Rodar."

Ehren gave him a skeptical look. Maybe Dannel and Jenorah had kept their children deliberately naive about their two countries. Or maybe Laine had just never paid attention, which was more likely. "In a way, I *am* talking about the Levels of Hell—or the Heavens, depending how you feel about politics."

"I know how *I* feel," Jada muttered.

Ehren's mouth quirked, but otherwise he ignored her. "The Solvan government is based on nine levels of operation—from the First Level ministers to Ninth Level pit cleaners. The Upper Levels—First, Second, and sometimes Third—are the ones that directly advise and guide the king. Only in Rodar's case, the advisory aspect of their powers seems to have slipped over into actual power—Rodar wasn't handling too much on his own, from what I understand."

"And from what *I* saw," Jada said with a decisive and somewhat scornful nod.

"I suspect that tendency was cultivated," Ehren said, thinking again just how convenient Benlan's death had been for Varien's interests, resolving once more to get to the bottom of it all.

"Ehren?" Jada asked quietly.

He looked over at her. She was holding her horse's reins close to the bit, her relaxed arm bobbing around with the movement of the animal's head, but her face somber, a reflection of his own. He shook his head. "Just trying to put the pieces together, Jada. Wishing we had more substantial evidence to take to Rodar."

"It's enough for him to act on," Jada said, intractable. "And that's what we should do, you know—take it straight to Rodar."

"That's what we *are* doing," Laine said.

She shook her head. "We're going to the lodge. Everyone's there—the ladies who are tripping over each other to catch the royal eye but who don't want to hunt; the cooks and servants; the off-duty Guards—and Varien, burn him. How'd he figure out what we were up to, anyway?"

"If he knew exactly what we were up to, we'd be caught by now," Ehren said shortly. "But your point is taken. There are a lot of people to trip over at the lodge."

"Right. But *I* know Rodar's favorite hunting spots. There're a couple of meadows, and he likes to have the houndsmen and whippers drive the game to him. If he's here, and he's hunting, he's going to start the day in one of just a few spots—and if we're quick enough, we can check them all before the whippers get him his game. The hunting," she said with a wry expression, "seems to be getting a little thin in this area."

"The creatures here would no doubt be better off if Rodar spent a little more of his time at court, attending to Solvany's needs," Ehren said absently. He was thinking of Jada's suggestion, and picturing the participants in such a hunt. Some of the court nobles, the young men, especially. Moderately loyal, but not fighting men. Definitely Guards, maybe as many as ten, if Varien had stirred them up—although maybe not, since he seemed to have them out checking the entire area, as well. The thinner they were spread, the better.

And Varien himself? Where would he be? And what sort of complications could he present, if he was with Rodar when Ehren approached?

There were some questions they just couldn't answer. And some answers that they were going to have to make up as they went along.

Ehren stirred, discovered the other two looking at him, and nodded. "Pick the likeliest of them, Jada. We'll spend the night there."

It didn't turn out to be as easy as that. Jada scouted ahead, trying to find the best route to the chosen meadow. It was late afternoon, and the gathering clouds suggested another bout of rain. Ehren was stewing over the idea—and the fact that rain of any significance would likely delay their plans a day—when he realized Laine's expression had gone distant, and that it spoke of magic. "What?" he said sharply.

Laine didn't bother to look at him. "I'm not sure," he said, scanning the area ahead of them. "It seems to be . . . moving. I can't pin it down."

"Toward us?" Ehren's hand landed lightly on his sword, though he well knew there were spells against which a sword was no protection.

"I'm not sure," Laine repeated, closing his blue eye. Then his expression cleared—the look he always got when his Sight kicked in—and just as suddenly he went berserk. Ehren was so flabbergasted he just stared, as Laine dropped Nimble's reins and scrambled away, his face mad with . . . fear? Fear of *what*?

"*Laine*," Ehren said, his voice sharp again, and totally unheeded as Laine tripped over his own feet and a low branch, fell heavily—but never stopped moving, never stopped his effort to get *away*. Scrabbling forward, he regained his feet and sprinted into the woods.

Ehren didn't bother to call after him. Leaving the startled horses, he matched Laine's sprint, long legs gaining ground and the bad one screaming at him. He took Laine down in a tackle that threw them both heavily against a thick hickory, and flaky bark rained down on top of them as they slid against its trunk.

The noises in Laine's throat weren't human, the contorted expression on his face barely so. He fought Ehren without comprehension, only naked fear—and Ehren learned first-hand that there was plenty of strength in Laine's sturdiness. He threw himself across the younger man, grabbed him at the sides of his neck, and shouted in his face. "Stop *Looking*, Laine! Stop Looking!"

The barest glimpse of intelligence flashed across Laine's features; Ehren shouted at him again.

As suddenly as the fit had come, it was gone. Laine relaxed beneath him, breathing hard. Carefully, Ehren released his hold. "All right?" he asked.

Slowly, Laine nodded, looking befuddled. "I—I've never felt anything like that before. It was . . . so strong. There was nothing I could do to fight it. I feel like such a—a coward."

Ehren climbed to his feet, wincing; he offered Laine a hand up. "There's no point. It was magic, Laine. No doubt a spell like that could drive a man to do *anything* in his attempt to escape it—jumping off a cliff, killing someone he loves who happens to be in the way . . . I've heard of such things, but I've never seen it." He brushed crumbled hickory bark off the back of his neck and gave Laine a wry twist of a grin. "Until now."

"It's hard to believe," Laine said, still dazed. He held out his hands, as if he expected to find they weren't his, and looked the rest of his body over in a similar manner. "I hadn't realized magic came in such insidious forms."

Ehren made a derisive sound deep in his throat. "It's one reason to put Varien out of business. And lately, those reasons have been piling up." Then he stopped trying to get that last tricky bit of bark that was stuck beneath his collar, for Laine had stiffened, his eyes gone apprehensive.

"It's back," he whispered. "Could it . . . could it follow us?"

"Damn that man to the Ninth Hell," Ehren growled. "Yes, it's possible. If he's set the spell to key on one of us—and he doesn't know about you." He scanned the woods that had Laine so alarmed. "At least, he *shouldn't* know about you."

"Let's talk about that later," Laine said, shifting nervously. "It's damn hard not to See the thing once I've focused on it . . . and it's definitely closing in on us."

"Running works for me," Ehren said.

"Running sounds *great* to me." Laine jogged a few

backwards steps, ran into a tree, and turned around to give navigation his full attention. Ehren snagged his arm and redirected him.

"Back to the horses," he said. Laine didn't waste his breath with a reply, but nodded and followed, casting anxious looks over his shoulder.

He soon fell slightly behind Ehren, whose long strides came in a fast, slightly syncopated rhythm, but when Ehren checked on him, Laine just waved him on.

"We've left it behind," he said. "But if it catches up again . . ." He paused, gulping in a few audible breaths as he ran. "We can't run forever. Sooner or later—"

Ehren didn't waste his breath. A few more moments, a slight course correction, and they were running up on the horses, who took their intrusion with some suspicion and much snorting. "Easy, boys," Ehren said, soothing them between breaths. When Laine had Nimble and was catching up on his own breathing, Ehren said, "There's got to be a limit to the spell—time limit, or distance. I've no intention of getting caught by it."

"The spells in the mountains have been wandering for hundreds of years," Laine said pointedly.

Ehren grimaced, rubbing his leg. "True enough. But they weren't keyed spells . . . that's got to take more energy, or more direction."

"You *know* that?" Laine asked with some surprise.

Ehren shook his head. "No."

Laine muttered, "Wonderful," and dug a piece of hickory bark out of his shirt. Then, "Are we just going to stand here?"

"This is where Jada expects us to be." Ehren jerked the tie loose on his saddlebag, and rummaged around inside. He needed something dispensable. Unfortunately, all the dispensable things had been left with Laine's packs and mule, on the other side of Kurtane.

"Ehren . . ." Laine said, with distinct unease.

"All right, Laine . . . go ahead, just stick to the game trail. It's me the thing's after."

"You're going to let it get you?" Laine asked, true horror in his voice.

"Not if I can help it," Ehren replied, pulling a narrow length of clean linen from the bottom of the bag. He'd been carrying it ever since he rode away from Dajania's wagon, in case he needed to redress the leg. The healing spell had made that unnecessary, but he'd kept it on general principles—with the kind of trouble they were stirring up, having a handy bandage had seemed like a good idea. He only hoped that possessing it for so long had imbued it with whatever essence the spell was sniffing out. "Wait, Laine—can you still see it?"

"You better believe it, and it's mighty burning close." Laine's voice came from a hundred feet off, and even at that distance, his tension was clear.

"Tell me when it's on the edge of triggering distance," Ehren said, tightening his hold on Ricasso's reins. He dropped the cloth to the ground and moved a few feet back, shooing Shaffron up the trail. Shaffron snorted indignantly and swished his tail in Ricasso's face, trotting only a few steps away.

"All right," Laine said. It was only another moment before he added, "*Now*, Ehren. Move it!"

Ehren moved it. Dragging Ricasso behind, swatting Shaffron's bobbing hindquarters ahead, he jogged down the trail until he met up with Laine. "Did it work?" he asked, glancing behind and moving aside to see past Ricasso. Everything looked just as it had.

Laine must have thought otherwise, for he made a noise in his throat and added, "It's stopped . . . it's just sort of— whoops!"

Ehren detected nothing. "What? Is it moving again? *What?*"

"It triggered," Laine said somberly. "It's scaring the Hells out of that patch of ground. How'd you do that?"

"Gave it a decoy," Ehren said. "Something I've had for a while. It's definitely keyed to me, then. Varien's not taking any chances." He shook his head. "This is the sort of thing he can do without anyone else noticing. Unless someone hires another wizard to find these things and read the signature on them, he can take us out without incriminating himself in the least."

"You think he'll send more?"

"He might. If I was him, I'd send a couple more even though this one triggered, just to make sure we didn't somehow blunder out of it." He gave Laine a searching look. "You're going to have to stay on your toes, I'm afraid. Jada may get us to the king, but you're going to be the one to get us past Varien."

Laine sighed, and ran a hand down Nimble's neck, never looking away from Ehren. Although humor-crinkled eyes defined the one expression Ehren most associated with Laine, recently his face had been all too somber—just as it was, now. Laine said, "Then we'd better hope you don't run out of things to throw down as decoys."

And they'd better hope Varien didn't catch on.

Chapter 16

Laine and Ehren intercepted Jada as she returned, heading for the spot where she'd left them.

"Why'd you move?" she asked instantly. "Trouble?"

"Definitely," Laine said. He glanced at Ehren, who shrugged. Jada tucked away the stray hair that habitually fell over her eye, and gave Laine an impatient look. "Varien's sending spells after Ehren. Or," he added, suddenly realizing their assumption, "*some*one's sending spells after Ehren. We just tricked one of them—didn't want you caught in it."

She frowned, and looked at Ehren for the missing pieces. "Someone's *sending* spells?"

"Make a spell, key it to someone, and turn it loose," Ehren said. "We're assuming it was Varien."

"Seems a safe enough assumption to me," Jada grumped. "But—how'd you get away?"

"Laine spotted it," Ehren said, glancing up at the clouded sky. "We'd best hope that rain holds off, because I'm sure that wasn't the last spell, and Laine's our only hope of avoiding them."

"Oh?" Jada said tartly. "And how is that?"

"I can See them coming," Laine said simply, then spoke quickly to forestall her questions as her jaw dropped. "Just leave it at that, Jada, and actually, if you can forget you

317

know it, that might be better." When he'd been working with Ansgare, there didn't seem to be any point in denying his abilities. But now that he knew where they came from, he didn't want anybody asking the sort of questions that might lead to answers best left alone. Ehren and Jada knew who he was, and so did the T'ierand. Knowing there were people in the world who would wish him dead just because of his heritage, that almost seemed like a crowd. If Ehren had followed orders instead of instinct, Laine and his family would be dead already.

"I agree," Ehren said with a nod. "I think it's safe to say that *any*thing you learn about Laine, you should consider a confidence, Jada."

She looked slightly affronted. "As if I'd betray him."

"Betrayals come in insidious packages," Ehren said. "And with some people, it only takes a single word out of place."

Jada tossed her head, annoyed, but Ehren ignored her. "And you, Laine—you're going to have to watch what you say, as well. You're not used to keeping your Sight a secret."

"No," Laine said ruefully. "I'm not." He stroked Nimble's tangled mane and thought about the ways his life had changed this summer. He had learned what real fear was, for one thing. He'd never even imagined he was capable of such utter terror as that spell had just invoked in him, and he'd only been *Looking* at it, not been under it. He wished he could perceive the sendings more clearly, instead of as a funny little itch at the corner of his vision—they'd be easier to track. On the other hand, maybe it was just as well that they were hard to see. "You know, Ehren . . . I can spot any other spells that come our way . . . but I don't think I'll *Look* at them."

Ehren snorted, a mixture of amusement and appreciation. "*That*," he said, "is what I call a good idea." Then, looping Ricasso's rein loosely over a thin, flexible branch that the horse would probably eat in another moment anyway, Ehren went back to Shaffron, and began fussing with the packs.

"I found the trail that'll get us to the hunting meadow," Jada said loudly, in an obtuse question that came through clearly on her face; she gave Laine a glance that seemed to dismiss him. Still smarting over Ehren's admonishment, he decided.

"In a minute," Ehren said, grunting as he shifted the packs; Shaffron grunted too, a noise of surprise at the tug. "Shouldn't have made this thing so secure . . . though no doubt I'd be saying otherwise if things started falling out as we traveled."

"No doubt," Jada muttered. She and Laine stood and listened to Ehren's efforts for a few more minutes, and then he reemerged from the other side of Shaffron, holding the stained and torn pants he'd replaced in T'ieranguard.

"Bait," he said to Laine, who understood. Jada frowned at him as he slipped his belt knife from its sheath and cut the stained cloth into squares. "If any more spells sniff us out, they ought to key in on this just as well as on me. Unless," he added with a frown, "Varien figures out what we're doing."

"Don't beg trouble," Jada told him, and turned her mare around in the narrow trail. Ehren raised an eyebrow at Laine, who grinned back at him. He knew better than to argue with any woman of Jada's skills when she got the wind up her back.

They set up a cold camp at a stream, a short distance from the meadow. After they'd eaten some borderline cheese and bread that crunched more than it tore, Ehren walked the perimeter of the meadow. It was a large area, a quarter-mile across, with sparse, tall grasses and meadow flowers, and the occasional upcrop of the rock that ran beneath the shallow dirt and discouraged the trees. There had been royal hunts staged from this meadow for at least a hundred years.

The underbrush in the immediate area had been thinned with the extent of the off-season hunting; when the deer started rutting, Ehren knew, the hunting would only increase. The foresters must be having a fit. Ehren could only hope Rodar didn't ignore *all* his counsel so completely.

As it was, there would be no approaching on horseback, and they would have to be excruciatingly careful, or they'd be detected too soon and would never have the chance to get within earshot of the king. Reaching him physically was out of the question; Rodar would be surrounded by Guards, and Ehren had no intention of fighting his way through them. That would be worse than turning on family.

When he returned to camp, he discovered that Laine and Jada had reestablished peace, and were talking about something fairly safe—Ehren himself. Laine smiled cheerfully and guiltlessly as Ehren seated himself in front of the packs and stretched his leg out.

"If there's fighting tomorrow, will you be up to it?" Jada asked, giving the leg a pointed glance.

"Ask the T'ierand's guards," Ehren said.

Jada looked at Laine, who nodded with feeling. "Ah," she said. "I see."

"Or ask the T'ierand," Laine said, with mischievous eyes.

"Ah," Jada repeated. "I *see.*"

"I doubt that you do," Ehren told her. "I think it'd be best if we move in before they arrive tomorrow. It's going to be hard enough, moving around unseen in that trampled-down area. I don't want to be seen until I'm ready to be seen."

"Ignoring, for the moment, the fact that you're changing the subject," Jada said, "are you sure you want to seem that . . . *sneaky*? If I was guarding Rodar tomorrow, I'd trigger on sneaky a lot faster than a straightforward approach."

"We'll be straightforward enough," Ehren said. "*When* we're in the right place for it."

"Uh-oh," Laine murmured, in a voice that said much more.

Ehren stiffened. "Where is it?"

"Right down the creek," Laine said, climbing to his feet, his gaze riveted downstream. "And it's a fast one, Ehren—"

Ehren didn't waste any time. Stuffing a square of the

torn trousers into his sword belt, he headed for Ricasso, snatching up the startled horse's trailing lead rope and vaulting aboard. Ignoring Ricasso's indignant snorts, he put the horse right into a canter and headed away from the camp.

"That's far enough!" Laine called to him. "Any further and I won't be able to see clearly enough!"

Ehren promptly stopped. This was enough of a strain on all of them—he didn't need Laine in the position of guessing about what he was already trying not to look at. He dropped the square of cloth while Ricasso dropped his head and snorted several times in succession, clearly disgruntled at this whole odd procedure.

"Go!" Laine yelled.

Ehren went. Discarding niceties, he heeled Ricasso around forcefully enough that when the horse cantered off, he kicked up both his heels in protest. Fortunately, it was no chore to sit on the bay's wide back, and Ehren's soothing words got them settled into an even gait. By the time Ehren circled Ricasso around through the trees, the spot where the spell had triggered was obvious. He gave the wilted, blackened area a wide berth on his way back to the creek.

"What was *that*?" Jada said when he returned to them. The light was fading, but the affected area was large and obvious. Ehren thought he winded a stench on the breeze, something that put him in mind of a certain sumac patch in Loraka. From the expression on Laine's face, he was thinking the same thing. "I don't know," Ehren told Jada, "but I'm certain it's a good thing we aren't in it."

She gave the patch one last unhappy look, and nodded. "I guess we'll have to split watch tonight, Ehren—one of us ought to be up with Laine."

"To keep me awake, you mean," Laine said. Jada shrugged an apology, but he shook his head. "Don't worry about it. I don't want to take any chances, either."

"You take the first watch, Jada," Ehren said. "With any luck, we'll have that much time before Varien sends anything else at us—although with *more* luck, he'll figure me dead and leave it at that. As fast as that one was moving, we won't have much leeway." He slid off Ricasso's back and tied the horse nearby. "Sorry, son. I'll want you right at hand if I need you."

"Makes sense to me," Jada said. "First watch it is, then." She gave Ehren a stern look. "And don't you be taking my head off if I wake you up fast. If I had a choice I'd wake you with a ten-foot pole, so's I was sure to be out of range."

"I'll do my best," Ehren promised.

"I've heard that before," she grumbled, and he just grinned at her.

"Gotta be quick," he told her. "You gotta be quick." And then ducked the missile of stale bread she flung at him.

But Jada's watch went quietly, and when she woke Ehren it was with a quiet call from a safe distance. She settled right down to sleep, and Ehren worked out his stiffness with a quick walk around the edge of the camp, checking to see that the horses were all within a reasonable distance, and moving Ricasso so he could demolish the undergrowth in a fresh area.

He returned to sit by Laine, who hadn't said much; the strain was showing on his face. Ehren didn't envy Laine— on constant alert for something he wouldn't really be able to see, and something that was easy enough to miss during the daytime. He didn't envy him—and he didn't like having to rely on him. He preferred to rely on himself, and his own skills.

Above him came the pattering sounds of light raindrops on leaves.

"If it's raining," Laine said, "will they hunt tomorrow?"

"Depends on how hard it rains," Ehren told him.

Laine stirred; it was a dark night under the clouds and Ehren could barely see him. "Ehren . . . I can't do this for another whole day and night. Even if I somehow stayed awake, I'd probably miss anything that came our way."

"I know," Ehren said. "Don't worry about it. It's not raining that hard." And it had better stay that way. Laine was right.

If Rodar didn't come out to hunt tomorrow, they'd have to go in after him.

But the rain stayed light and intermittent, and the spells stayed away. It was the grey of dawn when Laine suddenly perked up, and Ehren got to his feet immediately, going for Ricasso.

"Right down the creek again," Laine said wearily. "Not too fast."

Ehren moved swiftly, although he was a little gentler to his sleepy horse than the evening before. They rode out beside the spell of the previous evening, which seemed to have worn off, leaving in its wake a smear of darkened tree trunks and wilted leaves. When Laine signalled him to move, he'd only made it a dozen yards when a thunderclap of sound startled them both. It sent Ricasso skittering sideways, his head flung high, and Ehren snatching at his mane to regain the balance he'd left behind—but losing control of the runaway in the process. The halter rope was hardly as effective as a bit and bridle, and Ricasso pounded forward, barely dodging the trees in their path. When Ehren finally got him stopped, Ricasso was trembling, his breath coming in snorting huffs of fear. Gently, Ehren turned him around and headed back, with Ricasso prancing and tossing his head.

"You'd do your brother proud," Ehren told him, stopping him near the self-contained conflagration that would have annihilated their entire camp had Laine not seen the danger coming. Even with the heat of the fire against his face, chills ran down Ehren's spine. *Varien*.

Back at the creek, Laine curried Nimble, his face pale. Jada, too, seemed shocked by the violence of the spell. Her own horse was saddled, and she sat by Ehren's packs, chewing on tough dried meat and watching Ehren approach.

"He's not playing around anymore," she said.

"No." Ehren cast a look over his shoulder to the fading flames. "Laine——" But when Laine turned to look at him, Ehren just shook his head. "Thank you."

"My pleasure," Laine said. He, too, watched the flames

for a moment, then scooped up his saddle and set it on Nimble's back. "I know you were planning on moving up on foot, but . . . I don't think the horses should be left behind. At least, not *your* horses."

"Hells," Ehren breathed. "You're right. We'll find a place to put them where they can't be seen." He wasn't going to chance losing the boys to *that*.

The morning light was still dim and diffuse, but it was past time to be moving out. Ehren made quick work of loading up Ricasso and saddling Shaffron while the other two waited. He donned only his greaves, thick leather gauntlets, and King's Guard ailette. His hair was tied back, the honor feather and beads securely attached. It was enough to remind them who he was, without shouting that he was looking for trouble. Jada nodded her silent approval when he was done, and they moved into the damp woods, heading for the meadow.

Jada entered the wet meadow, checking that Ehren's horses were truly out of sight. When she returned she was soaked up to her knees from the wet grasses, but looked grimly satisfied. "This whole area is in shadow, and will be, all morning. They'd have to be looking for us to find us, and even then, they'd have to come up close. And they usually gather at the other end of the meadow."

"That's how I remembered it," Ehren said, and then gave a short laugh at Jada's expression. "You think Benlan never hunted here? How do you suppose it came to be Rodar's favorite spot?"

"I . . . guess I never thought about it," Jada said.

"No." Ehren realized that none of the new Guards would have thought about it. To them, Benlan was a figurehead they'd served under for the first few months of training, or else the king who'd been killed right before they came to serve Rodar. Ehren was the only one left who'd known the king, really *known* him—served under him, hunted with him, stayed after long hours of Upper Level meetings and shared a glass of wine with him. If he died, the search for Benlan's killers would no doubt die as well.

No wonder Varien was so bent on getting him out of the way. If he'd had *any*thing to do with Benlan's death, Ehren was the last major threat to his safety.

"Ehren?" Jada said quietly, jarring Ehren out of his thoughts.

"Nothing," he said. "Just . . . thinking it all over."

"Yeah," she said, after a moment. "Me, too." He flashed her a look and discovered her expression was as somber as his, and abruptly grinned at her.

"We'll do all right," he said. "All we really have to do is get Rodar's attention. If you spent much time guarding him, it shouldn't be too hard. He'll want to talk to you, even if he puts me in chains to do it."

"I don't think we should let it come to that," Jada said tightly.

Ehren didn't answer. It wasn't his favored scenario, either, but he'd rather be in the hands of his fellow Guards than being hunted and killed by Varien's spells. On the other hand, being in the hands of his fellow Guards, unable to run, would be immensely inconvenient if Varien chose to send a spell after him.

They waited in silence for a while, suffering another short and fitful rain shower and increased concern that the day's hunting would be called off. It was late morning by the time Ehren heard the first sounds of riders in the woods.

The royal party arrived quickly after that. First, two Guards, riding point; they exchanged a few quiet words with each other and went straight to the center of the meadow, where they put their horses head to tail and surveyed the area. Laine was on the damp ground beside Ehren, and his tension became almost palpable. "Relax," Ehren muttered to him.

"Yeah, right," Laine muttered back. On his right, Jada nudged him. By then, the noisy riders had arrived—Rodar, with a handful of young men, all mounted on highly bred horses and outfitted in hunting greens that did nothing to subdue their presence. Their laughter and the jingle of their equipment could be easily discerned by any creature within a quarter mile. Ehren would be surprised if even a line of whippers and houndsmen managed to chase a deer through this meadow.

Not that he intended for this hunt to get that far.

Rodar had four more Guards positioned around him and his friends, and behind them were yet several more riders. Guards, male and female alike, had short shorn hair, variations on the theme Rodar had set. A timely reminder of the differences between them, Ehren thought. These were Guards, but they weren't *his* Guards . . . and they probably felt the same way about him. The huntmaster trailed them all, looking a bit despairing even at this distance.

And then came one more, not easily identifiable, but . . .

"Hells," whispered Jada. "Is that Varien? He came on the damn *hunt*?"

On the heels of her words, Laine whispered, "That's *him*. He's the one I saw, Ehren. The eyes . . ."

Benlan's killer.

Cold emotion washed down Ehren's spine. "Yes," he said to both of them, and his voice came out just as cold, and imbued with . . . if not hate, then a certain kind of loathing, and unyielding resolution. "He's not hunting tender deer, I can tell you that much."

"No," Jada murmured, giving him a nearly unreadable glance. Beneath it, Ehren thought he saw fear. None of them had expected Varien to act so openly. He sat his horse on the leftmost fringes of the royal party, composed and unconcerned.

He was there to protect the king from Ehren, no doubt. *Very* noble. "Varien will do his best to ensure we have no chance to talk to Rodar," he said, but his voice was resolute. Varien might *try* to stop him . . .

"*I* can," Jada said. "Let me go alone, Ehren."

"After what happened to Algere, you're just as rogue as I am." Ehren narrowed his eyes, looking hard at the man on Rodar's right. "Gerhard's there, too. He could be part of this thing."

"He may be imported from Loraka, but he's loyal. His

priority will be protecting Rodar." Jada's voice was low but assured. Ehren remained unconvinced.

"All right, then," he said anyway. "Nothing left but to do it." He stood, and his hand passed wistfully over the clean lines of his sword's stirrup hilt, then fell away, empty. Jada was scrambling to her feet as well. A hesitant beat behind them both came Laine. As one, they stepped into the clear, and walked toward the milling royal party.

One of the Guards snapped a short warning to the others, and Rodar's quartet immediately tightened around him. Laine faltered a step as the two Guards on point spurred their horses forward. Ehren and Jada's names hung in the air, sounding like curses; Gerhard called out an order that Ehren couldn't decipher, but that sounded dire.

"Steady," Ehren told Laine, giving Jada a hard look. "We're here to talk. As long as we remember that—"

"That's not it—look at—"

Something in Laine's voice made Ehren glance sharply at him; he instantly recognized the expression there. "Where?" he asked, dropping into readiness, a pose the Guards immediately misinterpreted.

Their swords, once inconspicuous, rose high, and Gerhard's voice was rough and commanding above the sound of pounding hooves. "Hold them there!"

"I can't—I can't—" Laine said, his gaze moving from Guards to the area between himself and Varien, who had dismounted to stand beside his horse.

He couldn't concentrate, that was it. "Damn," Ehren said under his breath, his hand hovering by his sword and wanting to snatch it free despite his resolve to handle this quietly.

"There!" Laine cried, and the clearing erupted into action as he flung himself before Ehren and the spell he'd Seen, and yelped as he was snatched up in midair, his arms and legs outflung and stretched tight. Jada's wordless cry of alarm rang in Ehren's ears, and the Guards pulled up hard, astonished, splitting up to flow to either side of the trio.

"No!" Varien's voice rang through the clearing as one of the Guards passed in front of Laine. "Fool!"

The Guard took one look at Laine's expression of terror—
another spell, Ehren realized—and stopped his horse in
midstride, frowning. The animal's head flung up, his eyes
rolling and his nostrils widened with fear—and then it was
too late. The spell triggered, and the air around the Guard
and horse turned smoky and dense. Laine, suspended only
yards in front of them, fought to turn his head aside, his
features twisted with horror.

Ehren slipped through the hole opened up by the separating
Guards; his sword had finally, somehow, found its way to
his hand. But steel was impotent against magic, and the smoky
cloud had turned into a swarm of black specks that dove
and whirled around the hapless Guard and his mount. Horse
and human screamed, confined within the cloud. They
seemed to blur, and the haze turned more pink than smoke,
thick enough that the frantic figures within were obscured.

When it cleared, they were gone. Laine was alone and
still tied by wizardly bonds. The metal of the Guard's gear
and horse's tack were all that remained unconsumed; it
lay scattered in the grass, winking greasily in the moment
of sunlight that broke through the clouds.

Laine fought and lost to the magic, his expression tight
with fear; when Ehren started toward him, he shook his
head—that much, Varien's spell allowed him. "Stop him,
Ehren," he said. "Just stop him, before it gets worse."

"I'll stop him, all right," Ehren growled. He cast Jada a
look, ignoring her pale face; his own expression spoke
volumes: *guard my back*. Then, sword in hand, he headed
for Rodar, moving with ground-eating strides.

"Halt!" cried the Guard behind him, her voice strained
and reluctant. Then, in surprise, "Jada, no!" In a moment
Ehren heard the sound of her body hitting the ground.
Jada at work. He walked inexorably onward, heading for
Rodar, but his eyes fastened on Varien.

Behind him, steel rang on steel, nearly obscuring Jada's
voice. "Let him *go*, Benna—*Varien* is the enemy here!"

"Come no closer," Gerhard commanded, moving between
the king and Ehren.

Rodar sat behind him on a horse that pawed the ground, snorting fractiously; he was tense, and Ehren was close enough to see the surprise in his eyes—surprise that the game of being king had suddenly turned into something much more dangerous. "Ehren," he said, barely audible, his voice uncertain and a little betrayed.

"I need to talk to the king," Ehren told Gerhard, stopping. His sword was at his side, but hung loosely in his hand, the tip down. "Guard's right."

Gerhard dismounted and released his horse, a deliberate move designed to put him on equal terms with Ehren; an *I am not afraid of you*. "You are outlaw. You have no Guard's right here." He nodded at the sword. "Drop the sword, Ehren."

Ehren shook his head, slowly, and looked at Varien, who seemed poised to act but whose devilish, wizardly hands were still. "I don't think so," he said. "I would have preferred to do this quietly" —in the background, Jada's sword rang an ironic counterpoint to his words— "but do it, I will. Rodar is safe from *me*, Gerhard. You've got the wrong outlaw."

Varien made a sharp gesture. "Get away from the king!"

Ehren stiffened, bracing against magical assault—

Nothing.

"No," Varien said, a humorless smile on his face. "You're far too close to the king for me to use magic; I would never risk my sovereign's life so. But your friend is another story." His expression was satisfaction, the face of a man who fully expected to win this fight—and to enjoy doing it. He nodded at Laine, still in magic shackles, and was rewarded with an instant cry of pain—and then another. And another.

Ehren set his jaw and kept his eyes on Gerhard. "Stop him," he said, his voice grating in his throat. Gerhard looked uneasy at the torture—he had an unobstructed view of Laine beyond Ehren—but clearly stood by both king and wizard. More loudly, Ehren said, "Rodar, *stop* the wizard!"

Only Gerhard answered, and it was almost drowned out by Laine's anguish. "Drop the sword, Ehren."

Rodar had had enough. "Leave the man alone, Varien,"

he said, a command he clearly expected to be obeyed, as queasy as he sounded.

Varien looked into Ehren's eyes and smiled coldly, not even acknowledging his king. Behind them, Laine gargled a raw noise. "Between your own comrades and my magic, you haven't got a chance." His voice was all silk and barely suppressed triumph. "Do you want your friend dead? Drop the sword, Ehren."

"Varien!" Rodar snapped, but this time his voice held surprise and uncertainty. Varien's gaze never wavered from Ehren, and his smile never faltered. *Do you want your friend dead?*

Ehren lunged for him.

Gerhard was just as fast, lunging between them. Ehren turned the lighter blade aside with a snarl of impatience but Gerhard came right back at him, lightning fast, landing a solid hit on Ehren's gauntlet and retreating while Laine's torment rang in Ehren's ears.

Ehren bore down on Gerhard in fury—a Guard's worst mistake. He wanted to smash Gerhard aside and go for Varien's head—but Gerhard skipped back out of his way, turning the struggle in the direction he would have it go, flinging his free hand up to keep the other Guards out of the fight. Instead, they gathered tightly around Rodar and herded him away. The point of Gerhard's narrow blade found Ehren's flesh in quick succession—arm, thigh, and a quick touch on his chest.

It was the sting of the last that broke through Ehren's anger. Panting, Ehren struggled to adjust his style to the Lorakan moves, keeping his wrist light and loose, letting Gerhard's blade slide off his own; he gave Gerhard the attack for the moment, and countered with swift parries his hand knew so well his mind didn't have to think about, blinking aside rage along with sweat.

Gerhard saw the difference. "Now," he said, wiping away the sweat on his own brow, *"now* we find out."

"That's not what this is—" parry, quick riposte, "—about," Ehren said.

Gerhard's answer was to press in close, forcing Ehren's sword aside with the forte of his blade, bringing his hilt up to smash against Ehren's head. Ehren jerked aside and took the glancing blow, shoving Gerhard back out of distance and automatically bringing his sword up to guard while he tried to blink his vision back to normal. Blood trickled down the side of his face; dimly, he noted that Laine had stopped screaming.

In that moment, with his own harsh breath filling his ears, with Gerhard stalking him, wary and about to strike, it was Varien who caught Ehren's eye, Varien who stood close and unconcerned, Varien with his smile and his hands twisting in some new and complex spell that no one else seemed to notice—no longer so concerned about working magic so close to his king.

No more time for this—Ehren closed the distance on Gerhard, gaining ground while they traded blows in the third and fourth lines. He'd seen Gerhard's students forget the importance of knowing your distance, and he kept his gain subtle, hoping . . . hoping—

Gerhard broke the rhythm by lunging low, and only then realized how close they were. And then it was too late, for Ehren had grabbed the outstretched arm, yanking Gerhard off balance as his foot swept behind Gerhard's forward leg and took him off his feet.

Gerhard landed hard on his back and Ehren jerked the sword out of his hand, flinging it toward the woods. His own sword tip rested at Gerhard's throat, and the Guard master dropped his hands to the ground by his shoulders, fingers spread wide in capitulation. The other Guards spurred their horses into motion toward Ehren, leaving only one man with Rodar. Ehren hesitated, hovering in an impossible choice. Varien and his spell had to be *stopped*— but dealing with Varien meant the mounted Guards would take him from behind—

Laine's newly raw voice cried a warning. "Ehren! The spell—Varien!"

The wizard was still smiling, and his hands were raised

in a theatrical flourish. *You can't do anything about it now*, his expression said, as clearly as his voice might have, while one raised eyebrow served to remind Ehren the Guards were bearing down on him.

Deal with Varien, and die by Guard hands. Dodge the Guards, and face Varien's magic—while Varien lived on.

Ehren made his choice without a second thought, holding Varien's coldly triumphant gaze and lifting his sword to first guard, hand at shoulder height, blade dropping diagonally across his body, edge out.

It looked awkward, it looked useless, and in the frozen moment of time when Ehren stared into Varien's eyes, the expression he found there told him so. And Ehren stared back, a hard, merciless look of his own; his voice was just as hard, and so low that only its intensity carried it to Varien. "This time, you lose."

There was no finesse in Ehren's movement, just fierce expertise. A step forward, a pivot, all the energy in his body going to the motion of his blade as it rose—he held Varien's gaze for one last moment before the rotation of his own body pulled him away, and saw the astonished disbelief there. And then came the satisfying bite of blade into skin and through Varien's neck—sharp steel driven by the force of Ehren's movement, hesitating at but not stopped by bone—and suddenly whipping free again, all the way around to strike dirt by Ehren's right foot. Something round and heavy hit the ground in the corner of his vision.

Ehren didn't turn to see what he'd done; he knew. The cries of dismay told him. So did the looks on the Guards' faces as they thundered up to him, not bothering with swords as they rode him down.

❦

Rough hands hauled Ehren to his feet, and when his chin sagged on his chest, someone yanked on his hair to raise his head. Harsh words in his ear meant nothing; what little wit he had was focused on the scene inside his head, the huge bulk of horses over him, of a horse rearing and

the hooves coming down at him, again and again, of trying
to roll out of the way—

There was enough wrongness, enough broken inside him
that he knew he hadn't been fast enough. Ribs grated; there
was the taste of blood in his mouth, and plenty soaking
his clothes. When the Guards on either side of him gave
him the chance to stand on his own, his legs behaved like
foolish noodles.

Jada, he wondered, trying to focus with the one eye that
seemed willing to open. *Laine*. He saw them, still across
the field—Jada, bleeding, relinquishing her sword to the
Guard who had bested her, and Laine, freed from the spell,
a heap on the ground but even now pulling himself upright.

Gerhard filled his vision; he had an honor feather in his
hand, and was looking from it to Ehren, a tight frown
wrinkling the space between his brows. "Rodar wants you
executed, right now," he said grimly, and waited, as though
hoping for reply or objection. Ehren couldn't seem to muster
anything but a groan, and when the grip on the back of
his head disappeared, his chin hit his chest again. In a fuzzy
wander of thought, he recalled that Benlan had been
avenged. It seemed enough. Something gurgled in his throat,
and he watched blood drip from his mouth to the ground.

"If the king wants him executed, he'd better do it quick,"
someone said.

There was a scuffle of feet, of someone joining them.
"Ehren!" Jada cried, fear in her voice.

"Hold her!" The order sparked the sounds of a brief
struggle; in the silence that followed, Jada gave one strangled
sob.

"Don't you realize what he's *done*? Do you think he's
really stupid enough to charge into a guarded hunting party
and kill Varien *for no reason*?"

In the background, Rodar's voice was quiet, considering.
"He was my father's favorite Guard."

"And what of me?" Jada asked. "Do you mistrust your
own judgment so, that you can shove aside all the trust
you've given *me*?"

Rodar's response was instantaneous, and closer. "What of the trust I gave Varien?"

"Did you, my liege?" Gerhard asked, and the honest searching in that voice surprised Ehren, who had counted Gerhard with Varien, no matter what Jada had said. "Did you truly trust the wizard?"

"He was my father's man," Rodar protested. "His years of service—"

"Your father," Ehren said, focusing all his energy to lift his head, just enough to look at Rodar, that's all he wanted—there. The young king was staring at him, scowling at him. But in his light eyes there was the seed of doubt. Ehren rattled through the blood in his chest, fighting for air. "Your father is dead. And Varien killed him."

Jada rapidly filled the silence of Rodar's astonishment. "We tried to come with weapons sheathed—*Varien* started the violence. Look what happened to Laine! Look what happened to Seth and his horse! One Guard dead today is enough. Please," she said, and now she was pleading. "Please, put him down. Quit hurting him. We can explain, we can prove ourselves, I swear it! Please—" and her voice broke.

"I—I withdraw the sentence of immediate execution," Rodar said, adding practically, "not that I think it'll make any difference to *him*, mind you."

In a disjoined, floating sort of way, Ehren thought he was right. And there was Laine, trying to get closer, a grip on his arm preventing him. He looked haggard, his blue and black eyes stark against his pale face—but he looked whole, at least. "Set him down," Laine said, an odd note of command in his voice. And after a hesitation, they did. Carefully, Ehren's Guards lowered him to the ground again, upon which he flopped like an obedient rag doll.

"Let me *go*," Jada demanded, and after another hesitation, she knelt by his side, unencumbered. She looked down at him a moment, then up again, long enough to say, "Give me that."

It was his feather. Carefully, Jada wove its narrow leather ties through Ehren's hair, close enough to the proper place.

"There," she whispered, putting her hand on his shoulder. Then she scowled upward. "No matter what you say, he's a King's Guard. He's the only one among *all* of you—Guards, ministers—even Benlan's *son*—who wouldn't give up looking for the man who killed his king. He damn well deserves all the honor you can give him. And it shouldn't have—" her voice started to break again, "—shouldn't have included being killed by two of his own!"

Suddenly there was a hand on Ehren's shin, just resting there. And another on his shoulder, and one over his chest, and a quiet grip on his ankle. *Guards.* Above him, Gerhard cleared his throat and said quietly, "Sire . . . your personal physician is at the lodge."

Rodar said, "Get him."

Chapter 17

Ehren was surprised to find Sherran standing over him in all her T'ierand authority, her fine brows arched in severe annoyance and her mouth pressed closed. *Foolishness, to get yourself in this state*, she seemed to be saying, and her scolding voice was sad. *How will you come back to me?* But she was a wavery and insubstantial illusion, and she didn't stay. His vision was filled with glowing bluish green light, and it swept over him like a floodwater and buried him, for a long time. When he came up again it was a gasping, sputtering rise with the light flowing down his hair and shoulders like liquid, dripping into his eyes and mouth and off his nose.

He took a sudden deep breath and realized he could.

"It's about time."

That was Laine's voice, with relief sneaking through. Warily, Ehren cracked his eyes open. They widened the rest of the way when he saw where he was.

The hunting lodge. The posh guest quarters in the hunting lodge. On a high, soft bed, in smooth, clean sheets. Laine sat in the corner, his chair tipped back so it rested against the wall, his chin resting on his fist. He looked, if not his usual hale and hearty self, levels better than the last time Ehren had seen him. Now, *haggard* had made way for the fatigue that would dog any man after what

Laine had been through between the Barrenlands and Kurtane.

"I was afraid he was killing you," Ehren said, discovering his mouth was dry and tasted funny; his words came out like his tongue was tipped with cotton.

"I was afraid he was killing me, too. But he wasn't . . . just playing with me." Laine tipped the chair down and reached for the pitcher that sat on the bedstand between his corner and the bed. "Shallai said you'd be extra thirsty for a while. All that blood you lost. And probably those herbs he got down your throat."

Ehren shook his head. "It took more than herbs to keep me alive." *Magic.*

"Yes," Laine said. "It did. A hell of a lot more, from what I saw. But you'd expect the king's personal physician to be up to that sort of thing, wouldn't you?"

You would, at that. Anticipating the water, Ehren sat up. Or tried to. The movement awoke so many tender, protesting places that his whole torso seized up. He took a deep breath, relaxed, and tried again, more carefully.

"Of course," Laine added, "even the king's physician has limits."

"So I noticed," Ehren grunted, carefully reaching for the goblet Laine offered him. His arm felt like it belonged on someone else's body and was his on loan, unfamiliar and uncooperative. Nonetheless, he managed to drain the goblet of water without spilling any on Rodar's sheets, and passed it back for a refill. "Do I want to know how long I've been here?"

Laine shook his head decisively. "No. But it's been a while. I've got to give your king credit, even if he is mostly an overgrown Shette, and with less common sense than she has, at that. We had plenty of time together out on that field, waiting for Shallai to come, and then waiting until it was possible to move you. He listened to us, and Gerhard listened to us, as soon as he began to understand . . ." Laine shook his head. "He ordered you brought here. He's confined all the members of the hunting party to the lodge, unless under Guard escort. He wants to hear every part of what you know before he returns to Kurtane, and he wants to have a strategy."

"He believes in Varien's guilt, then." Obviously.

"I think it was easier than believing Benlan gave his deepest trust and friendship to someone—you—who was stupid enough to kill the First Level Wizard without reason. Actually believing Varien was guilty came a little later." Laine looked down at his feet. "I let him read the journal."

Ehren nodded. "Good. But—what have you told them about . . ."

"About me?" Laine said, and tipped back into the corner again. Ehren decided it was the sort of thing designed to drive Shette crazy. No use in getting out of practice, apparently. "As little as possible. I told them about the Sight—but only that I'd seen Benlan's death. Nothing about my parents. It was easy enough—just told them it was the ring that triggered it all, because I was sensitive to such things."

"Easy enough," Ehren repeated, unconvinced. Likely not. Likely Rodar and Gerhard had enough of the answers they needed, that they chose not to pursue what Laine was not telling them. For now. But Laine was looking at him with the easy humor of old, and with the naivete to believe what he was saying. Ehren decided to let the issue rest. For now.

As if sensing Ehren had come to some sort of decision, Laine got to his feet. "Jada wanted to see you when you woke up," he said. "She won't stay long, I'm sure. It's just nice, after all these days of watching you lying there deciding whether or not to breathe, to actually talk to you. Besides, Rodar and Gerhard want to talk to you, too. And it's not polite to keep a king waiting."

No. Definitely not. Ehren marshalled his thoughts to order, and discovered that foremost among his own questions was the location of the chamber pot. Even kings had to wait for some things.

Autumn in Kurtane was as it had always been. The courtyards and gardens were a splash of color, the carefully tended foliage shouting reds and bright yellows. This day was crisp-aired and brightly sunny, and the paths were littered with carpets of brittle leaves. The vine-draped arches dropped leaves down the collars of the unwary, and no one went anywhere without announcing their arrival with crunching footsteps. The kind of day to be savored.

Ehren sat on a comfortable wooden bench in the midst of it all and knew this was no longer his home.

The courtyard was a busy one, much more so than it had been this spring, when he'd sat on this same wooden bench and contemplated his place here. The nobles and young apprentices moved with alacrity and purpose, and had time for no more than a surreptitious glance at him. But glance they did, as Ehren soaked up the sun and let it warm all the still-stiff places inside him.

He still knew what they saw, even if it was somewhat different from the man who had been here the previous spring. One of King Benlan's men, his last, who had now earned a place in Rodar's court—and wasn't sure he wanted it. A faded scarlet shirt, cleverly mended, but showing obvious signs of swordplay. Tall boots that had finally been resoled; today the greave straps were buckled to themselves and jingled only faintly when he moved. The sidelocks of his black hair—and never mind that strand or two of grey— were tied back; next to the honor feather there was another, much smaller feather, a secondary from the wing of the same royal bird.

Rodar wasn't shy about creating new tradition. A man could only wear so many beads, he'd declared, bestowing upon Ehren the secondary. It had been done at a small— for Rodar—celebration, when Ehren was still walking like an old man. When Ehren realized once again that the number of people in the room that he trusted and respected could be counted on both hands and a toe or two.

Crunch crunch. Someone else on the leaf-filled path, coming around the curve of the garden to where this bench sat up against a still-green hedge. Ehren recognized that carefree stride and didn't bother to turn his face away from the sun. "Laine," he greeted the younger man. "You about ready to go?"

"Tomorrow," Laine said. First to Sherran and Shette at Grannor . . . and then? Laine had openly admitted he wasn't sure. Back home to see his parents, undoubtedly. And then, maybe on to that caravan-route run with Ansgare—although Ehren privately felt that Sherran would co-opt him for some service or another to the Grannor. He was, after all, about to carry the first official words of communication between governments since the tensions a hundred years earlier, chosen only because Sherran already knew and trusted him. Solvany did not yet know of his heritage, only of his Sight— and of that, very little.

Rodar's missive was a humble one, drafted by his own hand in his first true act as a monarch: a request for help in the matter of the mage lure. He'd already sent word out amongst the wizards of Solvany, informing them of Varien's death, and the end of the mage lure supply. Unless Therand was willing to cooperate, anyone Varien had addicted to the drug now faced unpleasant death . . . but Ehren was willing to bet the T'ierand would try to obtain a supply of the drug, at least until alternatives could be explored.

"Guard escort all the way to the Barrenlands," Laine was saying, shaking his head. "You'd think they didn't trust me or something."

"It's not you they don't trust," Ehren said dryly. "The Upper Levels have been altogether too quiet since Varien died. Even the candidates for First Level Wizard are acting civilized. Someone's hiding something."

"They're *all* hiding something, as far as I can tell," Laine said.

A wry grin tugged at the corner of Ehren's mouth. "That's true, too."

Laine sat down next to Ehren, stretching his legs out in front of him. They sat in silence for a moment—or as near to it as they could get, with the paths as busy as they were, and the leaves crunching under everybody's feet. It was obvious enough without looking how many people paused to take a second glance at Ehren. "I don't get it," Laine said, finally. "You know there are ministers in the First Level— and no doubt below—who were helping Varien. But no one seems to be overly concerned with finding them. It's been over a month, and all the Guards have done is close off Varien's rooms and wait to install his replacement elsewhere."

"We're still learning from those rooms," Ehren said. "Don't you worry—we'll get through Varien's security spells and find the ministers who were in league with him. But for now, those people are hoping we don't have a clue. And they're doing their best to make sure things run smoothly, so we don't *get* any clues. As long as things go as smoothly as they have been, time is on our side."

"You're not worried that they're still plotting? What about Varien's connections in Loraka?"

Ehren shifted, rubbing his leg. Of all the things done to his body this summer, the old avalanche wound was the thing that bothered him the most—the scarring from the infection had affected the outer joint, Shallai had told him. The other things, the broken ribs, the internal injuries, the bone-deep bruises—had healed well enough—and on their own, once the physician had taken him out of danger. It was best that way, the surgeon had said. He sighed. "We may never discover just how deeply Loraka was into this, although we're trying. But their moment has passed. They've withdrawn most of their military presence, and we're building up ours, so . . ." He shrugged. "Once again, time is on our side. Without Varien to spearhead the whole thing, it's fallen apart." He looked at Laine with amused satisfaction. "Did you hear that the border incidents are falling off?"

Laine snorted. "That, I *did* hear, even if most of the rest of it manages to pass me by. Seems like Varien—and whoever—thought of a lot of different ways to stir up trouble, and used them all at once." He rubbed the back of his neck, and gave Ehren a sideways glance, one that showed a little self-deprecating humor. "You'd think some of the people around here would be a little more open with their information. I did my best to ferret some of this stuff out on my own, but court folks seem to be awful good at changing the subject, no matter how many times you turn it back in the right direction. After all, I *am* the one going back through the Barrenlands with Rodar's message to Sherran."

Ehren gave a gentle snort. "Can you really blame them? Right now, no one trusts anyone, and they're all trying to pretend that they trust everyone."

"I have to admit," Laine said, "I never thought of you as at home in this kind of atmosphere."

Ehren laughed outright. "I'm not." He shook his head, thinking about it for a moment. "It was different, under Benlan, somehow. . . ." Because he was among friends, he thought. People he knew, people he'd fought next to. Serving a man who was like an older brother to him, arranging for physical safety and not embroiled in the personalities in the court. Walking over them, in fact, when they got in the way of Benlan's welfare.

Which is what had probably gotten him into trouble in the first place. That and an unquenchable need to find the man who had killed his king.

"Shallai is just about to clear me for full duty," Ehren told Laine. "I've been ready for half a month, but he's . . . overprotective." That was mostly true. It was stiffness, now, mainly, and that wouldn't leave for a long time. Ehren met Laine's two-colored gaze, and shrugged. "Who knows? There are already agents in Loraka, trying to track down the wizard Typhean—the one Ileen mentioned. Maybe they could use some help. Besides, sounds to me like there's going to be some fresh activity with Therand—and her intriguing T'ierand—through the Barrenlands." He added a decidedly rakish grin, his thoughts on the spelled stone Sherran had given him. "You know I like to be where the action is."

Laine snorted. "It doesn't take Sight to see *that*."

Author's Note

Authors take their neonatal ideas, massage and plump them, weave in subplots, and turn them into books. Along the way we grow to believe in our characters, and sweat and grow and cry with them. There are very few things as satisfying as typing the last few words of a book, and knowing you've told the story as best you can.

But then comes the important part, the reader's part. That's who we're writing *for*, after all. Long after I've written those last words in *Barrenlands*, I'll wonder how they affect the people they're meant for...which is why my postal and current e-mail addresses are below:

Doranna Durgin
PO Box 26207
Rochester, NY 14626
(please send a SASE for reply)

doranna@sff.net

Or come visit at http://www.sff.net/people/doranna/